Travel Writing and Tourism in Britain and Ireland

Also by Benjamin Colbert:

BRITISH SATIRE, 1785–1840: Volume 3 (*editor*)

SHELLEY'S EYE: Travel Writing and Aesthetic Vision

Travel Writing and Tourism in Britain and Ireland

Edited by

Benjamin Colbert

First published 2012 by
PALGRAVE MACMILLAN

Palgrave Macmillan in the UK is an imprint of Macmillan Publishers Limited,
registered in England, company number 785998, of Houndmills, Basingstoke,
Hampshire RG21 6XS.

Palgrave Macmillan in the US is a division of St Martin's Press LLC,
175 Fifth Avenue, New York, NY 10010.

Palgrave Macmillan is the global academic imprint of the above companies
and has companies and representatives throughout the world.

Palgrave® and Macmillan® are registered trademarks in the United States,
the United Kingdom, Europe and other countries.

ISBN 978–0–230–25108–3

This book is printed on paper suitable for recycling and made from fully
managed and sustained forest sources. Logging, pulping and manufacturing
processes are expected to conform to the environmental regulations of the
country of origin.

A catalogue record for this book is available from the British Library.

A catalog record for this book is available from the Library of Congress.

10   9   8   7   6   5   4   3   2   1
21   20   19   18   17   16   15   14   13   12

Printed and bound in Great Britain by
CPI Antony Rowe, Chippenham and Eastbourne

Contents

List of Illustrations   vii

Acknowledgements   viii

Notes on Contributors   ix

Introduction: Home Tourism   1
Benjamin Colbert

1   Peripheral Vision, Landscape, and Nation-Building
in Thomas Pennant's Tours of Scotland, 1769–72   13
Paul Smethurst

2   Beside the Seaside: Mary Morgan's *Tour to Milford
Haven, in the Year 1791*   31
Zoë Kinsley

3   'Ancient and Present': Charles Heath of Monmouth
and the *Historical and Descriptive Accounts ... of Tintern
Abbey* 1793–1828   50
C. S. Matheson

4   Britain through Foreign Eyes: Early Nineteenth-Century
Home Tourism in Translation   68
Benjamin Colbert

5   The Attractions of England, or Albion under German Eyes   85
Jan Borm

6   The Irish Tour, 1800–50   97
William H. A. Williams

7   'Missions of Benevolence': Tourism and Charity on
Nineteenth-Century Iona   114
Katherine Haldane Grenier

8   Holiday Excursions to Scott Country   132
Nicola J. Watson

9   'Every Hill has Its History, Every Region Its Romance':
Travellers' Constructions of Wales, 1844–1913   147
Katie Gramich

10 Famine Travel: Irish Tourism from the Great Famine to
    Decolonization   164
    Spurgeon Thompson

11 Meeting Kate Kearney at Killarney: Performances of the
    Touring Subject, 1850–1914   181
    K. J. James

12 'The Romance of the Road': Narratives of Motoring in
    England, 1896–1930   201
    Esme Coulbert

13 Home Truths: Language, Slowness, and Microspection   219
    Michael Cronin

Bibliography   236

Index   250

List of Illustrations

2.1   'Milford Haven', Samuel Fisher after Henry Gastineaux,
      from *Wales Illustrated, in a Series of Views, Comprising the
      Picturesque Scenery, Towns, Seats of the Nobility & Gentry,
      Antiquities &c.*, vol. 1 (London: Jones & Co, 1830), n. pag.
      Source: Zoë Kinsley private collection.   36

7.1   'Iona', from *Black's Picturesque Tourist of Scotland*
      (Edinburgh, 1875), 484. Source: National Library of
      Scotland.   116

11.1 'Map of Ireland and Detailed Map of County Kerry,
      showing Principal Tourist Resorts' (2011). Map created by
      Joshua MacFadyen. © K. J. James.   182

11.2 'Kate Kearney at the Gap of Dunloe', postcard, n.d.,
      postmarked 1904. Source: K. J. James private collection.   184

12.1 'The Car of the Moderns: Hillman Wizard Five-Seater
      Family Saloon £270', front cover of double-sided
      advertisement brochure (1930). Source: Coventry
      Transport Museum.   203

12.2 'Old Cottages off the Beaten Track in Sussex', from *The
      Autocar* 63.1760 (26 July 1929), facing page 160. © LAT
      Photographic.   209

Acknowledgements

Many of the essays here were first delivered as part of an international symposium, 'Travels in Britain and Ireland, 1800 to Present', organized by Glenn Hooper at the Open University, Milton Keynes Campus, on 30 May 2008. All the contributors owe Glenn their gratitude for conceiving this book project and for taking it as far as he did before circumstances required him to pass the editorship to me.

I would like to thank personally colleagues from the Centre for Transnational and Transcultural Research at the University of Wolverhampton, principally Glyn Hambrook and Jan Borm, for support, encouragement, and stimulating discussion; and Hilary Weeks for closely reading and commenting helpfully on parts of the book.

Thanks are also due to those who have provided the illustrations to this volume: the Cadbury Research Library, Special Collections, University of Birmingham, for kind permission to reproduce the cover image; Zoë Kinsley and K. J. James for making available materials from their private collections for Illustrations 2.1 and 11.2, respectively; the Trustees of the National Library of Scotland for Illustration 7.1; Joshua MacFadyen for creating a specially commissioned map, Illustration 11.1, and its copyright holder, K. J. James, for permission to use it here; LAT Photographic for kind permission to reproduce Illustration 12.1; and the Coventry Transport Museum for Illustration 12.2.

Notes on Contributors

Jan Borm is Professor of British Literature at the University of Versailles Saint-Quentin-en-Yvelines, where he is also Director of the research laboratory 'Centre européen pour l'Arctique' (CEARC) and Vice-Dean of the Faculty of Languages and International Studies (ILEI). He has published widely on travel writing and co-edited Bruce Chatwin's posthumous collection *Anatomy of Restlessness* (Jonathan Cape, 1996; paperback Picador, 1997). He has edited one of the two volumes of papers from the Borders & Crossings 2 Conference in Brest, *Seuils et Traverses* (Presses de l'Université de Bretagne Occidentale, 2002), and co-edited with Bernard Cottret and Jean-François Zorn a volume on missionary writing, *Convertir/Se convertir* (Nolin, 2006), and another with Bernard Cottret and Mark Münzel, *Christentum und der natürliche Mensch* (Corupira, 2010). He is the author of the portrait *Jean Malaurie, un homme singulier* (Nolin, 2005), the famous French explorer of the Arctic and specialist in Inuit civilization.

Benjamin Colbert is Reader in English Literature and Co-Director of the Centre for Transnational and Transcultural Research at the University of Wolverhampton. He is volume editor of *British Satire 1785–1840* (Pickering and Chatto, 2003), author of *Shelley's Eye: Travel Writing and Aesthetic Vision* (Ashgate, 2005), co-editor of the special issue, 'Literature Travels', in *Comparative Critical Studies* (2007), and he is currently editing *Women's Travel Writings in France after Napoleon*, 4 vols (Chawton Library Series, Pickering and Chatto). He has served on the Steering Committee of the International Society for Travel Writing (2006–11) and is Book Review Editor for *European Romantic Review*.

Esme Coulbert is currently an Arts and Humanities Research Council (AHRC) sponsored doctoral student working collaboratively with Nottingham Trent University and the Coventry Transport Museum; her research focuses on the motor car in early twentieth-century travel narratives.

Michael Cronin is Full Professor in the Faculty of Humanities and Social Sciences at Dublin City University, Ireland. He is author of *Translating Ireland: Translation, Languages and Identity* (Cork University Press, 1996); *Across the Lines: Travel, Language, Translation* (Cork University Press,

2000); *Translation and Globalization* (Routledge, 2003); *Time Tracks: Scenes from the Irish Everyday* (New Island, 2003; reprinted 2003); *Irish in the New Century/An Ghaeilge san Aois Nua* (Cois Life, 2005); *Translation and Identity* (Routledge, 2006); *The Barrytown Trilogy* (Cork University Press, Ireland into Film series, 2007); and *Translation Goes to the Movies* (Routledge, 2009). He is editor or co-editor of *Tourism in Ireland: A Critical Analysis* (Cork University Press, 1993); *Anthologie de nouvelles irlandaises* (L'Instant même, 1997); *Unity in Diversity? Current Trends in Translation Studies* (St Jerome Press, 1998); *Reinventing Ireland: Culture, Society and the Global Economy* (Pluto Press, 2002); *Irish Tourism: Image, Culture and Identity* (Channel View Publications, 2003); *The Languages of Ireland* (Four Courts Press, 2003); and *Transforming Ireland* (Manchester University Press, 2009). He is a Member of the Royal Irish Academy and co-editor of *The Irish Review*.

Katie Gramich is Reader in English Literature at Cardiff University. She has published extensively on women's writing and on the literature of Wales, in both languages. Her publications include *Twentieth-Century Women's Writing in Wales: Land, Gender, Belonging* (University of Wales Press, 2007) and a monograph on the Welsh writer *Kate Roberts* (University of Wales Press, 2011). She edited *Mapping the Territory: Critical Approaches to Welsh Fiction in English* (Parthian, 2010) and co-edited with Andrew Hiscock *Dangerous Diversity: The Changing Faces of Wales* (University of Wales Press, 1998). She also edits *Almanac: The Yearbook of Welsh Writing in English*. She is Chair of the Association for Welsh writing in English and co-organized with Claire Connolly the AHRC-funded Ireland-Wales research network. She is a Fellow of the English Association and of the Welsh Academi.

Katherine Haldane Grenier is Professor of History at The Citadel in Charleston, South Carolina. She is the author of *Tourism and Identity in Scotland, 1770-1914: Creating Caledonia* (Ashgate, 2005) and has contributed to *Victorians Institute Journal* and *Nineteenth Century Studies*. She is the co-editor of *That Gentle Strength: Historical Perspectives on Women and Christianity* (University Press of Virginia, 1990).

K. J. James is Associate Professor of History at the University of Guelph, Canada, where he is also a core faculty member at the Centre for Scottish Studies. He is the author of *Handloom Weavers in Ulster's Linen Industry, 1815–1914* (Four Courts Press, 2007), chapters on Irish social history and tourism history in edited collections, and several journal articles, including essays in *Labour History Review*, *Rural History*, and *Textile History*.

Zoë Kinsley is Senior Lecturer in English literature at Liverpool Hope University. Her research interests include home tour travel writing, early modern scribal culture, and eighteenth-century landscape poetry. She has published various articles on these subjects in journals such as *The Review of English Studies, Prose Studies*, and *Studies in Travel Writing*, is co-editor of *Mapping Liminalities: Thresholds in Cultural and Literary Texts* (Peter Lang, 2007), and author of *Women Writing the Home Tour, 1682–1812* (Ashgate, 2008).

C. S. Matheson is Associate Professor in the Department of English at the University of Windsor, Canada. She is the author of a monograph entitled *Composing Tintern Abbey* (forthcoming, University of Toronto Press) and co-author (with Alex McKay) of a forthcoming study of landscape and optical technology, *The Transient Glance: Claude Mirrors and the Spectacle of Landscape* (University of Toronto Press).

Paul Smethurst is Associate Professor at the University of Hong Kong, where he teaches travel writing, global fiction, and cross-cultural theory. His publications include *The Postmodern Chronotope* (Rodopi, 2000) and *Moving Nature: Travel Writing and the Natural World* (forthcoming). He has also co-edited two collections of travel writing: *Asian Crossings* (Hong Kong University Press, 2008) with Steve Clark, and *Travel Writing, Form, and Empire* (Routledge, 2009) with Julia Kuehn. He is currently working on *Bicycle*, a cultural history of the bicycle for Reaktion.

Spurgeon Thompson teaches at Fordham University. He has published articles on James Joyce, W. B. Yeats, James Connolly, and other Irish writers in *Irish Studies Review, Eire-Ireland, The Irish University Review*, the *International Journal of English Studies, The Irish Journal of Feminist Studies, Cultural Studies*, and *Interventions: International Journal of Postcolonial Studies*. His 2000 dissertation at the University of Notre Dame, 'The Postcolonial Tourist', was the first comprehensive study of Irish tourism and travelogues from the Great Famine to the present. He is editor of the 'Irish Cultural Studies' special issue of *Cultural Studies* (2001) and the March 2008 special issue of *Interventions* on James Connolly. He has also published articles comparing Cypriot and Irish writing, as well as an article on 'Cyprus After History' in *Interventions*.

Nicola J. Watson is currently Senior Lecturer in Literature at the Open University, having held posts at Oxford, Harvard, Northwestern, and Indiana Universities. Broadly based as a specialist in the early nineteenth century, her publications include *Revolution and the Form of the British Novel 1790-1820* (Oxford University Press, 1994); *At the*

Limits of Romanticism (Indiana University Press, 1994), co-edited with Mary Favret; an edition of Sir Walter Scott's *The Antiquary* for World's Classics (2002); *England's Elizabeth: An Afterlife in Fame and Fantasy* (Oxford University Press, 2002), co-authored with Michael Dobson; *The Literary Tourist: Readers and Places in Romantic and Victorian Britain* (Palgrave Macmillan, 2006); and most recently an edited collection of essays entitled *Literary Tourism and Nineteenth-Century Culture* (Palgrave Macmillan, 2009). She has also contributed many essays, articles, entries, and reviews for academic collections and journals. Her current research project is entitled *Transatlantic Pilgrims*, a book-length study of the investment of American culture in British literary geography.

William H. A. Williams has taught at Southern Illinois University, University College, Dublin, the Justus Liebig University in Germany, Arizona State University, and the Union Institute and University. He has contributed to many academic journals and is editor of *Daniel O'Connell, the British Press and the Irish Famine* by Leslie A. Williams (Ashgate, 2001), and author of *Only an Irishman's Dream* (University of Illinois Press, 1996), *Tourism, Landscape and the Irish Character* (University of Wisconsin, 2008), and *Creating Irish Tourism: The First Century, 1750–1850* (Anthem, 2010).

Introduction: Home Tourism

Benjamin Colbert

> A season comes in every year when Englishmen are
> converted into a nation of tourists. ... We are so far
> happy in the British Isles, that it is rather an advantage
> to those amongst us who love beautiful scenery for its
> own sake, to be turned back upon our own country. ...
> There are the Scotch Highlands and the English Lakes;
> there are North and South Wales, – Snowdon and
> the Vale of Festiniog; Chepstow and the Wye; – there
> is Devonshire with the Dart and the Exe; there are
> the southern counties with all their beautiful home
> scenery. All these points are more or less visited by
> all wanderers. There is one portion of the British Isles,
> however, which, as far as beauty and variety of scen-
> ery are concerned, yields to no other, but yet remains
> comparatively unknown. How few are the persons
> who, except for business purposes, have visited the
> southern and western districts of Ireland!
>
> *The Times* (18 June 1849)[1]

Travel begins and ends at home. The journey out and the homecoming
have long been framing devices in travel accounts, while home itself
remains a point of reference, perhaps more so the farther a traveller goes
(Marco Polo, as Italo Calvino perceptively represents him in *Invisible
Cities*, always speaks of Venice when describing Chinese cities to Kublai
Khan).[2] It is no different with 'home tourism', localized itineraries that
indicate a desire to discover closer at hand what is unfamiliar, yet at
the same time to harmonize, homogenize, and extend the purview
of home. Yet within the British Isles national, linguistic, and cultural

1

boundaries are indelibly inscribed. Travellers from and to the four nations – England, Ireland, Scotland, and Wales – have long found themselves at once 'at home' and on foreign ground as they move beyond borders that demarcate their senses of belonging. Historically, travel writers have responded variously to these dislocations. Sometimes they engage in proto-colonialist commentary on the civilization, cultivation, or modernity of those whom they encounter; sometimes they grope towards a selfhood that acknowledges and embraces otherness (what Michael Cronin has called a 'micro-cosmopolitan' identity[3]); and at other times they elide all questions of identity politics into an aesthetics of landscape, the 'beauty and variety of scenery' that *The Times* projected in 1849 as the measure of tourist desire.

The history of home tourism in Britain dates back at least to religious pilgrimage. Chaucer's Canterbury pilgrims, as Ian Ousby remarks, anticipate nearly all the attitudes and patterns of modern tourism: the fixed itineraries, the attention to predetermined sights, the trust in guides, the desire for keepsakes and souvenirs, and the longing for a higher purpose that justifies the whole.[4] An earlier example might be found in Gerald of Wales, who recorded his travels in 1188 'accompanying Archbishop Baldwin on a mission to acquire volunteers to embark on a Crusade', as Katie Gramich notes in her contribution to this volume. However, Esther Moir traces 'the *habit* of touring their native land' to English gentry in the sixteenth century, pride in the accomplishments of Tudor England and a desire to extend its power motivating their journeys.[5] While the Grand Tour held sway on the European Continent and provided gentleman tourists with well-established itineraries and patterns of self-fashioning, the home tour, as Moir argues, was the preserve of individualists who toured out of enthusiasm but with fewer guidelines and expected outcomes.[6] Refusing to be drawn into a traveller/tourist debate over the authenticity of experience, Moir is right to allow even these individualists their denomination as 'tourists'. Nevertheless, there does appear to be a qualitative difference between the period of habit-formation and that of institutionalization, when tourist sights become, in Dean MacCannell's phrase, 'sacralized'; when patterns of apperception and mobility become formalized; and when tourism begins steadily to extend below the aristocracy and gentry to include the middle and, later in the nineteenth century, the working classes.[7] Though rooted earlier, modern home tourism (and arguably tourism in general) flowers in the mid-eighteenth century as a popular leisure pursuit with a developing infrastructure of roads, inns, attractions, guides, guidebooks, engravings, narratives, and, with the rise of the taste for picturesque landscape, its own vocabulary and aesthetics. Picturesque tourism became an end in itself for some and a pleasing contrast with labouring Britain for others. Tourists also pursued agricultural, industrial, and scientific information;[8] or the homes, haunts, and tombs of writers.[9] Spas and coastal resorts became popular, as did beauty spots: the Lakes in Cumberland, the Scottish Highlands, Tintern Abbey and the Wye River valley, or the Lakes of Killarney in Ireland.[10] So many of the home tourist paths laid down then are with us now.

While there is a burgeoning scholarship on travel writing and tourism in Britain and Ireland, the principal studies – several by contributors to this volume – have had a regional, gender, or thematic focus.[11] The privilege of an essay collection is to take a wider prospect, and this one, bringing together the latest research from leading travel historians and travel writing specialists, is the first devoted solely to the home tour. The essays chart many of the key developments of modern tourism and travel writing in Britain and Ireland from the late eighteenth to the early twentieth centuries, rounded off by a retrospective and prospective essay that takes its vantage from the borderlands of Ireland in the 1980s. The volume as a whole covers a period of immense political, social, and cultural change in the British Isles. Political milestones such as the Acts of Union between England and Scotland (1707) and Great Britain and Ireland (1800), or the French Revolution and Napoleonic wars that followed, began a process in which tourism and travel writing played a central role in imagining or re-imagining the nations jostling for position in the mental geographies of the British and Irish peoples.[12] The essays here accordingly consider identity from various national perspectives, including those of foreign visitors from America and Continental Europe, and describe complicated negotiations between tourists' growing sense of Britain as a unified imperial centre, their desire for (or resistance to) homogeneity from within, and their recognition that language and representation intervene fundamentally in perceptions of belonging. Socially and culturally, the essays are also concerned with such issues as the aesthetic idealization of landscape and the *patria*, gender transgression and class stratification, the rise of mass travel and commercial culture, and the politics of touristic enjoyment. While no essay collection can claim comprehensiveness, this volume will be an indispensable guide to advanced students and scholars seeking an overview of modern home tourism in Britain and Ireland.

Home tourism is a special type of what Susan Pitchford calls 'identity tourism', 'in which collective identities are represented, interpreted, and potentially constructed through the use of history and culture'.[13]

Picturesque aesthetics, antiquarianism, and ethnology all serve this process by linking the surfaces and depths of touristic experience to wider frames of reference; Thomas West's comparison in 1778 of the Lake District to Continental scenery ('in miniature, an idea of ... the ALPS and APPENINES'),[14] for example, gestured to a larger perspective in which home tourism became an argument for national self-sufficiency. British peripheries in Wales, Scotland, and Ireland were brought together as living museums of an inter-related Celtic heritage by numerous tourists in the eighteenth and nineteenth centuries. Meanwhile, conjoining England to its Welsh and Scottish neighbours, encyclopaedic projects such as Edward Wedlake Brayley and John Britton's *The Beauties of England and Wales* (18 vols, 1801–18) and Richard Ayton and William Daniell's *A Voyage round Great Britain* (8 vols, 1814–25) re-centred the nation. Brayley and Britton – and the many subeditors who carried on the project when they no longer could – made a point of undertaking extensive travels and local interviews, cross-checking empirical with historical data. The retrospective introduction, produced by James Norris Brewer after the completion of the main body of the work, argued that the endeavour had 'performed the laudable task of ameliorating much that was repugnant in the crust of antiquity; ... and ha[d] proved that ponderous masses of monastic or castellated stone, nearly shapeless through age, and overgrown with ivy, are often fraught with tales of touching emphasis.[15] The compilers' excavations and analyses reinvigorate the picturesque, its regimented views and formalist principles, by layering historical meaning onto and beneath the surfaces that present themselves to the tourist. The volumes thus stand for and promote a textualized landscape subordinate to a grand narrative that elicits national feelings ('tales of touching emphasis'). Touring Britain, the volumes assure their readers, is not an act of superficial dilettantism, but amounts to a reading of the nation and the foundations on which it is built. Increasingly, readers looked to home tourism and travel writing more widely to provide this rich description, to connect the past and present in a single narrative, and to 'accredit' the participation of the tourist classes in the cultural life of the nation.[16]

The epitome of the textualization of landscape and the sign of touristic saturation is the guidebook, a term first used in 1814, according to the *Oxford English Dictionary*. 'We can no longer set forth as discoverers', remarked a reviewer for *The London Quarterly Review* in 1864, with reference to the extension of John Murray's guidebook series from Continental destinations to his 'red books' on the British Isles. In a manner reminiscent of the 1818 introduction to *The Beauties* just quoted, the reviewer celebrates the guidebooks' distillation of topographical and antiquarian study: 'Such books – which not only show us England as it is at present, but point out and describe for us the numberless relics of its former history – were only possible after many generations of antiquaries and topographers, and contain the very essence of their labours. Whilst travelling in England was never so easy, the means of real benefit by such travel were never more completely within the reach of all classes.'[17] The difference between Brewer's position and the reviewer's is the latter's acknowledgment of mass tourism and the access provided by guidebooks to the lore of previous generations. The democratization of taste that Tim Fulford has deemed the birthright of the picturesque[18] finds its apotheosis in the humble guidebook. Surfaces give way to depths that, in turn, open out into breadth.

The increasing importance and pervasiveness of guidebooks and travel narratives in the nineteenth century also testifies to the cumulative nature of tourism as a commercial phenomenon. These writings suggest a growing sense of the powers and responsibilities of domestic tourism: its effect on the psychological health of workers liberated from drudgery by their ability to go 'on holiday'; its role in circulating wealth, agricultural 'improvements', and industry; and its potential to help define a British modernity in which work and leisure played a mutually supportive role. Perhaps the greatest obstacle to the associations promoted between tourism and modernity, however, were tourists' confrontation with poverty. Popular aesthetic modes like the picturesque tended to airbrush labour from the domestic scene, writing nostalgic visions of common ground onto a landscape parcelled out into enclosures, as Ann Bermingham has influentially argued,[19] and primitivist discourses too were at hand with which tourists might explain away or gloss over an impoverished peasantry, especially in Wales, the Scottish Highlands, and Ireland. Ireland was especially problematic. In pre-Famine Ireland, poverty became more visible on the tourist track. It was an unsightly reminder that modernity did not necessarily bring with it improvement for all, and it called into question the laissez-faire morality that underpinned this modernity. The aesthetic, political, and economic responses to poverty in fact tell us a great deal about the ideological fault lines in the development of mass tourism and are a recurrent concern in several of the essays below.

The imaginative construction of the 'whole island of Great Britain', as Daniel Defoe's 1707 travelogue phrases it, is the subject of the opening essay in this volume. Paul Smethurst traces a line from Defoe to Thomas Pennant, both of whom conceived of Britain as a centralized power whose unity in an imperial context they take for granted. Though a Welshman, Pennant carries with him an essentially English metropolitan frame of reference, even as he traverses national peripheries. In Pennant's tours to Scotland between 1769 and 1772, the Scottish Highlands embody a primitivism commensurate to that reported back from the Pacific by James Cook's travel accounts, of which Pennant was an avid reader. Yet the measure of the modern for Pennant is agricultural improvement and Scotland too becomes fertile ground for the export of economic 'progress'. Linked to the centre by its susceptibility to improvement and distinguished by its outlandishness, Scotland represents the heterogeneous microcosm of the 'whole island' linked concentrically to the wider world.

Attention to coastal features of the 'whole island' in Ayton and Daniell's circumnavigation narrative evolves out of a growing fashion for sea-bathing that Alain Corbin dates from the 1750s.[20] Yet the coast could be treacherous and seductive, sublime and picturesque (and much of Ayton and Daniell's own first tour was conducted by carriage, when seas and winds would not cooperate). Zoë Kinsley develops the implications of the coast's liminality for women travellers, instancing a neglected travelogue, Mary Morgan's *Tour to Milford Haven* (1795). While popular satirists, poets, and other travel writers stressed the attractions of sea-bathing for women (and the attractions of their bodies on the beach to voyeuristic males), Morgan complicates the picture. Like Pennant, she is drawn to the peripheral nature of Wales and its coast, and indulges there in a cautious fantasy of the beach as a space of freedom from custom and from sexual restraint, yet ultimately she recoils from the sublime treachery of the sea, its promise of shipwreck, rape, and death. In Kinsley's view, Morgan's travelogue tallies with Jean-Didier Urbain's notion that the beach 're-centres' rather than destabilizes the self; Morgan's retreat from the coast symbolizes her embrace of a secure, inland identity.

Travelogues that dramatize self-fashioning would appear to be of a different order from guidebooks that stage-manage touristic experience. C. S. Matheson's essay, however, complicates this in turning to a particularly rich example, Charles Heath's *Historical and Descriptive Accounts of ... Tintern Abbey* which, with its eleven editions between 1793 and 1828, grew up alongside and contributed to the popularity of the Wye River valley as a tourist attraction. Rather than merely distilling the 'essence' of past antiquarians, historians, and topographers, Heath's guidebook proves to be dynamic, responding in successive editions to readers' feedback, to further research by Heath and others, and to new arrangements in tourist infrastructure. Heath's hasty production of the editions, including unpaginated insertions of the latest topical material, bespeaks furthermore an elision between textuality and orality, authority and sociability, as Heath embeds in the experience of Tintern Abbey the purchase of his book as well as his own persona as on-the-spot author/guide. As Matheson demonstrates, Heath increasingly interweaves references to himself into successive editions, breaking down the distinctions between the impersonal guidebook and autobiography, the most personal of genres.

In the next essay, Benjamin Colbert considers another phenomenon of home tourism, the interest amongst British readers in how they were viewed by foreign travellers. While continental travellers had long made the British Isles a destination, the number of such narratives translated into English for a British market increased dramatically after 1780. The marketability of these reverse ethnologies gave rise as well to a spate of fictional 'translations' in the manner of Montesquieu's *Lettres Persanes* or Oliver Goldsmith's *Citizen of the World*, yet wherein the tourist observers are not exotic visitors but fellow Europeans (for example, Robert Southey's Spanish persona in *Letters from England by Don Manuel Alvarez Espriella* (1807)). These proximate narratives become involved in party political representations of national identities, particularly during and immediately after the French Revolution, when Gallophobia characterized much mainstream discourse. However, Colbert identifies within the travelogues of two Francophone travellers, Jacque-Henri Meister and Louis Simond, a transcultural argument reflected by the visitors back upon their British hosts. Through the eyes of foreign travellers, the British see themselves as a travelling nation characterized by an 'insular cosmopolitanism', fundamentally programmed by a restless mobility to defy the physical and psychological limits of their coastal nation.

Of course, British translators, editors, and readers were especially adept at choosing and packaging foreign travel accounts that spoke to home affairs, politically and culturally. Turning from the British market for translation to continental, specifically German, accounts of England, the essay by Jan Borm describes a growing tradition in German travel accounts in which attractions are complicated by social critique, a recognition that cosmopolitanism among the wealthy is not universal in a class-divided, tradition-bound island nation. Tracing a line from Georg Forster to Johanna Schopenhauer (mother of the philosopher) to Heinrich Heine, Borm argues that German travellers are increasingly critical of British 'liberty' (so important to pre-French Revolutionary models of political reform), looking to post-revolutionary France instead for signs of a liberal, democratic future. While the 'practicality' of British approaches to property, industrialism, and commerce, as well as the persistence of the 'garden of England' trope continued to draw German eyes, travel writers wrote their island neighbour out of continental affairs, using it more for satire or as a critical foil rather than a discursive repository for new ideas and ideals.

As Ina Ferris has remarked, Ireland after its union with Great Britain was 'the foreign place that was also home'.[21] The cosmopolitan attitude Colbert discusses that was so flattering when retailed by foreign travellers was less in evidence when British travellers crossed the Irish channel. In his survey of the first fifty years of Irish home tourism after Union, William H. A. Williams describes the method of apprehending Ireland as the 'petit tour', modelled on the Grand Tour, an exhaustive enquiry into the social, economic, political, and cultural life of a land newly incorporated into British polity. Protestant visitors, however, also brought with them distaste for 'popery' and desired to sway the Irish to the 'true religion', one of many incompatibilities between visitor and visited that the Irish home tour threw into relief. Cultural misunderstanding arose too on the question of poverty, for historical reasons chiefly rural in Ireland and urban in England – a disparity English travellers were apt to put down to the chaos and primitivism of the Irish national character, a 'natural' predisposition. The contrast between poverty and natural beauty thus became a recurring feature of pre-Famine travel writing.

Poverty within more isolated tourist-dependent economies was equally apt to be explained by national character, but it could also enhance the story tourism tells about itself. Katherine Grenier's discussion of tourism to the Hebridean island of Iona illustrates how tourist fascination with relics and ruins associated with the spiritual history of St Columba, credited with bringing Christianity to pagan Scotland in the sixth century, becomes reconfigured as a desire to ease poverty through acts of charity and tourist-inspired economic aid. The sights of 'ragged children' selling pebbles and trinkets met every nineteenth-century tourist who disembarked on the island, yet accounts of the Iona tour over time begin to represent the children less as Gaelic beggars than Scottish entrepreneurs attempting to better their lot by engaging with tourism. Under the guidance of Thomas Cook, day-trippers to Iona were encouraged to contribute money towards a charitable society that intervened directly in the island economy by purchasing fishing boats and providing Christian education for promising youths. Publicizing the gratitude of these 'deserving poor' in his journal, *Cook's Excursionist*,

Cook promoted a vision of mass tourism as a force for economic revitalization and social progress.

Nicola J. Watson's essay considers the literary aspect of mass tourism in Scotland. Watson explores the making and unmaking of 'Scott country', from the initial success of Scott's *The Minstrelsy of the Border* in transforming settings along the Tweed into romantic localities, through to the Victorian passion for 'Scott-land', and finally to the cultural forgetting of Scott that began to make itself felt in the 1920s. Watson argues that the idea of 'Scott country' developed as a result of interconnected practices of annotating, adapting, and illustrating Scott's works, all of which practices fed into travel-writing and tourism itself. She examines how this sense of Scott country eventually became over-extended into England, Europe, and beyond, and considers the ways in which early twentieth-century writings consequently conceived 'Scott country' strictly within the limits of the verifiably biographical. No longer romancing the tourist nation, Scott became reduced to a footnote in Scottish history.

Katie Gramich exposes the overlay of romance and history in travellers' constructions of Wales in the Victorian and Edwardian eras. Both foreign and native accounts of Wales sought to reclaim the region from Romantic aestheticization (Wales was considered replete with sublime and picturesque 'scenes') as well as mid-century negative portrayals of its backwardness. Aided by a Celtic revival in British literature, travel writers paid closer attention to the cultural uniqueness of Wales but, in subtle and not so subtle ways, they underlined its otherness, idealized its peasantry as noble mountaineers, and, in later travelogues, prepared the grounds for Welsh nationalism by invoking cultural rootedness rather than acknowledging the political transformations underway in the South Wales coalfields and among the working classes generally. These positions – occupied in Gramich's analysis by an English emigrant *to* Wales, an Oxford don *from* Wales, and an American daughter *of* Welsh parentage – are in no way apolitical, but they do indicate an important class divide between tourists and their subjects, those who represent and those represented.

The next two essays turn again to Irish tourist discourse and its construction of national space. In his cross-sectional survey from the Great Famine to decolonization, Spurgeon Thompson argues that post-Famine tourism becomes 'post-political'; post-Union travel writing's imperative to explain Ireland and advance solutions to its economic problems is replaced by 'description, directions, and historical associations'. The famine itself – its causes, the suffering it produced – becomes a taboo subject; travel writing instead commodifies the depopulated land of Ireland, promoting opportunities for its exploitation by investors and tourists (often assumed to be one and the same). In this sense, romantic landscape aesthetics returns as advertising, a reification still very much part of the Irish tourist industry today, as Thompson notes. K. J. James focuses on the Irish beauty spot Killarney, and finds a surprising homogeneity between travellers of different nations in their representations of the Irish peasantry, and, like Thompson, links this to the commodification of tourism, the recycling of older forms of touristic response. Involved and implicated in mass outings (sponsored by railway companies or Cook's tours), tourists developed ways of distinguishing their own authoritative statements about Ireland from those presented by their Irish guides, whom they accused of having low commercial motives. For visitors to Killarney, drinking 'mountain dew' with descendents of the beauteous and seductive Kate Kearney – celebrated in song by the poet Sydney Owenson – became a performance not to be missed, but one that gave rise to standard disparagements in print. Past and present inscribed on the bodies of Kate Kearney's 'descendants' thus reinforced the authority, intelligence, and discrimination of the English tourist.

The homogenization of tourism through rail travel is a bugbear in much Victorian literature, yet technologies of mobility play an important role in the history of tourism. Perhaps a common denominator in the nineteenth century was the perception that macadamized roads, steam-driven ships and trains, and latterly the automobile increased accessibility to tourist sites and the speed with which one could arrive, achieving a compression of space and time. 'The definition of a man is a locomotive animal', wrote a contributor to *The New Monthly Magazine* in 1843, not altogether in jest.[22] In the penultimate essay, Esme Coulbert considers the transformations introduced by motor tourism from the turn of the century to the 1930s. As revolutionary as automotive technology undoubtedly was in liberating tourists from the constraints of package touring, motor tourism also recapitulates earlier patterns. At first the privilege of the wealthy, the car inevitably became commercialized, extending the possibilities of motor touring to the middle and lower classes. With commercialization came strategies in motor travel writing for self-valorization, an emphasis on the audacity of motorists off the beaten track and on 'the open road' at the expense of less adventuresome followers. Ambivalence towards the technology was also a feature: while early motorists prided themselves on being at the forefront of modernization, they increasingly sought out signs of an unchanging England in bucolic, pastoral villages.

The final essay by Michael Cronin finds in its chronological distance from the other contributions a purchase on them, and might well be read as a coda to the book. His subject is Desmond Fennell's *A Connacht Journey* and Colm Tóibín's *Walking along the Border*, the works of two Irish travellers, both published in 1987 and both concerned with complex border spaces in which multiple identities – colonial and post-colonial, English and Irish – create frictions through language. Like Colbert, Cronin explores the impulse of home tour readers and writers to defamiliarize, to re-see their home as if it were foreign, in what Cronin calls an 'ethnology of proximity'. Like Kinsley, Cronin is also concerned with liminal spaces replete with danger and desire; in the case of Tóibín's journey, the border between Northern Ireland and the Republic. Cronin's discussion of Fennell's travelogue engages with Williams's, Thompson's, and James's essays, too, in all of which the West of Ireland becomes figured by tourists as the mythic, pre-modern embodiment of 'Irishness'; here, Fennell confronts a palimpsest of linguistic overlays that require translation even to those like himself who consider it 'home' ground. Both travelogues lead Cronin, in contradistinction to Coulbert's depiction of the 'time-space compression' inaugurated by automotive technologies, to emphasize the importance of slowing down in a world where speed of access across great distance rather than proximity has become the hallmark of intimacy, the legacy of the period covered by this book. Cronin fittingly looks to home tourism for a new departure, a micro-modernity, in which deceleration, staying close by, and 'microspection' allow one to re-enchant a world grown uniform through globalization's relentless homogenization of space.

Notes

1. Qtd in *Description of the Lakes of Killarney, and the Surrounding Scenery* (London, 1849), xii–xiii.
2. Italo Calvino, *Invisible Cities*, trans. William Weaver (London: Vintage, 1997), 86–7.
3. See Michael Cronin, 'Global Questions and Local Visions: A Microcosmopolitan Perspective', in *Beyond the Difference: Welsh Literature in Comparative Contexts: Essays for M. Wynn Thomas at Sixty*, ed. Alyce von Rothkirch and Daniel Williams (Cardiff: University of Wales Press, 2004), 186–202.
4. Ian Ousby, *The Englishman's England: Taste, Travel and the Rise of Tourism* (Cambridge: Cambridge University Press, 1990), 7–8.
5. Esther Moir, *The Discovery of Britain: The English Tourists 1540–1840* (London: Routledge and Kegan Paul, 1964), xiv; my emphasis.
6. See Moir, *Discovery of Britain*, 3–4.
7. Dean MacCannell, *The Tourist: A New Theory of the Leisure Class* (Berkeley: University of California Press, 1999), 43–8.

8. See Benjamin Colbert, 'Aesthetics of Enclosure: Agricultural Tourism and the Place of the Picturesque', *European Romantic Review* 13.1 (March 2002), 23–34.

9. See Nicola J. Watson, *The Literary Tourist: Readers and Places in Romantic and Victorian Britain* (Basingstoke: Palgrave Macmillan, 2006), and Watson, ed., *Literary Tourism and Nineteenth-Century Culture* (Basingstoke: Palgrave Macmillan, 2009).

10. For coastal tourism, see Zoë Kinsley's essay below; for picturesque tourism, see Malcolm Andrews, *The Search for the Picturesque* (Aldershot: Scolar Press, 1989).

11. In addition to Andrews, Moir, Ousby, and Watson, already mentioned, important studies of home tourism include: (General) Zoë Kinsley, *Women Writing the Home Tour, 1682–1812* (Aldershot: Ashgate, 2008); (Ireland) Donal Horgan, *The Victorian Visitor in Ireland: Irish Tourism 1840–1910* (Cork: Imagimedia, 2002), Michael Cronin, *Irish Tourism: Image, Culture and Identity* (Bristol: Channel View Publications, 2003), Glenn Hooper, *Travel Writing and Ireland, 1760–1860* (Basingstoke: Palgrave Macmillan, 2005), William H. A. Williams, *Creating Irish Tourism: The First Century, 1750–1850* (London: Anthem, 2010); (Scotland) John Glendening, *The High Road: Romantic Tourism, Scotland, and Literature 1720–1820* (London: Macmillan, 1997), Alastair Durie, *Scotland for the Holidays: A History of Tourism in Scotland, 1780–1939* (East Linton: Tuckwell, 2003), Katherine-Haldane Grenier, *Tourism and Identity in Scotland, 1770–1914: Creating Caledonia* (Aldershot: Ashgate, 2005), Betty Hagglund, *Tourists and Travellers: Women's Non-fictional Writings about Scotland, 1770–1830* (Bristol: Channel View Publications, 2010).

12. See Susan Pitchford, *Identity Tourism: Imaging and Imagining the Nation* (Bingley: Emerald Group, 2008), 5.

13. Pitchford, *Identity Tourism*, 3.

14. Thomas West, *A Guide to the Lakes: Dedicated to the Lovers of Landscape Studies, and to All Who Have Visited, or Intend to Visit the Lakes in Cumberland, Westmoreland, and Lancashire* (London, 1778), 5–6.

15. James Norris Brewer, *Introduction to the Original Delineations, Topographical, Historical, and Descriptive, Intituled The Beauties of England and Wales* (London, 1818), vii–viii.

16. For 'cultural accreditation' on the Continental tour, see James Buzard, *The Beaten Track: European Tourism, Literature, and the Ways to 'Culture'* (Oxford: Clarendon Press, 1993), 110–11.

17. 'Travelling in England', review Article VIII, *The London Quarterly Review* 231 (July 1864), 115 (American edn, New York, 1864, Google Books, Web, 17 Feb. 2011).

18. Tim Fulford, *Landscape, Liberty, and Authority: Poetry, Criticism, and Politics from Thomson to Wordsworth* (Cambridge: Cambridge University Press, 1996), 142.

19. Ann Bermingham, *Landscape and Ideology: The English Rustic Tradition, 1740–1860* (Berkeley: University of California Press, 1986).

20. See Alain Corbin, *The Lure of the Sea: The Discovery of the Seaside, 1750–1840*, trans. Jocelyn Phelps (London: Penguin, 1995).

21. Ina Ferris, *The Romantic National Tale and the Question of Ireland* (Cambridge: Cambridge University Press, 2002), 18.

22. 'A Few Thoughts upon Tourists', *The New Monthly Magazine* 69.275 (Nov. 1843), 290.

1
Peripheral Vision, Landscape, and Nation-Building in Thomas Pennant's Tours of Scotland, 1769–72

Paul Smethurst

> Thus from a Mixture of all kinds, began
> That het'rogenous Thing, *An Englishman*:
> In eager Rapes, and furious lust begot
> Betwixt a painted *Britain* and a *Scot*.
> [...]
> From whence a Mongrel half-bred Race there came,
> With neither Name, or Nation, Speech or Fame.
>   Daniel Defoe, 'A True-Born Englishman' (1716)

While it might have had a strong sense of external identity and an increasing global presence, domestically, Great Britain in the early eighteenth century was less a geographical or political unity, than an 'imagined community'.[1] Like Defoe's Englishman, it remained a most 'het'rogenous thing', although home tours were gradually bringing the disparate identities and ancient histories of England, Wales, and Scotland into a common imaginative frame. In his *A Tour through the Whole Island of Great Britain* (1724–26), Defoe explicitly calls for economic and political union, claiming that Scotland's future prosperity must depend on closer ties with England and integration with the British Empire in the aftermath of the Act of Union (1707). This essay examines how Defoe, and later Thomas Pennant, used the home tour in the eighteenth century to incorporate Scotland, politically, economically, and imaginatively into the 'island of Great Britain'. Some fifty years after Defoe, Pennant continued the theme of integration, by which time the history of Scotland and its relations with England had reached a particularly interesting juncture. In the wake of the Battle of Culloden (1746) and with the dismantling of the ancient clan system, land reform was now of paramount importance to the country's future. Furthermore, Celtic culture was in danger of receding (and being disingenuously revived in the 'works of Ossian'). While attentive to this historical moment, Pennant's wide-ranging interests led him to locate his tours of Britain in discourses that reach beyond the domestic scene. There is an element of global vision in his Scottish tours, which he connects with eighteenth-century contexts of exploration, natural history, landscape aesthetics, Georgian modernity, and colonial expansion.

Like Defoe and Samuel Johnson, Pennant had an interest in overseas exploration voyages, and this would influence his decision to visit Scotland. In the far north of Britain, travel still had the allure and hardships of more distant exploration, which was much in the public mind. Pennant and Johnson were writing in the immediate aftermath of James Cook's *Endeavour* voyage (1768–71), and the cross-fertilization of scientific ideas and imaginative speculation is palpable. As a prominent naturalist, zoologist, and Fellow of the Royal Society, Pennant was directly connected to Cook's enterprise. He fixed the natural world in the same scientific gaze as Cook's own naturalists and played a significant role in the accumulation of scientific knowledge in Europe.[2] Johnson had read the account of Pennant's first tour of Scotland in 1769 and knew of his second in 1772 before setting off on his own long-awaited journey with James Boswell in 1773. Acknowledging that 'he's the best traveller I ever read; he observes more things than anyone else does',[3] Johnson might have felt a sense of belatedness – Pennant had already been there and written about it. But Johnson's purposes were different. He was concerned about arriving too late to witness and record a disappearing Highland culture. It was another kind of belatedness.[4]

Pennant is much closer to the ground than Johnson in several respects. In his tours, knowledge gained can be equated, or *mapped*, to the traveller's progress across (and *beneath*) the physical terrain. He is in this sense more of an explorer than either a tourist browsing curiosities or a naturalist scrutinizing singularities. Language had been a barrier for Pennant on his first tour of Scotland, so he took a Gaelic specialist with him on his second, and even in his homeland of Wales he needed an interpreter: an indication of the proximity of strangeness within the island of Britain. To cope with the surfeit of the unfamiliar in Scotland, he borrowed the observational and corroboratory methods of travelling naturalists. In the account of his second tour to Scotland in 1772, he incorporates verbatim Sir Joseph Banks's earlier description of the striking basalt formations on the island of Staffa.[5] Elsewhere he includes information from prominent naturalists and antiquarians who responded to his advertisement in the *Scots Magazine*.⁶ The account of Pennant's voyage to the Hebrides in 1772 is presented in much the same way as the journals of Cook and Banks: factual and objective, yet with an underlying tension of danger, dramatic revelation, and the uncanny. Just as Cook gives a detached account of the near shipwreck of the *Endeavour* on the Great Barrier Reef, Pennant can calmly relate a life-threatening situation on his voyage to the Hebrides.⁷ Similar objectivity is evident when facing the immense disappointment at not being able to reach the Northern tip of Scotland and so complete his survey of 'our island'.⁸ Despite this setback, Pennant went on to cover 1200 miles on his second tour and produce two volumes of detailed observations viewed with considerable interest across English society.

Natural history was now highly fashionable, with George III, leading politicians, and the aristocracy all enthusiastic followers. In 1763, *The Critical Review* declared it 'the favourite study of the times'.⁹ But the involvement of rulers and politicians suggests more than simply a fashion; natural history was also a matter of national and international importance for Britain.¹⁰ Food security and industrial progress are major concerns, and in those parts of Britain untouched by the southern wave of modernization Pennant sees poverty, idleness, and starvation. Although principally a naturalist, Pennant's focus in Scotland is less on nature as it is, than on finding ways to improve it. On his second tour in 1772, he 'pointed out everything [he] thought would be of service to the country', and noted that improvements were already evident since his first tour three years earlier: 'societies have been formed for the improvements of fisheries, and for the founding of towns in proper places', but in a candid reference to the sometimes political rather than rational use of investment, he warns that 'vast sums will be flung away; but incidentally numbers will be benefited and the passions of patriots tickled.'¹¹

For most tourists following in Defoe's and Pennant's footsteps (or hoof-prints), the eighteenth-century home tour provided an opportunity to engage in more superficial aspects of natural history, antiquarianism, and towards the end of the century, picturesque tourism. Yet the home tour in the late eighteenth century was acquiring a further impetus connected with Defoe's and Pennant's search for national progress. As Britain's imperial presence spread around the globe, a domestic urge sprang up to travel across the island nation at the centre of this empire. The home tour signalled interest not only in the topography and local curiosities of the country, but also in witnessing a *modern Britain* at the forefront of industrial and agricultural progress. More extensive home tours to Northern England and Scotland were made easier towards the end of the century by the improved turnpike roads and printed guide-books. Such developments in travel were evidence in themselves of progress. Although the domestic tourist would later have an ambivalent relationship with other aspects of industrial modernity, it was still common during the eighteenth century to combine visits to sites of natural beauty with side-trips to mines, factories, and brickworks.[12] These confirmed the emergence of Britain as an industrial force and reminded travellers of how national interests were connected to global trade. At the beginning of the century, Defoe was already aware that economic prospects for Scotland (and by extension, Britain) were related to colonial expansion: 'the lands in Scotland will now be improved, their estates doubled ... and the West-India trade abundantly pours in wealth upon her'.[13]

Following Defoe, Pennant made informed observations on how Britain generated its wealth at home and how this was increasing through agriculture and industrial improvements; he would also, with Johnson, trigger a tourist boom in Scotland as predicted by *The Monthly Review*:

> [T]ours to the Highlands, and voyages to the isles, will probably become fashionable *routes* of our virtuosi, and those who travel for amusement. Mr. Pennant has led the way, Dr. Johnson has followed; and with such precursors, and the sanction of such examples, what man of spirit and curiosity will forbear to explore these remote parts of our island, with her territorial appendages – of which, indeed, and of the public advantages which *might* be derived from them, we have hitherto been shamefully ignorant.[14]

In combining usefulness and curiosity, the objectives of the home tour in the eighteenth century were very similar to those of exploration. At the periphery, this was even more so, as curiosities and natural phenomena could be found which were as strange to an English traveller as anything to be found in the South Seas. The far north of Scotland epitomized the unmodernized periphery, which Defoe says 'our geographers ... are obliged to fill ... up with hills and mountains, as they do the inner parts of Africa, with lions and elephants, for want of knowing what else to place there'.[15] This imaginative association between a home tour in Britain and exploration in Africa, points to a frequently observed parallel, noted by Martin Martin, Edmund Burt, Banks, Pennant, Johnson, and others that the Highlands and Islands of West Scotland were 'as little known to its southern brethren as

Kamtschatka'.[16] This local remoteness engenders both vulgar and scientific forms of curiosity. The scientific approach to natural history and ethnography in the eighteenth century actually increased the public appetite for vulgar curiosity, and encouraged tourism. Even Pennant, while usually dismissive of superstition, leaves open the possibility of spectres, elves, and fairies, as if wilfully re-enchanting the landscape. In the far north-west coast of Scotland among the mountains, bogs, and sea lochs, he distances himself, and us, from the superstition of 'less enlighten'd times', but at the same time installs the unseen spectre in the imagination of the future tourist:

> It is not wonderful, that the imagination, amidst these darksome and horrible scenes, should figure to itself ideal beings, once the terror of superstitious inhabitants: in less-enlighten'd times a dreadful spectre haunted these hills, sometimes in the form of a great dog, a man, or a thin gigantic hag called *Glas-lich*.[17]

In a similar vein, he draws attention to the phenomenon of 'second sight' which he finds is 'firmly believed at this time' in these sequestered parts of the Hebrides. His 'informant' gives him an example of a man hearing the hammering of nails into his coffin immediately preceding his death.[18] The presence of fairies and elves is entertained by the enlightened scientist, as he reports the old women of Jura 'preserve a stick of the wicken, or mountain ash, as a protection against elves';[19] and Pennant finds himself 'again enraptured with the charms of *Faskally*, which appears like fairy ground, amidst the wild environs of craggy mountains, skirted with woods'.[20] Consciously or not, Pennant re-enchants the natural world in equal measure to his analytical and utilitarian abstraction of it. As a result, the peripheries of Scotland and Wales would soon prove fertile ground for both serious naturalists and ethnographers, and the increasing hordes of wide-eyed tourists. Just two decades after his Scottish tours, Pennant wrote: 'I brought home a favourable account of the land [Scotland]. Whether it will thank me or not I cannot say, but from the report I made, and showing that it might be visited safely, it has ever since been *inondée* with southern visitants.'[21]

In parts of Wales and Scotland, the home tour might also put domestic travellers in touch with a disappearing Celtic culture, as well as with ancient Druid and Roman remains. These were often set within wild, mountainous landscapes, which would themselves become sites of interest for picturesque tourism. The tourist might escape modernity here and indulge in visions of an ancient past in landscapes which transcended contemporary reality.[22] By the end of the eighteenth century, scenic tourism was already beginning to assimilate the curiosities Pennant had revealed in Scotland, bringing a local-exotic within the frame of domestic tourist sites. Even the remote Western Isles and Highlands of Scotland, previously largely unknown even to most Scottish people, were included. The home tour was responsible here for an imaginative appropriation and domestication of the periphery, and in this respect at least, a conjunctive national identity was emerging.

This was helped by the structure and style of Pennant's narratives, which offer a more naturalistic, and possibly more patriotic, approach to travel writing. Unlike Defoe's constructed epistolary travelogue, based on the form of Grand Tour travel accounts, Pennant's narratives follow the method of the travelling naturalist, actively seeking and recording sites in the order they are encountered. His train follows the lines of his sometimes erratic and serendipitous routes, frequently digressing as particular sites become portals to discourses on natural history, antiquities, and land improvement. With increasing popular interest in the natural world, Pennant's topographical observations combined with phenomenological realism, were in great demand. By bringing the empirical protocols and epistemological aspirations of English exploration narratives into a domestic setting, Pennant's accounts of the 1769 tour to Scotland, and later his more extensive 1772 tour and voyage to the Hebrides, become patriotic if not nationalistic. The *Tour* of 1769 went to five editions, and both *Tours* were well-received critically in their time. To more modern eyes, the weight and breadth of Pennant's combined *Tours* of Scotland might indicate a structural awkwardness, with encyclopaedic detail threatening to overwhelm the sense of *being there*. To accommodate Pennant's 'awkwardness', Alan Chalmers comes up with an ingenious formalist twist, suggesting that the 'textual problem', in which detail obscures the chronology of the travels, might parallel 'Scotland's contemporary uneasy relations with its own past and future', which is indeed one of Pennant's themes.[23]

Pennant's *Tours* of Scotland, Wales, and England were important in bringing disparate national identities and ancient histories into a common imaginative frame. In an age of exploration and colonial expansion, the topographical realities rendered by home tours facilitated the *territorialization* of the island of Britain. As a construct, Great Britain had previously lacked a sense of the country as a whole which extended beyond the English centre of the Thames valley and the gently rolling countryside of southern England. If this was equivalent to a body, the heartland wanted limbs, backbone, and remote appendages. The Western Highlands and Islands fulfilled that function and were often referred to in these terms. Furthermore, the furthest tip of this island body took on symbolic freight as the extreme edge and liminal boundary. Its associations with the primitive, the mythological, and the supernatural were then perfectly fitting. Yet, despite the geographical wholeness Pennant's tours engender, their point of view is essentially *English* (notwithstanding Pennant's Welshness). As Pennant's gaze pans out to its 'appendages', we could argue that an English national identity (still rooted in southern England, London, and the growing Georgian towns and cities) is being defined against a proximate other discovered in the peripheries and the countryside. Meanwhile, Welsh, Scottish, and regional English identity are left to gird themselves against the pressures of transculturation and cultural appropriation from interloping urban English tourists.

Despite the sense of invasion and colonization that such tours impressed upon those in England's peripheries (for example, as a Scot, Boswell railed against Pennant's representation of his homeland), domestic tourism helped to produce by the late eighteenth century a more cohesive image of the island of Britain as a whole. From an English, and to some extent a British, perspective, particular topographies induced symbolic attachments to a shared homeland without necessarily making it more homogenous. Indeed, the reverse is true when the mode is one of *differentiation*, as is commonly the case in travel narratives organized around sequential encounters with local difference. Pennant uses such a mode to map out his theory of progress and regress in the context of improvement and Georgian modernity. Flourishing places are evidence of the influence of rational modernity and mercantilism, whereas sites of destitution, poverty, and migration demonstrate the failure to apply systems of improvement.

Modern approaches to the natural world in eighteenth-century Britain would begin to cast nature as 'other' rather than as a coextensive unity providing humanity with its essential biomass. Through the progressive Whiggish ideology that influenced Pennant and other English travellers, the countryside when wild, untended, and unimproved, represented a regressive milieu. English tourists could find plenty of examples in the peripheries of Britain, and Pennant would even discover a literal translation of the primitive swamp in the Highlands of Scotland. Here he associates the boggy valleys hindering their progress with a regressive culture. General Wade's military roads, on the other hand, symbolize the civilizing and progressive force of Georgian modernity.[24]

A moral as well as political dimension underlies the landscape descriptions when Pennant describes the old chieftains' objections to the new military roads:

> These public works were at first very disagreeable to the old chieftains: it lessened their influence greatly ... But they had another reason ... Lochaber had been a den of thieves; and as long as they had their waters, their torrents and their bogs, in *a state of nature*, they made their excursions, could plunder and retreat with their booty in full security.[25]

As in Shakespeare's *Macbeth*, whose historical connections Pennant explores fully on his second tour, the heath suggests a lawless place outside the world of rational and historic forces, and an ancient world destined to turn. Pennant is a modern, and this marginal landscape affords no aesthetic possibilities. More importantly, from his Whiggish point of view, it represents a wasted opportunity with respect to land use. The 'state of nature' is a repeating motif in his tours of Scotland and always meets with a negative response. For both Defoe and Pennant, travel had not yet become the metaphor for escape that it would become in romantic and modern travel narratives, and countryside in a 'state of nature' produces not lyrical raptures in the traveller, but yearning for enclosures and efficient husbandry. When Pennant finds such a view, as he does in Perthshire and the Central Highlands, he is enchanted: 'A most delicious plain spreads itself beneath, divided into verdant meadows, or glowing with ripened corn; embellished with woods.'[26] The byword of the age was *improvement*, especially as applied to agriculture, mining, fisheries, and manufacture, and it is through a progressive utilitarian frame that Pennant observes the potential for improving trade and rental incomes.

Defoe and Pennant, and to some extent Johnson, describe the landscape but are much less interested in landscape *per se* than will be the ensuing tourists. Topographical curiosities, such as the naked 'paps' of Jura, were less an attraction to the aesthetic eye than the means to gain elevation to complete a survey of the surrounding terrain. However, by the end of the eighteenth century, such landscapes were drawing thousands of tourists to the countryside. By choosing to ground his many observations in the topographical realities of Scotland, Pennant connected with an aesthetic in which landscape was becoming a vehicle for expressing modern ideas. The land itself was being exploited by modern techniques of husbandry, rotation, and enclosures, and microscopically scrutinized in natural history. Meanwhile, the picturesque emerged initially as a painterly approach to topographic realities and evolved into an imaginative construct outside, but corresponding with, these realities. Although grounded in real terrain, the picturesque allows subtle inflection in its verbal or pictorial projections of internal emotions and desires, expressions of progress/regress, and frames for local or national attachment. Picturesque tours were thus engaged in a process of self-identification and patriotism. Somewhat bizarrely, an expanding empire with an increasingly metropolitan character maintained a national identity steeped in the aestheticized nature of England's immediate periphery (Scotland, Wales, and the Lake District). As Anne Janowitz points out, the word 'country' came to signify both rural terrain and nation at this time, and out of this conflation 'was born the myth of rural England, as well as the myth of the homogeneous coherence of the nation'.[27]

Representations of landscape might express national identity or conform to aesthetic fashion, but they can also reflect social and political realities. Defoe's travels in Scotland predate Pennant's and Johnson's by fifty years or so, yet the theme of nation-building as post-conflict reconciliation is still evident. Pennant says he was trying to heal old wounds as well as look to future prosperity: 'I laboured earnestly to conciliate the affections of the two nations, so wickedly and studiously set at variance by evil-designing people.'[28] It is in this spirit of suture that both Defoe and Pennant trace paths back and forth across the borders of Wales, England, and Scotland. Defoe announces that he journeyed across the 'whole ISLAND' of Great Britain to produce a guidebook 'fitted for the Reading of such as desire to Travel over the ISLAND'.[29] In describing his second tour of Scotland and voyage to the Hebrides, Pennant begins with Chester and does not reach the Scottish borders for some 70 pages. On his return from Scotland, he traces his journey through northern England to his home in Downing, Wales. Pennant seems intent on imaginatively reconciling the three nations of the Union, and seeking common ground through which to join, transcend, or *bury* their differences within a progressive national vision. For Pennant, one of the chief areas of common ground is literally the earth, with native soil in a political and metaphorical sense being derived from concrete examples. The essential relations between people and the land on which their living depends bring Pennant time and again to the efficient use of land resources across the nation as his main theme. The pressing needs of the contemporary invariably supplant his other interests as a naturalist and antiquarian.

It is as an antiquarian that Pennant brings to light the tomb of the last prioress in a nunnery near the Bay of Martyrs on Iona, noting the intricate carvings and Latin inscriptions on its face. He does not remark on the desecration of the church housing the tomb which is presently used as a cattle shelter. But the waste of the cow-dung lying 'some feet thick' offends his progressive landowner's eye:

> [T]he islanders are too lazy to remove this fine manure, the collection of a century, to enrich their grounds. With much difficulty, by virtue of fair words, and a bribe, prevale [*sic*] on one of these listless fellows to remove a great quantity of this dung-hill; and by that means once more expose to light the tomb of the prioress.[30]

He has already given an historical account of St Columba and the massacre of the monks by the Vikings. In bearing witness to this history, he brings it into the present, with all the touristic ramifications this entails. The melancholy induced by the wanton destruction of a religious community is something the whole nation can feel. There can also be a shared sense of outrage, by dint of the perpetrators being foreign invaders, and yet Pennant is possibly more passionate about the wasted opportunities for agricultural improvement. This is a passion that becomes more intense as he proceeds northwards in the Western Highlands, where he finds local inhabitants destitute and starving for want of modern farming methods that serve more than the narrow interests of the landlords. At the northernmost point of his voyage to the Hebrides, at Ledbeg in Sutherland, he describes a pitiful scene:

> This tract seems the residence of sloth; the people almost torpid with idleness, and most wretched: their hovels most miserable ... yet there is much improveable land here in a state of nature: but till famine pinches they will not bestir themselves: they are content with little at present, and are thoughtless of futurity.[31]

This habitation of abject misery is reminiscent of Cook's descriptions of the Patagonian Indians at Tierra del Fuego, but all the more shocking for being so close to home, and, according to Pennant, quite avoidable. While recognizing that famine will lead to migrations in the short term, Pennant is confident that improved and more equitable land management would lead to greater prosperity.

The function of natural and ancient history in Pennant's tours is not to escape contemporary reality, but to enrich it materially through ideas for improving the soil and food production, and, metaphorically, through symbolic attachments to the landscape. I would argue that his metaphorical schema for the representation of Scottish landscape is connected to his mercantilist vision of a united Britain, which he shares with Defoe. This has a political dimension when he seeks to erase recent bloody conflicts between England and Scotland, the signs of which are still evident in the landscape. For example, on his first tour of Scotland in 1769, he passes over Culloden Moor, reporting that this is 'the place that North Britain [Scotland] owes its present prosperity to, by the victory of April 16, 1746'. He barely mentions the ensuing massacre: 'But let a veil be flung over a few excesses consequential of a day productive of so much benefit to the united kingdoms.'[32]

Pennant's political stance is also reflected in his description of the plain of Raynach, where he observes a diminished countryside, partly barren, with 'no trees of any size':

This was once the property of Robertson, of Struan, who had been in the rebellion of 1715; had his estate restored, but in 1745 rebelling a second time, the country was burnt, and the estate annexed to the crown; he returned a few years after, and died as he lived, a most abandoned sot.[33]

The 'rebel' Robertson is banished and left with a harsh and primitive existence in a wild and barren nature, as if both he and the countryside have deserved their fate. By contrast, the castle at Braemar forms part of a beautiful prospect from Invercauld, now firmly in the grip of government forces:

On the northern entrance, immense ragged and broken crags bound one side of the prospect; over whose gray sides and summits is scattered the melancholy green of the picturesque pine, which grows out of the naked rock ... A little lower down is the castle ... formerly a necessary curb on the little kings of the country; but at present serves scarce any real purpose, but to adorn the landscape.[34]

The castle has no function but an aesthetic one; it registers history *under erasure*. Through picturesque framing, the castle as a site of English military oppression is reduced to an aesthetic object, detached from its historical context. By contrast, en route to Athol House, Pennant passes through a 'most picturesque scene, with the pendant form of the boughs waving with the wind' and a 'beautiful little straith, fertile, and prettily wooded'. Then arriving at the house, we learn that it 'held a siege against the rebels in 1746' and inside he finds the house 'highly finished by the *noble* owner'.[35] Such aesthetic appreciation of the natural scenery through the picturesque is for Pennant generally reserved for the thriving estates of southern Scotland.

If recent history is partially erased and aestheticized by Pennant, or under erasure, this is in contrast to his treatment of the sites of ancient history. He delves into the deep past and native soil of Scotland, literally exhuming Druid, Roman, and Celtic remains, and he reveres the 'classical ground' of Roman antiquities. In what must have been something of a conflict of interests for the antiquarian and landowner, he even complains that the Roman camp at Strageth has been 'defaced with the plough', when his natural tendency elsewhere is to celebrate the cultivation of the land.[36] Giving far more weight to ancient history than recent conflict between England and Scotland, he notes the site of the 'British' defence of the island against the forces of Agricola, as if from this famous battle the myth of a united Britain might be resurrected for modern times.[37]

Pennant finds that the ancient inhabitants of Sunderland in North-West Scotland did not attempt to defend the native soil, but rather retreated into it, completely burying themselves in funkholes built for the purpose. This evidence of literal entrenchment appeals to Pennant's near obsession with native soil, and yet as an image of primitivism, it offends his modern outlook, leading him to describe the 'buried' men as being 'almost in a state of nature' and 'the whole scenery of this place ... unspeakably savage, and the inhabitants suitable'.[38] Although he tries to instil a shared sense of belonging in Scottish soil, he seems more comfortable disinterring the remains of 'classical ground'. His fascination with the hidden strata of Roman civilization in Britain owes something to his familiarity with the classical literature of Tacitus and Virgil, and later he is also interested in the sites of Scottish history that relate to Shakespeare's *Macbeth*. Whether he is doing so consciously or not, Pennant ennobles the native soil with these literary allusions, and connects with his posited audience of educated gentlemen.

The Druidical sites, again because of their proximity to the earth, materially and spiritually, intrigue him, but he can only find tenuous links to their origins in Latin texts. Pennant tantalizingly links the Druidical site on Skye through Pliny and Plutarch to the 'purity of the *Celtic* religion',[39] such that again Scottish soil finds aggrandizement through connection with classical ground. Local knowledge, largely derived from oral cultures and enigmatic carvings, has blended with myth and hearsay over the centuries. Finding an *Anait* on Skye, his 'informant' tells him it was designed for the worship of the earth. The sanctity of the soil and the relics it delivers are of particular interest to Pennant as he seeks connections across temporal and geographical borders through a shared ancient past and nature worship. For Pennant, these connections are reinforced by the scientific realities of an extensive and conjoining geological past, dramatically revealed by Banks's description of Staffa. Geological knowledge combines here with an appreciation of nature as the school of art, where blocks of basalt offer a greater lesson in 'regularity' than the whole 'Grecian school'.[40]

Through typical temporal disjunctions mapped to the present spatiality of his journey, Pennant moves from the *Anait* to describe in a single paragraph: lunch; a boat ride across Loch Grisernis, where he notes the fishermen's nets are made of 'purple *melic* grass'; and his arrival at Kingsburgh, 'immortalized by its mistress, the celebrated FLORA MAC-DONALD, the fair protectress of a fugitive adventurer'.[41] By making Scotland redolent with ancient history and the already romanticized recent history of Flora MacDonald and the 'fugitive adventurer', he allows the past to impinge on the present here as an almost disconnected spectacle. His topographical descriptions remain focused on the real and visitable Scotland, and this is the solid ground between his antiquarian excursions and such ghostly, filmic histories. Where recent history has become romanticized or aestheticized, sites become portals into a past grown inaccessible to the contemporary visitor. This past nevertheless exerts a strong pull on touristic curiosity, and while continuing to see the future in real landscapes, Pennant also enriches Scottish soil *touristically* with ancient history and myth.

As we have already seen, improvement is always writ large in the landscape for Pennant. His vitriolic attacks on irresponsible Scottish landlords sharply contrast with his praise for modernizers who fully exploit the natural resources of the country. At the end of the voyage to the Hebrides, which marks the end of the first volume of his 1772 tour to Scotland, he invokes the spectre of an old Chieftain: 'A figure, dressed in the garb of an antient [*sic*] warrior, floated in the air before me.'[42] Through the mouthpiece of the Chieftain, Pennant gives an account of the glorious feudal past: of warlords, battles, and loyalties given and received. He then explains how the feudal government was ended (by the imposition of English law after the crushing of the Jacobite Rebellion, although this is not made explicit) and the trappings of power removed from the once mighty chieftains: '"The target, the dirk, and the claymore [*sic*], too long abused, were wrested from our hands, and we were bid to learn the arts of peace; to spread the net, to shoot the shuttle, or to cultivate the ground."' To substitute for the loss of feudal power, the chieftains looked for profit in the lands the English had not confiscated: 'by a most violent and surprizing [*sic*] transformation, [the chieftains] at once sunk into rapacious landlords; determined to compensate the loss of power, with the encrease [*sic*] of revenue; to exchange the warm affections of their people for sordid trash.'[43] The apparition then gives advice for the future development and improvement of Scotland through the assistance of the English, while warning the Scottish lords not to become 'effeminated' or '"become ridiculous by adopting the idle fashions of foreign climes"'.[44] The main complaint is against those landlords who take a quick profit from the land and spend it abroad, abandoning their 'vassals' to poverty, hunger, and migration.

The function of the spectre's speech is not so much to dwell on the past or complain about the rapacious landlords, but in line with his main theme, to exhort Scottish landowners to play their part in his vision of a prosperous and united Britain. He calls upon Pennant to urge his countrymen (English more than Welsh) to help develop Scotland to the benefit of Britain and the empire as a whole: 'THOSE should extend your manufactures; and THESE would defend your commerce ... they would weave the sails to waft your navies to victory; and part of them rejoice to share the glory in the most distant combats.'[45] This would all be possible, the spectre suggests, if the 'improving state of the vassals of an *Argyle*, an *Athol*, a *Breadalbane*, and a *Bute*' were to become the norm.[46] The curtailment of feudal power might give the highlanders immediate cause to 'bless the hand that loosened their bonds', because 'tyranny more often than protection' is what they had received in return for their vassalage. But Pennant remains a supporter of 'the tender relation that *patriarchal* government experiences', that he finds in the estate of Mr Macleod of Dunvegan.[47] Pennant is a Whig, but certainly not a 'leveller'. Like his fellow landowner, Uvedale Price, whose estate in Hereford also straddled the borderlands of Wales and England, Pennant is conscious of the delicate balance of running an estate beneficently and profitably. Both men instinctively look to landscape for material and metaphorical possibility, and with Price the two are sometimes interchangeable. When he suggests 'all parts [to remain] free and unconstrained, though some higher than others, some in shade, some rough, some polished',[48] he refers to an aesthetics of landscape and through this to his political stance against 'levelling'.

Price defines the principles of the picturesque, but for him the aesthetic has a function in the actual improvement of real landscapes. When Pennant describes Kelso, he likewise links the aesthetics of the picturesque to the environment, and to improvements in the rural economy:

> The environs of *Kelso* are very fine: the lands consist of gentle risings, inclosed with hedges, and extremely fertile. They have much reason to boast of their prospects … from *Pinnacle-hill* is seen a vast extent of country, highly cultivated, watered with long reaches of the *Tweed*, well wooded on each margin. These borders ventured on cultivation much earlier than those on the west or east, and have made great progress in every species of rural economy.[49]

This is a real and present landscape, but it is also, for Pennant, a vision of the future. In the miserable environs of Sunderland, where the land has not been cultivated, the inhabitants must live hand-to-mouth with no sense of futurity, until forced into migration. By contrast, the environs of Kelso can 'boast of their prospects'. The word 'prospect' was of course a key term in picturesque landscape aesthetics, denoting a viewpoint or outlook extending towards the horizon. By switching the indicators of space and time, it also denotes a view of the temporal horizon – the future vision that in this case most conforms to Pennant's ideal.

Pennant cannot be described as a picturesque tourist, but he certainly provides a road map for the pursuit of likely 'prospects' and 'stations', to use the scenic tourist's lexicon. He is not attracted to countryside in a state of nature, and, as we have seen, he prefers cultivated farmlands and estates in which prosperity manifests itself through a reinvented nature. But he is also drawn to the aesthetic of diversity and proximate otherness, which connects with an important principle of the picturesque: what Uvedale Price might term 'sudden variation' or a 'variation of light and shade'.[50] There is a striking example of Pennant's mode of differentiation/reintegration following his description of a prosperous fishing village in the far north-west of Scotland, where he has also witnessed abject poverty:

> So unexpected a prospect of the busy haunt of men and ships in this wild and romantic tract, afforded this agreeable reflection: that there is no part of our dominions so remote, so inhospitable, and so unprofitable, as to deny employ and livelihood to thousands; and that there are no parts so polished, so improved, and so fertile, but which must stoop to receive advantage from the dreary spots

they so affectedly despise; and must be obliged to acknowledge the mutual dependency of part on part, however remotely placed, and howsoever different in modes or manner of living. *Charles Brandon's* address to his royal spouse may well be applied to both extremes of our isle:

> Cloth of gold, do not despise,
> Altho' thou art match'd with cloth of frize.
> Cloth of frize, be not too bold,
> Altho' thou art match'd with cloth of gold.[51]

This could be read as a vision of the island of Britain in which Scotland plays the lesser role of 'frize' (frieze: a coarse woollen cloth) to England's gold, but there is a more subtle reading. From the situation of a traveller who has covered some 1200 miles mostly on horseback, Pennant has clearly observed great diversity of terrain and variation in livelihood across Scotland and northern England. Yet he has not fallen into the trap of early ethnographers in the South Seas of assuming a deterministic relationship between humanity and the environment.[52] His message is that the environment can be improved, and livelihood increased no matter how unpromising the land. Furthermore, the variation in prospects for different parts of the island is for Pennant proof of his theory of improvement and his desire for a union of coherent incongruity – a picturesque aesthetic organizing a nationalistic, and by extension, an imperial vision of the island of Great Britain.

In the context of eighteenth-century improvement, nature is no longer a barrier or a constraint that separates communities, but can, in a rational world, be moulded to the common good. With Pennant, the desire for social and political harmony through improvement is reflected in his tendency to read landscapes through the lexicon of late eighteenth-century aesthetics. His travel writing marks a pivotal moment in changing attitudes to beauty in the landscape, and this is connected with his vision of harmonious correspondence between elements: in art as in life.

Notes

1. A cultural artefact as defined by Benedict Anderson in his *Imagined Communities* (London and New York: Verso, 1991), 2.
2. See Pennant's *British Zoology*, 4 vols (1768–70), *Arctic Zoology* (1784–85), and *Outlines of the Globe* (1798–1800). Pennant's circle included Gilbert White, Carl Linnaeus, Joseph Banks, Horace Walpole, Voltaire, and the Comte de Buffon.

3. Peter Levi, 'Introduction' to Samuel Johnson and James Boswell, *A Journey to the Western Islands of Scotland* and *The Journal of a Tour to the Hebrides* [1775, 1786] (Harmondsworth: Penguin, 1984), 14; and again in Thomas Pennant, *A Tour in Scotland 1769* [1771] (Edinburgh: Birlinn, 2000), ix.

4. For further comparison, see Alan Chalmers, 'Scottish Prospects: Thomas Pennant, Samuel Johnson, and the Possibilities of Narrative', in *Historical Boundaries, Narrative Forms: Essays on British Literature in the Long Eighteenth Century*, ed. Lorna Clymer and Roeber Mayer (Newark: University of Delaware Press, 2007), 199–214. See also Thomas Jemielity, 'Thomas Pennant's Scottish *Tours* and [Samuel Johnson's] *A Journey to the Western Isles of Scotland*', in *Fresh Reflections on Samuel Johnson: Essays in Criticism*, ed. Prem Nath (Troy: Whitston Publishing Co., 1987), 312–27.

5. Thomas Pennant, *A Tour in Scotland and Voyage to the Hebrides*, 2 vols (Chester: John Monk, 1774), 1: 299–309.

6. See 'Introduction' by Charles W. J. Withers, in Thomas Pennant, *A Tour in Scotland and Voyage to the Hebrides 1772* [1774], ed. Andrew Simmons (Edinburgh: Birlinn, 1998), xvii.

7. Pennant, *A Tour in Scotland and Voyage to the Hebrides*, 1: 376.

8. Pennant, *A Tour in Scotland and Voyage to the Hebrides*, 1: 367.

9. Qtd in Keith Thomas, *Man and the Natural World* (London: Allen Lane, 1983), 283.

10. For an assessment of the importance of plant economy to Britain's colonial expansion, see Richard Drayton, *Nature's Government: Science, Imperial Britain, and the 'Improvement' of the World* (New Haven and London: Yale University Press, 2000), 108.

11. Thomas Pennant, *The Literary Life of Thomas Pennant Esq., by Himself* [1793] (Dublin: J. Christie, 1821), 27.

12. Esther Moir, *The Discovery of Britain: The English Tourists 1540–1840* (London: Routledge & Kegan Paul, 1964), 98.

13. Daniel Defoe, *A Tour through the Whole Island of Great Britain* [1724–6] (Harmondsworth: Penguin, 1971), 637.

14. Ralph Griffiths, *The Monthly Review* 51 (January–February 1775), 459.

15. Defoe, *A Tour through the Whole Island of Great Britain*, 663.

16. Pennant, *The Literary Life*, 19.

17. Pennant, *A Tour in Scotland and Voyage to the Hebrides*, 1: 397.

18. Pennant, *A Tour in Scotland and Voyage to the Hebrides*, 1: 323.

19. Pennant, *A Tour in Scotland and Voyage to the Hebrides*, 1: 245.

20. Pennant, *A Tour in Scotland and Voyage to the Hebrides*, 2: 55.

21. Pennant, *The Literary Life*, 19.

22. As a geologist, Pennant was particularly aware of time in the landscape.

23. Alan Chalmers, 'Scottish Prospects', 206.

24. For an appraisal of Wade's road-building see Pennant, *A Tour in Scotland 1769*, 142. In his second tour of 1772, he was not always so complimentary, complaining at times of unnecessary loops and diversions.

25. Pennant, *A Tour in Scotland 1769*, 136 (emphasis added).

26. Pennant, *A Tour in Scotland and Voyage to the Hebrides*, 2: 20.

27. Anne Janowitz, *England's Ruins: Poetic Purpose and the National Landscape* (Oxford: Blackwell, 1990), 4.

28. Pennant, *The Literary Life*, 23.

29. Defoe, from title page of the first edition of vol. 1 (1724) in *A Tour Through the Whole Island of Great Britain*, 41.
30. Pennant, *A Tour in Scotland and Voyage to the Hebrides*, 1: 282.
31. Pennant, *A Tour in Scotland and Voyage to the Hebrides*, 1: 365.
32. Pennant, *A Tour in Scotland 1769*, 103.
33. Pennant, *A Tour in Scotland 1769*, 67.
34. Pennant, *A Tour in Scotland 1769*, 82.
35. Pennant, *A Tour in Scotland 1769*, 73.
36. Pennant, *A Tour in Scotland and Voyage to the Hebrides*, 2: 101, 91.
37. Pennant, *A Tour in Scotland and Voyage to the Hebrides*, 2: 97.
38. Pennant, *A Tour in Scotland and Voyage to the Hebrides*, 1: 256.
39. Pennant, *A Tour in Scotland and Voyage to the Hebrides*, 1: 341.
40. Pennant, *A Tour in Scotland and Voyage to the Hebrides*, 1: 301.
41. Pennant, *A Tour in Scotland and Voyage to the Hebrides*, 1: 342.
42. Pennant, *A Tour in Scotland and Voyage to the Hebrides*, 1: 421.
43. Pennant, *A Tour in Scotland and Voyage to the Hebrides*, 1: 424.
44. Pennant, *A Tour in Scotland and Voyage to the Hebrides*, 1: 425.
45. Pennant, *A Tour in Scotland and Voyage to the Hebrides*, 1: 427.
46. Pennant, *A Tour in Scotland and Voyage to the Hebrides*, 1: 425–6.
47. Pennant, *A Tour in Scotland and Voyage to the Hebrides*, 1: 337.
48. Uvedale Price, *An Essay on the Picturesque, as Compared with the Sublime and the Beautiful, and, on the Use of Studying Pictures, for the Purpose of Improving Real Landscape* (London: J. Robson, 1794), 28.
49. Pennant, *A Tour in Scotland and Voyage to the Hebrides*, 1: 276.
50. Price, *An Essay on the Picturesque*, 44–5.
51. Pennant, *A Tour in Scotland and Voyage to the Hebrides*, 1: 398.
52. As did Johann Reinhold Forster, for example, in his *Observations Made During a Voyage Round the World* [1778], ed. Nicholas Thomas, Harriet Guest, and Michael Dettelbach (Honolulu: University of Hawai'i Press, 1996), 9–10.

2
Beside the Seaside: Mary Morgan's *Tour to Milford Haven, in the Year 1791*

Zoë Kinsley

> ... now alike, gay widow, virgin, wife,
> Ingenious to diversify dull life,
> In coaches, chaises, caravans and hoys,
> Fly to the coast for daily, nightly joys,
> And all impatient of dry land, agree
> With one consent to rush into the sea.[1]
> > William Cowper, 'Retirement' (1782)

In his social satire, 'Retirement', William Cowper suggests that the coast was particularly alluring for women who, whatever their circumstances, were somehow united by a communal desire to plunge into the sea. In reality, the experiences of those who travelled to the British coast were, of course, much more complex, and its various faces – resort towns, ports, beaches, cliffs – produced a range of responses, and inspired multiple traditions of representation. This essay considers some of these responses and representations emerging at the turn of the nineteenth century, and makes a detailed consideration of one home tour narrative, Mary Morgan's *Tour to Milford Haven* (1795).

While Cowper's poetry is an important influence on Morgan's writing – she quotes from *The Task* on the title page of her travelogue – the *Tour to Milford Haven* nevertheless offers a corrective to his masculinist interpretation of the way in which women relate to the British coast. In the preface to her work, Morgan fiercely defends the rights of female authors, positioning herself within a strong tradition of women's writing. However, she implicitly resists Cowper's notion that all women relate to the landscapes of travel in the same way by emphasizing the variety, rather than the homogeneity, of travellers' descriptions of the home tour. As part of that discourse of difference she insists upon the uniqueness of her account.[2] What is significant about Morgan as a commentator on the seaside is the way in which her travelogue traces a shift in her own ideas about the coast: as detached observation of place gives way to intimate familiarity, so the enthusiastically Romantic tone of her early responses becomes undercut by an increasing sense of disillusionment. Consequently, her work not only offers an alternative perspective on women's relationship to the seaside to that offered by Cowper, it also qualifies a popular strain in current criticism which constructs the beach as 'liminal', a transgressive space defying certain demarcation, where conventional social and spatial structures are eschewed or disrupted and alternative ones rehearsed.[3] While Morgan's travelogue highlights the transgressive, it cannot sustain a discourse of positive liminality. Rather, coastal space is subsumed within a stronger, dominating narrative of fear and danger which culminates in the traveller's physical and metaphorical rejection of the coastline in favour of an experience of place which she characterizes territorially as inland, and conceptually as therefore 'safe'. In contrast to Cowper's depiction of women rushing to the sea, Morgan decisively withdraws from it, and in doing so denies the neat correspondence between female desire and the coastal landscape offered in his poem.

2.1   'Neglected' space? The British coast at the turn of the nineteenth century

> While the inland counties of England have been so hackneyed by travellers and quartos, the Coast has hitherto been most unaccountably neglected, and, if we except a few fashionable watering-places, is entirely unknown to the public.[4]

So writes Richard Ayton in his introduction to *A Voyage Round Great Britain* (1814–25), narrating the twelve-year home tour exploration undertaken by the landscape painter and engraver William Daniell, illustrated with 308 aquatint engravings of coastal scenes.[5] Daniell's comprehensive circumnavigation of the British coastline was designed to increase interest in the coast, and to highlight the complicated and often ambiguous place of 'our seas and shores' within the popular imaginary. Ayton argues that it is both surprising and lamentable that the coastline plays a significant role in the narrative of British identity formation, yet receives little serious study. The coast is also depicted as a space where divergent and often conflicting impulses and imperatives tussle for dominance, as is epitomized by this distinction drawn between seaside tourism on the one hand, and an appreciation of the sublime on the other:

> Those parts which are frequented for the purpose of sea-bathing, are chosen where the shore is flat and convenient for bathers and bathing machines; where the country is divided into smooth paths for ladies to walk on, and safe paths for gentlemen to ride on; ruggedness and sublimity, features for which coast scenery is most to be admired, would be subversive of the objects for which these places are visited.[6]

The convenience, safety, and gender divisions of bathing resorts are established as antithetical to the 'neglected' sublime terrain to be found elsewhere along Britain's periphery, which is associated with danger and difficulty.

The divergent trends in coastal tourism identified by Ayton and Daniell in the second decade of the nineteenth century originate in late eighteenth-century travelling and vacation practices. During the course of the eighteenth century local authorities shaped and managed beaches as leisure spaces. Among the earliest interventions in the coastal landscape was the provision of bathing machines, a practice which became popular from the mid-eighteenth century. While 'the primary purpose of the beach in embryonic resorts was as the starting and return point for the therapeutic journey in the bathing machine', by the last decades of the eighteenth century the beach and adjacent ground emerges as a tourist destination in and of itself. This practice frequently involved the appropriation of coastal territory from local inhabitants for reinvention as 'pleasure' spaces for visiting travellers and holidaymakers, as was the case with the Steine promenade and pleasure ground at Brighton, the development of which began in the 1770s. The land behind the seafront was 'transformed from a working area used by the fishing community into a respectable resort promenade ground'.[7] So emerges the beach and its surrounding territory as a space of convenience, safety, and social exclusion, as is bemoaned by Ayton and Daniell, and satirized elsewhere by the likes of Tobias Smollett, Cowper, and Jane Austen.[8]

In the last decades of the eighteenth century, therefore, British seaside resorts were being rapidly developed and popularized as social spaces; yet, at the same time, within literature and the arts the seashore was becoming a powerfully symbolic Romantic space of self-discovery, a meditative, marginal location for sublime and solitary experience. As Alain Corbin has argued:

> The sea-shore offered a stage on which, more than anywhere else, the actual spectacle of the confrontation between air, water, and land contributed to fostering daydreams about merging with the elemental forces and fantasies of being swallowed up, as it unfolded the mirages of what Ruskin was to call the pathetic fallacy.[9]

Charlotte Smith needs to be seen as an early but influential proponent of this Romantic tradition. In the 1780s she begins to explore the British coastline as a liminal and uncertain space characterized by 'moody sadness' and 'lamentation', in which she finds an echo, and a means of expression, for her own sense of marginality and fragmentation.[10] The cliff-top and shoreline locations in her *Elegiac Sonnets* (and, indeed, in her novels) are often violent environments, yet her poetic speakers do not retreat from the potential brutality of the coastline: they embrace it and in doing so discover an opportunity for self-knowledge, but also for self-obliteration. Like writers such as George Crabbe and Percy Bysshe Shelley after her, Smith fully recognizes the seductive nature of the sea as suffocating and liberating, beautiful and monstrous.[11]

Home tour narratives produced at the turn of the nineteenth century frequently pay testimony to the coastline as a space of social interaction and diversion of the sort being encouraged by emerging touristic infrastructures, but *also* as a site for intensely personal emotional, sensuous, and aesthetic experience as explored by contemporary poets. Travellers commonly embrace both emergent traditions of coastal experience and representation. The travel writings of Ann Radcliffe and William Gilpin provide good examples of this synthetic approach, and also illustrate a third strand of signification, one which emphasizes the national and political importance of the coastline.

Like her account of the Lake District published within *A Journey Made in the Summer of 1794* (1795), Radcliffe's unpublished descriptions of the South English coast, which she travelled extensively with her husband from the late 1790s, reveal characteristic interest in and sensitivity to the aesthetics of landscape and space. She lingers on the hazy tones of the sea from Dover on a clear day – 'the long shades on its surface of soft green, deepening exquisitely into purple' – but also relishes the thundering darkness of the storm observed from Steephill on the Isle of Wight: 'Nothing sudden; nothing laboured; all a continuance of power, without effort'.[12] Radcliffe records intensely pleasurable encounters with nature and the elements, yet she also celebrates the coastline as a space for energetic social observation and interaction. She narrates the activities of tourists 'exhibit[ing] themselves' by the sea, alongside the hectic noise and bustle of naval men: 'the sailors' *he-ho*, the shrill whistle, and the rattle of cordage'.[13] Her repeated mention of the navy is a reminder that Britain's coastline is of particular national and strategic importance during times of conflict, such as these early years of the wars with revolutionary France.

William Gilpin similarly presents the South English coastline as a site where patriotic confidence and loyalties can be confirmed in the face of threats of invasion from the Continent. His *Observations on the Coasts of Hampshire, Sussex, and Kent* (1804) – published in the year that Bonaparte declared France an Empire, and was preparing to invade England's south coast – celebrates the '*clamor nauticus*' of Dover harbour. Gilpin constructs a fantasy of European containment and global dominance: Portsmouth harbour 'would contain all the shipping in Europe'; the view from Portsdown-hill is 'grander in its kind than perhaps any part of the globe can exhibit'.[14] However, despite protestations of aesthetic, commercial, and military superiority, the traveller simultaneously recognizes the ways in which both local and national identities become permeable in the liminal terrain inhabited by coastal communities:

> The inhabitant of Dover ... is a kind of connecting thread between an Englishman and a Frenchman; partaking in some degree of both. His customs, and manners are half English and half French. His dress also borders on that of his opposite neighbour. In Dover you may eat beef with an Englishman; or ragouts with a Frenchman. The language of both nations are equally understood.[15]

Gilpin stresses connection and exchange in a discourse of mutuality which pays testimony to both the geographical proximity and the cultural interaction between two nations at war but separated by only twenty-one miles of sea. In doing so he nuances the nationalistic strain developed elsewhere in the travelogue and underscores the complex nature of shoreline experience at this time: the British coast in this period may have served as a 'vital defence and a highly effective frontier',[16] yet it was also the point at which national identity became most susceptible to permeation.

2.2   Bathing bodies: transgression and seaside sensuality

Mary Morgan travelled with her husband from their home in Ely, Cambridgeshire to Haverfordwest in Pembrokeshire, South-West Wales, in order to visit her husband's family. From there she explored the surrounding coastline, including Milford Haven (see Illustration 2.1) and St Bride's Bay. Her experiences are recorded in the epistolary travelogue *A Tour to Milford Haven in the Year 1791*, published by subscription in 1795 and containing letters written between late June and mid-October 1791. Morgan, like many of her contemporary travel writers, filters her home tour experiences through both her own poetry and that of others; more unusual is the strain of anxiety that emerges in her writing. What distinguishes her work from that of Radcliffe and Gilpin is her cautious negotiation of the emerging Romantic poetic tradition of coastal representation which places emphasis on the individual, and on intense interaction with the elements.

When Morgan visited it in 1791, Milford Haven, described by some as 'the finest natural harbour in Europe', was on the cusp of a programme

Illustration 2.1 'Milford Haven', Samuel Fisher after Henry Gastineaux, from *Wales Illustrated, in a Series of Views, Comprising the Picturesque Scenery, Towns, Seats of the Nobility & Gentry, Antiquities &c.*, vol. 1 (London: Jones & Co, 1830), n. pag. Source: Zoë Kinsley private collection.

of development to be instigated by Sir William Hamilton, the founder of the town, and his agent and nephew Charles Francis Greville.[17] In the early 1790s the area was a busy harbour poorly equipped to deal with the volume of shipping traffic it received.[18] Hamilton was given the authority to build a proprietary town at the site in the year preceding Morgan's tour, and Milford Haven evolved – albeit in fits and starts – in the years that followed. Mary Morgan's account of this part of the Welsh coastline is therefore an important record of a region about to experience great change.[19]

It is not, however, the contemporary projects for Milford's future that dominate Morgan's account; rather, Milford Haven's particular resonance arises from its Shakespearean associations. 'It is impossible to traverse the shores of Milford Haven, without thinking of poor Imogen', she writes, referring to *Cymbeline*, part of which is set in the Welsh harbour. 'With what pleasures did I enter the caves under the protection of my Posthumus! But she, alas! was only deceived into a belief that she should find *her's there*'.[20] In retracing the steps of Imogen, Morgan not only enacts a form of literary tourism in which she 'performs' the literary work itself, but also rewrites the story to suit her own circumstances. Whereas Imogen, estranged from the husband for whom she searches, enters the coastal cave alone, exhausted and melancholy, Morgan is in the company of her husband, her 'Posthumus'. She therefore 'experiences' the literary text by enacting part of its action in the location in which the play is set, yet is ultimately reassured of the preference of her own situation in comparison to Shakespeare's unfortunate heroine.[21] Such an example tells us much about the key role played by literary association and intertextuality in Morgan's travelogue. The Pembrokeshire coastline's caves, beaches, and cliffs, which she describes in detail and at length, are imbued with a mythic and literary significance that is fundamental to the way in which she perceives herself in relation to them. In her repeated visits to the shoreline, and her narration of those excursions, a complex emotional and imaginative relationship to the coast is worked out.

Among the most complicated of Morgan's coastal descriptions are those of the sea itself, particularly human interaction with it. By the time Morgan travels to Wales, the 'therapeutic and health-enhancing qualities of sea water' had long been trumpeted by physicians.[22] The popular belief in the protective and restorative powers of sea water – only to be much later superseded by the cult of sea air, and then of the sun – meant that bathing was an extremely popular seaside pastime for both men and women.[23] However, although her account relates that her husband bathes in the sea frequently during their stay in Haverfordwest, there is no record of Morgan herself setting foot in the water – her descriptions are, therefore, observational rather than participatory.

Morgan's first account of sea bathing comes in a letter dated 20 August 1791 addressed to Matthew Robinson, the nephew of Elizabeth Montagu, the wealthy author and 'bluestocking' (with whom Morgan also corresponds, and stays, during her tour). In it she describes three women she observes bathing in the sea in an unspecified location on the Pembrokeshire coast, a depiction which is typical both in its recourse to literary myth and its emphasis on the narrator's detachment from the scene. The description is worth quoting in full because it illustrates the way in which her experience of the coastline can be complicated by her reading of place through text:

> I cannot omit telling you one thing, which surprised me very much, as I think it would have done you, if you had been witness to it. After having amused myself in the caves and on the rocks as long as I chose, I walked some way down on the beach, and on look-ing towards the sea, I saw, at a considerable distance, three people seemingly walking in it; but upon approaching nearer them, I found they were three females in bathing dresses, sporting like Nereids in the water, and with as little apprehension. They were hand in hand, moving in somewhat of a minuet step and attitude, and at intervals curtseying to let the sea wash over them. Thus they continued hold-ing fast together, till they bathed their fill. Had there been two only, I should have believed they were Salmacis and Hermaphroditus.[24]

The opportunity to observe strangers enjoying the pleasures of immer-sion in the sea is an unexpected diversion for Morgan. This guilty pleas-ure which she relates for the vicarious enjoyment of her correspondent would, Jean-Didier Urbain argues, become central to the way in which the European beach functions in later decades:

> On the beach, society puts itself on display, looks at itself as a whole and in parts, and stages itself for itself, outside of any context. The beach site is a decontextualized theater structured by the narcissistic dialectics of seeing and being seen.[25]

Written before the 'dialectics of gaze and appearance' become fully embedded within the structures and practices of the seaside on this part of the Welsh coastline, Morgan's narrative nevertheless reveals an awareness of the theatrical nature of the activity she takes part in as onlooker. By describing the women's movements as akin to dance steps, and drawing attention to their curtseying, she formalizes a scene which a sentence earlier she suggests is characterized by joyful abandon. The traveller's insistence that the women's bathing is in some way choreographed reveals her sense of them as performers on a stage.

Up until this point Morgan's use of literary allusion supports her depiction of the trio as a positive model of female companionship: 'holding fast together' they are like the Nereids of Greek myth. That image of sisterly comradeship is undermined by the final sentence of the description, however, in which the mythic frame of reference becomes dark and disturbing. By suggesting that these women remind her of Ovid's story of Salmacis and Hermaphroditus, Morgan associates the scene with violence and sexual deviance. The parallel drawn between the women bathing off the Pembrokeshire coast and Salmacis and Hermaphroditus is not explained or elaborated; however, the reader familiar with Ovid's story would be puzzled, perhaps shocked, by this analogy and its implications. In many ways the parallels seem too few for Morgan's mythic interpretation to be convincing. Salmacis is a Naiad or water nymph who attempts to rape the young Hermaphroditus after he resists her lustful advances; after praying to the gods that they may never be parted her wish is fulfilled when they are metamorphosed into one being: 'Both Bodies in a single Body mix, / A single Body with a double Sex'.[26] Morgan therefore requires the reader to imagine that she is looking at a man and a woman, rather than three women, and she exports an inland river story to the seashore. However, there are elements in the myth and its setting that echo Morgan's location on the strand, and her transformation of the scene of women bathing into a fantasy of sexual transgression anticipates a trend that has, it has been argued, become fundamental to the structures and expectations of seaside tourism.

In Ovid's *Metamorphoses* it is the shore of the river where the tragedy of Hermaphroditus unfolds and his fate is sealed:

> The Boy now fancies all the Danger o'er,
> And innocently sports about the Shore,
> Playful and wanton to the Stream he trips,
> And dips his Foot, and shivers as he dips.[27]

In these lines, taken from Addison's translation of Ovid which Morgan knows and refers to elsewhere in the *Tour to Milford Haven*, the movements of Hermaphroditus are reminiscent of those attributed to the women Morgan observes in the waters off the Welsh coast. The paradoxical representation of Hermaphroditus as both innocent and wanton could also apply to the bathers Morgan describes. Their close communion with each other and the sea, their courtship of the waves and submission to the sea's rhythms, and indulgence in that pleasure until satiated all carry sexual connotations that are reinforced by association with Ovid's tale. The shore is also the site of Hermaphroditus's undressing, where he reveals his naked form to Salmacis and ignites the passion which will result in his violation:

> Now all undrest upon the Banks he stood,
> And clapt his Sides, and leapt into the Flood:
> His lovely Limbs the Silver Waves divide,
> His Limbs appear more lovely through the Tide;
> As Lillies shut within a Crystal Case,
> Receive a glossy Lustre from the Glass.
> He's mine, he's all my own, the Naïad cries,
> And flings off all, and after him she flies.[28]

The first six lines of this passage draw us in to focus on the body of Hermaphroditus as an aesthetic object, and as an object of desire. In doing so they implicate the reader in the act of lustful voyeurism in which Salmacis is engaged. We are in turn reminded of Morgan's own position on the strand, gazing upon the playful limbs of the bathers in the waters off the Welsh coast, and left to wonder about the possibility of her own sexual arousal on that other shoreline.[29]

From the earliest establishment of touristic infrastructures at British seaside resorts in the latter half of the eighteenth century, there has been an awareness of the beach as a place of sensual experience and potential sexual transgression.[30] Efforts on behalf of the authorities at established resorts to stop mixed bathing did little to prevent spectators gazing at women's bodies, and the satirist John Williams (pseud. Anthony Pasquin) suggests in his *New Brighton Guide*, published a year after Morgan's *Tour*, that the ogling of female bathers was standard practice at some resorts:

> The coast is like the greater part of its visitors, bold, saucy, intrusive, and dangerous – The bathing machines, even for the ladies, have no awning or covering, as at Weymouth, Margate, and Scarborough; consequently they are all severely inspected by the aid of telescopes,

not only as they confusedly ascend from the sea, but as they kick and sprawl and flounder about its muddy margin, like so many mad Naiads in flannel smocks[.][31]

By describing the women in her letter to Robinson, and by subsequently publishing that letter within her travelogue, Morgan commodifies them as an erotic seaside pleasure. However, hers is not a satiric text in the vein of *The New Brighton Guide*, and her position as a female observer, coupled with her association of the bathers with both male and female sexuality, makes Morgan's a much more complex and ambiguous text than Williams's. Morgan's reference to Ovid's story seems to function as a means of expressing female behaviour which she struggles to align with traditional gender roles. Salmacis's indolent vanity, along with the predatory nature of her pursuance of Hermaphroditus, contrast strikingly with the positive model of 'virgin-huntress nymph' offered elsewhere in Ovid's *Metamorphoses*: she is presented as rejecting that conventional model of femininity.[32] The reference to Salmacis and Hermaphroditus could, therefore, be read as shorthand for female deviance. It also, however, draws attention to Morgan's own potentially aberrant behaviour as spectator at a coastal site where voyeurism is yet to become normalized into the practices of the beach, and hints that the violation that takes place during Morgan's exploration of the seashore is in fact enacted by the gazing traveller herself.

The long history of the eroticization of the sea and its shore has much to do with the coenaesthetic nature of the individual's experience of them. However, while the beach is imagined and popularized as a place of desire, heightened sensuality, and transgression, sociologists have argued that actual behavioural practices are very different from that fantasy:

> People do not go astray at the beach; instead, they rediscover one another. They do not decenter; quite to the contrary, they recenter, refocus on their habits, their friendships, their loved ones, their partner's body, their own body. They allow a measure of doubt to arise, a possibility. But they ultimately re-establish, resettle, recenter themselves.[33]

This theory, largely based upon modern attitudes towards the seaside, is borne out by Morgan's late eighteenth-century narrative. In the paragraph immediately following her description of the women bathing, she shifts her attention to the local social calendar, promises to furnish her correspondent with 'a different amusement from descriptions of solitary caves and romantic rocks', and details her husband's recent activities.[34] Such a change in subject matter transfers the reader's attention from the mythic world of Naiads and sexual violence to the domestic detail of Morgan and her husband's life while staying with his family; the letter ends with the traveller's views on Welsh mountain air. This 'recentering' of the text reminds us of the familial imperatives of Morgan's tour, and the geographical shift of focus away from the coastline effects a curtailment (albeit temporary) of the traveller's imaginative engagement with place.

The second significant discussion of sea bathing to be found in *A Tour to Milford Haven* focuses upon Morgan's husband. In an early letter written from Haverfordwest, Morgan positively describes the opportunities offered by her husband's bathing routine: 'It gives me an opportunity of making observations upon many curious and sequestered places, which otherwise perhaps I should not have seen'. A month later she writes:

> One very agreeable thing on this coast is, there is very little occasion for bathing-houses. Every bay and every cave affords the most private and commodious dressing-room, and twenty people might undress in different grottos, and go out and bathe without knowing of each other's being near.[35]

Morgan celebrates this tract of South Welsh coastline as virgin territory, as yet undefiled by the structures of fashionable, sanitized seaside resorts epitomized by bathing houses. Once again the seashore prompts fantasies of undress and nakedness: the imagined pleasure of private, unobserved bathing is here made erotic by the possibility of the proximity of other undressed bodies.

After this imagined scene of 'twenty' people undressing, Morgan turns to describe the reality of her husband bathing, which she narrates as viewed from the cliff-top:

> It is hardly to be imagined what I felt on seeing him dropping, as it were, lower and lower down the tremendous precipice, till he almost became as small as a gnat or the point of my needle. After some time I entirely lost sight of him. But having undressed in a cave in order to bathe, he again made his appearance, though he seemed no bigger than a child of a year old, owing to the immense height of the cliff upon which I sat, and the distance I was from him.[36]

Morgan's increasing anxiety in this passage directly correlates with the decreasing size of her husband as she observes him from her position of detachment on the headland, and evokes the language of defamiliariza- tion. Animalistic and material metaphors give way to infantilization as the anguish she describes becomes that of an over-protective mother, while simultaneously evoking the separation anxiety experienced by young children. Morgan's husband here enacts the ritual of submersion and regression that has been characterized as central to the Romantic discourse of the seashore. In the moment that he 'throw[s] himself headlong from a huge rock into the ocean', he submits himself to full elemental contact with the sea.[37] Mary Morgan's status as observer and narrator of this scene complicates our interpretation of it, however. Her husband's desire to plunge into the sea demonstrates a typically Romantic urge for contact with the elements – what Corbin describes as a 'longing for ... coenaesthetic return'.[38] However, that moment of pleasurable submersion is figured as one of pain and distress for his wife; while her husband experiences pantheistic union with the water, Morgan is agonized by the sensation of disunion affected by the visual loss of her husband:

> The horror I felt at that moment is not to be described, and I resolved never to put myself to such painful sensations again. The sea at this place is prodigiously magnificent, and the whole of the sea is grand; but I have had enough of the sublime to satisfy me for some time.[39]

In rejecting the sublime, Morgan simultaneously abrogates the mascu- line model of sea-bathing epitomized by her husband. This is a signifi- cant moment in her travelogue, and in her engagement with the Welsh coastline. From this point on she physically and metaphorically turns her back upon the seashore: its temporary pleasures are relinquished, overshadowed by the overwhelming terror initiated by observance of her husband's submersion in the sea.

2.3 'The storm lurks beneath': fears of the dangerously deceptive

Morgan repeatedly emphasizes the fearfulness she experiences during her tour, and suggests that her pleasure is limited by what she self- deprecatingly describes as her own cowardice. Writing from Hook, on the Western Cleddau river, she enumerates the aspects of her situation which evoke trepidation: she is 'fearful of walking about the premises, lest I should stumble into a coal pit'; 'the roads are so extremely bad ... that I dare not venture on horseback'; she is afraid to approach the shore of the river because of the slipperiness of the rocks; she dare not set foot in the road because there are so many bullocks pulling coal carts. Each fear concerns her movement within her environment, and each limits her mobility. The most persistent provocation of Morgan's terror in her narrative, however, is water. Her writing reveals a deep mistrust of travelling on water – that 'fickle' 'element' – and she repeatedly struggles to reconcile the beauty of river and coastal landscapes with the potentially destructive power of the water they contain.[40]

Morgan explicitly tells her correspondents that she is 'extremely fearful of water', and the discourse of danger which she develops around the theme of river and coastal waters centres on the idea of their deceptiveness:

> [T]he rivers in this country have a remarkable deception in them: they are transparently clear, and have such a smooth pebbly bottom ... you think by stooping a little you can gather up the polished variegated ones in your hand. But alas! if any unwary damsel or inexperienced stranger should be tempted to beguile their way by such an innocent recreation, they would find themselves fatally mistaken; for these rivers are sometimes so dangerously rapid, that they might be hurried down the stream, and never more heard of.[41]

As is the case in Ovid's story of Salmacis and Hermaphroditus, the danger of the river is rendered more disturbing by its beauty and lucidity, qualities traditionally associated with virtue and truth.[42] The impulse to reach one's hand into the water is demonstrative of a desire for connection with nature, and also evidences the touristic urge to collect souvenirs. Morgan describes these 'innocent' pleasures as being thwarted by the river itself, which she portrays as paradoxical and deeply disquieting.

The same anxieties that dominate Morgan's discussion of rivers haunt her responses to the sea, and ultimately come to define her attitude towards the Pembrokeshire coast. When she first catches sight of the sea at St Bride's Bay, Morgan's reaction is one of 'inexpressible' 'astonishment and delight': unlike the Norfolk coast with which she is familiar, the Welsh coastal landscape offers variety enough to dispel 'dreariness and horror'. However, during the course of her narrative this initial positive judgement, based upon the aesthetics of place and the 'promise' of 'commerce and society', becomes undermined as greater familiarity brings with it an increasing sense of fear and unease. This comes to a climax when she experiences the horror of watching her husband descend into the sea from the cliff-top: 'this, with my other painful sensations, determined me to bid a final adieu to the rocky shores of Little Haven'.[43] It also prompts her to compose a poem which she includes in her travelogue. In this verse she elaborates the theme of dangerous deceptiveness which has come to dominate her views on the sea. The poem gives an insight into her relationship to the coastline, and indeed the symbolic value of the sea in popular poetry:

> To thy shores, Little Haven, adieu,
> To thy o'er-hanging cliff's rugged side;
> Thy grand scenes can the stranger admire,
> When pursu'd by the swift rolling tide?
>
> To thy rocks, Little Haven, farewell:
> Ah! Farewell to thy wide spreading main;
> To thy coast I no more will return,
> Nor e'er view thy white billows again.
>
> . . . .
>
> May my feet no more print thy gold sands,
> Tho' thy waves be as emerald green;
> For I know that the storm lurks beneath:
> Soon they black as the jet will be seen.
>
> To thy smooth sea for ever adieu;
> It may rage, tho' it now seem to sleep:
> Then flee, gentle Cæsar, this shore,
> And ne'er venture again in its deep.[44]

The poem demarcates the coast into various zones of experience – cliffs, rocks, main, bays, caves – all of which produce different responses within the main text of Morgan's narrative. However, implicit within each stanza is a sense of mistrust. Her praise for the aesthetic qualities of coastal space – the 'wide-spreading main', 'fair beach', and 'emerald' waves – is undermined by a second strand of signification, via which the sea is figured as a seductive temptress whose threatening presence is felt in every area of this coastal territory, and whose advances must be resisted. The fact that she feels 'pursu'd' by the waters – a term which suggests being hunted, but also courted – implies a sense of vulnerability in the face of an elemental authority which is feminized as alluring but also figured as predatorily masculine. It is this slipperiness, this ambiguity, which is at the heart of Morgan's distrust, and ultimate rejection, of the coast. Beneath its alluring surface lie dangers which are rendered more terrifying because they are concealed: the sublime prospect scene at St Bride's Bay, Morgan's first glimpse of the Pembrokeshire coast, proves to be a delusion. In this denunciation of the sea's beguiling nature can be traced a rejection of two essentially masculine discourses of coastal contact: the self-sufficient, utilitarian myth of individualism evoked by the Crusoe-like reference to footprints on the 'gold sands'; and the emerging Romantic tradition of heroic, elemental interaction with nature.

Writing two decades after the publication of Mary Morgan's *Tour to Milford Haven*, Richard Ayton and William Daniell urge travellers to explore the coastline of their home nation. They promote the rugged areas of the coast as the 'most to be admired', and offer those sublime landscapes as a positive alternative to the routine and safety of bathing resorts. Morgan's narrative in many ways anticipates and chimes with those sentiments: she celebrates the fact that the South Welsh coastline is as yet unencumbered by the institutionalized structures of seaside tourism, and her early letters reveal her indulging fantasies of nakedness and potential sexual transgression. In this sense she is a more radical commentator on the coastline than a travel writer such as Ann Radcliffe, and can be likened to Dorothy Richardson who celebrates the coast as a place of intense personal pleasure where social boundaries can be transcended.[45] However, the subtlety and complexity of Morgan's literary response is in many ways unusual, and can perhaps be most clearly aligned with a writer such as Charlotte Smith who, while working with other literary forms, similarly presents the seashore as an ambiguous space where women experience both pleasure and pain. Morgan's *Tour to Milford Haven* demonstrates that the subversive qualities applauded by Ayton and Daniell can be destabilizing for the traveller, and she finally rejects the South Welsh coastline in a manner that is violent and emotional. The transgressive potentialities of the coast, embraced by her husband and symbolized by his solitary and naked submersion in the sea, stimulate negative feelings of loss and disempowerment in Morgan herself. Her narrative constructs her 'adieu' to the coast in terms of a self-enforced wrenching away from a zone of contact which has seduced and beguiled her, but which she has ultimately found disturbing. Unlike the women of Cowper's poem who run *en masse* towards the sea, Morgan flees from it. In doing so she emphasizes the temporary nature of any feelings of transgression and liberation engendered by her journey to the coast, and denies the universality of the model of female seaside behaviour offered by Cowper.

Notes

1. William Cowper, 'Retirement', in *The Poems of William Cowper*, ed. John D. Baird and Charles Ryskamp, 2 vols (Oxford: Clarendon Press, 1980), 1: 519–24.
2. Mary Morgan, *A Tour to Milford Haven, in the Year 1791. By Mrs Morgan* (London: John Stockdale, 1795), ix–xiii.
3. See, for example, Rob Shields, *Places on the Margin: Alternative Geographies of Modernity* (London and New York: Routledge, 1991), 84.
4. Richard Ayton, 'Introduction', *A Voyage Round Great Britain, Undertaken in the Summer of the Year 1813 … By Richard Ayton. With a Series of Views … Drawn and Engraved by William Daniell, A. R. A.*, 8 vols (London, 1814–25), 1: iii.
5. Ayton 'occupied two summers' in accompanying Daniell on his tour, and contributed to the first two volumes of the work. See Anon., 'Memoir', in Richard Ayton, *Essays and Sketches of Character* (London: Taylor and Hessey, 1825), iii–xiv, vii; and T. F. Henderson, 'Ayton, Richard (bap. 1786, d. 1823)', rev. M. Clare Loughlin-Chow, in *Oxford Dictionary of National Biography*, Oxford University Press, 2004, Web, 14 June 2010.
6. Ayton, 'Introduction', *A Voyage Round Great Britain*, iii–iv.
7. Fred Gray, *Designing the Seaside: Architecture, Society and Nature* (London: Reaktion Books, 2006), 147, 118, 131–2.
8. See Smollett's description of the bathing routines at Scarborough in *The Expedition of Humphry Clinker* (1771) (London: Penguin, 1985), 212–14; Cowper's satirical portrayal of the beach in 'Retirement', quoted at the beginning of this essay; and Austen's posthumously published *Sanditon* (see Jane Austen, *Lady Susan/The Watsons/Sanditon* (London: Penguin, 1974)).
9. Alain Corbin, *The Lure of the Sea: The Discovery of the Seaside 1750–1840*, trans. Jocelyn Phelps (1994) (London: Penguin, 1995), 164.
10. Charlotte Smith, 'Sonnet LXX. On Being Cautioned against Walking on an Headland Overlooking the Sea, because it was Frequented by a Lunatic', in *The Poems of Charlotte Smith*, ed. Stuart Curran (New York and Oxford: Oxford University Press, 1993), lines 7, 9.
11. For discussion of Smith's representation of the coast in her *Elegiac Sonnets*, see Zoë Kinsley, '"In Moody Sadness, on the Giddy Brink": Liminality and Home Tour Travel', in *Mapping Liminalities: Thresholds in Cultural and Literary Texts*, ed. Lucy Kay, Zoë Kinsley, Terry Phillips, and Alan Roughley (Bern: Peter Lang, 2007), 41–67; 46–8. Letter 22 of George Crabbe's poem *The Borough* (1810), telling the story of Peter Grimes, is set in a dark and desolate coastal landscape influenced by Crabbe's Suffolk home. See George Crabbe, *The Complete Poetical Works*, ed. Norma Dalrymple-Champneys and Arthur Pollard, 3 vols (Oxford: Clarendon Press, 1988), 1: 363. In Shelley's 'A Vision of the Sea' (1820) the raging ocean devours the ship with both 'splendour

and terror'. See P. B. Shelley, *Poetical Works*, ed. Thomas Hutchinson, corr. G. M. Matthews (Oxford and New York: Oxford University Press, 1970), 597, line 20.

12. Ann Radcliffe, extracts from [Tour to the Coast of Kent, Autumn 1797] and [Journal of a Tour, made in the summer of 1801, to Southampton, Lymington, and the Isle of Wight], cited in Thomas Noon Talfourd, 'Memoir of the Life and Writings of Mrs Radcliffe', in Ann Radcliffe, *Gaston de Blondeville*, 2 vols (Philadelphia, 1826), 1: 3–123; 13 and 34–5. Radcliffe's journals narrating her south coast tours have not survived; we therefore only have access to these travel accounts via the extracts in Talfourd's memoir. See R. Miles, 'Radcliffe, Ann (1764–1823)', in *Oxford Dictionary of National Biography*, Oxford University Press, Sept. 2004, Web, 21 June 2010. For Radcliffe's account of her Lake District tour, see *A Journey Made in the Summer of 1794, through Holland and the Western Frontier of Germany ... to which are added, Observations During a Tour to the Lakes of Lancashire, Westmoreland, and Cumberland* (Dublin, 1795).

13. [Tour to Portsmouth, the Isle of Wight and Winchester, Autumn 1798], in Talfourd, 'Memoir', 24, 20.

14. William Gilpin, *Observations on the Coasts of Hampshire, Sussex, and Kent, Relative Chiefly to Picturesque Beauty: Made in the Summer of the Year 1774* (London, 1804), 83, 13–14.

15. Gilpin, *Observations*, 79.

16. Linda Colley, *Britons: Forging the Nation 1707–1837* (London: Pimlico, 2003), 17.

17. Charles Frederick Cliffe, *The Book of South Wales: the Bristol Channel, Monmouthshire, and the Wye*, 2nd edn (London, 1848), 259.

18. K. D. McKay, *A Vision of Greatness: The History of Milford Haven, 1790–1990* (Haverfordwest: Brace Harvest Associates, 1989), 11.

19. The history of Milford Haven is not solely a story of expansion and prosperity, however. From its inception in the late eighteenth century it has experienced both economic booms and periods of severe economic, commercial, and industrial decline. See McKay, *A Vision of Greatness*.

20. Morgan, *Tour to Milford Haven*, 301.

21. Nicola J. Watson has traced the touristic vogue for visiting a site associated with a fictional text to the end of the eighteenth century. See *The Literary Tourist* (Basingstoke: Palgrave Macmillan, 2006), 132.

22. Gray, *Designing the Seaside*, 20–1; and Richard Russell, *Dissertation on the Use of Sea Water in the Diseases of the Glands*, 4th edn (London: W. Owen, 1760), v–vi.

23. See John Travis, 'Continuity and Change in English Sea-bathing, 1730–1900: A Case of Swimming with the Tide', in *Recreation and the Sea*, ed. Stephen Fisher (Exeter: University of Exeter Press, 1997), 8–35, 11–12; Gray, *Designing the Seaside*, esp. chapters 1 and 6; and Corbin, *Lure of the Sea*, esp. chapter 3.

24. Morgan, *Tour to Milford Haven*, 212–13.

25. Jean-Didier Urbain, *At the Beach*, trans. Catherine Porter (Minneapolis: University of Minnesota Press, 2003), 193.

26. Ovid, 'The Story of Salmacis and Hermaphroditus', trans. Joseph Addison, in *Ovid's Metamorphoses, in Fifteen Books. Translated by Mr. Dryden, Mr. Addison ... and other eminent hands*, 4th edn, 2 vols (London: J. and R. Tonson, 1736), 1: 4.138.

27. Ovid, 'The Story of Salmacis and Hermaphroditus', 136.
28. Ovid, 'The Story of Salmacis and Hermaphroditus', 137.
29. Morgan implicates herself in her allusion to Nereids by dramatizing herself descending onto the beach from 'caves' and 'rocks': Nereids 'generally resided in grottos and caves', see J. Lemprière, *A Classical Dictionary; Containing a Copious Account of all the Proper Names Mentioned in Ancient Authors*, 11th edn (London, 1820), 494. By doing so she reinforces her own position as a sexualized, gazing subject.
30. See Corbin, *Lure of the Sea*, 77.
31. [John Williams; pseud. Anthony Pasquin], *The New Brighton Guide* (London: H. D. Symonds and T. Bellamy, 1796), note, 6–7. Like Morgan, he transposes the naiad from inland waters to a coastal setting.
32. See Matthew Robinson, 'Salmacis and Hermaphroditus: When Two Become One (Ovid, *Met.* 4.285–388)', *The Classical Quarterly*, New Series 49.1 (1999), 212–23.
33. Urbain, *At the Beach*, 265, 270.
34. Morgan, *Tour to Milford Haven*, 213.
35. Morgan, *Tour to Milford Haven*, 203, 288.
36. Morgan, *Tour to Milford Haven*, 288.
37. Morgan, *Tour to Milford Haven*, 289.
38. Corbin, *Lure of the Sea*, 167.
39. Morgan, *Tour to Milford Haven*, 289.
40. Morgan, *Tour to Milford Haven*, 230–1, 251.
41. Morgan, *Tour to Milford Haven*, 139.
42. 'A River here he view'd so lovely bright, / It shew'd the Bottom in a fairer Light, / Nor kept a Sand conceal'd from Human sight', Ovid, 'The Story of Salmacis and Hermaphroditus', 135.
43. Morgan, *Tour to Milford Haven*, 200–1, 290.
44. Morgan, *Tour to Milford Haven*, 290–1.
45. See Dorothy Richardson, 'Tour in the East Riding of Yorkshire &c 1801', John Rylands Library, Deansgate, Manchester, Eng. MS 1126; also my discussion of Richardson's description of Bridlington Quay and Scarborough in *Women Writing the Home Tour, 1682–1812* (Aldershot: Ashgate, 2008), 148–50.

3

'Ancient and Present': Charles Heath of Monmouth and the *Historical and Descriptive Accounts ... of Tintern Abbey* 1793–1828

C. S. Matheson

To modern readers the term travel writing – certainly travel *literature* – refers to narratives spun out of the experiences of travel, rather than the books of information or guidance travellers consult in their journeying. Guidebooks provide filters or lenses that are offered to the tourist at a particular site and juncture. Here, insists the travel guide, is the information that will deepen your experience of this place – here is what you need in order to know where and who *you* are. Look this way, please. Yet for all of their authority and assertiveness, guidebooks are ephemeral productions. The specific advice of one edition may be unhelpfully dated by the next. Their copy is subject to forces even more relentless than authorial perfectionism or editorial imperative: think for example of seasonal changes to public transit, the state of roads, the rise and fall of local businesses, the waywardness of rivers, or the vagaries of opening hours. The air of knowledgeable certainty that guidebooks can project in this parlous world is one of the genre's best bluffs. And unlike travel narratives, travel guides do not have the luxury of turning their blunders to advantage.

This essay will examine the manner in which the author, printer, and publisher Charles Heath of Monmouth balanced ephemerality and authority in a popular guidebook, and what his efforts contributed to shaping the form in the Romantic era. Heath's *Historical and Descriptive Accounts of ... Tintern Abbey*, which ran to eleven editions between 1793 and 1828, reveals a great deal about the conditions and evolution of the guidebook in Britain. It was Heath, 'Bookseller, Antiquarian, Historian', who 'first brought into the notice of tourists the antiquities, scenery and numerous objects of attraction in the neighborhood of Monmouth', or so his epitaph reads.[1] Just as the Wye Valley, Wales, is the birthplace of

British domestic tourism, so the region is a nursery of the British travel guide.[2] Thomas Gray's descent of the River Wye by boat in the summer of 1770, during which he famously saw 'a succession of nameless beauties', was recorded in correspondence published soon after his death in 1771. This association with Gray attracted tourists to the region while William Gilpin's *Observations on the River Wye* was still circulating in manuscript. Wye tourism and tour-publication exploded in the decades following the first edition of Gilpin's *Observations* (1782). By 1810, French tourist Louis Simond complained, vividly, that 'Wales and the Wye are visited by all tourists; we are precisely in the same tract, and meet them at all the inns, – stalking round every ruin of castle or abbey, – and climbing every high rock for a prospect; each with his Gilpin or his Cambrian Guide in his hand, and each, no doubt, writing a journal. This is rather ridiculous and discouraging.'[3]

Simond's observations reveal the complexity of the guidebook's negotiation with its audience. A guidebook has a rude relationship to the material world and with readers who are sent bodily from place to place and sensation to sensation – even to the point of clustering atop high rocks like a colony of compliant birds. It provides the stranger seeking aesthetic experiences with practical advice, safely tethering a desire for novelty to bollards of necessary information. In Heath's Tintern Abbey guide, visitors are told of the noble personages buried underfoot in the ruins as well as the best place to procure a luncheon, or coached into sensations of awe after they are reminded that their tour boat will depart with the tide in two hours' time. Guidebooks attend to the mechanisms and institutions of travel (which they have a hand in constructing) even as they address and administer to the individual. And crucially, as Simond's experience demonstrates, they must achieve some discursive balance between their obligations. Simond's belief in the singularity of his Wye quest is shaken by the visible evidences of its communal nature – all the 'stalking', 'climbing', 'writing' tourists who are 'precisely in the same tract' (textually and geographically) as himself. His frustration rises as the illusion of his originality dissipates, fanned away perhaps by the mass flourishing of copies of Gilpin's *Observations* or the *Cambrian Traveller's Guide* up and down the river.[4] Simond finds himself uncomfortably placed between fashion and his need for self-fashioning – caught as it were between printed guides and the writing of his own journal.

Guidebooks stand at a crossroads between what is known or can be communicated about a place and what yet remains to be said. No work occupies this charged space of retrospection and promise as completely as Heath's *Historical and Descriptive Accounts of the Ancient and Present State of Tintern Abbey*, to give the volume its sonorous, cumulative title. The thirty-five-year career of Heath's guide spans the high decades of picturesque tourism in Wales, documenting Tintern's ascendancy among the stations of the Wye tour (especially the celebrated forty-mile stretch of the river between Ross-on-Wye and Chepstow at the mouth of the Severn) and what evolved there in response to the seasonal tide of visitors. The little dynasties that arose around the feeding, accommodating, and guiding of tourists – not to mention the selling of artefacts – are recorded as if in some alternative parish register. Changes in transportation are also documented in Heath's pages. The first edition of the guide opens with the arrival of tourists from Monmouth by hired pleasure-boat – imagine batches of 'ten cheered hearts / Stowed side by side' as one poet describes – while the 1828 text concludes with directions for catching a steam packet across the Bristol Channel. Intervening editions respond to the fashion for pedestrian tours (1801), the opening of a new Chepstow-Tintern turnpike (1823), or substantial road-works that smoothed carriage excursions from Monmouth (1828). Each improvement generates new copy in the form of updated directions; but more subtly, each improvement changes the character of the tour and alters what the guide must aesthetically and intellectually manage.

Heath's volume has a significant place too within Romantic visual culture, for its eleven editions offer a rich, serialized narrative of viewing practices as enacted at a constant location. *Tintern Abbey* is a site-specific guide, designed to be physically carried about the ruins and vicinity in a manner reminiscent of art-exhibition catalogues. In proposing 'to impart innumerable circumstances, which the contemplation of such a scene naturally excited in the mind of every curious and observant traveller', the guide locates and anticipates the requirements of its audience. The content, arrangement, and material character of the volume all have a bearing upon the performance of spectatorship at the Abbey.

What are the 'innumerable circumstances' that a late eighteenth-/ early nineteenth-century viewer at Tintern would be 'naturally excited' to know? The first edition of Heath's guide is a modest, 88-page anthology of materials that can be broadly grouped into the categories of antiquarian scholarship, aesthetic theory, tour narrative, poetry, and local anecdote – although these divisions are as permeable as the contemporary disciplines themselves. An excerpt from Francis Grose's *Antiquities of England and Wales* (1772–6), for instance, details the foundation of the monastery, supplies the dimensions and discusses the architectural order of the Abbey church, yet concludes (with a poetical excerpt) that the Abbey is not quite 'Gothic' enough: 'it wants that gloomy solemnity so essential to religious ruins; those yawning vaults and dreary recesses which strike the beholder with a religious awe, and make him almost shudder at entering them, calling into his mind all the tales of the nursery'. Measurement, classification, pronouncement, sensation, and narrative all have their moment in Grose's passage – as they do more broadly for the reader of *Tintern Abbey*. In Heath's 1793 text, aesthetic instruction and demonstration is firmly housed within antiquarian scholarship, a pattern repeated variously throughout all editions of the guide. Heath addresses the 'Man of Observation': the 'antiquarian traveller' who finds respite from the rigors of 'historic reflection' and exercise of the 'thinking faculties' in the contemplation of Nature.

Stephen Bending observes that 'ruins become increasingly popular objects of attention in the eighteenth century, and it is here that a shift has been charted from an "antiquarian response" early in the century, to a far looser "associative response" in terms of the picturesque by its end.'[5] At first glance Heath's guide – poised between the 'innumerable circumstances' of Tintern's past and the 'natural' excitement generated by their contemplation – seems to exemplify this shift. Yet it is not the case that one form of scrutiny simply replaces the other, even over the length of a century; nor that a point of transition between 'Enlightenment' or 'Romantic' tourism can be precisely marked. Alternating between these tendencies in the text is as natural for Heath as walking. In the 1801 guide, a pedestrian tourist approaching Tintern from the north passes through the port-village of Brockweir; as he reaches the settlement's edge he is informed (in a footnote, appropriately) that the present causeway is believed to be built upon a Roman road. From here the physical track and Heath's commentary lead away from the hard surfaces of history and towards a moment of private sensation: 'For near a mile the path leads thro' an extensive wood (the Wye flowing at its feet), at the end of which we are surprised by a beautiful view of the *object of our destination* – any description of which, at this moment, would be an intrusion on the feelings of the reader.'[6] In a verdant space between historical landmarks the reader is surprised by 'feelings'; between two features begging antiquarian explanation – Roman road and Gothic abbey – the author falls discreetly, even companionably silent. The vigorous hybridity of Heath's approach persists to the last edition of *Tintern Abbey* (1828), in which he likens 'the faculties of the mind ... to the butterfly within its shell, till knowledge like the sun had called its powers into action.'[7] What bridges the categories of 'antiquarian' and 'associative' in Heath's guide, or rather what carries these twinned responses convincingly into the next century, is the inclusion of the mediating figure of the author-publisher.

In a retrospective account of the genesis of *Tintern Abbey*, Heath relates that his own introduction to the Abbey was wholly 'unguided'. Arriving at Tintern in 1790 and applying for admission to the ruins at the Beaufort Arms, Heath learns that the appointed caretaker and key-holder – landlord George Gethen – is absent and his family 'sorrowing over a recent domestic affliction'. Heath is turned into the ruin without the usual hired attendant for a solitary, but unsatisfactory, wander: 'I surveyed again and again every part of the fabric with the most insatiable curiosity: but not having read any part of its history, I wanted some intelligent guide'. Heath conceives his text as a proxy for this figure of the local attendant, the *cicerone* whose knowledge and presence lend efficacy to the viewer's curiosity. Tintern Abbey can only be seen in depth when the present state of its fabric and past circumstances are stereoscopically mixed. Looking back more than a decade later, Heath reflects that although 'highly gratified' in having accomplished a visit, 'with ten-fold pleasure should I have enjoyed the scene, had there THEN been such an account as THIS I have now collected'.[8] It seems a small step from the person of a guide discoursing in the ruins to a printed guide sold at the ruins, as Heath's volume was from its second edition. Such untroubled transitions between the cultures of communication are wholly typical of Heath's practice.

The price of Heath's text – two shillings – was modest enough that a visitor might consider investing in *both* types of guides at Tintern.[9] Heath made a virtue of the inexpensive production of his volume: 'I confess it would have been very easy to have swelled out the materials into a respectable volume, by printing them in a large character, with extensive margins, and afterwards to have extended the sale price by expensive engravings; but I must here repeat my opinion, *that all information, to be useful, should come recommended in the cheapest form possible* – an axiom I have never swerved from, in the topographical accounts of Monmouthshire I have presumed to lay before the Public'.[10]

The 'cheapest form possible' was a small octavo pamphlet (although crown quarto and demy octavo are both advertised), done up in a rough, pale-blue stock that has been likened to the paper used for sugar packaging.[11] The stitched paper covers and modest title pages of the guides, decorated only with a few rules or a narrow border of printer's flowers, are also consistent with Heath's utilitarian aesthetic. The work is designed to be used freely, for 'it takes up little room, and if lost is of no value', unlike large and expensive works in topography that are 'little calculated as companions on a tour'.[12] One Elizabeth Jones of Norwood turned her copy of the 1823 guide into an itinerary by neatly jotting tour dates above the printed entries, a hands-on rather than an off-hand treatment of the text.[13]

The press-work itself does little to justify the 'Caxton of Monmouthshire' sobriquet awarded Heath by one enthusiastic Victorian bibliographer.[14] Poor registration throughout all the editions makes for unrestful pages; the contents page roves about in the volume and pagination is inconsistent. Some editions (pre-1800) are wholly paginated, some wholly unpaginated, and some partly and/or inaccurately paginated as Heath uses up surplus sheets from a previous edition.[15] The 1799 edition is only paginated where Heath has incorporated sheets from the 1798 effort (vide pages 19–32 and 55–60), although these recycled numbers do not match their new position in the 1799 volume. The 1816 edition is paginated throughout, but has three portions of unpaginated text added near the beginning, middle, and three-quarter mark of the volume. Some of these new insertions reference recent events, such as the repercussions of the enclosure of Trellech common-lands following an 1810 Parliamentary Act, or the 'exclusive' of Heath's participation in an excavation near the Abbey's altar the previous May. News and lore are thus typographically distinguished; reading editions of the guide sequentially allows one to see how events are shaped into anecdote and finally set into history in Heath's pages. In some cases the comments of distinguished tourists, guided about the ruins by Heath himself, enter the printed text as testimony of the Abbey's power. It is a lovely thought that what is said in a place becomes part of its meaning.

Fittingly for a work detailing a Cistercian or 'white monk' foundation, Heath's output is riddled with 'friars': white patches on a page caused by imperfect inking of the type.[16] In addition the 'reader is solicited to exercise his Candor over a few Typographical Errors' – in one case on a title page and another on a prospectus – with Heath remarking, 'Some Apology might be made for Haste – but for Inadvertencies, I hope I shall be forgiven'.[17] Indeed, it is hardly Heath's fault that there is an 'inadvertency' on his tombstone outside St Mary's Priory Church, Monmouth.[18]

Heath's 'haste' in the production of the guides resulted from a combination of seasonal pressures – the dating of one preface suggests that renewal of the guides was timed to the start of the tourist season – as well as in-house practices. He states in the 1799 *Excursion down the Wye* that he did not set his letter-press from a copy-text, but rather his thoughts were 'transferred to the composing-stick, and afterwards put ... to press, without any further concern than literal correction'.[19] Such details evoke the atmosphere of a busy provincial book and print-shop, the multi-tasking required of one who was 'first and foremost a jobbing printer', not to mention an occasional tour guide, manager of a circulating library, and purveyor of stationary, tea, newspapers, patent medicine, fishing tackle, and artist's colours.[20] Heath confides wistfully in the *Excursion* that 'the mind of a person in the constant exercise of the retail trade has many claims upon his attentions, whereas the man of letters sits down in his study to meditate and revise his thoughts with-out the train of them being interrupted by casual intrusion'.[21] Typically however, Heath fashions the 'casual intrusions' occasioned by his busi-ness and even the accelerated production of the Monmouthshire guides into positive features by making them part of the responsiveness of the genre. His apparent casualness in this respect pushes communication back towards the mode of oral conversation. When Heath mentions 'the facility of communication which I hold with the Public, by means of my Press', we should remark upon his priorities.[22]

Heath describes the origin of his topographical guides in a preface to the 1803 edition of *Tintern Abbey*:

> The Spring of the succeeding year [1791] fixing me as a Printer at Monmouth – Tintern became the favorite object of my leisure moments, and many happy hours were passed under the shade of its venerable walls. As the season proceeded, my house was much resorted to by the respectable travellers who passed thro' the town, requesting me to afford them any information relating to the beau-tiful scenes they intended to visit in Monmouthshire, which my residence might enable me to impart – adding, that even fragments would prove acceptable. Encouraged by such solicitations, and find-ing my own mind in unison with their wishes, I immediately entered on the attempt to collect its scattered history. Mr. Page (then) of Dingatstow, favored me with Grose's Antiquities – my correspond-ent in town supplied me (though not then to be had in the regular trade) with Mr. Gilpin and Mr. Wheatley's works – accident threw in my way the poetical part – while a gentleman near Monmouth lent me the books from whence the notices of the monastic orders were extracted. With these materials I went to press; and as the number of copies printed was small, they did not long remain unsold.[23]

Publication is formulated here as an extension of Heath's sociability – literally so in that conversations with a flesh-and-blood public occurred during the high 'season' of tourism, inside of a sociable space 'resorted to' by respectable travellers (most famously Lord Nelson in 1802). The slight political adjustments required to set Heath upon an equal, conversable footing with his clients – and those who lent him books – are briskly accomplished in the paragraph. A reference to Heath's livelihood in the first sentence is immediately balanced by his appearance in the character of a leisured man, one whose pleasure in the Abbey justifies full participation in the interests and enthusiasms of his 'respectable' patrons. Heath's mention of his 'house' and 'residence' in the passage plays well in this respect too. In the first two years of Heath's establishment in Monmouth, his house in Munnow Street doubled as his place of business, although by the time of the publication of the first Tintern Abbey guide he was working from a shop in the market-place.[24] Although it is literally the case that Heath's house in this early period was a destination for travellers seeking information, rather than a separate commercial space in the Monmouth market-square, references to Heath's house blur, rather usefully, the social distinction between customers and private callers at his door.[25] The little ambiguity around Heath's word 'residence' is significant in another respect, for it also reads as the duration of the author's life in the region, and therefore as the basis for Heath's evolving authority. The mix of assurance and expediency from which Heath's scheme of topographical publication emerges in this passage is wholly characteristic of the travel guide genre. As Heath describes, the wishes of an itinerant readership, craving information but prepared to accept even 'fragments', are answered by a rapid programme of research, collection, and printing – almost as if print publication is a bespoke business. His rhetorical compression of the production schedule of the guides and the small size of each quickly-sold edition keeps the book within the parameters of his original exchange. Even the promotion and sale of his topographical volumes is brought resolutely back to this primary mode of commerce. As he explains in an 1817 guide to Ragland Castle: 'No effort has been used to extend the sale, beyond what has been claimed by visitors throughout the county; and I look back, with a high degree of delight, on the many valuable characters who have honoured me with their notice, solely from their knowledge of me as the author of these pages'.[26] Heath makes little distinction between oral and textual senses of publication here. Conversations with his public do not originate in print, but are obligingly carried there; his printed texts are not assiduously promoted but rather disseminated through the word-of-mouth-recommendations of 'visitors throughout the county'; his pages are successful because they generate further exchanges, contacts, and introductions for the sociable author himself.

Setting out the function of his original 1793 *Descriptive Account of Tintern Abbey* does require Heath to step outside of his 'residence' and position the work in relation to extant publications. He does this at first in conventionally apologetic terms:

> The Public are generally disposed to receive with Candour the endeavours of those who aim either to please or inform, when they do not assume a confidence to which their works have no pretension.
>
> In the publication of the following Sheets, little claim is made to Originality. Nothing more is aimed at than to collect the Remarks of All the Writers on this admired Ruin, for the information of those Travellers, whose curiosity leads them to visit it.[27]

But as *Tintern Abbey* progresses through its subsequent ten editions, Heath's professional sense of purpose evolves. He becomes more specific about the intellectual, practical, and commercial niches of the respective genres of history, illustrated tour, and his own brand of portable topography. Heath's invention of himself as a local and a topographer places him strategically between the competing authorities of the historian and the picturesque tourist. Unlike these inmates of the library or the pleasure boat respectively, Charles Heath is found at the ruin, marketplace, and county inns where his guide is purveyed. Heath's perception of the nature of his guides, and by extension the broader genre of the Romantic travel guide, is closely tied to an articulation of his identity. The accumulation of autobiographical content through the editions of *Tintern Abbey*, or rather the increasing presence of the author/publisher in the text, solves a number of political and generic issues. At the very least, autobiographical discourse allows Heath to reference the conventions of travel narrative while producing a hybrid text meant to supply travellers with a plot.

Creation of the *Tintern Abbey* guide is also an act of self-creation for Heath. The business of collection modestly described in the 1793 preface is supplemented in subsequent editions by the work of recollection, the harvest of a long engagement with the village and an Abbey 'viewed under every variation and change of the season, as well as times of the day'. A lovely analogy is supplied by Heath's description of the orchards then cultivated within the former abbey precincts. The autumnal 'luxuriance' or maturity of the crop produces what is locally known as a 'hit', which occurs '"when the rosy tribe of fruits are bending their parent trees to kiss the ground"'.[28] Recollection allows Heath to join the congregation of 'Writers on this admired Ruin', slipping decorously into the back pews while the significance of the Abbey is gravely and collectively intoned up front. Writers who are 'esteemed' in the earliest editions are later described more judiciously or collegially as 'accomplished'. Although stressing his role as a printer in the first editions – referring self-consciously to his 'sheets' in 1793 and in 1798 distinguishing himself as 'the printer of these sheets' when quoting a 'writer' who pays tribute to Gilpin – Heath gradually assumes a greater speaking part in the text.[29] The preface to the third edition of the Tintern Abbey guide ventures cautiously into the first-person:

> The Public are generally disposed to receive with candor the efforts of those who aim either to *please* or *inform*, when they do not assume improper confidence. The pleasure resulting from visiting this Ruin, was the principal motive that induced me to unite its scattered History: and if it should impart that satisfaction in the perusal, which it has afforded in collecting, I have all the reward I wish for. Charles Heath. Monmouth, 1801.[30]

1801 marks the tenth anniversary of Heath's establishment as a printer in Monmouth, a location chosen under the influence of his first deep draught of the Abbey and Monmouthshire antiquity. Reaching this milestone appears to have given Heath permission to reposition himself between the writers and readers, entering for the first time not just as a printer/publisher but as an author induced by his own experience to write and publish. In the language of the 1801 title page, Heath himself is now part of the 'whole' that was 'never before collected'. Gathering the 'scattered History' of the monument is now prompted by the recollection of his former pleasure in 'visiting this Ruin'. The history of composition offered here is as succinct as it is Romantic. Heath's original pleasure in his experience is transferred to his readers through the intermediation of the texts brought together in his guide, a stage that admittedly dilutes 'pleasure' into the more temperate sensation of 'satisfaction' for both his audience and himself. What is not stated, although assumed, is that readers' satisfaction will be upgraded to pleasure when the guide carries them to and round the Abbey.

A basic condition of any travel guide is that discovery and self-discovery are simultaneous possibilities; essentially both states must be in play for the text to be taken in hand. Or to phrase it more poetically, a travel guide is an instrument and the 'mute still air' that slumbers about its form is the consciousness of the traveller-elect. Travel guides offer readers the chance to be remade in the light of new experiences and knowledge. Heath's 1796 *Excursion down the Wye*, for instance, is designed to 'aid the traveller's Observations in this journey ... refresh the memories of those who have viewed the scenes; and to those who are less happy ... impart a variety of useful and necessary information'.[31] Not only does his text organize mental processes by programming the gaze and arranging memory, thus attending both to the life and the afterlife of the experience, it creates desire in the 'less happy' who have not yet ventured down the Wye. No one would wish to be left behind, well-supplied with 'useful and necessary information' to kick at the rungs of a school-room chair. In this manner all travel guides are aspirational, but none more so than a guide to Romantic Britain's pre-eminent site of aesthetic pilgrimage.[32] Heath himself says he was first prompted to visit Tintern Abbey by the sight of a painting viewed during a tour of Hagley Hall.[33]

As an author and publisher Heath is subject to the same processes or potentialities that he scripts for his readers. One might expect this in a travel narrative, which spreads its opinions and idiosyncrasies like a picnic blanket at each stop; but Heath is producing a guide that purportedly eschews 'Originality' in favour of plainer, more discreet 'information'. The mandate of the first edition is to 'please' and 'inform' without pretension or misplaced 'confidence'. Heath proposes to administer to the traveller's curiosity without arresting its motion by becoming its object himself. Yet the purpose of the guide and its market location seems tied to Heath's gradual recognition of his own role in the text of *Tintern Abbey* – and the fabric of Tintern Abbey as a place. In the expanded 1803 edition an autobiographical essay explaining 'the motives that occasioned the publication' becomes the gateway to the abbey, much as in a number of contemporary drawings and engravings the beckoning figure of the guide or companion waits for the viewer by the western entrance. By 1823, the penultimate edition of the guide, the contents have become 'alike interesting to the resident inhabitant as to the visitor ... The whole resulting from a continued endeavor, for [many] years, to illustrate this much frequented part of the kingdom, during which period the writer's life has been passed in it'.[34] The decades Heath spent in describing and illustrating the site are now a strand in the history of the monument. His own mother's death warrants a quiet footnote in the preface to the 1806 edition.[35]

The 1803 preface to *Tintern Abbey*, which builds the modest first-person address of 1801 into richer autobiographical disclosure, also shows Heath staking out the position of his guide more emphatically. Although itself a compendium of historical and descriptive sources on the region, *Tintern Abbey* is located through a careful survey – in mapping terms a triangulation – from more recent publications on Wales, specifically two works that for Heath represent opposing methodologies and levels of engagement with their subject. The first is David Williams's *History of Monmouthshire* (1796), to which Heath literally and metaphorically subscribed, and the second is Samuel Ireland's lavish *Picturesque Views on the River Wye* (1797) to which he emphatically did not.

Heath's references to the work of Williams and Ireland first appear in 1801, tucked deep in the volume as a tailpiece to his 'General Remarks on Tintern Abbey'. But by 1803, Heath's opinions of these rivals are shipped to the preface, an expression of the increasing confidence and presence of Heath's voice – and the expanding market for books on Wales. Professional and personal circumstances prompt Heath's engagement with Williams in the 1803 preface. *The History of Monmouthshire* was the period's first extended account of the region, and although five of Heath's small publications predate Williams's volume, it was Williams who became '*the* historian of the county', as Heath (with my emphasis) describes. Heath and Williams shared a connection to the Rev. Dr Phillip Griffin of Hadnock, an active amateur historian who introduced the two men at his residence in 1793. Heath must have been disappointed to learn that his patron's unpublished research was offered up to Williams for use in his volume. One forgives the plaintive notation Heath made in his copy of *The History of Monmouthshire*: 'Dr. Griffin would have assisted me in my collections for the county of Monmouth and the River Wye, if he had not held himself pledged to Mr. Williams by a Promise made long before I had the pleasure of being known to him.'[36]

Heath and Williams may have once shared political sympathies (Heath was rumoured to have 'quit his paternal home in consequence of his revolutionary principles')[37] as well as an approach to the subject of Welsh history. Williams's 'audaciously heterogeneous' treatment of county history, as Damian Walford Davies describes, is similar to the range of sources Heath abridges, references, and reproduces.[38] In *Tintern Abbey*, extracts from printed texts are joined to submissions from local antiquarians and corresponding scholars, transcriptions of original historical documents (some executed by Heath), local anecdote, poetry, and oral history, together with Heath's own recollections and observations. As Heath offers information on the Abbey, he also reproduces the network by which an exchange about the ruin is possible – even to acknowledging the loan of scarce or expensive books. This circulation of knowledge about the site, sociably managed by Heath, is fascinating given the literal circulation of its destined readership, and that record-making, in the form of journalizing and sketching, is so visibly an aspect of the Wye tour.

Heath's researches brought the author into contact with scholarly personages, providing limited (and coveted) access to gentlemanly circles of antiquarian investigation; but as a provincial jobbing printer, Heath was also conscious of the limitation of his resources. His topographical work was not motivated by 'the profits that were likely to result from my labours. It employed a large portion of time, which other pursuits at home would better have rewarded my assiduity; but, cherishing an enthusiastic love for antiquarian research, though my talents are very inadequate to the pursuit, pecuniary motives were but of secondary consideration'.[39] Identifying the Tintern Abbey guide as the offspring of his 'free time' rather than an offprint of his business interests is an important step in Heath's conception and positioning of the text. 'Placed in the centre of scenes I attempt to celebrate', says Heath, 'I have been induced, from the influence they hold over my mind, to devote those hours to which we give the epithet of *leisure*, to the constant search for such information, as would serve to advance my pages in the public estimation'.[40] 'Leisure' is a state that links Heath briefly – for labour reasserts itself by the end of the sentence – to the travellers he addresses in his guide and converses with throughout the season at his Monmouth shop. To be released from his usual occupation (one thinks of the respectability of *Sense and Sensibility*'s Edward Ferrars having no employment) and free to follow his intellectual interests aligns Heath – again briefly – with the amateur historians of his district. His formative first visit to the Abbey in 1790 occurred because he was 'disengaged at that period from business' and considering Monmouth as a place of residence.

We have seen that 'residence' is a term which allows Heath to characterize the nature of his authority as a guide and writer (tourists seek any information 'my residence might enable me to impart'), as well as a means of stepping round social distinction at a critical moment of self-definition. 'Residence' also becomes short-hand for the mandate of Heath's historical investigations, something set in opposition to the work of the non-resident author of *The History of Monmouthshire*. Heath complains that 'even the historian of the country, Mr. Williams, whose talents and recommendations gave him access to the first families, has but little increased the public stock of information relating to this Ruin'. This jibe at Williams's advantages, including access to Griffin's research on the region's pedigreed families[41] makes Williams's narrative seem the 'history from above' to Heath's livelier history on the spot. The 'public stock of information relating to this Ruin', in which Williams's work is deficient, are new facts or insights which might be readily disseminated to visitors.

If Williams disappoints, there is little to satisfy Heath in Samuel Ireland's 'expensive' *Picturesque Views on the River Wye, from its Source at Plinlimmon Hill, to its Junction with the Severn below Chepstow* (1797).[42] Ireland proposes to unify the 'detached views and single objects' celebrated by earlier writers and artists into a sequential, comprehensive tour.[43] The accuracy of his representations (including the record of some features destroyed in subsequent flooding) is offered as a corrective to what he calls the 'complicated sameness' of Gilpin's generalized representations.[44] Ireland's claim that additional value is given to the work through his delineation of lost structures (such as an arched bridge swept away at Hay-on-Wye) is a nod towards antiquarianism. The gesture is wasted on Heath: picturesque tours 'when we divest them of their descriptions of the face of the country add very little to the store of information'.[45]

It is not clear how much Heath knew about the controversy surrounding Ireland's involvement in his son William Henry Ireland's 'discovery' of a cache of Shakespearean documents in 1794 and the resulting forgery scandal.[46] Certainly there is evidence of sharp dealing in Ireland's use of Heath's 1796 *Excursion down the Wye*. Heath complains of Ireland 'arranging my pages, and new-dressing my expression, to make the work ... apparently his own, between Ross and Monmouth'. Perhaps it is poor morality to note that the duplication of one of his 'inadvertencies' alerted Heath to the plagiarism of his work. Ireland's shaky reputation as a part-time antiquary – and accessory thereof – is not redeemed by his behaviour as a Wye tourist in search of antiquities. Heath records with some asperity that Ireland acquired from Ann Bowen, daughter of a stone-mason involved in the original excavation of the abbey in 1756 and founder of a family business in artefacts:

> a Coin, of mixed metal according to her description, nearly the size of a penny piece; on the front of which was the figure of a man in armour on horseback, and on the reverse a *Church*; but when Mr. Ireland was at Tintern, he purchased it for a trifling consideration – with whom it now remains ... No other information on the subject has been communicated.[47]

Rivalry aside, this episode illustrates a significant difference between Ireland's and Heath's approaches to the subject of Tintern Abbey – the respective methodologies of a 'Writer of Travel' and a historically-minded writer for travellers. To Heath, history is not something to be purchased and exported, the token of a journey merely, but more rooted in place – literally an account to be read *in situ* in the case of a printed guide designed to be carried about the ruins. While this sounds a contradictory claim for a work based in part upon excerpts and abridgements from other texts, Heath's fidelity is to the place itself first and secondarily to the 'respectable Authors on the Abbey' he anthologizes. Sometimes even those 'most eminently qualified to write about the Abbey are not the most eminently observant'; an opinion which allows Heath to position his guidebook (and the genre more broadly) between fact and experience, knowledge, and a knowingness gained through the evidence of the senses. Heath is 'induced' to research and represent native scenes 'from the influence they hold over my mind'.[48] Collecting the 'scattered History' of Tintern Abbey is an act of repatriation, grounded in Heath's expectation that readers of (and with) the text will turn and return to the site itself. This premise determines the content, tone, and physical character of the volume.

Loss of even a coin-sized piece of the material history of the site rankles. Imagine a jagged hole, broad as a penny-piece, through one leaf of the volume where the story should be. What is so troubling to Heath is the sense that Ireland's private transaction has depleted what is collectively known about Tintern's past. With Ireland's purchase ('for a trifling consideration' no less) the coin ceases to exist as a local artefact. It is replaced by an unsatisfactory description and to make matters worse 'no other information on the subject has been communicated'. This abrupt termination of discourse is an attack on future editions of the guide, which lists oral and scribal communications among its sources, as well as an attack on Heath's practices as a writer. While Williams the historian is criticized for not increasing the 'public stock of information on the Ruin', Ireland the picturesque tourist is actually robbing the bank.

Heath's capital as an author is the depth of his regional knowledge – the legacy of 'a continued endeavour ... to illustrate this much frequented part of the kingdom, during which period the writer's life has been passed in it'. The distinction he draws between 'frequenters' of Monmouthshire and what he later names 'resident inhabitants' hardens into a philosophical distinction between the nature of his production and the work of tourists such as Ireland:

> In such a county as this as we are treating of, every foot of which is rendered interesting by History, the time allotted by Writers of

Travels for its investigation, can only excite the smile of the native. What can be expected from the information obtained in a pleasure boat, or the casual stopping at an inn, without any acquaintance in the place whose history they presume to illustrate?[49]

Heath offers himself as the 'acquaintance in the place' whose experience directs the curiosity of the traveller. Topography is not simply local description, but more actively a means of becoming local, a demonstration of what a native may learn, discern, and feel over time. In *Tintern Abbey*, Heath models a process which readers are invited to continue, 'his mind being in unison with their wishes' as he says in 1803. Fittingly, Heath himself became a figure in contemporary travel narratives. When Sarah Anne Wilmot was escorted by this 'philosophical librarian' in 1802, she found that 'by the attention of Mr. Heath we had the advantage of seeing the curiosities of the Country much better than ourselves'.[50] The 'intelligent guide' Charles Heath longed for on his own first visit to Tintern Abbey was clearly his later self.

Notes

1. Charles Sale, Gravestone Photograph Resource (Web), kindly supplied me with an image of Heath's monument at St Mary's Church, Monmouth.
2. For the Wye tour see Malcolm Andrews, *The Search for the Picturesque* (Aldershot: Scolar Press, 1989); C. S. Matheson, *Enchanting Ruin: Tintern Abbey and Romantic Tourism in Wales* (Ann Arbor: University of Michigan, Special Collections Library, 2008), Web, 14 September 2011; and Julian Mitchell, *The Wye Tour and its Artists* (Chepstow: Chepstow Museum, 2010).
3. Louis Simond, *Journal of a Tour and Residence in Great Britain, During the Years 1810 and 1811, by a French Traveller*, 2 vols (Edinburgh: A. Constable, 1815), 1: 208–9.
4. George Nicholson, *The Cambrian Traveller's Guide and Pocket Companion* (Stourport, 1808).
5. Stephen Bending, 'The True Rust of the Baron's Sword: Ruins and the National Landscape', in *Producing the Past: Aspects of Antiquarian Culture and Practice 1700–1850*, ed. Martin Myrone and Lucy Peltz (Aldershot: Ashgate, 1999), 85.
6. Charles Heath, 'A Walk on the Banks of the Wye from Monmouth to Tintern Abbey', *Historical and Descriptive Accounts of the Ancient and Present State of Tintern Abbey* (Monmouth, 1801), [13]. Hereafter cited as *Tintern Abbey*. All editions of Heath's works were published in Monmouth.
7. Heath, *Tintern Abbey* (1801), [13].
8. Heath, *Tintern Abbey* (1803), [ii].
9. Heath's unillustrated volume cost two shillings. Bent's *London Catalogue of Books with Their Sizes and Prices* (London: W. Bent, 1799) lists a duodecimo *Margate Guide* (likely the 1775 edition, 60 pages with plates and map) for 3s and an octavo *Guide to Scarborough* for 3s. Nicholson's octavo *The Cambrian*

Traveller's Guide (1808) cost 7s 6d: *Edinburgh Annual Register for 1809* 2.2 (1811), xxxii. By contrast, Samuel Ireland's illustrated *Picturesque Tour on the River Wye* contained 31 plates and cost 1 pound 16s: *Critical Review, or the Annals of Literature* 22 (March 1798), 282.

10. Heath, *Tintern Abbey* (1803), [iv]. Despite his disclaimer Heath considered this marketing strategy. The title page of the 1796 *Descriptive Account of Ragland Castle* announces that Heath 'is preparing for Press an elegant and enlarged Account, to be beautified with Plates from original Drawings, of this much admired ruin'.

11. Ifano Jones, *A History of Printers and Printing in Wales to 1810 and of Successive and Related Printers to 1923. Also, A History of Printing in Monmouthshire* (Cardiff: William Lewis, 1925), 226.

12. Charles Heath, *Excursion down the Wye* (Monmouth, 1796), [i–ii]. Hereafter cited as *Excursion*.

13. This copy is in the National Library of Wales. NLW xda 1356.2.h43.

14. W. H. Haines, 'Notes on the Bibliography of Monmouthshire', *The Library* (1896), Series 1–8, 244.

15. I use the term 'edition' not in the strict bibliographical sense of 'all copies of a book printed from substantially the same setting of type' but, following Heath, in the looser sense often used by publishers to 'distinguish among copies identifiable by publishing format ... change of publisher, textual revision, or some other feature, even if all the copies belong to the same edition in a bibliographical sense'. Where Heath has provided a new title page and made revisions to the text, I refer to the volume as a new edition. William Proctor Williams and Craig S. Abbot, *An Introduction to Bibliographical and Textual Studies* (New York: MLA, 2009), 151.

16. Jones, *History of Printers*, 225.

17. Heath, *Tintern Abbey* (1806), [ii]n.

18. Heath's monument, erected by 'his fellow townsmen' more than twenty-five years after his death, gives his year of death as 1831 rather than 1830.

19. Heath, *Excursion* (1799), [xii].

20. Edward Gill, 'Lord Nelson's Hat and the Country Printer', *Country Quest* (1911), 19; 'Charles Heath', *British Book Trade Index*, University of Birmingham, Web, 16 Nov. 2010; Jones, *History of Printers*, 224.

21. Heath, *Excursion* (1799), [xi].

22. Heath, *Excursion* (1799), [iv].

23. Heath, *Tintern Abbey* (1803), [ii–iii].

24. Heath began business in his Munnow Street house but moved to premises in the Market Place in 1793 and to 23 Agincourt Square in 1817. 'Charles Heath', *British Book Trade Index*, University of Birmingham, Web, 16 Nov. 2010. His relocation predates the publication of *Descriptive Account of Ragland Castle* (correctly dated 1792 according to Jones, *History of Printers*, 224) and *Tintern Abbey* (1793).

25. This blurring of domestic space and shop persists in later years. See Hermann Pückler-Muskau, *Tour in England, Ireland and France in the Years 1826, 1827, 1828 and 1829 ... in a Series of Letters by a German Prince* (Philadelphia: Carey, Lea & Blanchard, 1833).

26. Charles Heath, *Historical and Descriptive Accounts of the Ancient and Present State of Ragland Castle* (1819), [vi].

27. Heath, *Tintern Abbey* (1793), [ii].
28. Stebbing Shaw, *A Tour to the West of England* (1789), qtd in Heath, *Tintern Abbey* (1806), [75].
29. In the 1798 *Tintern Abbey* Heath comments: 'The Printer of these sheets joining with the Writer in paying a Tribute of Respect to such cultivated Talents, which have afforded him, among many others, such infinite pleasure, thinks it will not be displeasing to the Reader to introduce them here' (11). I am grateful to Germaine Warkington and Leslie Howsam for opinions on Heath's deployment of the term.
30. Heath, *Tintern Abbey* (1801), [i].
31. Heath, *Excursion* (1796), [i–ii].
32. I explore this subject in greater depth in a monograph, *Composing Tintern Abbey*, forthcoming from University of Toronto Press.
33. Joseph Heely's 1777 *Description of Hagley Park* places an unattributed painting 'A View of Tintern Abbey, near Piercefield' in the Green Bed-chamber (18).
34. Heath, *Tintern Abbey* (1823), [92].
35. Heath, *Tintern Abbey* (1806), [iv].
36. Charles Heath, autograph notes, *The History of Monmouthshire* by David Williams (London, 1796). This copy is in the Monmouth Museum. I am grateful to curator Andrew Helme for bringing these notes to my attention.
37. Heath, *Tintern Abbey* (1793), 55; qtd in Haines, 'Notes on the Bibliography of Monmouthshire', 363.
38. Damian Walford Davies, *Presences that Disturb: Models of Romantic Identity in the Literature and Culture of the 1790s* (Cardiff: University of Wales Press, 2002), 27, 41.
39. Heath, *Excursion* (1808), [vi].
40. Heath, 'General Remarks on Tintern Abbey', *Tintern Abbey* (1801), [72]. This passage is moved to the preface of the 1803 edition.
41. Williams acknowledges Griffin's generosity and describes his research as 'probably a model to the Historiographers of counties – a history of powerful and opulent families, written by a clergyman, uninfluenced by patronage or the desire of performance, and with a scrupulous regard to truth' (Williams, *Monmouthshire*, x).
42. Heath, *Tintern Abbey* (1803), [v].
43. Ireland, *Picturesque Views*, vi.
44. Ireland, *Picturesque Views*, viii–ix.
45. Heath, *Excursion* (1799), [x].
46. See Jeffrey Kahan, *Reforging Shakespeare: The Story of a Theatrical Scandal* (London: Lehigh University Press, 1998).
47. Heath, *Tintern Abbey* (1801), [59].
48. Heath, *Tintern Abbey* (1803), [v].
49. Heath, *Tintern Abbey* (1823), n. pag.
50. Qtd in Mitchell, *The Wye Tour and its Artists*. A partial digital facsimile of the diary of Sarah Anne Wilmot's visit to Gloucestershire, Monmouthshire, and the Vale of Glamorgan, 1802, may be found at *Gathering the Jewels: The Website for Welsh Heritage and Culture*, National Museums and Galleries of Wales, Web, 10 Sept. 2010. Item reference: GtJ27636.

4
Britain through Foreign Eyes: Early Nineteenth-Century Home Tourism in Translation

Benjamin Colbert

When Percy Shelley writes in *Alastor* (1815) of how a poet 'left / His cold fireside and alienated home / To seek strange truths in undiscovered lands',[1] the implicit irony – to be discovered by the poem's narrator as he reconstructs the poet's foreign excursions and death in exile – is that the alienated home has now become the undiscovered land where the strangest truths are to be found. By contrast, *Alastor*'s precursor, Wordsworth's *The Excursion* (1814), resembles a bole closing over a foreign body, the Solitary, the collapse of whose French Revolutionary sympathies have led him to retire, disillusioned, to the English Lake District. Not only unconvinced by Wordsworth's attempt to re-naturalize the Solitary by localizing him, Shelley dramatizes his Poet's unsettling foreignness. *Alastor*'s narrator is led to one conclusion: 'things / ... are not as they were' (lines 719–20). The Poet has had his influence on this new Wordsworth, who feels within himself what Madame de Staël has called, referring to British travellers in foreign parts, a 'necessary alienation', the state of mind in which incomprehension dulls the gloss of pre-conceived familiarity, that textual legacy of accumulated travel writings.[2] The politics of alienation are exemplified again in a March 1820 letter in which Mary Shelley satirically re-christens post-Napoleonic England as 'New Land Castlereagh', where those who refuse allegiance to the Tory state are branded 'aliens' or driven into exile,[3] a tableau that expresses the liberal expatriate's anxiety of belonging, mixed with indignation at oppressions that make expatriation a legitimate protest. But there is also a sense in the Shelleys' writing of a more profound alienation as a condition of the modern world, where the national and the cosmopolitan dialectically reveal the constructed and malleable nature of personal identity and allegiance.

Wordsworth's 1798 poem 'The Brothers' represents a proto-Shelleyan stance, for here Wordsworth explores what it means to look at Britain through foreign eyes. This poem underlies James Buzard's argument that the Romantic Period ushers in a modernity where 'one stops belonging to a culture and can only *tour* it'.[4] Bronislaw Szerszynski and John Urry more recently have called this the 'cosmopolitan condition', that is, 'the way that growing numbers of humans might now be said "to inhabit" their world at a distance',[5] aesthetically and psychologically. Returning home from a long captivity amongst the Moors of Barbary, the poem's protagonist, Leonard Ewbank, is mistaken for a tourist by the pastor, who relates a tragic tale for the stranger's entertainment, a tale that implicates Leonard's flight from home in a series of catastrophes lead- ing to his brother's early death. As a result, home becomes 'a place in which he could not bear to live',[6] and he flees abroad again; the native treated like a foreigner becomes one. This mimetic doubling of native and foreigner reappears in numerous guises in early nineteenth-century literature, from the English Opium Eater's encounter with the Malay at the heart of the Lake District; to Byron's wandering Spaniard, Don Juan, touring London; to the displaced French aristocrats in Charlotte Smith's *The Emigrants* (1793). Smith's émigrés stand in for a French population of some 20,000 in Britain during this period, with an active literary culture, including, between 1792 and 1815, French-language pam- phlets, books, newspapers, and journals.[7] Yet this paradise of exiles, as the French traveller Louis Simond found in 1810, was circumscribed in times of war by the Alien Acts, legislation requiring that foreigners log their movements and report to magistrates at three-month intervals.[8] Intended to protect the state from espionage, such Acts also objectify a fear that the foreigner might otherwise blend in too well, looking and acting like a native. Wordsworth's and Shelley's aliens, in different ways and for different purposes, remain unassimilated, isolated within soci- ety or exiled from it, but both writers gesture towards an earlier view of the foreigner that endows him or her with a power of vision detached from party politics, a means by which British imperial overseers of the world can be shown a panorama of themselves. As William Mavor remarks in his 1809 editor's introduction to *Travels through England and Scotland to the Hebrides. From the French of B. Faujas Saint Fond* [trans. 1799], 'a stranger ... is eminently qualified to place things in a proper point of view'.[9]

During the revolutionary and post-revolutionary years, the 'stranger' speaks not least through accounts of home tourism in translation, including foreign travel accounts in English and fictional works purporting to be by foreigners, together encompassing a neglected subgenre comprising thirty-six titles between 1789 and 1825 (compared with only two the previous decade). The travel writers are predominately French and German speakers, and their works include Johann Wilhelm von Archenholz's *A Picture of England* (Leipzig, 1785; trans. 1789); Pierre Étienne Louis Dumont's *Letters ... Written during the Author's Residence at Versailles, Paris, and London* (1792);[10] Jacques-Henri Meister's *Letters Written during a Residence in England* (Zurich, 1795; trans. 1799); Christian Goede's *The Stranger in England* (Dresden, 1806; trans. 1807); and Louis Simond's *Journal of a Tour and Residence in Great Britain* (Edinburgh, 1815). Among the ersatz travel books are Robert Southey's *Letters from England: by Don Manuel Alvarez Espriella* (1807); John Badcock's *Letters from London: Observations of a Russian* (1816); Peter George Patmore's *Letters on England. By Victoire, Count de Soligny* (1823); and *London and Paris, or Comparative Sketches. By the Marquis de Vermont and Sir Charles Darnley, Bart.* (1823). Translations of francophone travellers are concentrated in the 1790s (four titles) and in the decade after Waterloo (twelve titles). Especially in the aftermath of the Revolution, such works bespeak an interest in how transformations in French polity might affect French consciousness of their neighbour and traditional adversary. But they also present travellers who break down cultural stereotypes and avoid the one-dimensional categories of national identity characteristic of a wider, more prevalent Gallo-phobic discourse.[11] This essay focuses on two such travellers, Meister and Simond, whose works question essentialized notions of national identity even as they overtly engage in the discourse of national character, underscoring a wider tension in the genre between British insularity and cosmopolitanism, and reflecting what Kurt Mueller-Vollmer and Esther Wohlgemut have referred to separately as a post-Enlightenment, yet distinctly Romantic internationalism.[12] Within the genre of home tourism in translation, this amounts to what might be called 'cosmopolitan insularism' – the embrace of an internationalized, commercialized, mobile identity that nevertheless preserves its distinction from overseas others. Fundamental to this discussion, then, is the proposition that, in this period, a home-foreign binary, increasingly invoked in the name of nationalist party politics, is involved in a transnational or cosmopolitan alternative where construction of 'national identity' becomes a mode of exteriorized perception; perceiving oneself and one's place in the nation involves reading the nation itself as a 'foreign' subject.

Robert Southey is the first to recognize the kind of works discussed here as a minor canon, in a long review article of 1816 for the *Quarterly Review* later published under the title 'On the Accounts of England by Foreign Travellers and the State of Public Opinion'.[13] The review treats nine books, including Badcock's and Simond's, published between 1809 and 1816, but opens with a survey of the genre from Elizabethan times, a catalogue that details the chauvinism of foreigners and their linguistic ineptitude (as when Pierre Jean Grosley (*Londres*, 1770) interprets the Thames-side cry of 'Oars! Oars!', Southey writes, in 'the very worst sense which the sound can bear'). Southey softens when describing the 'perfect charity' of the 'Prussian Parson Adams', Karl Philipp Moritz, whose *Travels Chiefly on Foot* (Berlin, 1783; trans. 1795) starkly contrasts 'later French travels ... written with a very different feeling': 'a spirit of envious dislike ... more or less apparent in all'.[14] This charge brings Southey to the matter at hand, namely a group of French travel books that form, in his view, unpalatable alliances with British radical dissent: 'it is as much the virtue of the French to love their own country', he writes revealingly, '... as it is the vice of our oppositionists and *Ultra-Whigs* to take part on every occasion against England'.[15] The Tory view of the politics of alienation re-inscribes the foreign-native binary within a self-divided *patria*, where radical discontent gives way all too easily to rejection of 'home' values, treason, and emigration. But Southey is equivocal, for emigration encompasses as much the transfer and circulation of British values internationally as it does the last resort of scoundrels. Referring to Benjamin Silliman's *A Journal of Travels in England* (New York, 1810), therefore, Southey first acknowledges a 'commonwealth in which all distinctions of country should be forgotten' – what Peter Wollen calls the Enlightenment ideal of a 'transnational "republic of letters"' available to the genteel classes.[16] Southey then promotes the virtues of colonial emigration; in America, 'old settler' stock grafts Burkean values of 'prejudice and inheritance' onto American Revolutionary 'principle[s]' and 'duty', forming a republican hybrid that Southey associates with the Federalists, or in his words, 'the English party'. By contrast, he identifies a disreputable circulation in 'the modern swarm of emigrants, renegadoes and refugees' who transgress national boundaries, export discontent, and continue their war against the *patria* abroad. The American newspapers that fanned national feeling during the War of 1812, he believes, 'were edited, not by Americans, but emigrants, Scotch, Irish, and English'.[17]

Southey's Britain seen through foreign eyes (from malcontents within and travellers without) sets up terms for a partisan critique of Louis Simond, a French citizen who had resided in the United States before returning to France via Britain in 1810. Simond's transnational identity and the hybrid nature of his book in fact pose a sophisticated challenge to Southey's Tory world view, as do two translations of francophone works published in 1799 that Southey ignores in his survey. The first of these is Barthélemi Faujas de Saint-Fond's *Travels in England, Scotland and the Hebrides* (1799), remarkable here for its own advocacy of a transnational commonwealth.[18] Faujas pointedly begins his book with an anecdote of his visit to Sir Joseph Banks's London salon, the 'rallying point' of international correspondence and exchange, where foreign gentlemen of all nations are received. On this occasion, Banks receives a parcel from China containing some 'lapideous matter', and Faujas uses this for an excursus on the 'disinterested' international networks of scholarly exchange by which fragments of the same 'adamantine spar' end up in the Museum of Natural History in Paris.[19] The parcel also contains a robust varietal of hemp, chiefly valued in England, as Faujas remarks, for the sake of 'her navy, which constitutes her power'.[20] Fearful of imminent invasion by France, British readers in 1799 would have needed no prompting – and the translator provides none – to realize the potential implications for the *French* navy of Banks's gift of a sample of these same hemp seeds (Faujas notes his intention of distributing them to growers in Paris and estate holders in the South of France). But Faujas's point is that the spirit of Anglo-Gallic collaboration should be the spirit of the age even if it is not, and in a footnote he admits that he has been prevented from publishing the successful results of the trials 'by the melancholy remembrance ... that of eleven persons to whom I gave some of the seed from China ... eight have been dragged to the scaffold',[21] a reflection that locates the ideals of transnational cooperation in the scientific culture of the *ancien régime*.

The second book that Southey overlooks, Jacques-Henri Meister's *Letters Written during a Residence in England* (Zurich, 1795; trans. 1799), might well have drawn his ire had it been the product of the later period, although Meister very subtly repudiates politicized national feeling. Meister (1744–1826), resident in Paris from 1769 to 1792, was Swiss by birth and is known principally as editor, along with Baron Grimm and Diderot, of the *Correspondance littéraire* (1754?–1813), a clandestine manuscript journal whose subscribers included sovereigns of northern European powers, such as Catherine II.[22] Meister edited the *Correspondance* from 1773 to 1813, and in 1813 saw a collected edition up to 1790 through the press – his editorship, like his correspondence with the proscribed Madame de Staël during the Napoleonic years, remaining a secret.[23] Meister travelled to England in 1789 and again in 1792, and some if not all of the ten letters composed on the subject of his first tour, by his own account, 'appeared in the *Journal des Indépendans*',[24] before being 'printed together in a small volume ... in 1791, at Paris'.[25] The 1813 edition of *Correspondance* includes the first three letters under the May, August, and September 1790 issues and the serialization is likely to have continued into 1791;[26] letters 7 and 10 were translated into German by Archenholtz for his journal, *Minerva* (Hamburg, 1792–1858); still others were translated by Heinrich August Ottokar Reichard (1751–1828) for his miscellany, *Olla Potrida* (Berlin, 1778–87), this time attributed to 'an emigrant lady ... assisted by her brother'.[27] Thus, a peculiar international circulation had commenced even before the first Zurich edition of 1795, published anonymously in French.

The subterfuges involved in its early textual history indicate a malleability of purpose that the 1799 translation in no way belied. The account of the first visit to England comprises ten letters to an unnamed friend that present Meister as a partisan of English liberty, law, and the British constitution: 'I had not walked fifty yards on English ground before I thought I felt sensations of freedom and the dignity of human nature rising in my breast, which I had never experienced before; not even on the day when ... I trampled on the ruins of the Bastille'. Assuming the philosopher's mantle, Meister offers his readers 'rather what I thought than what I have seen',[28] yet his distinctions between English and French manners are punctuated and illustrated by visual memories nonetheless: men and women *choosing* to ride on the roofs of coaches reveals them as the hardiest of travellers; a boxing match in Pall Mall carried out with strict adherence to rules signifies the harmony between liberty and constraint under law; the Thames 'bearing thousands and thousands of vessels ... from every part of the world' sums up the nation's commercial might and cosmopolitanism built upon the security of insularity.[29] It is not all adulation. Communal drinking and dining habits (such as wiping fingers on tablecloths rather than napkins) tests his equanimity; the theatres appear to him 'like so many shabby tennis courts'; and criminal jurisprudence in which capital punishment is served for minor offences while hardened criminals exploit loopholes to go free tarnishes the British Constitution (offset, Meister argues, by the 'sagacity' of judges and juries).[30] When the early letters were written and first published in 1790–2, Meister's arguments were part of what Rachel Hammersley calls 'the complex debates concerning the best kind of republicanism for the circumstances' in the period before the Jacobin ascendancy in Paris,[31] but from the vantage of 1799 – the year in which the translation was published – more prominently emerging from these letters is Meister's attachment to the ideas and appearances of social and political justice rather than to the biases of national identity. 'Whether luckily or unluckily for myself, I find I am rather a cosmopolite than a citizen',[32] he declares, emphasizing the desirability of exteriorized perception – seeing one's own country at a distance.

Besides Meister's sacrifice of detail for reflection and his implicit support for an English-influenced constitutional republic in France, there is nothing particularly unusual about this home tour until letter 6 when, in the midst of discussion of public charitable institutions, he breaks off mid-paragraph upon receiving a letter from Lady C***** criticizing his journal letter of March 1791, published in the *Correspondance littéraire*. In a note, the translator identifies the interlocutor as Lady Elizabeth Craven, Margravine of Anspach (1750–1828),[33] author of the popular *Journey through the Crimea to Constantinople* (1789). Craven reviews and reproves the superficialities of Meister's previous letters – his comments on the legislature, elections, women's fashions, and the like. 'You were in England only three weeks', she chides:

> you were astonished with what you saw; you were not sufficiently acquainted with the country to describe it, unless you supposed you could amuse and instruct your readers by giving them a description of the world in the moon or any other world you have only seen through a telescope, and that a telescope after the French fashion: for you have lived so long in Paris that … you reason, and you form systems entirely in the French manner.[34]

Craven recommends that Meister revisit, this time searching for the individual rather than the representative, avoiding a too orthodox discourse of national manners. 'We are not to be described in a mass', she writes, 'but by an infinite variety of minute particulars'. He should reconsider London, avoid the Court, and go into the country, visit the manufacturing towns, see harbours and dock-yards, dine with farmers, and observe English gentlewomen who, 'without declaring who they are, [succour] the distressed and unfortunate every where about them'.[35] It is a remarkable letter, all the more so because Meister defends his impressionistic method while acknowledging the justice of her position. Craven's letter thus works contrapuntally if not dialectically with Meister's; her 'English' and his 'French' sensibility playfully manipulating each others' personae.

Subsequent letters, equally noteworthy, include one on Shakespeare that anticipates Madame de Staël's and Stendhal's more renowned departures from French neoclassicism by a quarter of a century.[36] But letter 10, the conclusion to the first visit, voices the question implicit in so many of the works in this genre: 'Should a person be a stranger in a country, or a native, to be able to give the best account of it?'. Meister's answer deftly incorporates Craven's views into his own, balancing the 'astonishment' of a stranger's first impressions against the prejudices inherent in the native's habitual regard, and concluding that the traveller must record impressions but 'hazard an account of nothing' until 'thoroughly acquainted' with a country's language, religion, politics, customs, and manners.[37] Meister's keen sense of epistemological relativism and (almost) romantic irony prevents even this synthesis from being his last word. He first complicates the notion of national difference by claiming that urbanization, travel, translation, and commerce 'have made the several nations of Europe, as it were, one people'. Then, he reaffirms the persistence of national character beneath circumstantial unities. And finally, unravelling what he had said about the traveller's duty of immersion into religion, politics, and manners, he reasons that to judge modern Europeans by these standards is to form 'a false estimate'. The modern European is 'estranged' *('nous sont devenues presque étrangères')* from these institutions and the traveller must therefore judge character from 'the spirit of our theatrical entertainments, the style of our romances, and the taste of our witticisms'. For revolutionary France, even this is in flux: 'To determine whether the same may be said of us twenty years hence, we must know whether our new constitution will alter our character, or whether our character will alter the constitution'.[38]

Meister thus redefines travel writing as a dialogue between particulars and generalities, information and aesthetics, and, ideally, between natives and foreigners, as Craven's interpolated letter exemplifies. Far from deploying a stable hermeneutic or coherent subjectivity, however, the travel writer is fragmented and changeable, relying on the appearance of unity within diversity to signify national character, yet supplying only a dubious consistency him or herself; as Meister puts it in the opening chapter of the second tour, 'as to my opinions ... They are changeable, and we too must change with them'.[39]

The book ends with another dialogue, this time with the 'Countess de V——',[40] in which the correspondents exchange dream visions. Meister's concerns a visit to William Beckford's country seat, Fonthill Abbey, transformed into 'the mansion of an enchanter', where Beckford is an idealized cosmopolitan figure, embodying the theatricality, romance, and wit that inform the traveller's true estimate of a people: he 'touches the harpsichord' like Piccini, speaks French 'with all the genius and glow of Diderot', and English with 'all the rhetorical powers of the ... House of Commons', yet all of these charms are coloured by an English melancholy.[41] For her part, the Countess relates how she fell asleep on a collection of prints after turning over one representing 'Saint Jerome sleeping in the desert, surrounded by tigers'. Her remark alludes to an earlier letter in which Meister relates an anecdote of a Paris showman who revolutionizes his Royal tiger display with a new show-cloth, on which is 'substituted ... these words, *"Here is to be seen the large national tiger"'*.[42] The Countess's vision works as a revolutionary allegory of cross-cultural, even meta-cultural alliances; Beckford is transmuted, first, into the placid Jerome, untroubled by cross-channel upheavals, and then into the Countess's father who is given leave to visit her from the temple of Elysium (a parallel to Fonthill). The father delivers a kind of postcard, 'a canvas frame of an oval shape' produced in the following manner:

> Whenever we, who remain here upon earth, honour the memory of these departed spirits ... the incense burnt here reaches the altar, and the perfumes on it take fire, the ethereal vapour from which arises to the magic frame, and impresses on it the likeness of the person by whom this mark of respect is shown.

The Countess discovers but does not reveal the likeness and presses it to her breast when the drum of revolutionary Discord awakens her. 'All that remained', she writes, 'was this portrait ...' which 'you will find, on your return ... placed in your bedchamber'.[43] So ends the *Residence in England*, the final tableau suggesting yet another level of knowledge serviced by travel letters and sketches, the human, affective bonds that unite author and reader, beyond political boundaries and historical change.

The 'Advertisement' to the 1799 translation contains several intriguing but evasive clues to the translator's identity, but its emphasis on a particular site of translation similarly locates Meister's book historically and affectively:

> The translation contained in the following sheets constituted the amusement of some anxious hours, during an irksome residence at Bremen, whilst the remains of the late unfortunate British continental army were embarking at Bremerlche, [sic] in the year 1795, on their voyage to England.[44]

The evacuation of British forces from Bremen in April 1795 terminated the disastrous Flanders campaign begun the previous year under the Duke of York's command.[45] That the translator remained behind, not arriving in London until the following year, reduces the likelihood of his or her connection with the British, but the translator's commiseration with them underwrites the vision of unity with which Meister's letter to Countess V—— ends. So too does the date of publication, 1799, one year after the French invasion of Switzerland, at a time when the threat of a French landing on British shores remained palpable. In these contexts the Swiss expatriate Meister's complex dialogism argues for and exemplifies cross-cultural rapprochement in the face of the violent divisions within Europe that were all too easily appropriated for exclusive patriotism and national feeling. By contrast, rather than a Burkean equilibrium of distinct national types held in harmony by conservative ideology, Meister radically re-envisions a reciprocal internationalism modelled on commercial circulation, artistic accomplishment, and cross-border affections.

Although French Revolutionary excesses spur Meister to look to Britain for models of constitutional liberty, his cosmopolitan vision is an implicit promise that Britain can never be, nor ever should be, the sole preserve of liberty. Louis Simond's *Journal of a Tour and Residence in Great Britain, during the Years 1810 and 1811, by a French Traveller* (1815) shares these concerns, yet he identifies more closely with Britain than he does with France, in particular with liberal Whig political and cultural interests associated with Francis Jeffrey's *Edinburgh Review*. Like Meister's, Simond's hybrid identity exerts manifold pressures on his claim to represent France: his twenty-year residence in the United States; his composition of the *Journal* in English, translating it into French for publication in Paris only after its Edinburgh debut; his marriage to an Englishwoman (the niece of John Wilkes); and, by the time the *Journal* was published, his relation by marriage to Jeffrey himself. In fact, Simond self-consciously represents a France that is no more, as he journeys to recover his *patria*, schooled however not by the nostalgia of the French émigré population in England for *ancien regime* privilege, but by the republican aspirations of the United States.

For Simond, as for Meister, the discourse of English manners is ready to hand: English melancholy, seriousness, and taciturnity. Yet true to Craven's formula, Simond luxuriates in 'minute particulars' of city and country, and he too is a relativist when adjudicating on English travellers' sententious comparisons of self and other. The French may be chided for spitting on the floor, he observes, but the English keep a chamber pot in the dining room (and use it); 'the same principle ... stigmatised as *charlatanerie* in France', he points out, 'might, on the hustings of an English election, have appeared like love of the people'; 'men of all countries are not extremely unlike', he concludes.[46] But the characteristic of the British that Simond returns to concerns their insular cosmopolitanism: they are a people characterized by their propensity to travel, to write about their travels, and to read guidebooks and tours about their home (Simond notes at Cambridge how 'there is no place of any note in England which has not its printed guide').[47] John Scott, in his *Visit to Paris in 1814* (1815), remarks that this 'travelling propensity' – his phrase – is perceived by the French as a 'species of derangement', and Southey, in his *Letters from England* (1807) coins a term for the condition, *oikophobia*, fear of home.[48] Simond, too, resorts to the pharmacopoeia, and calls this travelling mania 'the English *maladie du pays*': 'a sense of weariness and satiety all the time they are at home'.[49] The downside of this restlessness is that, as Simond notes later, 'the *amor patriae*, in its full force, exists only for those who never travelled',[50] but English discontent proves, in his analysis, to be the counterpart of its freedom of the press, the circulation of ideas and information, and commercial power. 'Nobody is provincial in their country', he argues: 'The English see from their windows across the channel all that passes on the Continent; hear all that is said, and read all that is published, without translation, and in its original form'.[51]

The tensions within this idealized vision of a panoramic Englishness can be seen when Simond attempts, *pace* Meister, to explain and exalt British wit and genius through an appreciation of Sir Walter Scott. Among the first wave of 'genteel tourists' who toured the Trossachs in the light of Scott's recent sensation, *The Lady of the Lake* (1810), Simond responds to a landscape, as Nicola Watson puts it, 'saturated by fiction'[52]: 'we remarked a narrow and wild pass ... along the base of Ben-Ledi, which we pronounced the very spot of the ambuscade of Roderick Dhu – the whole scene between him and Fitz-James was before us'.[53] Simond's recollection of this moment prompts a meditation on English and French poetry and poetics, on the impossibility of translating English verse into French, a language whose only true poets, he argues, are prose writers such as Rousseau and Madame de Staël. But with the untranslatability argument, Simond sacrifices his privileged vantage; the foreigner, writing in English and experiencing its poetry with the sensitivity of a native, has *gone* native. He has become part of the nation that can experience the world 'without translation' but cannot be translated itself.

Fellow-feeling and transnational identity cut no slack with Simond's Tory hosts, who denied his feeling for poetry and treated his hybridity with contempt. Walter Scott's only notice, some years later, pronounces him 'intelligent, but rather conceited, as the manner of an American Frenchman'; Thomas De Quincey, using Simond's own theories against him, damns him for having a 'French inaptitude for apprehending poetry at all'; Southey calls him 'a wretched connoisseur, and a miserable critic' and labelled him the 'Gallo-American traveller'.[54] This rancour owes a great deal to Simond's deference to Jeffrey's literary criticism; while arguing against factionalism, Simond identified himself with one of the principle factions in the literary culture wars of the age. Although Simond does not follow Jeffrey outright in condemning the Lake poets during his tour of the region, he did meet and does mention Wordsworth, Coleridge, and Southey in conjunction with their youthful pantisocratic plan to 'traverse the Atlantic ... to breathe the pure air of liberty', noting how Southey still retained traces of the reformer, as 'the new insect, fresh out of his old skin, drags still some fragments of it after him'.[55]

Southey paid Simond back in kind, not merely with his remarks on Simond's literary criticism, but by reading the *Journal* as already historical, 'a tale of the times that are gone', discounting what in Simond's analysis does not fit Southey's present concerns in 1816, particularly his attack on the radical press (which Simond subsumed into more general reflections on the strengths, weaknesses, and ultimate versatility of the British constitution). Southey can thus acknowledge Simond's 'political observations, with the respect that they deserve',[56] but denies that the book will have value for British readers; and he is wholly silent on Simond's cosmopolitanism. Instead the review ends with a parody. Southey replaces Simond's relativist comparison of French and British national character with a stark homology between French Revolutionary conspirators of 1789 and English radicals of 1816, a rhetorical flourish developing Southey's conceit of the radical as a foreign body within the body politic.

By 1817, when Simond published a second edition of his *Journals*, a new tone of triumphalism among British travellers to France had become so pervasive that Simond included an appendix devoted in part to combating what, in a series of allusions principally to John Scott's *Visit to Paris*, he calls 'exclusive patriotism and geographical morality'.[57] In this context, the *Journal* reasserts its vision of a cosmopolitan subjectivity and its privilege of distance; Britain seen through foreign eyes can help correct the way British travellers perceive the foreign, teach them better to see themselves, and prevent travel writing itself from becoming the new factionalism. Yet the ease with which Southey brings Simond's tour into line with the cultural politics of the day underscores the rarity of a dia-logical theory of the foreign-native travel account, like his or Meister's, and how the Shelleys' representations of exile or alienation become more common weapons in the critique against British insularity in the charged political atmosphere after the post-Napoleonic settlement.

In the 1820s, home tourism in translation nevertheless remained a space for experimentation with the boundaries of identity between France and Britain. Jean Emmanuel Charles Nodier's *Promenade from Dieppe to the Mountains of Scotland* (1822) frames itself as a journal dedi-cated to Nodier's absent wife, affective ties designed partly to deflect criticism from the impressionistic subjectivity of his 'journal abruptly sketched' which rather reinforces national difference than otherwise and is most animated when linking, conventionally, the primitivism of the Scottish Highlanders to the poetry of Ossian.[58] *London and Paris, or Comparative Sketches. By the Marquis de Vermont and Sir Charles Darnley, Bart.* (1823) ostensibly collects an exchange of letters from a Frenchman in London and an Englishman in Paris, yet the 'dialogue' played out between them amounts to less a dialectical rapprochement than a comedy of national stereotypes leading to greater mutual tolerance. Patmore's *Letters on England. By Victoire, Count de Soligny* (1823) uses fictionalized French persona – a provincial who the 'translator' assures us 'is *not* ... a citizen of the world'[59] – to engage in cultural criticism without the automatic vilification accorded those in William Hazlitt's London circle, notoriously branded the 'Cockney' School by *Blackwood's Edinburgh Magazine*.

Meister's belief that cultural assessment should replace national stereotype or Simond's that a nation's poetry might be the locus of its identity finds its most effective successor and summary in Joseph Amédée Pichot's *Historical and Literary Tour of a Foreigner in England and Scotland* (1825). Pichot argues that poets, artists, and authors contrib-ute to 'the explanation of an epoch' and are an index to its 'physical discoveries and improvements'; the genius of Byron, Scott, and James Watt, modern poetry and the power of steam, belong to the same pro-gressive movement.[60] Although he remarks on the 'miserable exile' a traveller feels in leaving home and his own fears of being accused of 'anti-national prejudice',[61] Pichot subverts easy binaries between native and foreigner. His immersion in English literature is such that through it he can think, observe his surroundings, and meditate on the future of his own country's literature, when the classical rules will become adapted to new social, political, and intellectual circumstances, the harbinger of a French Romanticism. In this sense Pichot's opening portrait of his travelling companion, a young woman of English birth schooled lately in Paris, able to feel 'the beauties of Racine, Fenelon, Bernardin de St. Pierre, Chateaubriand, &c.' as well as 'the literature of her own country', becomes a portrait of Pichot's ideal citizen and reader, as it was for Meister and Simond before him: the national whose subjectivity is founded on a transcultural identity. 'The muse of Albion', as Pichot imagines his young companion, could not have represented England so well had she not become 'partly a Frenchwoman'.[62]

Notes

1. Percy Bysshe Shelley, *Alastor; or, the Spirit of Solitude*, lines 75–7, in *The Poems of Shelley*, ed. Geoffrey Matthews and Kelvin Everest, vol. 1 (London and New York: Longman, 1989), 467.
2. Qtd in John Scott, 'Review of *The Diary of an Invalid* ... by Henry Matthews', *London Magazine* (July 1820), 59–60.
3. Mary Shelley, 'To Mariane Hunt', [24 March] 1820, in *The Letters of Mary Wollstonecraft Shelley*, ed. Betty T. Bennett, 3 vols (Baltimore and London: The Johns Hopkins University Press, 1980), 1: 137–8.
4. James Buzard, *The Beaten Track: European Tourism, Literature, and the Ways to 'Culture', 1800–1918* (Oxford: Clarendon Press, 1993), 26.
5. Bronislaw Szerszynski and John Urry, 'Visuality, Mobility and the Cosmopolitan: Inhabiting the World from Afar', *The British Journal of Sociology* 57.1 (2006), 115.
6. William Wordsworth, 'The Brothers', line 421, in *William Wordsworth*, ed. Stephen Gill (Oxford: Oxford University Press, 1984), 167.
7. Simon Burrows, 'The Cultural Politics of Exile: French Emigré Literary Journalism in London, 1793–1814', *Journal of European Studies* 29.2 (1999), 157, *Expanded Academic ASAP*, Web, 6 February 2011. See also, Simon Burrows, 'Émigré journalists and publishers', in *An Oxford Companion to the Romantic Age: British Culture 1776–1832*, ed. Iain McCalman (Oxford: Oxford University Press, 1999), 496.
8. Louis Simond, *Journal of a Tour and Residence in Great Britain, during the Years 1810 and 1811, by a French Traveller: with Remarks on the Country, Its Arts, Literature, and Politics, and on the Manners and Customs of Its Inhabitants*, 2 vols (Edinburgh, 1815), 1: 191–2.
9. William Mavor, *The British Tourist's, or, Traveller's Pocket Companion, through England, Wales, Scotland, and Ireland* ... 3rd edn (London: Richard Phillips, 1809), 5: 2.
10. Although presented as a translation from the German of Henry Frederic Greenvelt, *Letters* was a collaboration between Dumont, Samuel Romilly, and James Scarlett. Romilly may have translated some of Dumont's letters from the French. The German pretext was used to conceal Dumont's revolutionary associations and to give the letters from France a patina of objectivity.

11. For Gallo-phobia, see Linda Colley, *Britons: Forging the Nation 1707–1837* (London: Pimlico, 1994).

12. See Kurt Mueller-Vollmer, 'On Germany: Germaine de Staël and the Internationalization of Romanticism', in *The Spirit of Poesy*, ed. Richard Block (Evanston: Northwestern University Press, 2000), 51; and Esther Wohlgemut, *Romantic Cosmopolitanism* (London: Palgrave Macmillan, 2009). Mueller-Vollmer writes: 'Romanticism embraced ... a new cultural discourse that was international and transcultural in nature, while at the same time extolling the individuality of the participating national cultures' (151).

13. Robert Southey, 'Art. XII. 1. *Letters from Albion to a Friend on the Continent* ...', *Quarterly Review* 15.30 (July 1816), 537–74; *Essays, Moral and Political, by Robert Southey*, 2 vols (London: John Murray, 1832), 1: 251–323. Hereafter cited as Art. XII.

14. Southey, Art. XII, 541, 543, 544, 544.

15. Southey, Art. XII, 548.

16. Peter Wollen, 'The Cosmopolitan Ideal in the Arts', in *Travellers' Tales: Narratives of Home and Displacement*, ed. George Robinson, *et al.* (London: Routledge, 1994), 189–90.

17. Southey, Art. XII, 555, 536.

18. Barthélemi Faujas de Saint-Fond, *Travels in England, Scotland and the Hebrides, Undertaken for the Purpose of Examining the State of the Arts, the Sciences, Natural History and Manners in Great Britain*, trans. fr. French, 2 vols (London: Printed for James Ridgway, 1799).

19. Faujas de Saint-Fond, *Travels*, 5, 7.

20. Faujas de Saint-Fond, *Travels*, 16. The hemp is smuggled out of China under cover of the scientific parcel for Banks, so the free exchange celebrated by Faujas is at the expense of Chinese protectionism.

21. Faujas de Saint-Fond, *Travels*, 19.

22. For an overview of Meister's life and works, see Yvonne de Athayde Grubenmann, *Un Cosmopolite Suisse: Jacques-Henri Meister (1744–1826)* (Geneva: Librairie E. Droz, 1954).

23. Meister was sole editor of the *Correspondance* from 1790 to 1813. From 1794 the journal was published from Zurich. Meister's reluctance to own his editorship publicly may be owing to the proximity, as perceived by French authorities, of his foreign correspondence with espionage.

24. A prospectus for the *Journal des indépendans* published as supplement No. 40 to *Journal de Paris* No. 86 (27 March 1791) advertised the new periodical as available from 2 April 1791 on Tuesdays and Saturdays. The prospectus stressed that, although published and distributed by the *Journal de Paris*, the *Journal des indépendans* was editorially distinct. The new journal claimed a non-partisan love of liberty and interest in the success of the revolution.

25. Jacques-Henri Meister, *Letters Written during a Residence in England* ... (London: Longman and Rees, 1799), xxix. See also Jacques-Henri Meister, *Souvenirs d'un voyage en Angleterre* (Paris: Chez Gatty, 1791).

26. The first letter appeared under the title, 'Quelques Lettres à mon ami, sur mon voyage d'Angleterre'. See *Correspondance littéraire, philosophique et critique, addressée à un souverain d'Allemagne ... par Le Baron de Grimm et par Diderot*, vol. 5, pt 3 (Paris: F. Buisson, 1813), 392–7, 477–83, 506–13.

27. Meister, *Letters*, [xxix]. For Archenholtz's translation, see 'Ueber Shakespear', *Minerva* 2 (May 1792), no. 2, 264–72; 'Ideen des Reisenden', *Minerva* 1 (Jan 1792), no. 1, 60–8. For Reichard, see 'Briefe einer Dame über England', *Olla Potrida* (1793), Pt. 4, 75–119. Meister's claim that Reichard included 'all [the letters of the 1789 tour] into his *Olla Podrida* [*sic*]' ([xxix]) is not entirely accurate. Reichard translates only letters 1–6, including the interpolated letter from Lady Elizabeth Craven. A translation of letter 10, 'Gedanken eines Reisenden', appears as if it were an unrelated item (also anonymous) immediately before the longer section attributed to the emigrant lady (see 71–5).
28. Meister, *Letters*, 2–3, 2.
29. Meister, *Letters*, 11, 22–3, 17.
30. Meister, *Letters*, 12–13, 16, 36–8.
31. Rachel Hammersley, *French Revolutionaries and English Republicans: The Cordeliers Club, 1790–1794* (Woodbridge: Boydell Press for the Royal Historical Society, 2005), 163.
32. Meister, *Letters*, 14.
33. Separated from Lord Craven since 1783, Elizabeth Craven resided between 1787 and 1791 principally at the Margrave's court at Triersdorf, from which place – oddly in a book otherwise devoid of dates – the letter is most likely dated, 'T—, 13 April 1791'. Meister's insertion of Craven's letter so dated calls attention to the retrospective nature of travel writing; letters that appear to be written on the spot are revealed as instalments prepared for the periodical press.
34. Meister, *Letters*, 79.
35. Meister, *Letters*, 83, 84.
36. See René Wellek, *A History of Modern Criticism 1750–1950*, vol. 2: The Romantic Age (London: Jonathan Cape, 1970), 216–7.
37. Meister, *Letters*, 130, 131.
38. Meister, *Letters*, 131, 133, 134.
39. Meister, *Letters*, 136.
40. The Countess is most likely a semi-fictionalized Madame Marie-Angélique de Vandeul, the daughter of Meister's mentor, Diderot, who died in 1784. For Meister's close relationship with Madame de Vandeul around this time, see Grubenmann, *Un Cosmopolite Suisse*, 38–9.
41. Meister, *Letters*, 306–7.
42. Meister, *Letters*, 317, 22.
43. Meister, *Letters*, 322, 324.
44. Meister, *Letters*, xxiii.
45. See Gordon Corrigan, *Wellington: A Military Life* (London: Continuum, 2001), 30–2.
46. Simond, *Journal*, 1: 50, 2: 28, 129.
47. Simond, *Journal*, 1: 188.
48. John Scott, *A Visit to Paris in 1814; Being a Review of the Moral, Political, Intellectual and Social Condition of the French Capital*, 2nd edn (London: Longman, Hurst, Rees, Orme, and Brown, 1815), 4; Robert Southey, *Letters from England*, ed. Jack Simmons (London: Cresset Press, 1951), 164.
49. Simond, *Journal*, 1: 3.
50. Simond, *Journal*, 1: 139.
51. Simond, *Journal*, 1: 185, 188.

52. Nicola J. Watson, *The Literary Tourist: Readers and Places in Romantic & Victorian Britain* (Basingstoke and New York: Palgrave Macmillan, 2006), 155.
53. Simond, *Journal*, 1: 324.
54. Walter Scott, *The Journal of Walter Scott, 1825–32*, new edn (Edinburgh: Douglas & Foulis, 1927) , 626 (entry for 6 July 1828); Thomas De Quincey, 'Society of the Lakes' (1840), qtd in Frederick Burwick, *Thomas De Quincey: Knowledge and Power* (New York: Palgrave, 2001), 37; Southey, Art. XII, 555.
55. Simond, *Journal*, 1: 355.
56. Southey, Art. XII, 553, 555.
57. Simond, *Journal of a Tour and Residence in Great Britain during the Years 1810 and 1811*, 2nd edn, 2 vols (Edinburgh: Archibald Constable, 1817), 2: 487. Reversing Scott's unfavourable comparison of French society to a 'glass-bee-hive' (*Visit to Paris*, 53), Simond condemns the jingoism of English travellers: 'Swarms of youthful and active politicians, out of the overflowing bee-hive of Great Britain, have passed over to the continent, and there, settling upon the unfortunate natives of France, prick and torment them into new ways of building combs and making honey *a l'Angloise*' (2: 488).
58. Jean Emmanuel Charles Nodier, *Promenade from Dieppe to the Mountains of Scotland. By Charles Nodier. Translated from the French* ([Edinburgh]: William Blackwood and T. Cadell, [1822]). 210, 163–4.
59. Peter George Patmore, *Letters on England. By Victoire, Count de Soligny*, 2 vols (London: Henry Colburn, 1823), 1: iv. Emphasis added.
60. Joseph Jean Marie Charles Amédée Pichot, *Historical and Literary Tour of a Foreigner in England and Scotland*, trans. fr. French, 2 vols (London: Saunders and Otley, 1825), x–xi.
61. Pichot, *Historical and Literary Tour*, 2, 4.
62. Pichot, *Historical and Literary Tour*, 4.

5
The Attractions of England, or Albion under German Eyes

Jan Borm

Anglomania was a well-worn trope in the eighteenth and nineteenth centuries, both in England and abroad. A memorable piece of self-congratulatory prose can be found in James Boswell's *Life of Johnson* where the author's hero is referred to as expanding on English superiority, compared to France notably, in the year 1770: 'He was of opinion, that the English cultivated both their soil and their reason better than a..ny other people: but admitted that the French, though not the highest, perhaps, in any department of literature, yet in every department were very high.'[1] The allusion to Voltaire's famous dictum at the end of *Candide* (*'cultiver son jardin'*) is particularly daring, given the Frenchman's admiration for English culture as expressed in his *Lettres philosophiques* (1734).[2] This spirit of cross-Channel competition seems to have lasted until the present day, though a recent example taken from an essay by Julian Barnes tries to make up, at least to a certain extent, for such Anglo-centric condescending: 'Doubtless there was an element of cultural snobbery in my initial preference for things Gallic: their Romantics seemed more romantic than ours ... Rimbaud versus Swinburne was simply no contest; Voltaire seemed just smarter than Dr Johnson'.[3] Whatever the case may be, the attractions of England were a common topic of reflection amongst travellers of the Enlightenment and the Victorian age writing within and against that frame of mind. German travel writing of the period is no exception to the rule. Three German travelogues will come under closer scrutiny here in view of the tropics of the English (home) tour: Georg Forster's *Ansichten vom Niederrhein* (3 vols, 1791–4), Johanna Schopenhauer's *Reise durch England und Schottland* (2 vols, 1813–14), and Heinrich Heine's *Reisebilder* (1826–27 and 1830). For coherence's sake, only subjects in relation to England will be discussed here, focalization oscillating between expressions of political Anglophilia and social criticism, two of the principal themes of German discourses on Albion.

Georg Forster (1754–94) reached international fame through his account of the second voyage of Captain Cook, *A Voyage Round the World* (1777), largely acclaimed by the reading public in Britain, Germany, and elsewhere, Dr Johnson's somewhat inconsiderate remarks notwithstanding.[4] Forster was accompanied by young Alexander von Humboldt, who regarded the former as his mentor in many respects. *Ansichten vom Niederrhein, von Brabant, Flandern, Holland, England und Frankreich, im April, Mai und Junius 1790* has been called Forster's masterpiece.[5] Georg had accompanied his father Johann Reinhold, a distinguished naturalist and Calvinist minister in the German community of Nassenhuben, just outside Gdansk, on a journey to Russia as an adolescent and then on the second voyage of Cook, after the two had established themselves in England in the 1760s.[6] *Ansichten* is therefore the work of an informed traveller who returns to a country he is familiar with. The English part of the journey is represented in the third volume of the travelogue by way of posthumously published notes. The travellers spent some time in London and then went on to the Midlands (Birmingham and Soho, Derby, and so on), returning south via Blenheim and Oxford and crossing the Channel from Dover to Calais. Forster's notes deal with cultural phenomena, but also manners and national character, a favourite trope of the period that appears rather problematic in retrospect. The moderate authentic English character, as he puts it, is likely to always end up paying more attention to reason, no matter how prominent the preconceived views of the English may be, or their bad habits and passions.[7] Forster goes on to consider English tolerance when it comes to foreign fashion, insisting on the remarkable English capacity for resistance to foreign influence. Forster's encyclopaedic spirit of observation then covers a variety of subjects, including Westminster Abbey, Windsor Castle, and Herschel's telescope in Slough, before turning to what he calls the interior of England, including Birmingham and a tour of the Midlands via Bath, the opulence of which he notes on the way,[8] as well as trade and commerce in Bristol, the charms of Gloucestershire, and Worcester, described as a very pleasant small country town.[9]

Though Forster is by no means averse to picturesque travel, his attention focuses more regularly on issues of commerce and industry, as well as politics. It is worth noting that Forster does not appear particularly radical in his views on rotten boroughs and parliamentary reform, just a few years before he ended up representing the Republic of Mainz at the French Convention in Paris where he died as a revolutionary, banished from German lands, in 1794: 'The reproach of unequal representation has been made too often in respect to the English Constitution, to be repeated here'. A little further on, Forster explains his position: 'The author of the present state of Birmingham considers those drawbacks as to representation one of this manufacturing city's biggest advantages, since the workers' industry will never be disturbed by the spirit of party politics and elections'.[10] Among other sites visited are the following: the views of the Black Mountains to be enjoyed from the park of Hagley Hall, as though 'God's endless garden was unfolding beneath the wanderer's feet', a rather rare version of the 'garden-of-England' trope; and the splendour of Oxford's colleges termed 'barbarian', a monument, in a way, to that blind faith in tradition or old forms on which, according to Forster, England's political existence seems to depend.[11] Moderation should strike the keynote in order to balance extremes, Forster adds.[12]

His narrative obviously merits still closer readings, but the above-mentioned remarks may suffice to illustrate some of the author's main concerns in a text that, as Gerhard Steiner has argued, set the tone and standards for German travel writing in the century to come. According to Steiner, *Ansichten* played a seminal role in the evolution of travel writing (in German at least) from 'views' or 'pictures' to scientific representation as the privileged mode of comparative geographical and anthropological studies, acknowledged and developed further by Alexander von Humboldt. Forster has also sometimes been considered to be the fourth major German writer of classicism, together with Goethe, Schiller, and Lessing. His style was appreciated by many readers and fellow writers in German lands, never mind Dr Johnson's somewhat unkind remarks.[13] Steiner considers Forster's way of expressing his own social and political interest by literary composition as one of the chief characteristics of his narrative that set new standards; the travelogues of authors such as Ernst Moritz Arndt, Adelbert von Chamisso, or Heine seem impossible without Forster's groundbreaking work.[14] Whether one should subscribe unconditionally to Steiner's views is a question that cannot be debated here at length, but Forster's prominent role in the history of German travel writing appears manifest enough at least in respect to one of the other writers discussed here, Heinrich Heine.

Before we turn to the poet, another important though less well-known figure of German letters, Johanna Schopenhauer (1766–1838), the mother of the famous philosopher, should come under consideration. Johanna travelled with her husband and their adolescent son Arthur through Europe in the years 1803–5. They spent several months in London in 1803 before going on a tour of England and Scotland from July until September. Both mother and son kept a diary. Her husband died shortly after their return home from this prolonged journey. Johanna was encouraged to write by friends and published a version of her journals in 1813 and 1814, becoming a well-known writer in later years.[15] The ways in which the published version may or may not correspond to her notes taken some ten years before are of no concern here, but rather the views we get in her travelogue.

London is her first major focal point, the city imposing itself on the traveller more than any other right from the start as an extremely busy urban centre of almost one million inhabitants.[16] Like Forster, Schopenhauer is struck by the lively scenes of busy London life to be witnessed in the streets, feeling almost topsy-turvy from the wheeling and dealing, to paraphrase her German term ('Gewühle').[17] Given the overwhelming size of the city, its splendour and individual character offering a wealth of details to the viewer, Schopenhauer steps back from wanting to draw a broad sketch, announcing that she offers nothing but her own impressions to the reader. Nonetheless, her largely descriptive text tries to bring over at least an idea of the profusion of elements that offer themselves to the traveller's eye – shops, fashion, characters, and life style – moderately paying attention also to issues of social class. This is where her text actually starts to reflect more openly her personal views. The busiest part of the population, craftsmen and shopkeepers, are portrayed as leading rather sad lives on the whole. Such generalizing may appear particularly problematic today, but has to be read as standard practice in her day, as it remains indeed up to a certain degree in everyday conversation.[18] The reasons for such sadness, according to her, are the high level of taxation and the rise in living expenses owing to the particularly elaborate tastes in fashion, forcing many to restrain themselves up to the point of living in what would be considered elsewhere as poverty.[19] Working hours often have to be extended to midnight and there is little time for distraction, if any. The wealthier merchants are obviously an exception, as Schopenhauer hastens to add. As to the grand and distinguished, there is nothing much to be said, she reckons, since they are not to be considered in any country as members of the nation, as they are everywhere the same, whether one looks at Russia, France, England, or Germany.[20] Schopenhauer adds an interesting comment on her own approach, affirming that she was always striving to discover the manners of any given nation, and that one should not search for details too high or low in this respect, but rather focus on the (English) middle class, or the English upper middle class to be more precise, as she points out herself.[21] The question of national character is dealt with by way of the theatre. English comedy in particular is taken as a faithful reflection of the private and public sphere, even though the rendering appears often somewhat excessive.[22] Several theatres are described in some detail, including The Haymarket, one of those summer venues for the 'poor nobodies' as she puts it, no doubt tongue-in-cheek,[23] who have to remain in town for the whole summer. Concerts, museums, and exhibitions are other subjects dealt with at some length, as well as some famous sites such as Saint Paul's Cathedral, Westminster Abbey, the Tower, Greenwich, and Windsor, including an account of the Royal Family's Sunday afternoon walk in public.

A climactic moment in terms of the picturesque is reached when the traveller contemplates the Thames from Richmond Hill. There might be many grander, larger, and more romantically beautiful views, Schopenhauer exclaims, but none which surpass this particular one in terms of charm. A kind of *joie de vivre* takes hold of the spectator and the highest possible form of culture ornaments this broad valley, animated by one of the most beautiful rivers and surrounded by gently rising hills covered in forest: 'Even England does not offer any second view of the kind which are to be found nowhere else than on this island since where could one find such fresh green in the gardens and meadows, fields and forest'.[24] The charms of the scenery observed may be unquestionable, their unique status as an irrefutable illustration of supposed English cultural superiority less so, unless one reads this rather lyrical outburst against the background of the garden-of-England trope, a striking example of which can be found in a passage on Greenwich from Daniel Defoe's *Tour Through the Whole Island of Great Britain*, where Defoe describes his 'first step into the county of Kent, at a place which is the most delightful spot of ground in Great Britain ... made compleatly agreeable by ... the continual passing of fleets of ships up and down the most beautiful river in Europe'.[25] (Too bad, then, for the beautiful, blue Danube.) Schopenhauer's outing to Richmond is part of a more general exploration of the surroundings of London, including an attempted pilgrimage to Alexander Pope's home in Twickenham that Forster had also visited but which leads to disenchantment in Schopenhauer's case, since it had been sold and refurbished since. Fortunately, there are other sites such as Sion House and Chiswick to allow the traveller to dwell in dreams of Augustan grandeur.

The second part of her account is dedicated to her impressions from England and Scotland. Birmingham is the first notable halt on the way north, the city being portrayed as the emblem of English industrialization: 'one could almost claim that there is not a single village in cultivated Europe, perhaps no single house, in which one would not find some object produced by the industry of this city, be it only a button, a pin or a pencil'.[26] She then moves on fairly quickly to a rather enthusiastic description of Mr Boulton's Soho Manufactory and Mint, a site also visited by Forster. From a portrait of the enlightened philanthropist and philosopher as entrepreneur we move on to dreary-seeming Manchester, 'dark and covered in coal steam'. Work, the making of a living, and craving for money seem to be the only ideas one can come across here she suggests. Generally speaking, the refined sense of sociability is more or less foreign to such manufacturing cities where the men seek to recover after work by taking to the bottle in taverns while the women keep to their own circle.[27] Still, Schopenhauer is keen to discover a variety of industrial sites and offers descriptions from which pronounced social criticism is strikingly absent, as her rendering of her visit to a cotton spinnery where 'everything is carried out in the easiest of manners thanks to machines each one of which struck us as a miracle of industry'.[28] Even child labour on the precincts is mentioned without any comment. The picture is slightly altered, though, when it comes to describe miners in Leeds. This time round the garden-of-England trope is definitely out of sight, Schopenhauer representing the Yorkshire landscape as an arid, uncultivated waste void of any signs of pleasant vegetation. Miners are assimilated to moles and pitied by the traveller for having to lead such short, miserable lives.[29] Still, the following paragraph strikes a friendlier note on visiting Wakefield, remembering its 'good vicar'; so do longer chapters on the amenities of English inns, questions of etiquette in Bath, promenades, and 'amusements'.[30]

Johanna Schopenhauer is manifestly trying to address a readership that is supposed to adhere very largely to the notion of progress, with only little concern voiced about forms of social injustice or exploitation. We are far from William Blake's *Songs of Innocence* (1789) or Friedrich Engels's *The Condition of the Working-Class in England* (1844). True enough, Blake's poetry was still not very well known by readers in Europe in the early nineteenth century and Schopenhauer is writing at a moment where the age of political reform has hardly begun in England, but it appears useful to bear in mind such references to illustrate the fact that there are subjects of public debate (such as child labour) that she does not engage with at any particular length. Her travelogue is largely concerned with expressions of the public spirit to be observed notably in London, numerous descriptions of sites, and landscapes, thereby complying with what readers might expect from her volume as far as its guidebook function is concerned. Her personal impressions stand more in line with sentimental travel in the second half of the eighteenth century than they do with the satirical vein of some other texts of the Enlightenment, such as Tobias Smollett's admittedly fictive *Expedition of Humphrey Clinker* (1771) which does read nonetheless as a proto-condition-of-England (and Scotland) novel in certain respects, a subject with which Heinrich Heine's *Reisebilder* is also largely concerned.

Heine's 'English Fragments' (1828), published in his *Reisebilder*, start off with a conversation on the Thames, at a moment when the narrator is taking in the green banks of the river from a boat, 'nightingales awakening within every corner of my soul. Land of liberty, I exclaimed, greetings!'.[31] Heine is no doubt alluding to Augustine's famous metaphor in his *Confessions* of memory as a kind of palace stored up to the full, ruminating on bygone ages of splendour and genius. 'Liberty is possibly the religion of the new age and it is once again a religion which has not been preached to the rich but to the poor'.[32] The narrator – let us call him the poet – is then addressed by the 'yellow man' next to him on the boat as a 'young enthusiast' who obviously needs some lecturing on English moderation, since this 'religion of liberty' is always adapted, according to the yellow man, by every nation according to its local needs and national character.[33] The English are characterized by the poet as a homely people. An Englishman is thus content with the kind of liberty that grants him personal rights and guarantees his own person, property, marriage, faith – hence, 'My house is my castle'[34] – as opposed to the French, who may be prepared to give up individual rights if only the sacred principle of *égalité* is respected, and to the Germans, who seem to care neither about liberty nor equality but only about speculative ideas. As one can see immediately, Heine's observations are evidently political in outlook, his biting satire being one of the hallmarks of his pen. Under his eyes, the home tour becomes a frame of reference for comment on domestic, German affairs.

The second fragment declares London to be an ideal field for the philosopher's, rather than the poet's, spirit of observation since one can learn more from standing on the corner of a street in Cheapside than from all the books to be found at the Leipzig book fair. Heine also draws a picture of London as the busiest of places or a place swarming with busybodies: 'if London were the right hand of the world, the active, mighty right hand of the world, then that road leading from the Stock Exchange to Downing Street is to be considered the aorta of the world'.[35] The poet's view, however, appears in stark contrast to such opportunities to contemplate London street life driven by the English (or British) spirit of commerce. Heine's poet is more inclined to deplore 'the sheer seriousness, colossal monotony, mechanical movements and dreary joy even of exaggerating London which oppresses the imagination while breaking one's heart'. Standing on that corner of Cheapside alluded to above, the poet has a vision of London's pulsating life as a rat race of sorts, or what he terms a permanent flow on 'Beresina Bridge' (in allusion to the disastrous retreat of the Napoleonic army from Russia), where everyone is engaged in saving his own frail existence, stamping over dead bodies and clinging to life as long as possible.[36] In comparison, Germany would appear a much quieter, homely place to live, where people and dogs find time and space on public squares to engage in social interaction, as one might phrase it today. With Heine, everyone is in for a fair share of abuse, his vivifying prose not halting in front of any geographical or cultural boundary.

Having opened such intercultural perspectives, Heine then focalizes on social themes, comparing the 'west end of town' to 'plebeian quarters'. The foreigner remaining in the former is not likely to notice anything or only very little of the 'widespread misery' that prevails in London, beggars excepted, that one may encounter here or there in those wealthy parts of town that the English nobility is described here as using only as a sort of *pied-à-terre* when spending some time in the capital; Italy being its summer retreat, Paris a kind of salon for (high) society, regarding the world in general as its property – if not oyster.[37] 'Poor poverty!' the poet cries out: 'How painful hunger must be there where others indulge in the greatest of excess! And with an indifferent hand someone threw into your lap a crust; how bitter the tears must be that you need to soften it up!'.[38] Heine's call is powerful indeed and even daring in suggesting that there might just be more of the humane in the heart of a criminal expelled from society than in those cool, irreproachable citizens of virtue in whose pale hearts the capacity to do evil may well have been vanquished, along with that to do any good too.

In the following fragment, Heine has a go at national character. The English are portrayed as trying on the skin of frivolity that the French only just managed to get rid of, or rather one half of the population seems to try to do so, while the other is holding on to the Puritan vein,[39] his narrative becoming not a tale of two cities but of two tendencies within the nation. Still, according to the German poet, the feeling of appertaining to one people also characterizes the English nation.[40] Other fragments deal with Sir Walter Scott, a visit to the Old Bailey observing the grim procedures there as Dickens was going to do a few years later, the National Debt, the opposition, religious emancipation, Wellington, and liberation. At the end of the latter section, Heine returns to his notion of liberty being the religion of this new age, in which France, not England, is given the key role to play. Jesus Christ is no longer the God of this faith, but its high priest. The French are the chosen race (Heine was both Francophone and Francophile), the first gospels and dogmatic rules have been recorded in their language. Paris is the New Jerusalem and the Rhine the new Jordan, separating the consecrated land of liberty from that of the Philistines.[41]

What about the English, then? Are they reduced to a simple role of observers in what appears somehow as a mainly continental affair? Heine's English fragments end with a comparison between France and Germany, as though England were only a pretext to engage in comparisons between the two nations whose cultures are at the core of Heine's own work. By way of answer, one may be permitted to return once more to the fragment on the English opposition. In the early days of what has since been termed the 'Age of Reform' or improvement, the English spirit continues to dwell in the dark middle ages, as Heine has it, the sacred idea of equality amongst human beings still not having enlightened the English mind, reformers and radical reformers or radicals excepted.[42] This is in stark contrast to the picture Alexander Kinglake draws at the end of *Eothen* (1844) a few years later. Kinglake relates the experience of crossing the Pass of the Lebanon in the 1830s, only some twelve years after the first Reform Act in the published account, by opposing the 'old and decrepit world' of the Orient, 'religions dead and dying', to what lay out there ahead, naturally to the West: 'Before me there waited glad bustle and strife ... religion a cause and a controversy, well smitten and well defended – men governed by reasons and suasion of speech – wheels going – steam buzzing'.[43] This reads very much as the Age of Reform keeping up the steam of the Age of Reason, which it certainly did in a number of respects; a hymn to progress that is too busy praising to spend much time reflecting on those left out of what may seem to some a frantic movement, nor on the human effort required to make it work.

To respond to the question raised above from still another angle, let us look briefly at one last text in conclusion: Theodor Fontane's *Ein Sommer in London* (1854). Its author, one of the most prolific German writers of the second half of the nineteenth century, towards the end of his book also attempts a series of comparisons between England and Germany.[44] The focus is on politics, which, from a nineteenth-century point of view at least, invariably involve questions of national character, a notion that may strike us as too generalizing to be useful today but which was a common feature of travel writing at the time: 'England is aristocratic,

Germany democratic. We talk day after day about English liberty and desire a *Habeas corpus* act and parliament, which has more rights than just simply to tal'.[45] According to Fontane, there is no country which is further removed from democracy than England, despite the liberties of her citizens, nor keener to court the aristocracy for favours and to copy its glamour and prestige. This would explain, then, what the author terms the 'stereotypical forms of English life', that is, the modest being in competition with the illustrious, the poor with the rich, and still, the inferior bow to the Lords, considering the descendants of a Baronet or Members of Parliament as objects worthy of particular consideration and devotion.[46] But then again, English pragmatism is highlighted, as opposed to German idealism,[47] no doubt in reference to Heine's remarks referred to above. Yet even so, England supposedly places appearances above truth, millions of her citizens adoring vanity and hollow forms of representation. Nonetheless, the English are practical from 'tip to toe' and are conquering the world not in quest of fame and adventure like most conquerors do, but to gain a practical advantage from the gathering together of all these treasures and a comfortable place by the fireside on top of that.[48] My home is my castle, after all!

What kind of a picture emerges then from England under the German eyes considered here? The view of a country, it would appear, admired for being one of the driving forces of progress in Europe, political (1066, Magna Carta), economic (the Industrial Revolution), and cultural (Shakespeare and Company), while venerating traditionalism as much as Anglicanism as a specifically English version of faith. German travellers of the long eighteenth century seem to hold the Augustan age in awe or to share the values of its elite up to a certain degree, engaging in a more personal sense of place following Sterne's model of the sentimental traveller. Later nineteenth-century travellers seem more immediately concerned with the condition of England in their narratives, comments to be read as a kind of foil to conditions in Germany and elsewhere. To many readers, there was much to be admired in Britain and their expectations certainly needed to be addressed if the book were to enjoy widespread circulation. Heine's verve stands out in terms of literary composition, though the charms of Forster's, Schopenhauer's, and Fontane's texts should in no case be neglected. This is a concession – which the editor of the second English edition of Karl Philipp Moritz's *Travels Chiefly on Foot Through Several Parts of England in 1782* was also prepared to make – as regards the writing of travel: 'Besides the more obvious advantages likely to result from our occasionally listening to the remarks and opinions of other travellers ... it might not perhaps be without its use sometimes to consult them, if it were only on the force of composition'.[49] German writing is held in esteem by the same editor for its 'minute prolixity', but English travelogues are considered to be 'superior to those of most other people'. What one might be forgiven for terming an English complex of cultural superiority crops up time and again in some of the sources discussed above. Fortunately, such efforts to oppose cultures have largely given way to more comparative approaches that the present volume also purports to contribute to by opening new intercultural perspectives.

Notes

1. James Boswell, *Life of Johnson*, ed. R. W. Chapman (Oxford and New York: Oxford University Press, 1998), 442.
2. Voltaire admires England as the birthplace of liberty as he understands it: 'La liberté est née en Angleterre des querelles des tyrans' (*Lettres philosophiques*, ed. René Pomeau, Paris: GF Flammarion, 1964, 62).
3. Julian Barnes, Preface, *Something to Declare* (London: Picador, 2002), xii–xiii.
4. Boswell, *Life of Johnson*, 860 (entry dated Sunday, 21 September 1777): 'I talked to him of Forster's *Voyage to the South Seas*, which pleased me.... JOHNSON: No, Sir; he does not carry *me* along with him: he leaves me behind him: or rather, indeed, he sets me before him; for he makes me turn over many leaves at a time'.
5. See Gerhard Steiner's postface to the edition referred to in this chapter, Georg Forster, *Ansichten vom Niederrhein*, ed. Gerhard Steiner (Leipzig: Dietrich'sche Verlagsbuchhandlung, 1979), 686.
6. The family was of English origin but went into exile in the seventeenth century.
7. Forster, *Ansichten*, 570–1: ' ... *ein Beweis für die Milde des ächtenglischen Charakters, der am Ende der Vernunft doch immer Gehör giebt, so laut auch seine Vorurtheile, seine üblen Gewohnheiten, und seine Leidenschaften zuweilen dagegen reden*'.
8. Forster, *Ansichten*, 586: '*Der Luxus ist in Bath so gross, als in London*'.
9. Forster, *Ansichten*, 592: '*ein sehr nettes Landstädtchen*'.
10. Forster, *Ansichten*, 598; my translation.
11. Forster, *Ansichten*, 609, 644, 639: '*Kein Volk hängt so blindlings an alten Formen, wie das Englische; es knüpft den Begriff seiner politischen Existenz daran*' (639).
12. Forster, *Ansichten*, 639.
13. Steiner, postface, in Forster, *Ansichten*, 689.
14. Steiner, postface, in Forster, *Ansichten*, 689.
15. See Konrad Paul's postface in Johanna Schopenhauer, *Reise nach England*, ed. Konrad Paul (Berlin-Ost: Buchclub 65, 1982).
16. Schopenhauer, *Reise*, 68.
17. Schopenhauer, *Reise*, 70.
18. May it be mentioned here in passing only that the idea of the impossibility of reaching a satisfying degree of precision or accuracy in referential textual

representation is one of the central themes of James Agee's extraordinarily intense narrative in the volume *Let Us Now Praise Famous Men: Three Tenant Families* that he co-published with the photographer Walker Evans in 1941.

19. Schopenhauer, *Reise*, 92.
20. Schopenhauer, *Reise*, 93.
21. Schopenhauer, *Reise*, 94, 107.
22. Schopenhauer, *Reise*, 115.
23. Schopenhauer, *Reise*, 137.
24. Schopenhauer, *Reise*, 225–6.
25. Daniel Defoe, *A Tour Through the Whole Island of Great Britain* (1724–6), ed. Pat Rogers (London: Penguin Classics, 1986), 113.
26. Schopenhauer, *Reise*, 253.
27. Schopenhauer, *Reise*, 264.
28. Schopenhauer, *Reise*, 265.
29. Schopenhauer, *Reise*, 269.
30. Schopenhauer, *Reise*, 298 (chapter title).
31. Heinrich Heine, *Reisebilder*, ed. Jost Perfahl (München: Winkler Verlag, 1969), 361.
32. Heine, *Reisebilder*, 361.
33. Heine, *Reisebilder*, 361–2.
34. Heine, *Reisebilder*, 362.
35. Heine, *Reisebilder*, 366.
36. Heine, *Reisebilder*, 366, 367.
37. Heine, *Reisebilder*, 369, 370.
38. Heine, *Reisebilder*, 370.
39. Heine, *Reisebilder*, 373.
40. Heine, *Reisebilder*, 374.
41. Heine, *Reisebilder*, 424–5.
42. Heine, *Reisebilder*, 400.
43. Alexander William Kinglake, *Eothen: Traces of Travel Brought Home From the East* (London: Picador Travel Classics, 1995), 270.
44. Theodor Fontane, *Ein Sommer in London* (Dessau: Katz, 1854).
45. Fontane, *Ein Sommer*, 268.
46. Fontane, *Ein Sommer*, 268–9.
47. Fontane, *Ein Sommer*, 270.
48. Fontane, *Ein Sommer*, 271.
49. Anonymous, preface in Charles P. Moritz, *Travels Chiefly on Foot through Several Parts of England in 1782*, 2nd edn (London: G. G. and J. Robinson, 1797), x.

6
The Irish Tour, 1800–50

William H. A. Williams

In the annals of Irish tourism, the decades from 1800 to 1850 reflect continuity with the past but also reveal a period unique unto itself. Constituting the second half of the first century of Irish tourism, these years saw the development and expansion of trends that began in the eighteenth century. However, framed between the Act of Union and the Irish Famine, the Irish Tour took on some distinctive characteristics in response to an Ireland that emerged and then disappeared within the span of five decades.

The origins of the Irish Tour lie in the mid-eighteenth century with the appearance of the first Irish travel narratives modelled on the emerging English 'pleasure tour'. By the time Philip Luckombe assembled his *A Tour through Ireland in 1779* (1780), he had managed to plagiarize much of his text from earlier works, such as *Hibernia Curiosa* by John Bush (1767), *A Tour of Ireland in 1775* by Richard Twiss (1776), and *A Philosophical Survey of the South of Ireland* by Thomas Campbell (1777). In fact, between 1750 and 1799 at least a hundred Irish travel accounts of varying lengths had appeared in print (around 400 were published between 1800 and 1850).[1] Most were written by British and Anglo-Irish travellers who were somewhat belatedly inspired to focus on Ireland for two very different reasons: dramatic changes in landscape aesthetics and a growing interest in and a concern for Ireland's political and economic future. These themes carried over into the period from 1800 to 1850.

It is hardly an accident that the Irish Tour emerged and expanded at a time when Western appreciation of nature experienced a philosophical and aesthetic revolution. With the articulation of the concepts of the sublime and the picturesque during the latter half of the eighteenth century, travellers began to seek out the wilder or at least the less-tamed aspects of nature. Mountains and dark glens that had once inspired fear and even loathing among travellers now evoked wonder. Ireland's mountains, sea cliffs, lakes, and glens enticed visitors, many of whom had already explored the scenic areas of England, Wales, and Scotland.[2] By the end of the century, travel writers already had identified and described most of Ireland's major scenic attractions, such as the glens of Wicklow and Antrim, the valleys of the Blackwater and the Suir, the Rock of Cashel, the Lakes of Killarney, and the Giant's Causeway – sites that would continue to draw tourists for the next two hundred years. In 1800, only the West of Ireland remained to be opened to tourism.

Estate tourism provided another element of continuity as the Irish Tour entered the nineteenth century. In both Britain and Ireland the great country houses were among early tourist attractions, and even the more modest 'seats' of country gentlemen graced the tourist's journey on both sides of the Irish Sea. While Ireland had fewer of the magnificent piles that attracted visitors in England, the 'big houses', nonetheless, were featured in many Irish travel accounts. Irish proprietors, moreover, helped to organize the ground for tourism in Ireland, indirectly by building roads and inns, and directly through opening their estate lands for visitors. Some estates, in fact, also contained the lakes, falls, glens, and mountain views most sought after by tourists. For example, Killarney's early emergence as a tourist destination may be largely credited to the organizational and promotional efforts of the Browne and Herbert families who controlled much of the area. Estates continued to be a part of the Irish Tour into the new century, although after 1820 interest in them appears to have slackened. With the opening up of the West, tourists were more inclined to pursue their search for the sublime and the picturesque without needing or even wanting the mediation of vistas provided by carefully laid out estate parks. In this respect the Irish Tour after 1800 differed from the English home tour. By the time Victoria came to the throne the combination of nationalism, historical fantasies about the 'Olden Time', and convenient train travel for day trippers had made England's great estates more popular than ever. In Ireland, on the other hand, the estates of the Anglo-Irish could never be identified with the sort of Irish nationalism being articulated by Daniel O'Connell.[3]

Visitor interest in antiquities represented another element of continuity as the Irish Tour entered the new century. By 1800, ruins had become an extension of the tourist's search for the sublime and the picturesque in both Britain and Ireland. In this respect Ireland was blessed (if that is the proper word) with ruins extending from the prehistoric into the early modern period. The country abounded with cromlechs or dolmans, abandoned abbeys, shattered castles, and tower houses, all virtually an extension of nature thanks to the intrusion of ivy and invading trees. As the picturesque evolved into a technique for visually organizing, describing, and depicting nature, ruins were useful in anchoring a view or framing a scene. Moreover, romantic fascination with decay, fleeting time, and faded glory lent crumbled buildings an air of fashionable melancholy.

Although fascination with picturesque antiquities was a part of British touring culture, few Irish ruins held the same meaning for English visitors as those they had seen at home. Britain's abandoned monasteries and ruined castles represented milestones in the growth of a nation and the triumph of a reformed church. In Ireland such structures signified the conquest of a nation and the suppression of its religion. Of course, most English visitors were not overly burdened by knowledge of Irish history, a situation that some travel writers after 1800 recognized and did their best to amend. In works such as Richard Colt Hoare's *A Tour in Ireland* (1806), T. Croften Croker's *Researches in the South of Ireland* (1824), Thomas Reid's *Travels in Ireland in the Year 1822* (1823), Anne Plumptre's *Narrative of a Residence in Ireland during the Summer of 1814* (1817), Leitch Ritchie's *Ireland, Picturesque and Romantic* (1837), and Rev. Caesar Otway's *Sketches in Ireland* (1827), *A Tour of Connaught* (1839), and *Sketches in Erris and Tyrawly* (1841), authors either devoted whole chapters to Irish history or worked historical information into their narratives.

By the end of the eighteenth century the international situation had made the Irish Tour more inviting than ever. Tensions between Britain and France had rendered portions of the Continent closed to Britons, making Ireland an attractive alternative for those in search of romantic scenery. However, even if Ireland had been as flat as the Netherlands and as featureless as the North German Plain, with nary a lough, mountain, or fell, there would still have been an Irish Tour and a resulting, if smaller, travel literature written by British visitors. Regardless of scenery, the long and difficult relationship between the two islands would have ensured a steady stream of visitors intent on investigating Ireland's economy and society. Some travel writers in the second half of the eighteenth century had sought to address British ignorance regarding Ireland's problems, and these efforts continued unabated into the new century. To some extent this socio-economic concern represented an extension of older touring habits, carried over from the Grand Tour and adopted by the middle class, which by 1800 had emerged as the mainstay of British tourism. Originally designed to provide social polish and some knowledge of statecraft for the sons of the British aristocracy, the Grand Tour had been focused on the great cities and the political centres of Europe. Having initially climbed the nearest tower or steeple in order to gain the lay of a city, the newly-arrived 'Milords' visited libraries, palaces, fortresses, and cathedrals; sketched ruins; and sought interviews with knowledgeable people.[4] While travellers arriving in Ireland hardly expected to find a Rome or a Paris, many visitors, nevertheless, began their visits by investigating Ireland's cities and towns. As they moved around Ireland, following what could be considered a sort of 'petite tour' (as opposed the Grand Tour), visitors often took in and reported on markets, workhouses, barracks, Protestant churches, and Roman Catholic 'chapels', schools, mines, iron works, and, in Ulster, linen mills.[5]

In spite of the obvious continuities with the eighteenth century, there were certain distinctive features that characterized the Irish Tour during the period 1800 to 1850. For example, while its origins were in the touring habits fostered by the Grand Tour, after 1800 the 'petite tour' took on new significance for British visitors, imparting a special character to Irish tourism in the pre-Famine decades. By 1801, the relationship between Great Britain and Ireland had undergone a dramatic change. Largely in response to the United Irishmen's Rising of 1798 and the accompanying French invasion of the island, the British government forced through the Act of Union. This abolished the Irish Parliament and made Ireland a part of the United Kingdom, with a reduced number of Irish members sitting in the Imperial Parliament at Westminster. Ireland's problems now appeared, at least in theory, to be Great Britain's as well. As Glenn Hooper has suggested, the need to improve English knowledge about Ireland suddenly seemed imperative, if there was to be any hope of real integration of Ireland into the United Kingdom.[6] This greatly complicated the Irish Tour. While a British visitor to Naples might have been horrified by the poverty he encountered, there was nothing he could or needed to do about it. It was not his responsibility. Irish poverty could not be shrugged off so easily. Even seekers after the sublime and the picturesque often felt impelled to take note of Ireland's social and economic conditions. Therefore, while the combination of natural beauty and poverty was hardly unique to the Irish Tour, it made for a difficult mix that would colour British attitudes towards Ireland and its people during the pre-Famine period.

Two other closely connected factors that shaped the Irish Tour between 1800 and 1850 involved the expansion of Ireland's transportation network and the subsequent opening up of the West. Although most visitors in the eighteenth century had admired Ireland's roads, the country in 1800 still lacked an adequate system for transporting visitors. However, by the 1820s the expanding routes of mail coaches and, in the southern part of the country, a growing posting network of unenclosed cars greatly improved internal travel. The introduction of passengers on the country's two canal routes linking Dublin to the Shannon River system provided relatively comfortable transportation tied in to a chain of hotels owned by the canal companies. Stream travel took a while to establish itself inside Ireland; construction of the national rail network only began in the 1840s. Nevertheless, trains linking English cities to western ports and the steam packets that crossed the Irish Sea greatly facilitated Irish tourism after 1820.

Spared the wear and tear inflicted by an English-style form of industrialization, the relatively smooth roads of Ireland were among the few things that British visitors tended to admire unreservedly, unless, that is, they attempted to travel in the western part of the country. In 1800, much of the island's western sea board – south-west Munster, Connaught, and the most western parts of Ulster – remained barely accessible to the average traveller. Even the most dedicated eighteenth-century tourists tended to avoid Connemara. However, partly in response to the economic downturn following Waterloo, the government began to expand the country's road network westwards during the 1820s. Progress was slow, however. Henry D. Ingles chose to walk through Connemara in 1834 rather than test his carriage on the region's miserable roads. And as late as 1840, the anonymous author of *The Sportsman in Ireland* complained bitterly of the roads there. However, within a few years the newly completed road system through the area elicited praise from writers such as William Makepeace Thackeray and the Halls, Samuel Carter and Anna Maria, who found travel through Connemara convenient and relatively comfortable.[7] While many of Ireland's popular tourist destinations had been identified and established by the end of the eighteenth century, the exploration and description of the West of Ireland was mainly the product of the pre-Famine decades.

The opening up of the West influenced the Irish Tour in two ways. First, it helped to solidify the idea that the West represented the essence of Ireland, although this did not always suggest positive connotations. In the 1690s, John Dunton, one of the few Englishmen around that time to visit the Ihr Connaught, claimed that it presented the Irish 'in all of their original barbarities'. Richard Twiss, touring the country in 1775, refused to venture into Connemara because he had heard that it was peopled by 'savages'.[8] As the West became more accessible, however, it gained a more positive mystique. The major Irish tourist destinations established in the eighteenth century had generally offered relatively lush picturesque landscapes. The treeless, bog-strewn mountains and rugged sea cliffs of the West presented starker scenes, alien but also fascinating to most visitors, thereby expanding the tourist experience in Ireland. At the same time the West's new accessibility, occurring as the British were 'opening up' parts of Asia and Africa, seemed to spark the colonial imagination within some visitors. For example, the possibility of developing Connemara intrigued settlers, such as Henry Blake's family (who published a book on Connemara in 1825), as well as visitors, beginning with Henry D. Inglis in 1834.[9]

Cultural colonialism in the guise of religion represented another aspect of the Irish Tour in this period; one also connected to the opening of the West. Ever since Henry VIII's Reformation, the subject of religion, inevitably combined with politics, has been a dominant factor in Irish history. Between 1800 and 1850, religion became a principal motivating factor for certain visitors to Ireland. While some travellers focused on scenery, on agriculture, or on economic development, a few travel writers made what were essentially religious tours of Ireland. For example, even though Rev. Baptist Wriothesley Noel's 1836 trip through the midlands promised an investigation of poverty among the peasantry, much of his tour involved visits to Protestant churches and schools.[10] Supported by English and Anglo-Irish Evangelical clergy and laity, a militant Protestant movement emerged in Ireland during the 1820s and continued through the immediate post-Famine period. The movement was partly in reaction to an emergent Catholic voice under the leadership of Daniel O'Connell, which had resulted in the passage of Catholic Emancipation in 1829. Under the banner of the 'Second' or 'New Reformation', Evangelicals, eager for converts, focused on the West of Ireland. They recruited Irish speakers as Gospel readers and established 'colonies' that offered economic support, Protestant cultural values, and modern agricultural practices as inducements to bring Irish peasants into the 'true' church. Some of these Protestant outposts, such as Rev. Alexander Dallas's colony on the shores of Lough Corrib in Galway and especially Rev. Edward Nangle's community at Dugort on Achill Island in Mayo, became well known, attracting curious and often sympathetic tourists. Dugort even boasted a hotel for the accommodations of visitors.[11]

Given that most of the British visitors to Ireland were Protestants, religion often figured in even the most general travel accounts. Many tourists visited St Patrick's College at Maynooth, the principal centre for training Irish Roman Catholic priests. Itineraries often included Protestant churches and even Catholic 'chapels' along with schools, invariably run by one persuasion and another. Although few visitors approved of the obvious growth of Roman Catholic influence, most tried hard not to appear bigoted in their criticism. For some, however, the spectre of Popery seemed at times overwhelming. Contemplating major Catholic pilgrimage sites such as Lough Derg (St Patrick's Purgatory) in Donegal and Croagh Patrick on the shores of Clew Bay in Mayo, writers such as Rev. Caesar Otway, Inglis, and Thackeray described what can only be called 'confessional landscapes' where the essence of Romish 'superstition' seemed to permeate the very landscape, oozing from the rocks and bogs.[12]

What made the Irish Tour in this period truly unique may be suggested by a startling fact: in contrast to the rest of Europe, a visitor to Ireland in 1900 would have entered a country whose population was actually smaller than it had been in 1800, when it stood at around five million. On the other hand, those touring between 1820 and 1845 encountered a population that was climbing rapidly to its historic peak of around eight-and-a-half million by the eve of the Famine. By 1851, however, the country already had lost two million people to death and emigration, and the population continued to slide until the end of the century, when it stabilized around four-and-a-half million. This not only illustrates the ravages of the Famine but also suggests the distinct appearance of the crowded social landscape of rural Ireland that greeted visitors during the decades before the Famine, a landscape that was virtually swept away by the middle of the century.

Visitors from Great Britain would have been accustomed to the visual effects of rapid population growth. However, the social and economic patterns of Ireland's demographic changes did not parallel those of the larger island. Ireland's ability to shape its economy had been greatly curtailed by the Act of Union. Apart from the area around Belfast, Ireland did not experience significant industrial growth after 1800. The country's cities and towns did not expand at rates similar to those of Britain, especially England. Instead, much of Ireland's rapid increase in population took place in rural areas, but even there, Ireland was different. Large-scale farming based on the enclosure movement did occur on both sides of the Irish Sea; however, many Irish landlords, especially those with holdings in the less productive areas west of the Foyle and the Shannon, favoured subdividing their lands among numerous small-holders, thus increasing rents instead of consolidating and improving their fields. A seemingly endless supply of peasants bidding up rents acted as the base of a pyramid consisting of squatters and conacre farmers (share croppers) at the bottom and subtenants, tenants, and landlords at the top. As a result, large sections of rural Ireland presented a crowded and disorderly appearance virtually unseen in England's agricultural regions.

This was especially true of the 'clachans' or rundale villages that could be encountered in most parts of Ireland, but which were particularly characteristic of Connacht and western Ulster. Also found in parts of Scotland, the rundales were settlements in which member families pooled their resources in order to rent and work marginal land that did not lend itself to modern, large-scale farming. The inhabitants tilled the land in unfenced strips parcelled out among the families, while grazing cattle and sheep on rough common pasture. A village headman, the *argid rí* (money king), oversaw the distribution of plots and the collection and payment of the annual rent to the landlord. The cabins clustered nearest the road on the least arable plots, giving the clachans their characteristically careless, jumbled appearance. What the Irish peasants saw as a workable solution to the scarcity of affordable land the British visitors regarded as a kind of rural slum. Lacking virtually all of the infrastructure and amenities of the typical English village, visitors took the clachans to represent the slovenly chaos at the bottom of Irish life.[13] Many of the clachans were wiped out by the Famine.

While some travellers in the late eighteenth and early nineteenth centuries thought that Ireland was demographically static, by the 1830s it had become obvious that the country's population was growing dramatically. Although Ireland's fertility rate peaked around 1820, the demographic momentum continued to expand Ireland's population until the onset of famine conditions in the winter of 1846, when excess mortality and panic-driven emigration gripped the country. In 1841, M. F. Dickson claimed that the Clare coast from Kikee to the Carrigaholt seemed like one extended, crowded village.[14] Much of the increase seemed to occur at the bottom of the economic ladder. For example, the 1841 census identified two-fifths of Irish dwellings as fourth-class houses (one-room mud cabins), while three-quarters were categorized as either fourth- or third-class (two- to four-room mud dwellings).[15] And while it is not clear to what extent Ireland represented the terminus of Britain's used clothing trade (as alleged by some travel writers), all visitors found the Irish peasant remarkable for his rags. As for food, one-quarter to one-third of the country's population lived on the margin, surviving largely on potatoes, a crop that, even when abundant, did not last a full year. Travellers were surprised to discover that, during the 'hungry months' of July and August before the new potato crop could be lifted, those who had nothing took to the road to beg from those who had only a little. Some tourists learnt to differentiate between these seasonal beggars, who rarely solicited from tourists and the 'professionals' who greeted visitors at hotels and popular tourist spots.[16]

For those touring between 1800 and 1850, poverty in Ireland seemed ubiquitous. It greeted tourists everywhere, crowding the docksides, spilling out from the slums and back lanes of the cities and towns, clustering around the rural clachans, and emanating from the cabins that marked the entrances and exits of the towns and which lay scattered along the roadsides. In the British mind poverty had long been synonymous with Ireland. However, during the pre-Famine decades many British travel writers tended to regard Ireland's poverty as unique, far worse than anything that might be found back home. T. K. Cromwell insisted that 'the condition of the Irish labouring classes is infinitely below that of the English'.[17] Irish poverty was certainly very visible and widespread. Nevertheless, it is difficult to credit the visitors' frequent assertion that no place in England, not even the St Giles section of London, was as poverty stricken as almost any part of Ireland. In fact, living conditions in England's industrial slums often resulted in a lower life expectancy than generally found in rural Ireland. It seems that British insistence upon the uniqueness of Irish poverty represents a case of 'tourist amnesia', whereby visitors, comparing the best of Britain with the worst of Ireland, managed to ignore problems back home. After all, one does not generally travel abroad in order to be reminded of the shortcomings and failures of one's own country.[18]

There is also some evidence that British tourists, through their ignorance of the nature of Irish society, exaggerated the extent of Irish poverty. Unlike many of their Protestant counterparts, Roman Catholic farmers in Ireland were less likely to spend their money on houses or clothing. Those who had surplus funds tended to invest in livestock, on education for their children, or on preparation for emigration. Visitors, to their surprise, occasionally discovered that the ragged occupant of a tumble-down cabin might be a 'man of sixty cows'. Observers commonly insisted that rural Ireland lacked a middle class, when it was, in fact, largely invisible to the strangers.[19]

One problem that tourists had in gauging the extent of Irish poverty lay in the relative nature of poverty itself. Although the Irish peasant dressed in rags, his cabin, no matter how poor it looked, often cost him little to erect. As Cormac Ó Gráda has pointed out, turf, the peasant's fuel, was virtually free and his primary food, potatoes, could be grown in almost any type of soil through spade cultivation alone. Moreover, the Irish peasants' monotonous diet of potatoes generally left them better fed than their British counterparts, who enjoyed a more varied fare.[20] Cultural bias prevented most British visitors from understanding that Paddy's potato was more nutritious than bread, the staple of English farm labourer.

Inevitably, poverty became an integral feature of the pre-Famine Irish Tour. Not only was it anticipated but, once on the ground, many travel writers incorporated observations and descriptions of poverty into their accounts. Moreover, the 'petite tour', by focusing on Ireland's social and economic problems, made discussion of poverty unavoidable. This went beyond visiting and reporting on workhouses, slums, clachans, and beggars, however. The very cabins of the peasantry became sites of tourism. It was not unusual for a visiting lady or gentleman to dismount from their vehicle and seek admission into a tumble-down roadside dwelling. Once inside, visitors became caught up in the ritual of Irish hospitality. The family offered them the best it could afford – one of the better-quality potatoes grown only for market, some sour milk, or a taste of smoky *póitín*. The visitor in turn would leave a sixpence or in some cases a shilling, the money perhaps pressed into the hands of the children, as adults sometimes refused to accept recompense for their hospitality. These roadside encounters were important, since they provided a more intimate acquaintance with Irish poverty than could be gleaned from parliamentary reports or even from the road itself. More important, the cabin visits made it easier to put an individual face on Irish poverty, and the proffered hospitality, no matter how minimal, encouraged at least some tourists to acknowledge a certain dignity among Ireland's peasantry.

While poverty was an inevitable and certainly a proper subject for visitors whose primary interests lay in investigating Ireland's economic and social problems, it also presented a problem for those travellers intent on admiring the country's scenery. Beggars and ragged peasants often crowded the most popular tourist destinations. Moreover, the most spectacular mountains and seascapes were seldom found amid the more agriculturally prosperous sections of the island. As Ireland's population grew, the poorest peasants often pushed their way into the least fertile areas where their rags and wretched cabins contrasted sharply with the beauties of the surrounding scenery. Admittedly, those writers anxious to depict picturesque Ireland sometimes resorted to techniques and rhetorical strategies that helped them to compartmentalize, if not quite ignore, the poverty they encountered. The romantic notions of visitors, such as Lady Henrietta Chatterton, sometimes tempted them to mini-mize the hardships of the peasants, even envying them the supposed rustic simplicity of their lives. Adept at framing peasants within the windows of the houses she visited, Chatterton, having turned them into 'pictures', often invented stories about them.[21] Nevertheless, a surpris-ing number of writers felt forced to describe the poverty they encoun-tered, regardless of their dedication to the picturesque tour. As Leitch Ritchie wrote at the end of his 1837 travelogue, in spite of Ireland's natural beauty, the poverty and suffering he had seen would leave him with 'many a bitter thought and many a melancholy hour'.[22]

Indeed, if one theme can be said to dominate travel writing about Ireland between 1800 and 1850, it is the contrast between the country's natural splendour and its human poverty. Although not uncommon in earlier travel accounts, this theme became more prominent as Ireland's population growth manifested itself and as more visitors found their way into the West of Ireland. The unpleasant, even shocking juxtapo-sition of spectacular scenery and grinding poverty was not, of course, encountered only in Ireland. The seasoned traveller would have seen it all before. However, the powerful appeal of the sublime and the pic-turesque, encountered within the fractious context of British-Irish rela-tions, produced a dynamic peculiar to the Irish Tour. Ireland was not merely a beautiful country marked by poverty. Many visitors found the country *irrational*. The very landscape seemed to testify to a misalliance between people and nature, just as Daniel O'Connell's popular mass movement to repeal the Act of Union exposed the 'irrational' character of the Irish people and their politics.

Landscape appreciation operated in complex ways among British tourists. By the end of the eighteenth century, visual culture in Britain had trained upper- and even middle-class eyes to assess more than mountains, lakes, glens, and seascapes. Agricultural land also fell under the tourist gaze. England's enclosure movement, beginning in the late seventeenth century and running well into the first half of the nine-teenth, had produced a new rural landscape with its own aesthetic. Dictated by the demands of the new system of complex crop rotation, checkerboard fields enclosed by stone walls and flowering hedgerows represented more than a method of farming. Enclosure also produced a visual effect that the English eye found pleasing and comforting. It symbolized a social order in which fields, trees, hedgerows, manor houses, cottages, and villages all seemed part of a well-ordered, hierar-chical society promising peace and prosperity. To the British visitor in

Ireland, the sight of an enclosed agricultural landscape provided a welcome suggestion that Ireland might somehow be successfully integrated into the United Kingdom. Unhappily, once out of Leinster and the eastern parts of Munster and Ulster, such reassurance was often missing. Western grazing land, for example, was economically productive, but to an eye trained to appreciate enclosed cultivated landscapes, such pastures with their large fields and sparse human population looked 'naked' and neglected. Also, as noted above, Irish landlords in the less productive areas often preferred to sublet their lands rather than invest in improvements. The resulting congestion of smallholdings with their rough cabins and unfenced, open fields stood in ugly contrast to the rich, well-ordered lands of the Home Counties of England. Finally, there were the bogs, which, thanks to the enclosure movement, had gained the epithet 'wasteland', which to the Victorian mentality, demanded improvement.

As a result, by the 1830s much of Ireland's landscape did not look right to British tourists. In part this was the result of seeing Ireland while thinking Britain. Trees, those much-beloved adjuncts to the English landscape, were scarce in many parts of Ireland. And even where there were well-demarcated enclosed fields, they were often divided by dry-stone walls or bare earthen 'hedgebanks' that lacked the attractive mixture of hawthorns and trees, which gave agricultural England its charming, reassuring appearance. Moreover, for many tourists the lack of aesthetic appeal in the extensive pastures of Tipperary and eastern Galway trumped the land's economic value. Finally, the endless bogs of the West, which wanted, according to Thackeray, 'but little cultivation to make them profitable',[23] were standing proof of an assumed Irish lack of enterprise. In fact, when the contrast between natural beauty and human poverty was combined with the agricultural biases outlined above, much of Ireland's rural landscape appeared as a rebuke to the Irish character. The Victorian mentality assumed that beauty and bounty went hand in hand. If one or the other was missing, something was wrong – the landscape was out of kilter – and the fault could not lie with nature. Although by the 1840s Ireland exported enough food to feed two million people in Britain, visitors often condemned Ireland's landlords and peasants alike for their backward, slovenly husbandry and their assumed failure to apply the virtues of hard work to the land.

Therefore, many travel writers in pre-Famine Ireland tended to portray Ireland, its landscape, and its people within a *moral* context, all too easily illustrated by the perceived contrast between the largely

Protestant sections of Ulster and the rest of the country. For example, Baptist Wriothesley Noel compared 'the nakedness and superstition of the South and West' to 'the prosperity and religious light of the North'.[24] Although not all writers were as overtly hostile to Catholicism as Noel, it was not unusual for observers in the decade or so before the Famine to describe parts of Ulster, especially Belfast, as being, in the words of Anna Maria and Samuel Carter Hall, 'in Ireland, but not of it'.[25]

Many factors combined to set Ulster off from the rest of Ireland, not the least being geography. Much of the province's southern border runs along a drumlin belt, the western portions of which can make for difficult farming. The best of Ulster's arable land lay north of this region. Passing into Ulster through the poor drumlin regions, many travellers found the eventual appearance of relatively good farms all the more striking. Likewise, leaving the North through the drumlin belt seemed to plunge the traveller instantly into the poverty that supposedly characterized the rest of Ireland. This is not to deny that the best of Ulster's agricultural lands around Londonderry, the glens of Antrim, and much of County Down were well farmed. Largely in Protestant hands, these holdings enjoyed privileges and protections in terms of tenure and rent not usually available to most tenants in Catholic areas in the West and South. And, as suggested earlier, there were also cultural differences that impelled Protestants to put more effort and money into appearances – houses, clothes, and land. However, the 'Ulster' upon which visitors lavished their praise represented only half of the province. Its less well-endowed western and southern reaches contained land and farms as poor as those found elsewhere in Ireland. Finally, the same travel accounts that lauded the supposedly unique appearance of Ulster usually contained descriptions of bountiful estate lands in Leinster and eastern Munster. In other words, the Ulster so often depicted in the travel books of the 1830s and 1840s was to some extent an artefact of the religious and social biases of Protestant British visitors, who turned their version of the province into a moral exemplar against which the rest of Ireland and its people were measured and found wanting.[26]

By the 1830s, the dynamics of the Irish Tour, as summarized above, revealed a shift away from the sense of excitement and even confidence regarding Ireland, which visitors had felt in the years immediately following the Act of Union. Glenn Hooper notes that even in the 1820s, fewer travel writers evidenced the sense of optimism that had characterized earlier accounts. Instead, visitors were increasingly likely to discuss the strangeness, even the alien nature of Ireland and its people.[27]

Yet, observers were not uniformly grim in their view of Ireland. Some, such as the Halls, authors of the popular *Ireland, Its Scenery and Character* (1841–3), maintained a generally rosy view of the country. More significantly, in the widely read account of his tour of 1834, Inglis mixed some hopeful notes in with his critical reports on low wages, high rents, and the alleged lackadaisical traits among the peasantry. In his introduction, he suggested that 'Ireland needs but a seed time of kind deeds in order that a harvest of abundant blessings may be reaped'.[28] As noted earlier, Inglis touted the possibilities for development in Connemara. Writing a year or so later, John Barrow, generally appalled by the poverty of the West, hailed the region's potential for becoming 'one of the most fertile and productive districts in Ireland'.[29] Other visitors, such as Thackeray, saw promise in draining bogs or in improving the area's inland waterways to support fisheries and mineral extraction.

Whatever the degree of optimism or pessimism that coloured travel accounts in the 1830s and early 1840s, no one actually predicted the catastrophe that would engulf the country after the appearance of potato blight in the autumn of 1845. When it struck and large-scale death and emigration began to grip the country the following year, some visitors were still slow to recognize the seriousness of the situation. The travel accounts of Therese Cornwallis West and Lord John Manners, both of whom toured in the summer of 1846, contained few descriptions of the blight-blackened fields reported in newspapers. Within a year or so, however, the crisis itself generated two types of travel literature that were new to Ireland. Early examples of what is now called 'disaster tourism' may be found in the accounts of those who toured Ireland expressly to gauge the effects of the Famine. In some cases, visitors, such as the American Asenath Nicholson and the British Quakers William Bennett and James Hack Tuke, tried to provide relief. Other writers, such as Rev. John East, author of *Notes and Glimpses of Ireland in 1847*, mixed visits to popular tourist destinations with observations of human suffering. Some visitors followed specialized itineraries focusing on particular aspects of the crisis. Rev. Sydney Godolphin Osborne confined much of his *Gleanings of the West of Ireland* (1850) to the Poor Law Union workhouses of the western districts.

Towards the end of the decade, another type of traveller appeared in Ireland, one inspired by the belief that while the Famine had been tragic it had, nonetheless, opened up possibilities for development, especially in the West. Although most of the books in this category were published after 1850, one of the first, George Preston White's *A Tour in Connemara, with Remarks on its Great Physical Capacities*, first appeared in 1849. Building on the enthusiasm for the region first expressed by the Blakes, Inglis, Barrow, and others, White combined appreciation for the spectacular landscape with confident assertions regarding the economic opportunities he believed the crisis had created for investors and settlers alike. Writing anonymously a few years later, Rev. John Harvey Ashworth published *A Saxon in Ireland, or the Rambles of an Englishman in Search of a Settlement in the West of Ireland* (1851). He, too, extolled the scenery but also focused on the supposed opportunities created by the collapse of the local landlords in the wake of the Famine and the break-up of their estates facilitated by the Encumbered Estates Act.[30] Writers like White and Ashworth believed that knowledgeable and dedicated English and Scottish farmers would settle in the area, drain the bogs, and turn the region into a veritable garden. Indeed, interested visitors could purchase special railway-excursion tickets to facilitate their search for investment opportunities in the West.[31]

As the Famine began to wind down and the first half of the nineteenth century came to an end, the great Irish contradiction between superb scenery and overwhelming poverty seemed gradually to resolve itself. The paupers had been swept off the land into workhouses, mass graves, or emigrant ships. Careless Irish landlords were bankrupt, and in Connemara the new 'Saxon' colony seemed to flourish. Even some of the bogs were drained. Colonial enthusiasm and ideology, however, could not repel the prevailing weather patterns (too much rain) nor replace boggy, peaty gley with better-drained, more fertile soil. In the face of falling grain prices after mid-century, pasturage rather than cultivation came to dominate the West, while its spectacular scenery drew more visitors than ever. Only roofless cabins and abandoned potato beds suggested a missing population, and eventually even these reminders faded amid the bogs and rushes. Over the ensuing decades, as emigration became institutionalized, the remaining population continued to dwindle, leaving a less conflicted, less 'irrational' landscape for tourists to enjoy.

Notes

1. These tallies are based on the author's analysis of items listed in John McVeagh, *Irish Travel Writing: A Bibliography* (Dublin: Wolfhound, 1996).
2. For landscape aesthetics and Irish tourism see Glenn Hooper, *Travel Writing and Ireland, 1760–1860* (Basingstoke, New York: Palgrave Macmillan, 2005), 17–58; William H. A. Williams, *Creating Irish Tourism: The First Century, 1750–1850* (London, New York: Anthem, 2010), 69–88.
3. For estate tourism in nineteenth-century Britain, see Peter Mandler, *The Rise and Fall of the Stately Home* (New Haven: Yale University, 1997), 23–73; for

estate tourism in Ireland see Williams, *Creating Irish Tourism*, 50–7, 60–5, 131–4.

4. For the Grand Tour see Chloe Chard, 'Introduction', *Transports: Travel, Pleasure, and Imaginative Geography, 1600–1830*, ed. Chloe Chard and Helen Langdon (New Haven: Yale University, 1998), 1–29; Judith Adler, 'Origins of Sightseeing', *Annals of Tourism Research* 16 (1989), 7–29.

5. For the Irish 'petite tour' see Williams, *Creating Irish Tourism*, 34–48.

6. See Hooper, *Travel Writing and Ireland*, 59–64.

7. See Henry D. Inglis, *A Journey throughout Ireland, during the Spring, Summer, and Autumn of 1834*, 3rd edn, 2 vols (London: Whittaker, 1835), 2: 264–5; Anon., *The Sportsman in Ireland, with his Summer Route through the Highlands of Scotland by a Cosmopolite*, 2 vols (London: Henry Colburn, 1840), 2: 57; Anna Maria and Samuel Carter Hall, *Hall's Ireland: Mr. and Mrs. Hall's Tour of 1840* [1841–1843], ed. Michael Scott (London: Sphere Books, 1984), 2: 412; William Makepeace Thackeray, *The Irish Sketch Book: 1842* [1843] (New York: P. F. Collins, 1902), 224.

8. See John Dunton, *Teague Land: Or A Merry Ramble to the Wild Irish (1698)*, ed. Andrew Carpenter (Dublin: Four Courts, 2003), 46; Richard Twiss, *A Tour of Ireland in 1775 with a Map, and a View of the Salmon-Leap at Ballyshannon* (London: Robson, Walker, Robinson, Kearsly, 1776), 144.

9. See the Blake Family of Renvyle House, *Letters from the Irish Highlands* [1825], ed. Kevin Whelan (Clifden, Galway: Gibbons Publications, 1995).

10. Baptist Wriothesley Noel, *Notes on a Short Tour through the Midland Counties of Ireland in the Summer of 1836* (London: J. Nisbet, 1837).

11. See Irene Whelan, *The Bible War in Ireland: The 'Second Reformation' and the Polarization of Protestant-Catholic Relations, 1800–1840* (Dublin: Lilliput, 2005); Mealla Ní Ghiobúin, *Dugort, Achill Island 1831–1861: The Rise and Fall of a Missionary Community* (Dublin: Irish Academic Press, 2001).

12. For the 'confessional landscape' see William H. A. Williams, *Tourism, Landscape and Irish Character: British Travel Writers in Pre-Famine Ireland* (Madison: University of Wisconsin, 2008), 21–8, 48–50.

13. For rundale settlements see Kevin Whelan, 'Settlement Patterns in the West of Ireland in the Pre-Famine Period', in *Decoding the Landscape: Papers Read at the Inaugural Conference of The Centre for Landscape Studies*, ed. Timothy Collins (Galway: Centre for Landscape Studies, 1994), 60–78. For tourist reactions to rundale villages see Williams, *Tourism, Landscape and Irish Character*, 99–101.

14. M. F. Dickson, 'Letters from the Coast of Clare', *Dublin University Magazine* 28 (July–December, 1841), 162.

15. James S. Donnelly Jr., *The Great Potato Famine* (Phoenix Mill, Sutton, 2001), 2.

16. For example see Leitch Ritchie, *Ireland, Picturesque and Romantic*, 2 vols (London: Rees, Orme, Brown, Green, Longman, 1837), 2: 24–5.

17. Thomas K. Cromwell, *Excursions through Ireland, Comprising Topographical and Historical Delineations of Leinster*, 3 vols (London: Longman, Hurst, Rees, Brown, 1820), 2: 131–2.

18. For 'tourist amnesia' see Williams, *Tourism, Landscape and Irish Character*, 110–11.

19. See Williams, *Tourism, Landscape and Irish Character*, 107–10.

20. Cormac Ó Gráda, *Ireland: A New Economic History 1780–1939* (Oxford: Clarendon, 1995), 23.
21. For an example see Lady Henrietta Chatterton, *Rambles in the South of Ireland during the Year 1838*, 2 vols (London: Saunders, Otley, 1839), 2: 218.
22. Ritchie, *Ireland*, 2: 263.
23. Thackeray, *Irish Sketch Book*, 308.
24. Noel, *Notes*, 4.
25. Hall and Hall, *Hall's Ireland*, 2: 343.
26. See Williams, *Tourism, Landscape and Irish Character*, 147–61.
27. See Hooper, *Travel Writing and Ireland*, 105–14.
28. Inglis, *Journey throughout Ireland*, 1: v–vi.
29. John Barrow, *A Tour Round Ireland* (London: John Murray, 1836), 244.
30. For Ashworth see Hooper, *Travel Writing and Ireland*, 157–62, 170–3.
31. See Williams, *Tourism, Landscape and Irish Character*, 178–89.

7

'Missions of Benevolence': Tourism and Charity on Nineteenth-Century Iona

Katherine Haldane Grenier

> How sad a welcome! To each voyager
> Some ragged child holds up for sale a store
> Of wave-worn pebbles, pleading on the shore
> Where once came monk and nun with gentle stir,
> Blessings to give, news ask, or suit prefer.
> Yet is yon neat trim church a grateful speck
> Of novelty amid the sacred wreck
> Strewn far and wide. Think, proud Philosopher!
> Fallen though she be, this Glory of the west,
> Still on her sons, the beams of mercy shine;
> And 'hopes, perhaps more heavenly bright than thine,
> A grace by thee unsought and unpossest,
> A faith more fixed, a rapture more divine,
> Shall gild their passage to eternal rest.'[1]

In his poem 'Iona (Upon Landing)', written after an 1833 trip to Scotland, William Wordsworth described a scene well-known to most nineteenth-century visitors to Iona: local children, clearly affected by the endemic Hebridean poverty, attempting to sell shells and rocks collected from the shore to newly arriving tourists. That 'sad welcome' compelled tourists, most of whom journeyed to Iona because of the island's role in Britain's religious history, to confront the realities of the Highland and Hebridean economic situation. Unusually in the history of nineteenth-century tourism in Scotland, however, many visitors responded to this encounter with local poverty not by turning away, but by taking measures to help alleviate it. This reaction was likely to have been inspired by the religious associations attached to Iona, but it also suggests a growing awareness of the extent to which tourism was an industry with a substantial economic impact. As Wordsworth's sonnet indicates, the children of Iona were cognizant of tourism's economic potential quite early in the nineteenth century. Tourists were Iona's chief import, as travel writer James Johnson pointed out in 1834, and the children's pebbles and shells, along with stories told by local guides, were the island's main exports.[2] While Wordsworth recognized the children's portrayal of themselves as merchants with commodities to sell, his quotation from Thomas Russell's 'Sonnet X' also likened them to beggars, 'the Babes from yon unshelter'd cot [who] / Implore thy passing charity in vain'. Most Victorian tourists who purchased the children's wares likewise understood the transaction as a charitable one, but one they undertook with a self-consciousness of tourism's commercial benefits for the local population. Under the guidance of Thomas Cook in the 1850s and '60s, many excursionists to Iona sought to direct the economic impact of tourism – and of their own charity – in a manner which helped islanders to become independent economic actors. Their manner of doing so, however, subtly privileged their own role in the development of the Hebrides.

Iona is a small island off Scotland's west coast, just beyond the Hebridean island of Mull (see Illustration 7.1). Its fame lies primarily in its connection with St Columba, an Irish monk who left Ireland for Scotland in 563 AD, possibly as an act of penance for participating in warfare. Columba eventually settled on Iona, the base from which he founded other monastic houses in the region and ruled a network of monasteries serving the pastoral needs of the Gaelic community of the area then known as Dal Riata. It is questionable whether Columba saw himself as a missionary to the Picts on the Scottish mainland, as his legend would have it. However, his followers established Christian churches in eastern Pictland within fifty years of his death, and their efforts reflect his spiritual zeal and enthusiasm.[3] Modern historians may debate some of the particulars of the traditions which grew up around Columba, but the nineteenth-century understanding of him as the first to bring Christianity from Ireland to the pagans of Scotland and thence to northern England positioned Iona as 'the mother-church of religion in Scotland'.[4]

Usually coupled with the island of Staffa, Iona was a must-see sight from the beginning of the development of modern tourism and travel to Scotland in the late eighteenth century.[5] Most tourists reached the islands by means of a tour run by the MacBrayne's Shipping Company, beginning as early as the 1820s. By mid-century, MacBrayne's offered daily summertime trips from Oban to Iona and Staffa, and the journey

CATHEDRAL CHURCH OF ST. MARY, IONA.

Illustration 7.1 'Iona', from *Black's Picturesque Tourist of Scotland* (Edinburgh, 1875), 484. Source: National Library of Scotland.

was popular enough that an 1860 description referred to 'the hundred tourists' on board the boat.[6] It was not always an easy trip. There was no pier on Iona until late in the nineteenth century, so the steamer anchored offshore and tourists clambered aboard smaller rowboats, which held 25–30 people. The boatmen had to find a landing place alongside seaweed-covered rocks jutting out from the island. Passengers then scrambled out of the unsteady boats, trying to find their footing on the wet, slippery rocks as the sea surged around them.

Having arrived on Iona, nineteenth-century tourists' time there was generally brief. Iona is a small island, roughly three miles long, and the sites of interest to most sightseers were situated within about a hundred yards of the landing site.[7] For most of the century, guides appointed by the Duke of Argyll, proprietor of the island, met the boat and led excursionists to the key attractions, hastening them back to the embarkation point once the hour's stop was over. The usual tour led visitors first to the ruins of a post-Columba nunnery, then to a small building known as St Oran's chapel, to see a graveyard said to contain the bodies of 48 Scottish monarchs, including King Duncan of *Macbeth* fame. Moving on to the ruins of the 'Cathedral', sightseers passed McLean's Cross, a large standing cross dating from the sixteenth century. The guide might point out a small hillock, 'Abbot's Knoll', from which St Columba was believed to have looked over the island and blessed it on the last day of his life. After exploring the remains of the small Cathedral, visitors were hustled back to the steamer, usually for the return trip to Oban.

Not only was the usual journey to Iona a quick one, there was little direct contact with artefacts related to St Columba. The ruins so eagerly perused by visitors were not the original structures built by Columba and his monks. Columba was buried on Iona, but his bones were later taken to Ireland. The spot where he first landed on Iona was reportedly marked by a circle of stones, but it was in a remote location on the other side of the island, inaccessible to most tourists. Thus, as many travel writers pointed out, Iona's importance lay less in what visitors actually saw, than in the associations aroused by their visit, the 'signifiers' which established a meaning for the island. Those associations were many. Journeys to Iona, for instance, enabled tourists to experience the unconquerable power of nature, manifested in the rough weather blowing off the Atlantic, and to immerse themselves in a deep sense of the past. However, those experiences could be had elsewhere in the Highlands. Iona's real attraction was its role in Great Britain's religious history. Staffa was often called a 'temple of nature', but Iona was the 'Temple of the Living God'.[8] All the Western Isles have some kind of novelty, said travel writer Jonathan Oldbuck, but 'it is on Iona you first learn that in Christ shall all be made alive'.[9] Victorian imaginations were fascinated by the idea of the tiny, isolated island surrounded by dangerous waves, peopled by a little group of devoted monks who preserved Christianity and scholarship in a barbaric time. Iona's remoteness and desolation was still apparent to nineteenth-century visitors, and the fact that so important a message could spread from so secluded a place magnified the power of the creed which Columba taught: 'From its wave-beaten shores the great pure light arose, which radiating thence on every side, never waned till the whole land was Christianized, and churches and chapels were established in every corner'.[10] To an age of some anxiety over the possibility of religious decline because of the effects of science, new Biblical criticism, industrialization, and urbanization, this vision of Iona was testimony to the power – and truth – of Christianity. The island was often described as 'sacred' or 'hallowed'.[11] 'Iona has always been deemed holy ground', said a newspaper article of 1860.[12]

As such, visits to Iona were opportunities for spiritual renewal. This expectation was partly created by Samuel Johnson's nearly canonical observation, made during his 1773 trip to Iona: 'That man is little to be envied whose patriotism would not gain force upon the plains of Marathon or whose piety would not grow warmer among the ruins of Iona'.[13] Johnson's sentiments were well known and many Victorians, often strongly influenced by Evangelicalism, found this an appealing possibility. Miss S. Taylor, who journeyed to Iona in the 1840s, expected to be 'struck with religious feelings' upon landing.[14] Sylvan's guidebook advised in 1848 that 'The reader of "Johnson's Tour to the Hebrides" will remember the raptures of the learned Doctor upon this island; and if he is in the least degree enthusiastic himself, will share them to the full on contemplating the relics of early Christianity and civilization with which it abounds'.[15] Tourist literature frequently depicted Scotland as a particularly religious (or spiritual) place, one of the many ways that the country appeared to preserve values that might be on the decline in the allegedly more modernized England. Both in the island's construction as the birthplace of British Christianity and as a place where one expected some level of spiritual encounter, Iona was a key part of that vision of Scotland.

One of the sources of spiritual renewal offered by Iona derived from the possibility of physical proximity to the places where St Columba lived, prayed, and worked. The whole island, said an 1882 article in *All the Year Round*, was dedicated to Columba's memory.[16] His holiness still seemed to linger there. '"Lives there a man with soul so dead" as to not catch a spark of enthusiasm as he stands upon the spot where St. Columba stood more than twelve centuries ago and repelled a heathen invader, not with carnal weapons, but by trolling forth in his magnificent voice the forty-fifth Psalm?'[17] Because Iona was still isolated, relatively difficult to reach, and sparsely populated, tourists could envision themselves as walking where Columba walked, in a landscape that seemed to have changed little in the intervening years. The view from 'Abbot's Knoll' was 'still the same as when viewed by Columba thirteen hundred years ago' said one visitor.[18] Tourist literature emphasized that St Columba lived an 'exemplary' Christian life and praised his 'pure patriotism', his 'love for souls', his 'forbearance and gentleness'.[19]

Although the expectation that travel to Iona might bring an encounter with the sacred evokes the idea of religious pilgrimage, nineteenth-century travel writers carefully distanced Columba from any Roman

Catholic associations. He was often identified as a Celtic Christian, and the faith he spread was imagined as a native – a British – faith: 'Those who delight in tracing the history of the ancient British or Celtic church – long before Augustine landed in Kent from Rome – must ever look with deep veneration on sea-girt Iona'.[20] Travel literature enumerated the ways in which Columba's monasticism differed from Roman Catholicism, and asserted that Columba and his fellows represented a purer form of Christianity than did the Roman church. Quoting the Duke of Argyll, *Black's Picturesque Tourist* of 1871 compared the 'fire, the freshness and the comparative simplicity of the old Celtic church' to the 'dull and often corrupt monotony of medieval Romanism'.[21] Given the continued prevalence of anti-Catholicism throughout the nineteenth century, the idea that Columba pre-dated Roman Catholicism not only made it easier for British Protestants to admire him, it suggested that the roots of British Christianity were untainted by Rome.[22] Many travel writers categorized Columba as a 'Culdee' or Celi De, who were semi-monastic holy men mythologized by Scottish Reformation leaders as defenders of the Celtic church against Roman influences.[23] This characterization of Columba further distanced British Christianity from Roman Catholicism, particularly since Reformation-era Calvinists had asserted a native Protestantism by claiming Culdees as Presbyterians before their time.[24]

An 1868 article about Iona insisted that Columba and his fellows should best be termed 'missionaries', not 'monks', to distinguish the work done on Iona from later 'superstitious usage'.[25] The many travel writers who joined in describing Columba as a 'missionary' or spoke of his 'missionary journeys'[26] not only further de-emphasized Roman Catholicism, they likened his efforts to the foreign mission movement of the nineteenth century, thereby deepening the sense in which the sixth-century saint could serve as a role model to devout visitors. The implicit association of Columba with Victorian missionaries may have held particular resonance for Scots who toured Iona, for the missionary enterprise was a key element of nineteenth-century Scottish national identity.[27] The 1863 edition of George and Peter Anderson's *Guide to the Highlands and Western Islands of Scotland* emphasized that Iona was not a monastery in the sense of a retreat for solitaries to work out their own salvation; rather, it was a 'great school of Christian education' designed to prepare and send forth a body of clergy trained to the task of preaching the gospel among the heathen and civilizing them by example.[28] Like modern heroes of the mission field, Columba, it could be said, left his home with a small band of fellow Christians to live among the pagans and spread the word of God. His success could offer inspiration to latter-day efforts to do the same. His task was thankless and dangerous, said an 1860 article in *The Leisure Hour*, 'but Columba is not the man to shrink from a godly enterprise because of the danger, and his perseverance is rewarded in due time'.[29]

In describing Columba's evangelism of the Pictish pagans, travel writers conflated the spreading of Christianity with the bringing of 'civilization' in much the same way as did nineteenth-century missionary literature. Just as Samuel Johnson celebrated Iona as the place from which 'savage clans and roving barbarians derived the benefits of knowledge and the blessings of religion',[30] nineteenth-century commenters lauded the sixth-century monastery for preserving learning and scholarship, as well as Christianity. As a consequence, even less devout Victorians, who could see in Columba a forerunner of Britain's imperial mission, could find him to be an inspirational figure. Iona was the 'shrine from which, amid the darkness of that early time, the light of civilization was spread throughout the north'.[31] Indeed, the spiritual experience expected on Iona was not necessarily a Christian one, although Christian language predominates in the tourist literature. The centuries-old graveyard, for instance, 'that stupendous scene of mortality', stimulated traveller William Winter to contemplate the transitoriness of human life, but his thoughts were not couched in a specifically Christian framework.[32]

The idea that Iona was an isolated island, distant from civilization, was central to the vision which attracted tourists in the nineteenth century. But as Scotland's tourist infrastructure grew over the course of the period, Iona became more and more accessible, and the reality of a trip there did not always fulfil visitors' expectations. The brevity of the steamer's stop allowed little time for spiritual meditation. Sightseers repeatedly commented that they would have liked more time to linger on the island, and spoke of the tyranny of the steamboat, whose scheduled departure cut into their 'pious reveries'.[33] Likewise, crowds of other steamer passengers, all trying to see the same things in a short amount of time, interfered with the expected spiritual atmosphere. Numerous excursionists grumbled that their visits were destroyed by the mob of other tourists. Miss Taylor, who had expected to be struck with religious feelings on the island, found that 'Holy meditation ill becomes a curious medley crowd hastening to survey all the remains of antiquarian mould, in one short half-hour of leave from a ship's captain'.[34] Such complaints, of course, were in part a strategy by which the writer differentiated him or herself from the hoard of mindless tourists, and claimed status as a more 'authentic' traveller.[35] The concerns were nonetheless valid. Could one experience the spiritual power of the sacred isle in an hour's hurried tour, surrounded by other tourists? Could Iona maintain its meaning as an isolated locale from which enlightenment and piety spread, if middle-class tourists could reach it on a comfortable day's sail with all the modern conveniences on board?

And, could one appreciate the spiritual atmosphere of Iona in the midst of the poverty so apparent on the island? As Wordsworth pointed out, the usual first impression upon landing on Iona was not the serenity of a sacred isle, it was the sight of local children crowding around the visitors, trying to sell shells, stones, and ferns allegedly collected from the spot where Columba originally landed on the island.[36] J. E. Bowman was swarmed by them as soon as his boat landed on the beach: 'Ragged filthy children thronged round us, offering for sale pebbles and crystals, but I saw nothing among them of the least value'.[37] In 1876, Edmund Gosse described the 'troop of wild children' who rushed at his party when they arrived, trying to sell ferns and shells, calling out the prices in 'droll' accents, which seemed to be the only English they knew.[38] Descriptions of these children were commonplace in Iona travel literature, available in travel accounts and some guidebooks throughout the nineteenth century. Such portrayals of direct meetings between tourists and indigent Highlanders and islanders are relatively rare in the travel literature of Scotland. Although most people only briefly mentioned their encounter with the children, then went on to enjoy Iona's attractions, the frequency with which tourists described the children and alluded to their economic condition suggests that visitors became particularly aware of Highland poverty while on Iona. In response, some tourists chose not to avoid the indigence they witnessed, but to contribute towards its eradication, an action possibly inspired by Iona's famed religious history.

Tourists to Scotland were generally very interested in Highlanders and islanders, regarding them as historical artefacts who lived just as their ancestors had and therefore preserved an ancient and rural way of life in a changing world. Many travel accounts of Scotland included ruminations upon Highland character and ways of life, but most of these observations rested more on preconceived expectations than on sustained encounters with the objects of their discussions. Tourists and travellers must surely have had regular contact with Highlanders and islanders, as innkeepers, servants, carriage drivers, tour guides, and even fellow passengers on trains and steamers. But visitors' accounts of their journeys are virtually silent on these interactions, which at any rate would be limited by language barriers and class differences, as well as by the structures of tourism. British sightseers could not help but know that considerable poverty existed in the Highlands and islands, and Thomas Cook claimed that it was impossible for tourists in the Hebrides to remain indifferent to the conditions they witnessed.[39] Many other sources, however, make it clear that Highland poverty could be construed in a manner which enabled travellers to be relatively unconcerned. Most of the key travel texts on the nineteenth-century Highlands asked readers to interpret poverty as central to the city/country and progress/tradition dichotomies within which Gaels' meaning lay. Tourist literature presented Highland black houses as a sign of crofters' commendable lack of greed and their contentment with their lot in life. Conversely, many Britons understood the indigence of the region to be a consequence of Highlanders' own indolence, which could be remedied had they the will. More fundamentally, although some sightseers did visit Highland homes as part of the effort to learn more about Highlanders and their social and cultural milieu, it is not clear that most ordinary sightseers had much contact with real conditions there. For the most part, the ritual of tourism in the Highlands focused primarily on historical monuments and on encounters with an allegedly wild and empty landscape, a manner of viewing the region which effectively wrote natives off the land.

The children of Iona, however, were difficult to overlook; one tourist said they followed his party 'everywhere', even to the water's edge at departure.[40] Periodic attempts were made to keep the children away from the tourists as they landed, but such efforts were unsuccessful until late in the century. In 1859 or 1860, for instance, a little stand was set up near the ruins of the nunnery, from which the children could sell their wares.[41] They evidently did not stay away from the landing site for long; in 1876, the children met Gosse when his boat landed. However, there are other reasons besides the persistence of the Ionian children that many sightseers became not only unusually cognizant of conditions on Iona, but willing to discuss them and to act on their knowledge. Wordsworth's poem may well have primed many to consider the children and their living conditions a part of the Iona experience. A few tourists quoted the poem in their descriptions of Iona,[42] and it is included in the 1840 version of one of the most popular guidebooks of the period, *Black's Picturesque Tourist*, although not in several other editions.[43] Poverty may also have been more apparent on Iona because of the way in which tourists were a kind of captive market there: they usually came at the same time, all together, and the arrival of the steamer was an important event on the island, making it easy for the children to find potential customers.

Ultimately, however, the willingness to discuss poverty on Iona was linked to the island's larger cultural symbolism as a sacred spot. As Wordsworth indicates, what was so sad about the welcome given to visitors to the island was less the actual indigence manifested by the children, but poverty *in that place*. Residents of Iona were not just poor, they were poor in a spot understood to have been the 'Temple of the Living God' and the centre of piety and scholarship in Scotland. The contrast between Iona's past (or perhaps, its imagined past) and its present made the condition of the little welcoming party all the more shocking, and testified to the island's decay since Columba's time.

Such contact with a piece of the reality of Hebridean life was clearly an unwelcome element of some tourists' trip to Iona, an attitude reflected in depictions of the children as annoying beggars and pests. Thomas Cook described how some visitors turned 'with apparent disgust from the exhibition of wretchedness which meets the eye'.[44] Others were more sympathetic, in ways they might not have been towards poverty among adults who could more clearly be blamed for their own condition. 'Poor children!' said one description, 'most of them have ragged clothes and pinched features; who could resist the impulse to gladden their hearts by exchanging a superfluous bit of silver for a handful of their trifles?'[45] In 1849, Abbot commented that 'the spectacle of their poverty and wretchedness, their eagerness to sell their little treasures, the roughness with which they were repulsed, and their looks of mournful disappointment' gave him more pain than the ruins gave him pleasure.[46] However, the tendency of some sightseers, especially late in the century, to portray the children as entrepreneurs, striving to make the best use of the opportunities available to them, undercut the image of lazy, improvident Gaels. This construction of the children's activities posited the purchase of their wares as a form of charity, an encouragement of their efforts, rather than a reward for begging: 'There was something affecting in the attempt of these poorly clad, but clean and orderly children, to pick up a few pence in exchange for the only articles they could find for sale'.[47] Some described the children as 'demure' or 'smart native girls'.[48] Thomas Cook referred to the 'little traders'.[49] This interpretation was easier to maintain late in the century, when the children stood behind a wooden board, numbered into strips as stalls for each, rather than crowding around the visitors as they landed.

In a successful effort to use tourism to help alleviate conditions on Iona, Thomas Cook combined the vision of Iona as a holy place with

the construction of islanders as entrepreneurs trying to better themselves. A one-time itinerant Baptist preacher and active member of the
Temperance movement, Cook began taking tour groups to Scotland
in 1846 and became an important promoter of Scottish tourism to
the English middle classes.[50] Between 1848 and 1863, Cook spent two
months every summer conducting four tours to Scotland, catering for
approximately five thousand people each season. In 1860, he estimated
that he had made forty or fifty trips to Iona since 1847, bringing thirty
to one hundred and fifty tourists with him each time.[51]

Cook first led excursionists to the Highlands in the fall of 1847,
soon after Victoria's first visit to Scotland. The 'condition of the poor
Islanders' of Iona, still struggling with the consequences of the potato
famine, he said, 'awakened kindly sympathies' of his party of tourists. On occasion, Cook's customers 'would give little presents' to the
'most abjected' residents, or buy stones and shells from the children
in an effort to help.[52] At some point in the 1850s, Cook formalized
these ad hoc charitable impulses by teaming up with the newly formed
'Society for the Relief and Encouragement of the Poor Fishermen
in the Highlands and Islands', a charitable organization headed by
Dr Alexander Fletcher, a Scottish clergymen then resident in London.
In the 1850s, the society started providing boats to fishermen on Skye
through a low-cost instalment plan. Members of the crew paid as little
as 10–12 shillings per year until their boat was purchased, at which
time the boat became the crew's property. The initial costs of the boats
were financed by donations; fishermen's repayments were used by the
charity to pay for nets, tackle, and repairs. The society was formally
organized in 1855 and widely publicized in Scottish and English newspapers. In succeeding years, the organization expanded its work to other
Hebridean islands; by 1859, the group had reportedly supplied 70 boats
to various Western Isles, mostly Skye.

Thomas Cook's involvement with the scheme centred on Iona and he
drew on the island's cultural significance to motivate tourists to contribute. Once the sightseers had toured most of the key sites of the island
and were gathered in the 'Cathedral', it was Cook's practice 'to catch the
moments of abstraction from the ordinary pursuits and every-day appeals
of common life, and there to call attention to the claims of our poor and
dejected brethren and sisters of this lone island upon the sympathy and
aid of Christian and benevolent visitors'. Those requests, he said, 'have
always met with a hearty response'.[53] The excursionists, 'holiday-making
and happy, are in a proper cue for the reception of such an appeal, and
respond liberally', said one of Cook's admirers.[54] In 1872, Cook claimed

that over the years he had raised four hundred pounds in contributions from tourists, as well as donations of books and tracts for the library.[55] His efforts provided twenty-six boats for fishermen on Iona and the nearby island of Mull; enough boats, Cook said, that almost every able-bodied man on either side of the Sound of Mull could support himself and his dependents.[56] Cook also helped educate a few 'promising sons of the island'. One young man was sent to a Church Missionary College at Islington and after ordination in the Church of England became a missionary in Ceylon. Others, Cook claimed, were similarly fulfilling positions of 'trust and sensibility'.[57] Cook may have been inspired in part by the efforts of an earlier advocate for Ionians, Legh Richmond. Richmond was an English clergyman who, reversing St Columba's work, became a sort of missionary to the island during a four-day trip in 1820. After preaching to islanders several times, Richmond returned home to raise funds to provide more amenities on Iona. He eventually built a school and a library, after the Duke of Argyll agreed to build a church.[58] Cook greatly admired Richmond; he wrote of his charitable work for Iona in his guidebooks, and the first boat which the Fishermen's Relief Society sent to Iona was named *The Legh Richmond*.

The contrast between the understanding of Iona as a sacred spot and the indigence of its inhabitants inspired others to take similar actions. The writer of an 1865 letter to the editor of *The Scotsman* described how, on an earlier trip to Iona, the writer had been so struck by the 'isolated and helpless condition of the fishermen' that he helped send two boats from the Fishermen's Relief Society to the island. He later founded a permanent society to support and encourage habits of temperance, economy, and perseverance on Iona and elsewhere in Scotland, and to help in cases of accident and sickness.[59] Cook always claimed that the excursionists he brought to Iona were eager to help, and he sometimes argued that they got involved of their own accord, motivated by Christian principles and by the atmosphere of the island.

We are conducted through the 'Nunnery', through 'Oran's Chapel' and the 'Cathedral', where are many monuments of Ecclesiastics and Devotees; and here in this Old Cathedral join every heart to sing the praises of the Great Eternal, whilst the whole congregation are moved with sympathy for the interesting people whose lot is cast upon this remarkable island. Many a moving scene have we witnessed within these time-honoured walls, and many a noble expression of good will for 'the poor children of Icolmkill' has here been involuntarily called into practical exercise.[60]

Cook conducted his tourists all over the Highlands (in a style often compared to a military campaign). The fact that he chose Iona as the place to ask for assistance for Highlanders and islanders testifies that visitors were unusually aware of local conditions there, and, because of the religious associations linked to the spot, particularly concerned about it. By making his pitch when and where he did, Cook called on visitors to act on the pious sentiments which many claimed were aroused by touring the ruins, reminding them that they were empowered to effect change in the Highlands. Giving to the fishing boat scheme promoted by Cook, or buying shells from the children as many tourists did, could be understood as acts of Christian charity, appropriate to the setting of Iona. With these actions, visitors counteracted the ways that poverty and the commercialization of tourism seemed to rob Iona of its spiritual atmosphere.

Furthermore, by asking his excursionists to invest in the futures of indigent Highlanders, Cook took a stand on a highly charged topic – and asked his tourists to do the same. Social and economic conditions in the Highlands and Western Isles were a much debated subject in the nineteenth century, although the 1850s and '60s was a less contentious period than during the Famine, or later during the Irish and Highland Land Wars. Cook claimed that he merely tried to awaken the 'generous sympathies' of visitors to Iona without getting into 'vexed questions' about depopulation and landlord responsibility.[61] But by raising funds to help Highlanders purchase equipment with which they could make a living, Cook and the Fishermen's Relief Society challenged many negative stereotypes of Highlanders and islanders. Highland and Hebridean poverty, the society asserted, was not the result of moral failings of the people, nor was it acceptable or quaint. Speeches in support of the enterprise defended islanders against the charges of laziness and lethargy often directed against them, and emphasized that the boats and supplies were not handouts. Rather, the society endeavoured to provide a people who were always willing to work, the ability to do so. Their supporters believed that with boats and tackle, Hebridean men will be 'amongst the most industrious and well-doing of British Fishermen'.[62] Advocates of the scheme pointed to the establishment of a savings bank on Skye as evidence of the moral improvement which was made there by 1856.[63] Since the ability to provide for oneself and one's family was central to middle-class Victorian notions of masculinity, the Fishermen's Relief Society's emphasis upon the industry and independence of Hebrideans counteracted the feminizing qualities of poverty, and of the racial construction of Gaels.

For visitors to Iona, a financial contribution either to Cook's campaign or directly through purchasing shells or rocks from the children, enabled one's journey to the sacred isle to be something more than a one-hour tourist jaunt. They might be on the island only briefly, but by demonstrating their concern for islanders through some form of philanthropy, the visitor could make a lasting difference in the Hebrides. On three occasions during the years that Cook was involved with the Ionian issues, he spent a few days on the island towards the end of the tourist season and held a large 'soiree' for denizens of Iona and along the Sound of Mull, with food donated by tourists and other supporters of his work, events which further illustrated the economic impact tourism could have. On those trips he visited the homes of fishermen and other islanders, conversed with two of the oldest men of Iona, went to church there, and socialized with residents at the soiree.[64] Although language barriers impeded communication between Cook and Hebrideans, he, at the very least, demonstrated an appreciation of Iona as a community whose people should matter as much as did the historic and spiritual sites. Indeed, Cook came to consider his work on behalf of islanders as the central focus of his tours there: 'Nothing has tended more to give character and interest to our visits to Iona than the opportunities they have afforded to lend a friendly hand of assistance to those isolated "children of the waves" by which the island and the neighboring shore of Mull are populated'.[65] Cook had long believed in the moral benefits of travel, and his activities on behalf of Iona grew out of his staunch belief that tourism should broaden the mind, break down barriers between nations, and promote Christian benevolence. He publicized his efforts through articles in his promotional newspaper, *Cook's Excursionist*, and through occasional letters to other papers, and continued to solicit donations of money and other supplies for islanders and for his end-of-the-year soirees.

At the same time, despite the genuineness of the concern which Cook, the Fishermen's Relief Society, and many tourists demonstrated, their efforts amounted to a reversal of the 'civilizing mission' which so many attributed to St Columba. Cook referred to his visits to Iona as 'missions of benevolence and Christian sympathy'.[66] Efforts to alleviate Iona's poverty posited the outside world as the necessary agent of change. Except for the Iona children who tried to sell souvenirs, the islanders were depicted by Cook and the Fishermen's Relief Society as passive recipients of others' aid. Whether or not boats, soirees, or libraries were the forms of aid desired by Hebrideans was not discussed. Islanders' gratitude towards their benefactors, however, was made clear in Cook's accounts of his work. When he went to Iona in 1857, for instance, two of the fishing boats which had been made available to island crews came to meet the steamer, colours flying at the mast and guns firing in salute. The men, women, and children of the island met Cook at the shore.[67] Heartfelt though such appreciation might be, the frequency with which Cook called attention to it served to reinforce the class and status differences between the recipients and the benefactors. Hebrideans' gratitude evinced their 'natural' respect for their superiors, a frequent trope in eighteenth- and nineteenth-century writing on the Highlands. The names of the boats, such as *The Legh Richmond*, *The Thomas Cook*, *The Duke of Argyll*, and *The English Tourist*, were chosen by the Fishermen's Relief Society and operated as constant reminders to islanders of the sources which enabled their jobs and incomes.

In like fashion, the notion that Hebridean industry needed to be 'encouraged' by others also served to highlight islanders' helplessness, despite the emphasis on the hard work and moral fibre displayed by fishermen once the boats were delivered. Cook designed his soirees in part with the goal of 'keeping up the awakened interest of the Islanders', which suggests a concern that Hebrideans might relapse into dependence on others without continued support from their patrons on the mainland.[68] Gifts of reading material such as the *Band of Hope Review* and Gaelic religious tracts furthered the 'improving' nature of those events.[69]

Scholars of travel and tourism frequently credit the 'tourist gaze' with the authority to define a people and a place. That power, however, is mediated by the interplay between tourists' expectations and the actuality of the place they find. The cultural significance which attracted sightseers to Iona lay in the island's past as an important religious site, a past which imparted a continued sacredness that tourists hoped to experience. Local children, however, took a hand in defining the island by focusing tourists' gazes onto contemporary economic concerns. Although these children and their indigence then simply became part of the expected experience of Iona, in the hands of Thomas Cook, Iona's historical and symbolic associations became a tool with which to encourage visitors' active intervention against poverty. The cultural significance attached to Iona called on tourists to look at Hebrideans in a way they might not otherwise. While their response to this call reflects ingrained notions of class and race, the fact that they heard it testifies to Iona's ability to assert itself against the tourist gaze.[70]

Notes

1. William Wordsworth, 'Iona (Upon Landing)', in *The Complete Poetical Works of William Wordsworth*, 10 vols (Boston: Houghton Mifflin, 1911), 8: 329.
2. James Johnson, *The Recess, or Autumnal Relaxation in the Highlands and Lowlands* (London, 1834), 108.
3. Alfred P. Smyth, *Warlords and Holy Men. Scotland, AD 80–1000* (Edinburgh: Edinburgh University Press, 1984), 84–115. See also Adomnan of Iona, *Life of St. Columba*, trans. Richard Sharpe (New York: Penguin, 1995).
4. George Eyre-Todd, *Scotland Picturesque and Traditional*, 2nd edn (Glasgow: Gowans and Gray, 1906), 307.
5. On the history of tourism to Scotland, see Alistair J. Durie, *Scotland for the Holidays: Tourism in Scotland c. 1780–1939* (East Linton: Tuckwell Press, 2003); John R. Gold and Margaret M. Gold, *Imagining Scotland. Tradition, Representation and Promotion in Scottish Tourism since 1750* (Aldershot: Scolar Press, 1995); Katherine Haldane Grenier, *Tourism and Identity in Scotland, 1770–1914* (Aldershot: Ashgate, 2005).
6. 'The Tourist in Scotland. A Day Among the Hebrides', *The Leisure Hour* 459 (11 October 1860), 645.
7. William Chambers, 'A Week among the Hebrides', *Chamber's Journal of Popular Literature, Science and Arts* (July 1858), 67.
8. S. Taylor, 'Journal of a Tour to Scotland' (1842), National Library of Scotland, MS 8927, 167. This phrase also appeared in a poem written by D. Moore which was sometimes quoted by guidebooks. See, David MacBrayne's Royal Mail Steamers, pub., *Summer Tours in Scotland* (Glasgow, 1896), 55.
9. Jonathan Oldbuck, 'A Visit to Iona', *National Review* (June 1892), 580.
10. Constance F. Gordon-Cumming, *In the Hebrides* (London, 1883), 77.
11. Malcolm Ferguson, *A Trip from Callander to Staffa and Iona* (Dundee, 1894), 164; Taylor, 'Journal', 169.
12. 'The Tourist in Scotland', 646.
13. Samuel Johnson, *A Journey to the Western Islands of Scotland*, ed. Peter Levi (New York: Penguin, 1984), 141.
14. Taylor, 'Journal', 166.
15. *Sylvan's Pictorial Handbook to the Scenery of the Caledonian Canal* (London, 1848), 39.
16. 'In Bonnie Scotland', *All the Year Round* 30.724 (14 October 1882), 280.
17. J. H. Overton, 'A Cruise among the Hebrides', *Longman's Magazine* 14.80 (June 1889), 176.
18. Ferguson, *Trip from Callander*, 100.
19. Adam and Charles Black, pub., *Black's Picturesque Tourist of Scotland* (Edinburgh, 1871), 467; George and Peter Anderson, *Guide to the Highlands and Western Islands of Scotland* (Edinburgh, 1863), 191.
20. W. D., 'Abbey Church of Iona and the Ancient British Missionaries', *Quiver* 3.145 (June 1868), 642.
21. Black, *Black's Picturesque Tourist* (1871), 468.
22. See D. G. Paz, *Popular Anti-Catholicism in Mid-Victorian England* (Stanford, CA: Stanford University Press, 1992).
23. Black, *Black's Picturesque Tourist* (1871), 481; John Menzies, pub., *Menzies' Tourist's Pocket Guide for Scotland* (Edinburgh, 1853), 551.

24. Michael Lynch, *Scotland: A New History* (London: Pimlico, 1991), 26.
25. W. D., 'Abbey Church', 642.
26. Black, *Black's Picturesque Tourist* (1871), 467; Eyre-Todd, *Scotland*, 303.
27. See Esther Brietenbach, *Empire and Scottish Society: The Impact of Foreign Missions at Home, c. 1790 to 1914* (Edinburgh: Edinburgh University Press, 2009).
28. Anderson, *Guide to the Highlands*, 190–1.
29. 'The Tourist in Scotland', 646.
30. Quoted in William Home Lizars, *Lizars's Scottish Tourist* (Edinburgh: W. H. Lizars, 1840), 249. See also Johnson, *Journey*, 140.
31. Eyre-Todd, *Scotland*, 303.
32. William Winter, *Over the Border* (New York: Moffat, Yard and Co., 1911), 209.
33. 'A Day in the Hebrides', *Dublin University Magazine* 32.190 (October 1848), 484.
34. Taylor, 'Journal', 167.
35. See James Buzard, *The Beaten Track: European Tourism, Literature, and the Ways to 'Culture', 1800–1918* (Oxford: Clarendon Press, 1993).
36. Gordon-Cumming, *In the Hebrides*, 99.
37. J. E. Bowman, *The Highlands and Islands: A Nineteenth-Century Tour*, Introduction by Elaine M. E. Barry (New York: Hippocrene Books, 1986), 116.
38. Edmund Gosse, 'Journal in Scotland' (1876), National Library of Scotland MS 2562, n. pag.
39. *Cook's Excursionist and Tourist Advertiser* (26 May 1859), 2.
40. 'In Bonnie Scotland', 281.
41. 'Tourist in Scotland', 646.
42. For example, Chambers, 'Week among the Hebrides', 68.
43. Adam and Charles Black, *Black's Picturesque Tourist of Scotland* (Edinburgh, 1840), 263.
44. *Cook's Excursionist* (26 May 1859), 2.
45. 'Tourist in Scotland', 646.
46. Jacob Abbott, *A Summer in Scotland* (Dublin, 1849), 218.
47. Chambers, 'Week among the Hebrides', 68.
48. Chambers, 'Week among the Hebrides', 68; Ferguson, *Trip from Callander*, 91–2.
49. *Cook's Excursionist* (26 May 1859), 3.
50. On Thomas Cook, see Buzard, *The Beaten Track*, 48–65; Piers Brendon, *Thomas Cook: 150 Years of Popular Tourism* (London: Secker & Warburg, 1991); John Pudney, *The Thomas Cook Story* (London: Michael Joseph, 1953); Edmund Swinglehurst, *Cook's Tours: The Story of Popular Travel* (Poole, Dorset: Blandford Press, 1982); Lynne Withey, *Grand Tours and Cook's Tours* (New York: William Morrow, 1997).
51. *Cook's Excursionist* (7 April 1860), 2.
52. *Cook's Excursionist* (7 April 1860), 2.
53. *Cook's Excursionist* (26 May 1859), 2.
54. 'My Excursion Agent', *All the Year Round* 11.263 (7 May 1864), 302.
55. *Cook's Excursionist* (9 July 1872), 3.
56. Thomas Cook, *Cook's Scottish Tourist Practical Directory: A Guide to the Principal Tourist Routes, Conveyances and Special Ticket Arrangements* (London, 1866), 83; *Cook's Excursionist* (July 1859 Supplement), 4.
57. *Cook's Excursionist* (26 May 1859), 2.

58. See Matthew Marshall, *Legh Richmond* (London: Religious Tract Society, 1893).
59. *The Scotsman* (1 September 1865), 3.
60. *Cook's Excursionist* (3 June 1858).
61. *Cook's Excursionist* (26 May 1859), 2.
62. *Cook's Excursionist* (7 April 1860), 3.
63. *Caledonian Mercury* (17 October 1856), n. pag.
64. *Cook's Excursionist* (26 May 1859), 2–3.
65. *Cook's Excursionist* (12 August 1861), 5.
66. *Cook's Excursionist* (23 August 1858), 5.
67. *Cook's Excursionist* (23 August 1858), 5.
68. *Cook's Excursionist* (7 April 1860), 2.
69. *Cook's Excursionist* (26 May 1859), 2.
70. Thank you to The Citadel Foundation for research funding, and to Paul Smith of the Thomas Cook Archives.

8
Holiday Excursions to Scott Country

Nicola J. Watson

Step out of the Victorian grandeur of Waverley station in Edinburgh today, glance up to your left, and you will see rising above you a tall, blackish spire, which gives the impression of being attached to a Gothic church mysteriously buried underground. If you walk to the bottom of it, you find a kiosk, and on payment of a small sum, you can buy a ticket to climb up through its levels and platforms up ever-narrowing stone stairs, to get the finest view of Edinburgh available other than the one from the top of the neighbouring mountain, Arthur's Seat.

This is the Scott Monument, one of the few surviving physical traces of the Victorian popular passion for the verse romances and historical novels of Sir Walter Scott between 1800 and 1830, a passion that petered out round about the 1920s.[1] Conceived on a massive scale (standing over 61 metres high, with 287 steps), ornamented with no fewer than sixty-four statues of Scott's characters, and arching over a huge marble statue of the Wizard of the North himself, it was designed both as a visual précis of his opus and as a national tribute to his comprehensive romancing of the past. It is not just the sheer size and height of the monument (the largest in the world ever erected to any writer) that bears witness to the Victorian sense of Scott's cultural importance, it is underscored also by the length of time over which the monument was progressively and expensively elaborated. First mooted just after Scott's death in 1832, work began on building the spire in 1838 (a year after pushier Glasgow had managed to put up a huge column topped with a figure of the poet outside *their* railway station); it would be completed in the autumn of 1844. The statue of Scott, an afterthought, was commissioned from one of the era's top sculptors, John Steell, and installed in 1846. Thereafter, one of the monument's landings was elaborately fitted out with stained glass in 1857, and subsequently developed as the Museum Room in 1871. Although in 1844 the monument was only adorned with four statues, by 1871 the total of statues had reached thirty-two. An additional thirty-two smaller statuettes were added in 1881 by public subscription; perching like opportunistic pigeons in every last available niche, they are testimony to the century's continuing and growing sense of Scott's position as *the* historian of the national romance. By the end of the century, therefore, Scott and his works were spectacularly realized at the heart of Edinburgh, Scott's birthplace, city home, and ancient capital of the nation.

The monument was designed to express the grandeur of Scott's vision and to make it co-extensive with national identity as the imaginative heart of Scotland; east, west, north, and south, Scott's characters gaze out over a Scotland which for the Victorians was suffused with a new 'romantic interest', as Lady Frances Shelley put it in a fan-letter to Scott as early as 1819.[2] In the nineteenth century it would have seemed inconceivable that the monument would outlast Britain's popular reading pleasure in Scott. Indeed, the inscription on the plaque buried beneath the foundations envisaged itself as insurance against every sort of apocalyptic disaster *except* the forgetting of Scott. Imagining a moment aeons in the future when it might be unearthed by archaeologists of a succeeding civilization because 'all the surrounding structures are crumbled to dust / By the decay of Time, or by Human or Elemental Violence', the plaque was to testify that it was on 15 August 1840 that the monument's foundation was laid in honour of Scott, 'Whose admirable Writings were … thought likely to be remembered / Long after this act of Gratitude / On the part of this first generation of Admirers / Should be forgotten'.[3] In 1902, it was still possible to write that 'every part of Scotland is Scotland', but a little over a hundred years later the very reverse of the situation those Victorian admirers envisaged has come to pass.[4] The monument has actually survived Scott's reputation, to become for the majority of tourists debouching from the station merely a blackened viewing platform, offering convenient views of Holyrood, Arthur's Seat, the Castle, and, beyond the New Town, the Firth of Forth, overlooking an Edinburgh no longer and forever Scott's 'ain town', and at the centre of a country no longer 'Scott country'. Even the name of the train station no longer recalls to the popular memory the extraordinary sequence of novels and tales by 'the Author of Waverley' that followed the anonymous publication in 1814 of Scott's first novel, *Waverley*, and continued until Scott's death in 1832.

My enterprise here is to revivify something of the inception, development, and decay of the Victorian sense of Scotland as 'Scott country'.

I shall be sketching the ways that, in romancing history and historicizing romance, Scott's narratives transformed the way that Victorians read Scotland, and in so doing, transformed tourism to the country. Under Scott's influence, established visual pleasures of landscape became newly saturated with traditionary and historic associations. These associations were helpfully strung onto a memorable narrative, attached to enchanting creatures of the imagination, and supplied with an inbuilt mode and language of emotional response, making them retrievable and repeatable as a complete virtual experience for the first time. Populating the already picturesque with historical romance, Scott thus, as Murray Pittock has argued, 'helped create a fictional and poetic framework for both cultural and landscape tourism'.[5] Looking back from the vantage point of 1847, William Howitt described the impact of the publishing sensation that Scott's works represented thus: 'The whole land seemed astir with armies, insurrections, pageantries of love, and passages of sorrow, that for twenty years kept the enraptured public in a trance ... of one accumulating marvel and joy'.[6]

Before setting out to explore what remains of the evidence for Scott-inspired Victorian tourist itineraries around 'Scott country', it is as well to note that the practice of literary tourism (by which I mean the practice of visiting, actually or virtually, sites with literary associations) did not necessarily exclude other sorts of travel – that principally invested in the picturesque or sublime of landscape for example, or that pursuing antiquities, or that interested in agricultural or urban development, or that pursuing pleasures whether those offered by sport or those offered by spas. Indeed, travellers would often dip between these modes of consuming the country they were exploring. Nor was nineteenth-century Scotland exclusively conceived as the imaginative domain of Scott; Burns had successfully asserted a prior claim to the territory of Ayrshire, and literary tourists throughout the century, especially those from France, were often as not in pursuit of aesthetic pleasures associated with the works of Ossian, poetry supposedly 'translated' from the ancient Gaelic by one James Macpherson that enjoyed a vogue in the late eighteenth and early nineteenth centuries.[7] However, in nineteenth-century Scotland, all these ways of consuming the natural and built landscape were tinged by the possibility of travelling and reading Scotland with reference to the works of Scott, which had in their totality set out to digest Scottish history, Scottish landscape, and Scottish manners, and in so doing, remade Scotland for an emergent nineteenth-century tourist sensibility. This sensibility is well-described by one early Victorian guidebook which remarks: 'The land which has been imprinted by the footstep of genius, or by the beings of its creation, can never fail to produce a deep and enthusiastic interest. The anxious eye searches for the haunts of those whom history has chronicled, and the fancy feels charmed to revel with the creatures of another's imagination'.[8]

For anyone interested in literary tourism, Scott is a central figure. He is crucial to the development of the phenomenon both because he inaugurates certain types of literary tourism in Britain and because he develops and exploits others to an unprecedented degree. Scott's birthplace was never enshrined as a tourist attraction because it was pulled down rather too early, but his grave did become a tourist destination.[9] With his choice of last resting-place at Dryburgh Abbey as especially appropriate not merely to his ancient birth and social pretensions but to his *oeuvre* as antiquarian and romantic, Scott exploited to the full a pre-existing sense of the drama of the poet's grave. With the building of his fantastical house Abbotsford, designed from the outset as a cryptic showcase for 'the Author of Waverley', Scott invented the notion of displaying the writer's house as a workplace of genius. With the enormous success of his narrative poems, especially *The Lady of the Lake* (1810) and the associated rush to view the Highland charms of the place in which Scott had set his romance, Loch Katrine, Scott inspired in his readers for the first time the urge to visit particular places in Britain in memory of events that had never happened outside the pages of a book. But the most spectacular of his effects was undoubtedly the diffusion of fictional characters and events drawn from his *oeuvre* across a range of historically verifiable and re-visitable places locatable first on the map of Scotland, then of England, and finally of largish parts of Europe, an achievement which arguably inaugurated the whole notion of the literary 'country'. In its heyday, the idea of 'Scott country' would bind together author and fictions within a single itinerary, whether actually travelled or simply imagined by a reader sunk within the comfort of an armchair.

8.1 Itineraries

Critics have long recognized that Scott's writings frequently both provide models for and draw on existing discourses of tourism. James Holloway and Lindsay Etherington suggested that the dreamy island retirees of *The Lady of the Lake* were themselves models for tourist pleasure in their shedding of professional and social identities.[10] John Glendening has noted the way that Edward Waverley, hero of the first of Scott's novels, *Waverley* (1814), acts very much like a tourist, 'a spectator and collector of second-hand experience', as he travels from his English home into Scotland. In chronicling Waverley's adventures as he is caught up in the Jacobite rebellion of 1745, Scott effectively sells Scotland to an English touristic constituency, Glendening argues, 'by relegating actual romance to the country's Highland past while simultaneously releasing for the present a sentimental, commodifiable echo or afterglow of romance appropriate for vicarious consumption'. Like a tourist, too, Waverley comes safely home.[11]

But although contemporaries frequently suggested that Scott's work invented the taste which he so spectacularly exploited, this would be to overstate the case. It was more that the sensibility was already there, waiting to be popularized. It is possible, in any event, to trace the very first stirrings of Scott tourism as early as 1801, when John Stoddart published his two-volume *Remarks on Local Scenery and Manners in Scotland during the Years 1799 and 1800*. Stoddart made a point of visiting the Border country, noting that 'it is no small addition to these lovely landscapes, that they are almost all stamped with poetic celebrity', an allusion to the border ballads that would be collected in Scott's volumes of *The Minstrelsy of the Scottish Border* (1802–3). He visited Smailholm Tower (mentioning the connection with Scott's early verse-romance 'The Eve of St John') and the environs of 'Loch Ketterine', not just because of its 'celebrity' as a beautiful landscape, but because it served as the setting for Scott's ballad 'Glen Finglas'.[12] Subsequent Scott tourism was strongly organized around three bestselling poems, *The Lay of the Last Minstrel* (1805), *Marmion* (1808), and *The Lady of the Lake* (1810). Elizabeth Grant recalled passing through the Border country on her way to the Highlands as a child in 1812 and her excitement in travelling through that 'classic ground': the family baggage contained all three poems.[13] Of these poems, by far the most influential in inspiring tourism was the last; on its publication, the Trossachs, known since 1759 and celebrated for its beauty since the 1780s, surged in tourist popularity.[14] Critical to this itinerary was the sense that the experience of place was an indispensable supplement to the reading experience: 'The best way to read "The Lady of the Lake" is to see the Trossachs; the best way to see the Trossachs is to read "The Lady of the Lake". There is a peculiar affinity between the poem and the country that makes each indispensable to each other'.[15]

With the publication of the Waverley novels as a series from 1814 onwards, enthusiasts began to develop itineraries that combined interest in more than one text. Admirers of *Rob Roy* (1817) could conveniently visit its setting as well as taking in the standard *Lady of the Lake* itinerary and strolling up to Bracklinn Falls above Callender to the site of Burleigh's hide-out in *Old Mortality*.[16] In 1818, for example, the actor William Charles Macready supplemented his tour of the settings of *The Lady of the Lake* with a detour to St Fillan's Well (mentioned in *Marmion*) and jaunts to Balquihidder (to see the grave of Rob Roy, the original of Scott's hero), Rob Roy's cave on the eastern shore of Loch Lomond, the crypt of Glasgow cathedral (where Frank Osbaldistone meets Rob Roy), and Glasgow's Salt Market ('the residence of Bailie Jarvie'). Two years later, in 1820, William Howitt, having visited Loch Katrine, was also guided around the Rob Roy locations by Patrick Graham, vicar of Aberfoyle, who eleven years previously had acted as guide to Scott himself.[17] In 1824, Mrs Hughes of Uffington visited the author at Abbotsford but also came north to visit Glasgow for the purpose of seeing places depicted in *Rob Roy*; her diary records seeing the crypt under the cathedral, the garden outside (scene of an aborted duel), and the bridge where the outlaw and Osbaldistone meet.[18]

As the series of the Waverley novels extended, so did the possibility of further hybrid tours. Edinburgh itself, for example, helpfully combined the settings of *Marmion* with those of *Waverley*, *The Heart of Midlothian* (1818), and the much later *Chronicles of the Canongate* (1827). The meeting of Lord Menteith in the *Legend of Montrose* (1819) is set in the pass of Leney, which also features in *The Lady of the Lake*. The Grey Mare's Tail waterfall appears both in *Marmion* and was identified as another model for Burleigh's hide-out in *Old Mortality* (1816); it debouches from St Mary's loch, itself the subject of a famous description in *The Lay of the Last Minstrel*. Such itineraries might even extend into England: one French traveller, Joseph Amédée Pichot, on arriving in London in the early 1820s, records the associations of Richmond, London, with Jeanie Deans and while travelling up to Scotland comments on *Ivanhoe* as he reaches Sheffield and Doncaster. Once in Scotland, he is more conventionally comprehensive: in addition to the Loch Katrine extended tour, he takes in the Borders, including a visit to Abbotsford itself as Scott's guest.[19] This effect was magnified by the notes and introductions written for the so-called Magnum Opus edition of 1830–2, which revised the entire series to date of the Waverley novels. They identified further originals for Scott's fictions, often imbuing places with associations derived from more than one work.[20] The Falls of Ledard (above the shores of Loch Ard) were now identified not only as the site of Helen MacGregor's picnic in *Rob Roy*, but also as the spot that Scott had had in mind in *Waverley* when he described his heroine Flora MacIvor staging her Gaelic song for the benefit of the dazzled Edward Waverley. The cave of Rob Roy was also now identifiable as the cave in which Waverley was held captive.

If the introductions and notes to the Magnum Opus increased the depth and range of associations between the fictions and localities, they also had the effect of combining the history behind the fictions with a history of Scott's life as a writer. The result was that the figure of Scott himself increasingly appeared in the foreground of this emergent Scott country. This was an effect that had a fairly long history; after the great success of *Marmion*, Scott's delighted publisher, Archibald Constable, had commissioned a much-reproduced portrait of him by Henry Raeburn, musing against a backdrop of the ruins of Hermitage Castle.[21] The long-standing usefulness of this tactic as representing a sense of Scott's transformation and appropriation of locale is underscored by two other versions of this portrait which are extant. A version made for Scott the next year showed the same figure but this time against a backdrop of the Yarrow; a French version of this portrait published in 1829 had changed this background to Melrose Abbey.[22] Scott had also been painted by Edwin Landseer as a literary tourist paying tribute to the Scots poet Thomas the Rhymer by musing in the 'classic, or rather fairy ground' of the Rhymer's Glen, a piece of real estate that he had taken care to purchase and annex as part of the Abbotsford estate and to which he often took his guests.[23] In designing the Magnum Opus, Scott would give a good deal of time and attention to the commissioning of expensive illustrations by cutting-edge artists, including the landscape specialist J. M. W. Turner. As Gillen d'Arcy Wood has remarked, Turner's topographical illustrations were designed not only to recognize tourist interest, but to model it by depicting Scott with his friends and other anonymous tourists 'as emblematic consumers of trademark Scott landscapes'.[24] These depictions of Scott combined with the flood of biographical material that appeared after Scott's death, including John Gibson Lockhart's lengthy biography; the result was that, for example, a visit to Clovenfords would yield not just a glimpse of the room in which Scott met up with Wordsworth, but Traquair House, supposed original for Tully-Veolan in *Waverley*, and the original for the cottage of the Black Dwarf. It would mean that for future tourists 'Scott country' would be occupied not just by Scott's creatures of the imagination, but by the Wizard of the North himself.

More generally, the sense of the topographical specificity of Scott's works was developed and furthered by visual depiction across a variety of media, commissioned both by the author himself in pursuit of commercial and reputational advantage and by others anxious to cash in where possible. Stage adaptations particularly exploited contemporary interest in accurate depictions of real scenery. In 1824, one grumpy but intelligent commentator ascribed the transformation of the environs of Loch Katrine by hordes of urban tourists to the contemporary dissemination of *The Lady of the Lake* and *Rob Roy* in the theatre:

> In the early days when I wandered first among these wild and lovely regions, there was an old romance in everything ... But the mystic portal has been thrown open, and the world has rushed in, dispersing all these fairy visions. ... Barouches and gigs, cocknies and fishermen and poets, Glasgow weavers and travelling haberdashers, now swarm in every resting place, and meet us in every avenue. As Rob Roy now blusters at Covent-Garden and the Lyceum, and as Aberfoyle is gone to Wapping, so Wapping and the Strand must come to Aberfoyle.... [R]ecollections of ... the smell and smoke of gas lights, and cries of 'Music, off, off' confound the other senses and recall base realities where there was once a delicious vision.... You talk of Rob Roy's cave, or of Inversnaid, or Ben Lomond, and your hearer immediately figures to himself a few feet of painted canvas and twenty-four fiddlers.[25]

Such visualization was not confined to the theatre. From very early on, Scott and his publishers commissioned illustrations to his poems and fictions which connected them ever more insistently to the places that had inspired them.[26] Topographical illustrations 'from designs taken on the spot' by John Schetky first appeared in 1808 by way of ornament to *The Lay of the Last Minstrel*. *The Lady of the Lake* was provided with not one but two sets of illustrations (by Westall and by Cook) in 1810 and 1811. The Magnum Opus was embellished with expensive illustrations, including by Turner; and this was a practice that would continue throughout the century in later editions of Scott's complete works, notably the Abbotsford and the Dryburgh. Running alongside the collected editions, expensive free-standing books of engravings began to appear. These included titles such as Pernot's *Vues Pittoresques de L'Ecosse* (1827), *Heath's Picturesque Annual* (1835), the handsome volumes of *Landscape-Historical Illustrations of Scotland, and the Waverley Novels: from drawings by J. M. W. Turner, Balmer, Bentley, Chisholm, Hart, Harding, McClise [sic], Melville etc etc. Comic Illustrations by G. Cruikshank. Descriptions by the Rev .G. N. Wright M.A. etc.* (1836) and Charles Tilt's *Illustrations: Landscape, Historical and Antiquarian to the Poetic Works of Sir Walter Scott* (1836). A notable feature of these books was the interspersion of documentary depiction of the location as it appeared at that time with 'historical' pieces that imagined Scott's characters against an identifiable backdrop. *Vues Pittoresques*, for example, occasionally shows figures drawn from Scott's works in the foreground, including one of the 'gallant grey' in the foreground of the Trossachs.[27] The net result was to build a sense of Scotland as 'Scott country', haunted by historical phantoms. Thus, *Heath's Picturesque Annual* advertised its project as follows: 'The country to be illustrated was Scotland – the country of Scott – the country where the spirits of history, summoned by his enchantments, haunt visibly its mouldering temples and ruined castles. ... It was determined to illustrate, at the same moment, SCOTT and SCOTLAND – to delineate, with the utmost possible fidelity, existing scenes, and yet to superadd a moral interest, by peopling them with the creations of genius'.[28]

Something of the practicable and conventional scope of Scott country as it had come to exist by mid-century can be glimpsed from an annotated copy of *Black's Shilling Guide to Edinburgh and its Environs* (1853) held in the Bodleian. It records on its back cover in neat handwriting its owner's own Scott-inspired excursions undertaken in September that year out of Edinburgh. She spent the day of the 21st travelling along the valley of the river Tweed south of Edinburgh, visiting Dryburgh Abbey, Melrose Abbey, and Abbotsford. On the 25th she forayed westwards to visit the Trossachs and Loch Katrine, and on the 26th she took the boat down Loch Lomond. On 2 October she returned down south. Three days, therefore, were sufficient to visit grave, home, and sites associated with *The Lay of the Last Minstrel*, *The Lady of the Lake*, and *Rob Roy*, and quite possibly this tourist may also have taken an interest in the Edinburgh locations that Scott evoked in *Waverley* and *The Heart of Midlothian*, though in the absence of further annotation, this is just guesswork. A grander tourist, Queen Victoria, made a similar set of excursions in the summer of 1867: on 22 August she viewed Melrose, Abbotsford, and Smailholm Tower in the Border country, and on 1 and 2 September she travelled up to the Trossachs and Loch Lomond to view sites associated with *The Lady of the Lake* and *Rob Roy*.[29]

8.2   Armchair itineraries

Energetic though Victoria was, she actually succeeded in visiting rather few of the locations associated with Scott and his writings, although they were certainly the most celebrated. Indeed, faced with the vast panorama of all the Waverley novels taken together, the most energetic of literary tourists might well fall back in the face of the physical and logistic rigours of 'doing' all of Scott country. Guidebooks, devised with practical considerations paramount, were unable to offer a plausible way of actually touring the whole of Scott country as conceived by contemporaries – even the glossiest gazetteer, such as John Marius Wilson's *The Land of Scott; or, Tourist's Guide to Abbotsford, the Country of the Tweed and Its Tributaries, and St Mary's Loch* (1858), belies its title and could, as its subtitle admits, only plausibly cover a fairly limited tract of country. Travelling the entirety of Scott country was increasingly possible less in fact than in fancy. More feasible was a comprehensive yet comfortable virtual tour enabled by the books of illustrations that I have already remarked upon. *Landscape-Historical Illustrations of Scotland, and the Waverley Novels*, for example, produces a virtual tour by chopping out Scott's scenic descriptions from his narrative, amplifying them with further guidebook-style information, speculating on probable originals if there is dispute, and appending them to facing illustrations accordingly. This book, although it limits the scope of Scott's writings, aspires to provide a comprehensive depiction of Scotland: the preface to *Landscape-Historical Illustrations* notes that 'wherever it was possible to ascertain the precise locality which constituted the original of the Novelist, our *Landscape* illustration has been designed from it; exhibiting, therefore, at the same moment, a true and characteristic View in Scotland' and remarks further that 'in speaking of Scottish scenery, our author has evinced the most unconfined topographical knowledge, and wandered, with the most varied fancy, over the romantic portions of every county in Caledonia; so that Illustrations of Scott may be considered identical with those of Scotland'.[30] By the early twentieth century, an appetite for increased comprehensiveness is evident in titles directed more at the armchair than the actual tourist, such as W. S. Crockett's definitive *The Scott Country* (1902) and James Baikie's *The Charm of the Scott Country* (1927). These were impracticable except for a real enthusiast; in 1913, Charles Olcutt published his account of a protracted tour with his wife in 1911 to all sites in Scotland associated either with Scott himself or with his poems and fiction as *The Country of Sir Walter Scott*: 'Knowing that he had derived his inspiration from an intimate knowledge of the country, we sought to follow in his footsteps as far as possible'.[31]

In the end, it was perhaps the potential scope of Scott country that was its undoing. There had been some sporadic interest in Scott's English settings throughout the century. Tellingly, this was mostly evinced by travellers from beyond Britain and tended to focus around the London and Stratford itinerary (this last offering reasonable access to the ruins of

Kenilworth Castle, inspiration for *Kenilworth*, 1821). Every now and then local pride would endeavour to appropriate the discourse of 'Scott country', as in Thomas Eastwood's *Ivanhoe-land* (1865) and a few other mappings of what was Scott's most popular novel.[32] Still, animating England with Scott's magic never seemed entirely plausible. William Sharp's periodical essay 'Scott-land', published with other pieces in a volume entitled *Literary Geography* in 1907, and accompanied as was now conventional with maps, including one of the 'Chief Localities of the Scottish Romances', one to accompany the poems, and one detailing Scott's English settings, mused at length upon the extent and nature of Scott country:

> It is not easy to define 'the Scott country.' If we admit that the lands which it comprises are those which in more or less degree owe somewhat to the magic of his genius, we have to cross not only the Scottish border and the Welsh marches, but to seek remoter regions in Belgium and northern France, by the Rhine, and in Switzerland and in sunny Provence, and eastwards again to Bavaria and the Viennese southlands ... in this wide sense, the Scott country extends from the Hebridean Isles and the coasts of Argyll and the Isle of Man on the west, to the Syria of the tales of the Crusades, and to the Byzantine empire of *Count Robert* and the India of *The Surgeon's Daughter* on the east; and from the Shetland Isles of *The Pirate* on the north, to Aix, the ancient capital of Provence, and to Toledo, the heart of Spain, on the south.

Sharp then considers the possibility of 'taking as Scott's country solely the lands intimately related to him by natural ties – the region of his birth and upbringing and habitual domicile'. Discarding that as a solution because it excludes 'the wider country (that is yet within our own kingdom) whereon he was equally at home, the country of his genius', he pauses over a formulation that Scott country is the 'country of the human heart', provides nonetheless a detailed tabulation of works and their settings for the use of 'those who would .... whether in fact or fancy ... perambulate Scott's country', and at last develops a definition which neatly binds together the biographical and the national:

> [T]he 'country' of a great writer ... is that where life first unfolded, and where its roots are, and which the heart enshrines. And that country, in the instance of Scott, is the little northern land of mountain and flood, from the Kame of Hoy in the North Sea to the Crooks of Dee beyond Solway Water.[33]

A year later, the same sense that Scott country is geographically over-extended also informed W. S. Crockett's narrower solution to the same problem: he argues that Scott's literary terrain is

> too large a space for the homage of the heart. There must be a more personal definition – one which can be grasped with a conscious affection. What is peculiarly the country of Sir Walter must be taken to be that where the greater part of his outward and actual as well as his imaginative life was passed, the region which lay closest to his heart and memory; which he knew best and loved most ... and where ... he sleeps well after the long, hard day.[34]

Like the Scott Monument, with its effigy of Scott below and efflorescence of characters above, both of these writers endeavour to bind Scott as author to his vast *oeuvre* and to his position as national historian by appealing to biographical fact.

The anxiety that both Sharp and Crockett betray was well-justified – the second decade of the century saw the beginnings of decay in the romances' power to enchant all ages, sexes, classes, and nationalities. This was arguably in part caused by the very thing that had made the invention of Scott country possible in the first place. The diffusion of Scott's characters across the landscape and their naturalization within it was originally rendered possible by their historical or quasi-historical status as escapees from historical fiction, but this meant that eventually Scott no longer held authorial copyright over them. As they and their stories morphed into received school textbook 'history', and as Scott's works themselves slowly ceased to be set texts in the nation's schools, Scott's authorial labour of imagination progressively vanished. Present-day Loch Katrine provides clear evidence of this: the modern information boards that punctuate the margin of the lake retail the documentary and traditionary material that Scott drew on for his poem, but make little reference to the poem itself. Scott's historically-minded footnotes have outlasted his romance. Similar evidence is provided by Smailholm Tower. It is filled at present with a display of costume dolls in glass cases. Among them Scott is depicted, first as the small boy sent to convalesce with his grandparents at neighbouring Sandyknowe Farm, and then as the young man who, in the company of his friends, set out to collect the ballads that he eventually published as *Minstrelsy of the Scottish Border*. Smailholm celebrates Scott as ballad-collector, but simultaneously forgets him as the great romancer of the nation. It acknowledges him as a conserver of Scottish history, rather than as the inventor of 'Scott-land'. Yet as those little costume-dolls suggest, it is biographical narrative that still just about maintains Scott's hold upon the landscape of today's Scotland. It lingers on in the shape of a plaque telling not so much of the nation's affection for Scott, but of Scott's affection for his nation; put up in c.1993, it can be found in the lay-by that overlooks the river Tweed and the Eildon Hills. The inscription reads:

> Scott's View. Sir Walter Scott loved the Borders landscape, history and people with a passion. He was the most popular writer of his age: when he died his funeral procession was over a mile long. It took his body from his home at Abbotsford to his tomb at Dryburgh Abbey down the hill to your left. Tradition tells how his horses stopped here on the way, just as they had done when their master was alive so he could enjoy his favourite view.
>> Breathes there the man, with soul so dead,
>> Who never to himself hath said
>> 'This is my own, my native land...'

Just for a moment, this plaque suggests, the traveller can still look through Scott's eyes, seeing Scott country re-emerge through the gathering mists of time, and feel an antiquarian surge of local and national passion.

Notes

1. This essay draws upon and extends work published in my *The Literary Tourist: Readers and Places in Romantic & Victorian Britain* (Basingstoke: Palgrave Macmillan, 2006).
2. Frances, Lady Shelley to Sir Walter Scott, 16 August 1819; qtd in *The Diary of Frances Lady Shelley 1787–1817*, ed. Richard Edgcumbe, 2 vols (London: John Murray, 1912), 2: 62.
3. A copy of this inscription is on display at the Writer's Museum, Edinburgh.
4. W. S. Crockett, *The Scott Country* (London: Adam and Charles Black, 1902), Preface.
5. Murray Pittock, ed., *The Reception of Sir Walter Scott in Europe* (London: Continuum, 2006), 3–4. For further general discussion of tourism inspired by Scott see Pittock, 'Scott and the British Tourist', in *English Romanticism and the Celtic World*, ed. Gerard Carruthers and Alan Rawes (Cambridge: Cambridge University Press, 2003), 151–66.
6. William Howitt, *Homes and Haunts of the Most Celebrated British Poets*, 2 vols (London: Richard Bentley, 1847), 2: 146.
7. On tourism associated with Burns see Watson, *The Literary Tourist*, 68–86.
8. *Lumsden and Son's Guide to the Romantic Scenery of Loch Lomond, Loch-Kethurin, The Trossachs, &c....* 3rd edn (Glasgow: Lumsden, 1838), 22.

9. Howitt (1847) quotes Robert Chambers's anecdote of a conversation with Scott regarding the demolition in 1825. Chambers reportedly 'took the liberty of expressing his belief that more money might have been made of it, and the public *much more* gratified, if it had remained to be shown as the birthplace of a man who had written so many popular books. "Ay, ay", said Sir Walter, "that is very well; but I am afraid it would have been necessary for me to die first, and that, you know, would not have been so comfortable"' (Howitt, *Homes and Haunts*, 2: 164).

10. James Holloway and Lindsay Etherington, *The Discovery of Scotland: The Appreciation of Scottish Scenery through Two Centuries of Painting* (Edinburgh: National Gallery of Scotland, 1978), 109. For an extension and variation on this reading see Watson, *The Literary Tourist*, 156–7.

11. John Glendening, *The High Road: Romantic Tourism, Scotland, and Literature, 1720–1820* (Basingstoke: Macmillan, 1997), 174, 180, 179.

12. John Stoddart, *Remarks on Local Scenery and Manners in Scotland during the Years 1799 and 1800*, 2 vols (London: William Miller, 1801), 2: 278, 307.

13. Elizabeth Grant, *Memoirs of a Highland Lady* [1898] (1950), 112–3; cited in Holloway and Etherington, *The Discovery of Scotland*, 92.

14. For the date of 1759, see Glendening on the evidence of Lord Breadalbane's letters (*The High Road*, 234). For more details of the tourist boom inspired by *The Lady of the Lake*, see Watson, 'Readers of Romantic Locality: Tourists, Loch Katrine and *The Lady of the Lake*', in *Romantic Localities: Europe Writes Place*, ed. Christophe Bode and Jacqueline Labbe (London: Pickering & Chatto, 2010), 67–80.

15. Charles S. Olcutt, *The Country of Sir Walter Scott* (London: Cassell, 1913), 70.

16. For a representative and detailed guide to the Trossachs and Loch Lomond tour as pursued in 1860, for example, see *Oliver and Boyd's Scottish Tourist* (Edinburgh: Oliver and Boyd, 1860). For the Borderland tour as it was pursued in the early years of the twentieth century, see *The Land of Scott Guidebook* (Galashiels: A. Walker & Son, c.1903). For the itineraries of both tours, as recommended by Thomas Cook in the 1850s, see *Franklin's Itinerary for the Trosachs and the Royal Route through the Highlands of Scotland* (Edinburgh and Glasgow: John Menzies, [1877]).

17. *Macready's Reminiscences, and Selections from his Diaries and Letters*, ed. Sir Frederick Pollock, 2 vols (London: Macmillan & Co., 1875), 1: 182–7; Howitt, 1: 153.

18. W. Forbes Gray, *The Scott Centenary Handbook: A Guide to Edinburgh, Abbotsford, and the 'Rob Roy' Country* (N.p.: n.p., n.d.), 115.

19. Joseph Jean M. C. Amédée Pichot, *Historical and Literary Tour of a Foreigner in England and Scotland*, 2 vols (London: for Saunders and Otley, 1825), 2: 243, 274, 366–92, 468–83.

20. On the touristic appeal of the Turner illustrations: 'It is this minute illustration, this transporting of ourselves to the actual locality of the scene that interests us'. *Quarterly Review* (July 1844), 168–99: 196–7. Cited by Gillen d'Arcy Wood, 'Working Holiday: Turner as Waverley Tourist', *Wordsworth Circle* 31.2 (Spring 2000), 87.

21. For Raeburn's portrait, see the Walter Scott Digital Archive, Edinburgh University Library, Web, 11 Feb. 2011.

22. *Illustrations de Walter Scott* (Paris: Henri Gaugain et Cie, 1829). See Gilles Soubigou, 'French Portraits of Sir Walter Scott: Images of the Great Unknown', *Scottish Studies Review* 7.1 (Spring 2006), 24–37.

23. For the Landseer painting, see George G. Napier, *The Homes and Haunts of Sir Walter Scott* (Glasgow: James Maclehose & Sons, 1897), 95; Washington Irving, *Abbotsford and Newstead Abbey* (Paris: A. W. Galignani, 1835), 39.

24. Wood, 'Working Holiday', 83–8: 85, 87.

25. John MacCulloch, *The Highlands and Western Isles of Scotland, containing Descriptions of their Scenery and Antiquities ... Founded as a series of annual journeys between the years 1811 and 1821, and forming a universal guide to that country, in letters to Sir Walter Scott, Bart.*, 4 vols (London: Longman, Hurst, Rees, Orme, Brown, and Green, 1824), 1: 194, 196.

26. On the illustration of Scott's works more generally, see Richard Maxwell, 'Walter Scott, Historical Fiction, and the Genesis of the Victorian Illustrated Book', in Maxwell, ed., *The Victorian Illustrated Book* (Charlottesville and London: University Press of Virginia, 2002), 1–51; Richard Hill, 'The Illustration of the Waverley Novels: Scott and Popular Illustrated Fiction', in *Scottish Literary Review* 1.1 (Spring/Summer, 2009), 69–88.

27. François Alexandre Pernot, *Vues pittoresques de l'Ecosse, avec un texte explicatif extrait en grand dessinées d'après Nature* (Bruxelles: Wahlen et Dewasme, 1827), 71, 83.

28. *Heath's Picturesque Annual* (1835), iii–iv.

29. Victoria, *More Leaves from the Journal of a Life in the Highlands from 1862–1882* (London: Smith, Elder & Co., 1884), 81–137.

30. *Landscape-Historical Illustrations of Scotland, and of the Waverley Novels ... 2* vols (London, Paris, America: Fisher, Son & Co., n.d.), Preface.

31. Olcutt, *The Country of Sir Walter Scott*, xiv.

32. William Holt Yates, *Ivanhoe Illustrated* (1846); Thomas S. Badger Eastwood, *Ivanhoe-land; being Notes on Men and Books connected with the Town and neighbourhood of Rotherham, in the county of York ...* (Rotherham: A. Gilling, 1865); Henry EcRoyd Smith, *The History of Coningsborough Castle, with Glimpses of Ivanhoe-land* (Worksop: for Robert White, 1887). The first includes an elaborate map.

33. William Sharp, *Literary Geography* (London, 1907), 57, 59, 60, 64, 70, 73.

34. W. S. Crockett, *Footsteps of Scott* (Edinburgh and London: T. N. Foulis, 1908), 5.

9

'Every Hill has Its History, Every Region Its Romance': Travellers' Constructions of Wales, 1844–1913

Katie Gramich

One of the earliest works which we might today classify as travel literature of the home tour variety was written about Wales by a Norman-Welsh author, Gerald of Wales, or Gerallt Gymro, as he is known in Welsh. Admittedly, Gerallt's travels in 1188 had what would nowadays be regarded as a sinister ulterior motive, in that he was accompanying Archbishop Baldwin on a mission to acquire volunteers to embark on a Crusade. Nevertheless, Gerallt produced during his travels idiosyncratic yet often highly perceptive commentaries in Latin on what he specifically calls 'this my native country ... describ[ing] the genius of its inhabitants, so entirely distinct from that of other nations'.[1] Gerald, in his *Itinerarium Kambriae* (1191) and *Descriptio Kambriae* (1193), may be seen as one of the earliest in a long line of observant pedestrian travellers curiously examining the landscape and settlements of Wales, along with the history and traits of its inhabitants. Like most travellers, he is by no means an unbiased observer, identifying his own birthplace, Manorbier in Pembrokeshire, as 'the sweetest spot in Wales', but also producing some trenchant comments whose astuteness still reverberates, such as (of the Welsh): 'If they would be inseparable, they would be insuperable'.[2] Gerallt is an informed, impassioned, hybridized native traveller, an erudite Anglo-Norman Welshman whose home tour travel books might stand as archetypes of this most slippery and unstable of genres.

In later centuries, the majority of the authors who turn their steps towards Wales are English or European travellers seeking out accessible Otherness, what Gerallt called that 'distinctness from other nations' which sits on their own doorsteps. Nevertheless, a number of much later Welsh people, like Gerallt himself, decided to tour the precincts of their *own* land: authors such as Owen Morgan Edwards, the brilliant Welsh-language author who set out in the late nineteenth century to 'raise up the old homeland to its former glory'.[3] English and Welsh travellers in Wales predictably construct distinct versions of the country in their travel narratives, though there are some intriguing similarities, too, as will be seen in the analysis that follows.

Victorian travel writing about Wales is noticeably different from the work of the many Romantic travellers who came in search of an experience of the sublime (though they often returned with something very different from that!). The Victorians appeared to be more interested in the sociological and the cultural, as opposed to the purely aesthetic, attractions of Wales. A writer such as Anne Beale, an English governess who settled in Carmarthenshire and identified strongly with her adoptive country, presented in her 1844 work, *The Vale of the Towey*, a sympathetic account of the Welsh peasantry to her English readership. After the devastatingly negative picture of Wales as a benighted and even barbaric country presented in the 1847 'Blue Books' government report on the state of education in Wales, the later nineteenth century saw a concerted effort by both native and foreign travel writers to rebuild the old, maligned land.[4] By the end of the century, thanks partly to the ministrations of native writers, like Owen Morgan Edwards, who mounted a campaign to restore Wales to the esteem he felt was her due, and partly to the vogue for Celticity propagated by English writers such as Matthew Arnold and Alfred Lord Tennyson, Wales was poised to become not just a tourist destination well endowed with Gothic relics, but an autonomous country clamouring for a disestablished church and even home rule.[5]

According to Welsh Biography Online, 'few English writers have written more appreciatively of Wales'[6] than Anne Beale (1816–1900), who was the daughter of a Somerset gentleman farmer and his wife. She first came to Wales as a governess to the three children of the Rev. David Williams, curate of Llandyfeisant, near Llandeilo in Carmarthenshire, in 1840 at the age of twenty-five. In her 1844 travel book, *The Vale of the Towey*, she describes her first arrival in Wales thus:

> When I came hither, a stranger, I was struck by the loveliness of the country, as well as by the character, manners, and language of its primitive inhabitants …
>
> … I was going into Wales for the first time, and … the novelty and beauty of the scenery, together with the pure mountain air, dispelled whatever feelings of sadness had seized upon me …
>
> I had not expected to be at once so much 'at home' as I felt myself when I arrived at my journey's end, nor had I anticipated the

warmth and friendliness of manner that characterise the Welsh, who are neither distant nor cold, but easily approachable.[7]

It is clear from her writing that Beale was immediately attracted to her new environment and, in effect, fell in love with the place and its people, using them as subjects for much of her prolific later literary work, which appeared from the 1840s to the 1890s. Her representations of Wales and the Welsh evidently met with the approval of her native Welsh neighbours, as evidenced by the enthusiastic treatment given to her and her work in an 1858 book on *Llandeilo Vawr and its Neighbourhood, Past and Present* by Gwilym Teilo. In a section subtitled 'Eminent Characters', Beale is afforded a six-page encomium, in which she is described as 'accomplished', 'amiable', and 'gifted', while her work in *The Vale of the Towey* is praised as 'display[ing] great powers of description, and of giving colour to natural objects'. 'The setting of the book', Gwilym Teilo explains, is 'a village in this immediate neighbourhood, and the characters, so wittily portrayed, are its inhabitants. The delineations of some of them', he adds, 'are as true to nature as artistic skill could daguerrotype them'.[8] Yet even in her most positive representation of Welshness, the 1876 novel *The Pennant Family*, as Moira Dearnley points out, 'her emphasis is on the need for love and understanding between the indigenous population and the "interloper"', which, as Dearnley observes, 'points inexorably, in this novel, to a continued process of anglicization'.[9] In fact, Beale's attitude towards Welsh betrays some ambivalence; like Matthew Arnold some thirty years later, Beale seems to approve of Anglicization, while at the same time waxing lyrical about 'the grand old Welsh language'.[10] She speaks approvingly, for example, of those 'among the native peasantry, particularly those who dwell in the mountains ... who speak their fine ancient language in its original purity'.[11]

One of the aspects of Welsh life which prevents Anne Beale from identifying wholeheartedly with her adoptive home is the fact that she is separated from the 'Welsh peasantry' by a class divide. Maintenance of her class position is clearly quite important for Beale – she cannot afford to 'go native' completely because she cannot allow herself to compromise her status as a gentlewoman. Perhaps this anxiety was particularly acute for her on account of her original, rather ambivalent status as a governess – neither quite of the gentlefolk, nor yet a servant (interestingly, the 1844 census lists Anne Beale separately from the three servants of the household). Beale observes that many of the people she calls 'the Welsh peasantry' are 'miserably poor', but she blithely goes on to say that 'my business is not with them',[12] indicating unmistakably her class difference. Similarly, the adjectives 'primitive' and even 'primeval' are frequently used by Beale in describing both the landscape of the Towey valley and its inhabitants. Though we might regard this use of language as indicating a supercilious, even a colonial, attitude towards Wales, it is evident that the adjectives are being used positively in order to valorize place and people, but at the same time they serve to underline the alterity of Wales and the Welsh. At other points in the narrative, though, she is perfectly prepared to claim possession of a Welsh identity in telling usage of the first person plural, for instance, in describing Llandeilo as 'our town'[13] and to the habits of 'we country-folk'.[14] Indeed, Beale laments, 'Alas! that our sister England should send her most depraved children into Wales to teach them the art of populous cities, as yet but little cultivated in this Principality, where robberies are few and far between'.[15] Again, this positions Beale herself both in and of Wales, with a relation of kinship to England, 'our sister'. Wales is here seen as morally superior, while elsewhere it is seen as culturally superior to England in its retention of old folk customs, festivals, and legends which 'are fast going into forgetfulness in England'.[16]

In the second edition of *The Vale of The Towey*, reissued significantly under the title *Traits and Stories of the Welsh Peasantry* in 1849, Beale writes a preface to explain why there is no reference to what she calls the recent 'agrarian excitement' in South Wales, by which she means the Rebecca Riots. She states that these sketches were written before the outbreak of violence and, moreover, that such behaviour is completely untypical of the Welsh. Tellingly, she speaks of the riots as an outbreak of a 'disease' which has now been 'cured', asserting that 'our tranquil vales and mountains' have now returned to their former pacific state. It is interesting that she uses the possessive 'our' here, indicating perhaps not only her own sense of belonging to Wales but also, perhaps, a sense that Wales is now once more enfolded into the cohesive national identity of Great Britain. For this is surely the nature of Beale's particular construction of Welshness: while she is an enthusiastic admirer of Welsh difference and, to a degree, a participant in that different culture, she is also a proud Briton and an upholder of Empire. She constructs an autobiographical travel narrative in which she 'came hither, a stranger' and was surprised not only by the unexpected grandeur of the landscape but by the friendliness of the natives. Unlike the English Romantic travellers who preceded Beale in their journeys to Wales in search of sublime scenery, Beale clearly becomes intensely interested in the *people* of Wales; hence, the change of title from *The Vale of the*

Towey to *Traits and Stories of the Welsh Peasantry*. As she puts it in the conclusion of the latter volume: 'Instead of druidical remains, old heroes, and old castles, I find myself engaged with the men and women of to-day'.[17] Given that the Blue Books report condemning the Welsh peasantry in overtly racist terms was first published in 1848, it is not beyond the bounds of possibility that Anne Beale, far from thinking of herself as upholding the findings of the Commissioners sent to Wales by the British government, might on the contrary see herself as refuting them, by showing what the benign Welsh peasantry were 'really' like. This is not to deny that Beale's ideology is imperialist, but it is to suggest that Beale's construction of a Welshness in which she herself had a role probably meant that she saw herself as the defender of the 'proud Cambrians' rather than their detractor.

In his 2001 work *On Cosmopolitanism and Forgiveness*, Jacques Derrida speaks about what he calls the 'law of hospitality', which he sees as a fundamental to culture because it rests on performative relations with others who are proximate but unknowable. In fact, Derrida goes further to assert that 'hospitality is culture itself and not simply one ethic amongst others', going on to elaborate: 'Insofar as it has to do with *ethos*, that is, with residence, one's home, the familiar place of dwelling ... *ethics is hospitality*'.[18] Thus, the experience of 'coming hither, a stranger', and of being welcomed, is essentially an ethical encounter which is transformative of both self and other; this is the drama which is unexpectedly played out in Anne Beale's unassuming little travel book about the Vale of the Towey.

If Anne Beale was inspired by her travel to Wales to adopt an elective Welsh identity, the Welsh identity of Owen Morgan Edwards (1858–1920) was entirely home-grown. Brought up in a tiny cottage near Llanuwchlyn in north-west Wales, he gained a scholarship to Oxford University, became a History don, and later, ironically enough, a Government Chief Inspector of Schools, though his own early schooling had been unhappy and traumatic, since he suffered frequently from being punished with the notorious 'Welsh Not' for speaking Welsh.[19] In his campaign to raise the consciousness of his fellow countrymen of their own language, history, and culture, Edwards became a veritable one-man publishing industry, founding and editing magazines, fostering the careers of other Welsh writers, and writing prodigious numbers of books himself. Interestingly, and unexpectedly, one of the primary genres he worked in was travel writing. In addition to publishing works in Welsh about his own European travels, he also published a number of volumes of travels within Wales itself. Two of these, namely *Tro i'r*

De (*A Trip to the South*) and *Tro i'r Gogledd* (*A Trip to the North*) were both published in 1907. In the conclusion to the latter, he addresses the question of why a Welshman like himself should bother to write a travel book about Wales. He justifies his project by stating that Wales is, in fact, precisely the country in which Welsh people travel least, yet which they would most profit from knowing. He ends on a sentimental note:

> *'Mae'r oll yn gysegredig' – pob bryn a phant. Mae'r gwlad yn rhywbeth byw, nid yn fedd marw, dan ein traed. Mae i bob bryn ei hanes, i bob ardal ei rhamant.*[20]

> ['It is all sacred' – every hill and hollow. The land is something alive, not a dead grave under our feet. Every hill has its history, every region its romance.]

In *A Trip to the South* he meets an American-Welshman called Daniel Jones who is visiting Wales, having been away in America for over sixty years. When praised for his ability to speak Welsh, he responds *'O 'ryn ni yn yr America'n cofio am Gymru o flaen bob peth. Ein harwyddair ni yn yr America yw, – 'Fy'n iaith, fy ngwlad, fy nghenedl'.*[21] ['Oh, we in America remember Wales before anything else. Our motto in America is "My language, my country, my people."'] The American Welshman praises the contribution of the Welsh to the building of America (for example, Thomas Jefferson was a Welshman by blood, while fifteen of the signatures on the Declaration of Independence were by Welshmen). But Edwards concludes *'Yr wyf innau'n hoff o grwydro, ond fy ngweddi olaf fydd am fedd yng Nghymru'.*[22] ['I am fond of travel but my last prayer will be for a grave in Wales'.] This link between Wales and America is important for Edwards in that it cuts across the continuing quasi-colonial relationship between Wales and England which he questions. The American Welshman stands as an emblem of fidelity and independence, and his conversation about memorial stones and gravestones is also representative of a recurrent preoccupation of Edwards as a traveller: he is an inveterate visitor of such stones, and they stand quite literally as *lieux de memoire*, places of national and cultural significance, connoting survival, perdurability, and the importance of a collective memory of who we are and what this place means. Nevertheless, Edwards often strikes a note of nostalgia and loss:

> *Bum yn syllu'n hir, oddiar ben bryn ar y mynyddoedd sy'n amgylchu Llanidloes, tarddleoedd yr Hafren a'r Wy. Cofiwn nad oes odid ardal ar*

*lannau'r afonydd hyn heb golli eu Cymraeg, ac y mae Saesneg yn ymlid
yr hen iaith yn galed i fyny at fynhonellau'r ddwy afon . . . Nid mater o
golli iaith ydyw i ardal golli ei Chymraeg, – cyll nerth ei mheddwl ar yr
un pryd.*[23]

[I gazed for a long time from a hilltop amid the mountains which
encircle Llanidloes, the sources of the Severn and Wye. I remembered
that there was scarcely a place on the banks of these rivers which had
not lost its Welsh, and that English was pursuing the old language
hard right up to the sources of the two rivers ... Losing Welsh in a
region is not a matter of language loss alone – it also loses the force
of its own way of thinking at the same time.]

The Welsh landscape for Edwards, then, is always culturally charged.
Edwards's Wales is a place with a distinct language, culture, and history;
it is also embattled. He tends to go on pilgrimages to sites, such as the
spring where Llywelyn the Last Prince of Wales allegedly took his last
drink before dying. Similarly, as he travels through the Towey valley
(the same valley which welcomed Anne Beale some fifty years previously) he thinks of the great literary figures that once lived there, such
as William Williams Pantycelyn, the hymn-writer. But Edwards is also
alert to the contemporary life of the country, as his astute comment on
the scene he witnesses on a railway station platform near Builth Wells
indicates:

*Dacw dyrfa o ymwelwyr Llandrindod yn disgwyl am eu tren, – pregethwyr
a blaenoriaid, – gwyr tewion gwyneb-goch; mwynwyr llygaid dyfrllyd, a
modrwyau yn eu clustiau; personiaid a phlu pysgota hyd eu hetiau; gwraig
radlon yn siarad Cymraeg, a'i mherch yn ei hateb yn Saesneg, wrth ddarl-
len nofel a elwir yn* 'Her Only Love'.[24]

[Over there's a crowd of Llandrindod spa visitors waiting for their
train, – preachers and deacons, – fat red-faced men; watery-eyed
lead miners with rings in their ears; parsons with fishing feathers
plastered all over their hats; a jolly woman speaking Welsh, and her
daughter answering her in English, as she reads a novel with the title
'Her Only Love'.]

Despite this perceptive observation of the contemporary scene, Edwards
is not a political revolutionary. When he visits the slate quarries in
Blaenau Ffestiniog, he finds the quarrymen on strike, yet he does not

engage with labour relations or politics at all, instead simply commenting on the quarrymen's unfailing courtesy, moral purity, literary culture, and continuing interest in theology. Edwards's project, in which
these travel narratives are an important component, is to foment *cultural* nationalism; despite his own labouring-class background, he has
little interest in class politics. The only thing that impresses him about
the deserted slate quarries is the atmosphere of eerie silence there.

Despite his political quietism, Edwards is by no means socially una-
ware. He satirizes the new sea-bathing culture which has begun to bring
large numbers of tourists from the English Midlands to the coastline of
North Wales. In *A Trip to the North*, he gives a vivid picture of *Y Bermo*
(Barmouth), commenting that everyone in the little coastal town now
ministers to the 'gentlemen visitors':

> *Wrth 'ŵr bonheddig, – rhif lluosog, 'byddigions' – yn y Bermo y meddylir
> gŵr yn siarad Saesneg, yn gwisgo clos pen glin, yn darllen papur newydd,
> ac yn ceisio mwynhau ei hun … Ychydig o bobl y wlad, rhagor a fyddai,
> sydd yn y Bermo. 'Byddigions' sydd yno yn awr – 'byddigions' ar y tywod
> yn gwrando ar 'fyddigions' yn nad-ganu ac yn lluchio eu heglau o'u cwm-
> pas, 'byddigions' ar y stryd, 'byddigions' yn y cychod, 'byddigions' yn yr
> orsaf, 'byddigions' ymhob man ond yn y capel … [ac eto] mor llawn o
> adgofion i'r Cymro darllengar yw'r holl fro, o ben Cader Idris yn y fan
> acw, gyda'i hen draddodiad am gwsg yr awen, at Llwyn Gloddaeth yn ein
> hymyl, cartref bardd nad yw ei wlad eto ond wedi cael prin amser i weled
> ei werth'.*[25]

['Gentleman' – plural 'gen'lemens' – in Barmouth means a man
who speaks English, wears plus fours, reads a newspaper, and tries
to enjoy himself. There are few visitors from Wales there these days.
Now it's full of 'gen'lemens', – 'gen'lemens' on the sand listening to
'gen'lemens' braying and fooling around, 'gen'lemens' on the street,
'gen'lemens' in the boats, 'gen'lemens' at the station, 'gen'lemens'
everywhere except in chapel … yet how full of memories is the whole
region to the literate Welshman, from the top of Cader Idris over
there, with its old tradition about sleeping there and being visited
by the Muse, to Llwyn Gloddaeth at our side here, home of a poet
whose value has only just been recognized by his country.]

Despite his evident Welsh patriotism, Edwards himself is positioned
in his text as a hybridized figure. Often mis-recognized by the Welsh
country people themselves as an English gentleman, he is the Oxford

don returning to his native land, observing, remembering, and delivering patriotic homilies. Above all, he is educating. His texts are also hybrid: anecdotal, topographical, historical, literary, and confessional by turns, they create a new self-reflexive travel writing which is energized by an overt cultural nationalist and recuperative ideology. Interspersed by pen and ink drawings, photographs taken by the author himself, and copious quotations from Welsh poetry and hymns, the texts attempt to create, as Robin Chapman has argued, a 'privileged discursive space' in which Edwards can cultivate his project to 'raise up the old land' to her former glory.[26] Often, in Edwards's travel narratives, the journey becomes a temporal as well as a spatial one: the return to the Welsh mountains is a farewell to modernity and a re-immersion in an ancestral history which is in danger of being forgotten. At the same time, the literal return to the springs of the great rivers in the mountains of Wales indicates for Edwards personally a temporary rejection of an Anglicized education and an adopted class position, an opportunity to return to a monoglot Welsh childhood perceived as being classless.

O. M. Edwards was a driven man, passionately committed to reminding the Welsh of who they were or at least of convincing them that they were the idealized, noble mountain people conjured up in his own narratives. As Anthony D. Smith has observed, one of the ways in which nationalist ideologies were forged by an educated elite 'was through a return to "nature" and its "poetic spaces". This nature and these spaces are quite specific; they constitute the historic home of the people, the sacred repository of their memories'.[27] Such is indeed the construct of Wales created in Edwards's travel narratives of North and South Wales, but his focus on Wales as 'the historic home of the people' becomes even more overt in yet another travel narrative, *Cartrefi Cymru (The Homes of Wales)* (1896).

The tone of this volume is, again, intimate and its style belletrist; he adopts a first-person narrative voice and in tones of disarming enthusiasm and, with outbreaks of purple prose worthy of the copious heather which decorates the cover of the text, he leads us to the homes of a dozen notable Welsh people. He takes us to the literal hearthstones of the nation, firmly placing that resilient Welsh character he champions in a domestic setting. In *The Homes of Wales* he visits the birthplaces of two hymn-writers, two preachers, three poets, two prose writers, a religious martyr, a composer, and a saint. Thus, he offers the reader a composite construction of Welshness, characterized by poetry, religion, and music. At the beginning of his pilgrimage to 'Dolwar Fechan', the former home of the hymn-writer Ann Griffiths, we meet the narrator at the local inn, an interior location which itself has a history:

> *Yr wyf yn eistedd mewn ystafell hirgul, gyda nenfwd isel, a ffenestri yn edrych allan i dri chyfeiriad, yn unig westy Llanfihangel yng Ngwynfa. Dyma brif ystafell y pentre, – yn hon yr ymgyferfydd pob pwyllgor gwledig, yn hon y bydd cinio rhent Syr Watcyn, yn hon yr ymgyferfydd y clwb, yn hon y traethwyd doethineb cenedlaethau o ffermwyr ar adeg priodas a chynhebrwng. Ond heddyw y mae'n ddigon gwag, nid oes ynddi ond y ddwy res hir o gadeiriau, y ddau hen fwrdd derw, a minne deithiwr blin yn ceisio dadluddedu ac ymlonni trwy yfed trwyth rinweddol dail yr Ind. Trwy'r drws agored gwelaf goesau meinion yr hen glochydd sy'n hepian wrth bentan y gegin, a thrwy'r tair ffenest gwelaf y gwlaw yn ymdywallt i lawr trwy'r coedydd tewfrig deiliog, trwy'r onnen a'r fasarnen, ac hyd gadwyni aur banadlen Ffrainc.[28]*

[I am sitting in a long, narrow, low-ceilinged room with windows looking out in three directions, at the only inn in Llanfihangel yng Ngwynfa. This is the most important room in the village – here every rural committee meets, here Sir Watkin's annual rent feast takes place, here meets every club, here the wisdom of generations of farmers at weddings and funerals is expressed. But today it is quite empty, just the two long rows of chairs, the two old oak tables, and myself the weary traveller seeking solace and restoration through drinking the wholesome steepings of the leaves of India. Through the open door I can see the thin legs of the old bell-ringer who is dozing by the hearth in the kitchen, and through the three windows I can see the rain pouring down through the leafy thick branches of trees, through the ash and the sycamore, and along the golden chains of the laburnum.]

This opening shows clearly that he is using literary and rhetorical devices such as repetition and periphrasis to create a sense of intimacy, a palpable atmosphere, as well as a sense of the past: this place, here, has its own history, repeated through the generations – it is almost as if the sounds of the voices heard here echo through the narrator's own. The strategic position of the old bell-ringer suggests the established ceremony of village life, its dignified marking of religious rite, and its intimate relation to the cosy domestic hearth. Outside, Nature just is, in all its fertile glory; the narrator is alert to all the resonances and beauty of this place, and transmits them to his reader.

He then goes on to recount his visit to Ann Griffiths's grave and house earlier in the day. For the author, the journey is as important as arrival at his destination: he walks through a haunted and historicized landscape; it is as if Edwards becomes Ann Griffiths, walking the same paths she walked, noticing the same things, such as the sound of the stream which might have inspired the rushing waters and fountains in the imagery of her hymns. The house, when he arrives, is disappointingly new but he is welcomed by an old woman who wants to feed him. Since he has walked eight miles from Llanfyllin, he asks for a glass of water, but is given an ambrosia-like milk:

> *Daeth a gwydriad o lefrith i mi, a'r hufen melyn yn felus arno. Lawer gwaith wedyn, pan yn yfed llefrith a'i hanner yn ddwfr a'i hufen wedi ei hel yn ofalus oddiarno, bum yn hiraethu am y glasiad llefrith a gefais yn Nolwar Fechan.*[29]

> [She brought me a glass of milk, with the yellow cream lying sweetly on top. Many times since, drinking milk which is half water with its cream having been carefully skimmed off, I have longed for that glass of milk I had in Dolwar Fechan.]

He is also given milk and hospitality in Pant y Celyn, the former home of William Williams, another prominent hymn-writer. The repeated gesture of Welsh hospitality at these hymn-writers' homes suggests subtly the way in which Protestant religion has fed and nurtured the Welsh, forming and sustaining them in the same way that milk nourishes the infant. This resonant scene is another example of the Derridean 'ethical encounter' which is created by the giving and taking of hospitality. As in Anne Beale's experience of 'coming hither, a stranger', and of having her identity transformed by Welsh hospitality, so here, Edwards's thirsty traveller has his feeling of selfhood and his national identity confirmed by his reception on the figurative and literal hearthstone of the nation.

In most of the houses he visits, he notices and describes old clocks and records the dates carved on walls or furniture – here, history is literally written on the material objects of the home. At the end of the text he expresses the hope that he has inspired some readers to take the same pilgrimages throughout Wales. As Robin Chapman has argued, 'by adopting the persona of traveller and visitor, Edwards relocates himself. Or, rather, bilocates himself. He is at once ... visitor and native, the pilgrim whose journey confers significance on the ordinary'.[30] Moreover, in a move characteristic of nationalist rhetoric, Edwards turns from the past to the future in the final pages of the text, calling explicitly for a National Museum, so that 'the homes of Wales' should not continue to be 'the only monuments to the heroes of Welsh history'.[31]

Five years after the publication of O. M. Edwards's pair of Welsh travel books, *A Trip to the North* and *A Trip to the South*, a collection of short stories entitled *Picture Tales from Welsh Hills* by Bertha Thomas was published in Chicago, soon after its first appearance in London. Thomas was an experienced novelist and journalist, but this was the first time she had turned to her father's native Wales for material for her fiction. The opening story of the volume, 'The Madness of Winifred Owen', is a first-person narrative told by a spinster taking a cycling tour through Wales in 1899. This is a characteristic opening: the figure of the cycling spinster immediately indicates that this is 'New Woman' fiction of the turn of the century, but what is interesting is the encounter between the 'New Woman' and a Wales which is immediately recognized as 'Other'. On the first page of the story, the narrator asserts that:

> It was in the summer of 1899, when the cycling fever was at its height in all spinsters of spirit. I and my Featherweight had come three hundred miles from our London home, nominally to look up the tombs of forgotten Welsh ancestors in undiscoverable church-yards; more truly for the treat of free roving among strangers in a strange land. So much I knew of the country I was in – that Wales, the stranger within England's gates, remains a stranger still.[32]

Bertha Thomas's travel writing takes a more overtly fictional form than does O. M. Edwards's, bearing a greater similarity to the proto-fictional sketches of Anne Beale's *Vale of the Towey*. Every story in the collection is framed by the figure of a traveller, a visitor to Wales, usually a female spinster but occasionally a male journalist and, in one case, an American woman from Kansas. This framing device mediates between the strangeness of the country and people encountered in the tales and Thomas's presumed English or American audience. While Edwards is talking, often in impassioned terms and in their own language, to his fellow Welsh people, Bertha Thomas is looking outwards and 'translating' the place for which she holds an evident affection for a potentially hostile but certainly ignorant outside world.

In the opening story, the brash New Woman narrator listens to the story of Winifred Owen and is left feeling admiration for this humble but resourceful woman; at the end the speaker describes herself as feeling 'commonplace and middle-class', an unusual pairing of adjectives. Interestingly, the story concerns the ruse the Welsh woman, Winifred Owen, works out in order to gain her father's permission to marry the English man of her choice. Winifred Owen herself marries her English sailor and spends a lifetime travelling the world before returning to the West Wales village whence she came, and where the narrator encounters her. The story is centrally about the experience of travel, between cultures and languages, as well as between countries and belief systems. The ideology of the text suggests that such travel is useful in dispelling preconceptions: the narrator herself comes to realize that her own brand of feminism, complete with bicycle and 'rational dress', is not the only form of agency that a woman can obtain: the apparently stolid, Welsh, Winifred Owen reveals other modes of feminist assertion.

Similarly, in the second story, 'The Only Girl', the spinster narrator and her companion, Edith, are left feeling slightly inadequate and wrong-footed by their experiences in Wales. Initially, they are lost in sudden fog on a hillside:

> 'Where are we?' asked Edith, timorously and low.
> 'In Pixyland,' I feebly jested, likewise.
> Then, in that lightless wild a sound arose – whether near or distant you could not tell – a sound indescribable, was it a voice? – meaningless, a whisper, an utterance; low, continuous, and though dimly articulate utterly unintelligible. It wasn't even Welsh! Anything so uncanny never broke upon my ears ... Spirit-talk – Pixy-talk.[33]

The exclamation that the mysterious utterance 'wasn't even Welsh!' is suggestive of the difficulty these progressive young women have in deciphering the culture of the Other, not just in linguistic terms but in ways much more deeply imbricated in social practices and beliefs. Edith and the narrator find refuge in the lonely farmhouse of Glascarreg, where Issachar Jones and his daughter, Catrin, live. Edith, who is a progressive thinker and a firm believer in eugenics, later voices the opinion that Catrin, who is 'feeble-minded', would be 'better dead'. Nevertheless, after the girl's death the family falls apart and they lose the farm; in retrospect everyone realizes how much they depended upon the misshapen and disabled girl, the 'only girl' of the title. Here, contemporary so-called progressive ideas emanating from London are held up to judgement against Welsh values and are found wanting.

The longest story in the volume, 'The Way He Went', is particularly illuminating for its juxtaposition of England and Wales and its portrayal of the way in which English education alienates Welsh children and cuts them off from their roots. This concern with potential loss of language and culture and with the deracination that may attend upon travel aligns Bertha Thomas's writing unexpectedly with that of O. M. Edwards. In 'The Way He Went', Elwyn Rosser is sent away from Trearvon, his widowed mother's Welsh 'farmstead' to Llanwastad College, a school 'run on English public school lines' and thereafter wins a scholarship to Oxford. (Again, the life story seems to echo that of O. M. Edwards.) Trepidation greets Elwyn's news that he is to go to Oxford, since the Welsh people of the neighbourhood regard England as a dangerous place; as Bertha Thomas puts it:

> In every European country but Elwyn's the English are well known for a terribly serious-minded nation – puritanical, taking their very pleasures sadly ... the land of prudish, dowdy women ... compulsory church-going ... rigid respectability ... In Elwyn's native circle a contrary conviction prevailed ... There, across the border, was the land of Play – or worse ... That England spells the world, the flesh and the devil was a time-honoured doctrine none cared to call into question.[34]

When Elwyn survives and succeeds at Oxford, he comes to the realization that he can 'never be at home in his real home again'. Travel is a significant element of the plot of this story, since Elwyn wanders all over Europe after leaving Oxford and seems most reluctant to return to his homeland, very much like those Welsh people O. M. Edwards rails against in the passage from *A Trip to the North* where he speaks of Welshmen 'passing for' English and 'keep[ing] their own country out of sight'.

As the title of Thomas's volume indicates, there are many pictorial descriptions of Welsh scenery and dwellings in *Picture Tales from Welsh Hills*; indeed, at times the narrative appears to become a travel guide to West Wales, aimed primarily at the American reader. One of the stories even has an American narrator, Ivy Harvey, who is from Kansas and spending a sightseeing holiday in Wales: 'The liner *Recordiana* set her down at Fishguard, South Wales. "Land of a hundred castles," read Ivy from her guide book. "Say, I'll stop and sample one or two of these before I jog on"'.[35] Ivy writes in travelogue style, being particularly taken with the picturesqueness of Carreg Cennen Castle, until she gets lost and impatiently wishes to meet 'a white man with an English tongue in his head'.[36] Again, as elsewhere in this volume, the implication is that the Welsh are racially as well as linguistically Other; given that Ivy is American, her use of the phrase 'white man' might additionally suggest an identification between the Welsh and the native American. Despite Ivy's exasperation, when she does find shelter in a Welsh country house, she is impressed by its antiquity: '"Those fixings were sawn before ever the Mayflower set sail", she thought enviously'.[37]

Both O. M. Edwards's and Bertha Thomas's early twentieth-century travels to Wales enact a retreat from modernity in terms of their construction of national space. Both writers acknowledge the existence of social change, though neither betrays much awareness of a nation shifting its allegiance from the nonconformist hegemony of Welsh Liberalism to the new international socialism emerging from the South Wales coalfield; a nation afflicted by industrial unrest, culminating in events such as the Tonypandy riots of 1910. Both the indigenous travel writer and the Anglicized visitor prefer to conjure up comforting visions, whether that be Wales as Pixyland or a Welsh Wales of deeply embedded literary and cultural stability. In this regard, both hearken back to the essentially consolatory travel narratives of Anne Beale half a century previously, narratives which are designed to reassure the English reader that Wales's alterity is fundamentally unthreatening. Nevertheless, O. M. Edwards's appeal to his own countrymen, in their native language, despite the conservative ideology it expresses, cannot help but be potentially challenging to the political status quo. That status quo includes the 'contributionist' ideology of national identity advocated by Matthew Arnold and embodied most spectacularly in the successful career of David Lloyd George. But that status quo also embraces the growing challenge of international socialism taking root in the industrialized valleys of South Wales, where the identity politics of working-class solidarity was beginning to oust Welsh cultural and linguistic specificity. Edwards's travel writing seeks to stem the tide of Anglicization which, in his view, will dilute Welshness to such an extent that there may be nothing left of that land which Gerald of Wales had described as 'entirely distinct'.

Notes

1. Giraldus Cambrensis, First Preface to Stephen Langton, Archbishop of Canterbury, *The Description of Wales*, 2, Etext, *Munseys*, Web; original Latin edition: *Itinerarium Kambriae* (1191).

2. Giraldus Cambrensis, *Description of Wales*, 24.
3. This is a translation of the line 'I godi'r hen wlad yn ei hôl' which originally comes from a poem by the very popular nineteenth-century poet, John Ceiriog Hughes, who also wrote works such as 'Dafydd y Garreg Wen', 'Nant y Mynydd', and 'Ar hyd y nos', later set to music.
4. See *Reports of the Commissioners of Inquiry into the State of Education in Wales* (London: William Clowes, 1848).
5. See Matthew Arnold, *On the Study of Celtic Literature* (London: Smith, Elder and Co, 1867) and Alfred, Lord Tennyson, *Idylls of the King* (London: Macmillan, 1889).
6. *Welsh Biography Online*, National Library of Wales, Web, 14 February 2011.
7. Anne Beale, *Traits and Stories of the Welsh Peasantry* (London: George Routledge, 1849), vii–viii, 2, 9. Originally published as *The Vale of the Towey, or Sketches in South Wales* (London: Longman, Brown, Green, and Longmans, 1844).
8. Gwilym Teilo, *Llandeilo Vawr and its Neighbourhood, Past and Present* (Llandeilo: D.W. & G. Jones, 1858), 46.
9. Moira Dearnley, 'I Came Hither, A Stranger: A View of Wales in the Novels of Anne Beale (1815–1900)', *The New Welsh Review* 1.4 (Spring 1989), 29.
10. Dearnley, 'I Came Hither, A Stranger', 29.
11. Beale, *Traits*, 10.
12. Beale, *Traits*, 22.
13. Beale, *Traits*, 50.
14. Beale, *Traits*, 63.
15. Beale, *Traits*, 111.
16. Beale, *Traits*, 75.
17. Beale, *Traits*, 321.
18. Jacques Derrida, *On Cosmopolitanism and Forgiveness*, trans. Mark Dooley and Michael Hughes, with a preface by Simon Critchley and Richard Kearney (London: Routledge, 2001), 17.
19. Edwards recounts his unhappy experiences at school in the autobiographical *Clych Adgof: Penodau yn hanes fy addysg* (*The Bells of Memory: Chapters in the History of my Education*) (Caernarfon: Swyddfa 'Cymru', 1906).
20. O. M. Edwards, *Tro i'r gogledd* (*A Trip to the North*) (Caernarfon: Swyddfa 'Cymru', 1907), 1–2.
21. O. M. Edwards, *Tro i'r de* (*A Trip to the South*) (Caernarfon: Swyddfa 'Cymru', 1907), 19.
22. Edwards, *Tro i'r de*, 36.
23. Edwards, *Tro i'r de*, 56.
24. Edwards, *Tro i'r de*, 68.
25. Edwards, *Tro i'r gogledd*, 66.
26. Robin Chapman, 'Margins, Memory and the Geography of Difference in O. M. Edwards's Cartrefi Cymru', unpublished lecture presented at the Association for Welsh Writing in English conference, Gregynog Hall, 2008.
27. Anthony D. Smith, *National Identity* (Harmondsworth: Penguin, 1991), 65.
28. O. M. Edwards, *Cartrefi Cymru* (*The Homes of Wales*) (Wrecsam: Hughes a'i Fab, 1896), 7.
29. Edwards, *Cartrefi Cymru*, 17.
30. Chapman, 'Margins, Memory and the Geography of Difference', 2008.

31. In the original Welsh: '*Cartrefi gwledig Cymru yw yr unig gofgolofnau i arwyr ein hanes ni*'. Edwards, *Cartrefi Cymru*, 140.
32. Bertha Thomas, 'The Madness of Winifred Owen', in *Stranger within the Gates*, ed. Kirsti Bohata (Dinas Powys: Honno, 2008), 1. Originally published as *Picture Tales from Welsh Hills* (Chicago: F. G. Browne & Co., London: T. Fisher Unwin, 1913).
33. Thomas, 'The Only Girl', *Stranger within the Gates*, 23.
34. Thomas, 'The Way He Went', *Stranger within the Gates*, 48.
35. Thomas, 'A House that Was', *Stranger within the Gates*, 131.
36. Thomas, 'A House that Was', 133.
37. Thomas, 'A House that Was', 135.

10
Famine Travel: Irish Tourism from the Great Famine to Decolonization

Spurgeon Thompson

Between 1845 and 1923, more than 569 travel narratives and tourist guides were published addressing Ireland. Most, in this period, were written in the years immediately after the Great Famine of 1846–50, in which, some estimate, more than three million people died of disease or starvation, or emigrated. The fact that, in the decade immediately after the famine, ten travel books or guides were published per year, nearly one every month, indicates that an attempt to culturally order the catastrophe that had happened in Ireland was taking place. Further, people were touring the country in greater numbers than they ever had – and ever would again, until the 1970s.[1] There are several ways to explain such numbers. For example, it is possible that the famine had very little direct effect on the number of tourists visiting the country, since in the decade previous to it there were almost as many tourists visiting as there were after it. Tourism would march on as an industry oblivious to human catastrophes, simply because the English middle classes were growing. It is also possible to blame the railways for the increase in numbers, for they would only come into operation in any significant capacity after the Famine. In one sense, it is impossible to make any generalizations until the mass of materials, all 569 travelogues, have been carefully analysed along with the context that enabled them. However, it is possible, upon looking at a small cross-section of these texts, to draw the provisional conclusion that the direct effect of the Famine, in clearing the land of its population – either by death or emigration – was to open it to tourists. The landscape, because depopulated, could become 'picturesque'. This essay examines a handful of these texts in detail.

Karl Marx summarized how Irish depopulation was seen by many economists in England in his famous attack on one who recommended that, at the height of the Famine, *not enough* people had emigrated from Ireland, yet that at least about a million more would need to go. Marx, summing up this way of thinking, put it like this: 'Therefore her depopulation must go yet further, that thus she may fulfill her true destiny, that of an English sheep-walk and cattle-pasture'.[2] Half a century later, it would be George Bernard Shaw, in *John Bull's Other Island* (1904) who would imagine Ireland as not only grazing country, but gazing country. The play, by its last act, fronts a vision of the country as a golf course for English tourists, its farmers transformed into caddies and shepherds. If Marx could not see what Shaw saw, it is because tourism to Ireland had not yet become an industry. In fact, Thomas Cook, the founder of modern mass tourism, was only experimenting with tourism in Scotland in 1846, where he led his first tour – and suffered his 'first fiasco', according to James Buzard.[3] Cook would, however, be successful the next year, leading tours to Scotland and the North of Ireland.[4] That is to say, Cook would lead one of his very first successful tourist excursions to Ireland during the worst year of the Famine, 1847. In any event, the economist Marx had been attacking, Lord Dufferin, was proved right in the end. The country was in fact transformed just as Marx had, in his sarcasm, predicted. Depopulated, it would become a country dominated by grazing ground. This grazing ground would fit neatly within popular landscape categories of aesthetics, in which the population was not, unless idealized, to figure prominently. Because of the starvation, death by typhoid, cholera, and other diseases, the evictions and the emigrations of millions of people, Ireland could become a pleasure ground. The 'beauty' of its landscape came at the cost of this unthinkable human misery.

After the 'greening' of the country in this way, guidebooks started to emerge immediately, mostly to accompany tourist excursions. *The Irish Tourist's Illustrated Handbook for Visitors to Ireland in 1852* is exemplary.[5] It makes its purpose clear in its introduction. About the handbook, it says:

> It makes no pretensions to literary merit of any sort, and it is not desired that it should be judged by any such standard. The design of its compilation has been, in the first place, to show the rapid, convenient, and economic means that now exist for travelling between every part of the United Islands ... and, lastly, to draw attention to the vast field for enterprise now existing in various portions of that country, for the safe and profitable investment of capital.[6]

The guidebook is no high-brow affair, as it claims from its opening. It uses clear, common-sense tourist terms that its middle-class audience understands, because they have been by now circulated and repeated for more that forty years: picturesque beauties, historical associations, and so on. It frames itself as the stuff of popular culture. Then, however, it changes registers. Not only will the tourist be proffered beauty, 'historical associations', and have access to rapid transport via new train lines in Ireland, but s/he will come into contact with places and sights that s/he can *actually purchase*. Furthermore, this investment can be done 'safely'. The Famine had made Ireland safely post-political, the guide assures.

In this guide we see one of the first forms of Irish tourist discourse proper. Until the Famine had devastated the country, few guides were produced that deployed such an idiom of 'development' while relying throughout on the banal clichés of the language of picturesque beauty promoters. Travel writing, on the other hand, had taken its form in an international context since the mid-seventeenth century; it would stretch to include personal narratives, mixed with the odd tide chart or currency exchange rate, set next to a proposed solution for all of the ills of Irish society, set side by side with a convenient road map or a sketch of an Irish servant with a coach timetable. Importantly, it was possible to discuss divisive political questions in pre-Famine travel writing, usually with an eye to resolving them. Countless English visitors came away with solutions drawn up, patronizing plans to help, exuding benevolence and naiveté. The canonical examples of such travel writing include Sir John Carr's *A Stranger in Ireland* (1805), Mr and Mrs S. C. Hall's *Ireland, Its Scenery, Character, &c.* (1842), and hundreds of others (among the 430 or so published before the Famine). It was, at least, flexible enough to accommodate straightforward political discourse.[7] There are exceptions, of course, like the 1810 *Post Chaise Companion through Ireland*, and others.[8] The 1852 *Handbook*, however, banishes politics for the talk of the professional landscape artist, the amateur historian, and the practical capitalist.

After the Famine, travel writers start doing one thing and tourist guides start doing another. The two part company, and the discourse of the latter prevails. The Famine acts as a wedge that drives home the split between political discussion and tourist discourse. After it, tourist discourse is liberated from the responsibility of open cultural politics, from the role of what Sir John Carr called the 'cordial cement' to reinforce the Union, or from the idea of *explanation* itself. In the place of explanation, we have description, directions, and 'historical associations'. In place of open talk, we have awkward silences.

10.1 Attracting capitalists and tourists

A text like Francis Bond Head's well-known *A Fortnight in Ireland* (1852) (with its gold-embossed shamrock cover but front-cover fold-out map of all the constabulary barracks in the country) reflects the rupture between explanatory categories and aesthetic categories.[9] As one of a handful of immediate post-Famine British travelogues, it is most valuable for the way that it gives us a view of the split as a process, as a dynamic regimentation *in discourse*: its dramatic oppositions reflect this process in action. It is tempting to understand the reason behind this split as part of an attempt simply to repress the tragic conditions of the Famine. The series of tourist guides that will be published in the years after the Famine seem to accomplish exactly this.[10] For capitalist discourse that a grazier economy can supplant a tillage-based economy is a natural progression from unsustainable economic conditions to more rational ones. Kevin Whelan reminds us of the facts of the matter in discussing the long-term effects of the Famine on the landscape:

> One was the eclipse of the arable by the pastoral sector: 1.8 million hectares under arable in 1851 halved to 0.9 million in 1911. Simultaneously, live cattle exports rose dramatically, helped by the advent of railways and steamships. ... From 50,000 in the 1830's, exports quadrupled to 200,000 in the 1840's, doubled by the 1860's and doubled again to reach 800,000 by the 1900's.[11]

We may want to say that 'pastoral' should also retain a double meaning here: the agricultural meaning of 'grazing' and the aesthetic meaning which romanticizes country living. This aside, the facts are astonishing. The Famine cleared the land to feed exponentially increasing amounts of exported cattle. This is, in capitalist terms, a rapid industrial progression, a rapid advance in beef production. In one sense, then, the bourgeoisie have no inherent interest in repressing the Famine or its effects, since its effects will clearly be an advance in agricultural production. What logical need would there be to repress these facts? Indeed, the capitalist celebrates them.

In the case of post-Famine Irish tourist discourse, however, what dominated was not a clear-cut capitalist idiom in which the Famine is openly acknowledged as a benefit for society, nor was it the repression of its horror. The guidebooks display the tendency not to discuss the past for fear of its meaning in the present. Texts written by hired pens, by bureaucrats working for railway companies, do the work of keeping the secret of the Famine. And in them, the repression characteristic of colonialist tourist discourse meets the businesslike rhetoric of development and improvement. Specifically, this means that tourist discourse takes up the role of *advertising* land. It becomes packaging. This packaging must conceal the Famine. 'Historical associations' can be substituted for history. The 'picturesque' can be substituted for the banal (mud cabins, rundale and clachan farming, tillage, and so on). Grazing cattle and sheep can be substituted for people.

The aestheticization of the landscape and the resort to the guides' uniformly descriptive mode are directly related to this commodification and retailing of *the land* in Ireland. Landscape discourse becomes spin, advertising. Of course, the main preoccupation of a new investor is whether the land in which he is to invest is arable or otherwise capable of agricultural development, but 'beauty' polishes this. Land thus becomes developable in two senses: that it can be used for grazing/farming or that it can be used for recreation and aesthetic appreciation. Indeed, the clearing of the land makes it possible to hunt, fish, and engage in other leisure pursuits, like oil painting for example, without hindrance. Cleared, the land can be also groomed to the model of the 'picturesque'. The grand narrative of civilization's ordering of the landscape after the Famine's clearances would be written in neat lines upon the landscape.[12] And the 'picturesque' is taken up by this narrative as one of its central forms, at least in tourist discourse. The concept of the picturesque by the 1850s, we should remember, is nothing more than a bureaucratic cliché. It underwent its most important articulations and contestations in the period from 1780 to 1800, when it was 'offered by its original proponents as a third aesthetic category to set against Burke's "Sublime" and "Beautiful"'.[13] By 1850, it had entered common sense and had rooted itself as perhaps the most important element of tourist discourse. By the mid-nineteenth century, tourism in Britain and to Europe was beginning to become systematically organized. The picturesque would dilute in meaning to a point where 'it can seem so ill-defined as to be virtually meaningless'. But, as Copley and Garside also point out: 'This lack of precise definition is not an indication of its cultural or ideological insignificance, however. On the contrary, it can be argued that the cultural importance of the picturesque stands in direct proportion to the theoretical imprecision of its vocabulary'.[14] It is the bureaucratic repetition of the term in such an 'imprecise' form that is one of the indications of its cultural importance, as well. As its quality dilutes, its quantity increases.

In the 1852 *Irish Tourist's Illustrated Handbook*, cited above, the picturesque takes on a meaning roughly equivalent to 'beautiful', for example. And it is used without reservation to advertise land for investment. This guide was published by the Chester and Holyhead Railway, whose only reason for existence was to facilitate trade and travel to and from Ireland (Holyhead being the main port through which the cross channel ferries, post, and shipping lines would run to and from Dublin). It was given free to all who bought what was termed the 'Tourist Ticket', which enabled visitors to use various railways in Britain and Ireland for a full month. It was an early form of what would later be called 'the package tour'. It is worth looking at its introductory section, entitled 'On Irish Travelling, Past and Present', for here we have an invaluable explanation for the boom in tourism to Ireland in the immediate post-Famine years. It explains:

> Though this is the fifty-first year of the Union, and though the scenic charms of the sister country have been household words on the Saxon tongue, or at least in Saxon type, for a far longer duration – within the last ten years only has Ireland attracted the attention of the general Summer tourist. Separated from England by a sea, which rendered every passage of sailing vessels a matter of risk much too great to be incurred by the ordinary pleasure-seeker, Ireland remained a *terra incognita* for years after the period of the essentially English habit of summer wanderings from towns had become confirmed ... [and long after tourists had started visiting the continent]. But steam, which developed the travelling abroad, no doubt created the travelling in Ireland. Still however ... this autumnal tourist commerce remained, for some years, exceedingly limited. English travellers commonly crossed the channel with no intention to go farther than Dublin. A few ventured into Wicklow, still fewer got as far as Killarney. For this there was [*sic*] several causes. In the first place, even with all the advantages of steam communication to bridge the channel, there were political reasons deterring that influx of inhabitants of England which, in consideration of the wonderful natural beauties of the country, was to have been expected.[15]

The guide then explains that the second reason tourists did not come was because the roads were poor, 'the coaches scarce, the inns execrable', and that few would endure this kind of accommodation. Indeed, 'all proper tourist parties, *i.e.*, including ladies, would not readily face such difficulties in a country where their own language was spoken, only twelve hours distant from England, and where they had unexcitingly to consider themselves "at home"'. Bad roads are endurable if one is in a place where one's language is not spoken, where one can feel the excitement of being not 'at home' but 'abroad', therefore. And then, it continues:

> But within the last ten years great changes, both commercial, political, and social, have taken place in this particular regard; and each season, for some years, has seen a large progressive increase in the number of Anglo-Irish [that is, English] tourists ... English capital, directly and indirectly, became invested in Irish enterprises. Political differences relaxed and grew weaker, and the two peoples no longer viewed one another in the light of foreigners.

Great progress has been made in the provision of amenities, it claims, and then: 'In the last two years [that is, 1850–51] as many strangers passed into Dublin from England as in any five years previously'.[16]

The guide's instructions continue to the point at which the idiom of capitalist improvement meets the discourse of the picturesque:

> By most of those needing a 'Guide' like this, Ireland will be regarded as a land of picturesque attractions, and frolic, and romantic associations; but the beautiful scenes about to be explored must not be gazed at as mere pictures ... Ireland now presents one of the most extraordinary social spectacles ever witnessed in the history of civilization. She is in a transition state. On the one hand, her native population has, in ten years, been diminished directly 20 per cent., and indirectly, in the sense of having lost the natural increase, by 30 per cent. On the other hand, the ownership of her soil is changing hands; the old encumbered being succeeded by a new and unencumbered propriety ... The labour market is thus eased of surplus hands who, in America, have found contentment and prosperity. Free capital is introduced for the development of agriculture. The railways present themselves to increase the value of the land in the districts which they traverse, to multiply the rural markets, to stimulate manufacture, to promote trade, and to put all Ireland in direct communication on one coast with England and Scotland, and on other shores with the buoyant and beckoning western world. Ireland, no doubt, is still reeling under the consequences of the famine of '46; but looking to material resources only, it is obvious that no country in the world has at this moment more distinct prospects of an onward career.[17]

The language of tourism and capitalist expansion have alloyed here. Importantly, this is not a racist, limpidly colonialist text; it can be distinguished, for example, from jingoist Francis Bond Head's work by its exclusion of any open talk of Protestant supremacy or 'idolatrous Catholic priests', as well as any talk of the racial predispositions of the native Irish, all favourite armchair rants of Head's. It is businesslike, rational, promoting investment and at the same time promoting the beauty of Ireland. This is exactly the kind of writing that we will find in tourist guides in the Irish Free State in 1925, in the Republic in the 1960s, and in the Ireland of the European Union from the 1990s until today.

Alongside the guidebooks of the immediate post-Famine period, we also see examples of this in other cultural practices; the most important was the Great Industrial Exhibition in Dublin in 1853. Mary E. Daly has written a brief description of this exhibition and is among the few to have produced any scholarship on the subject. The exhibition is not worth detailed attention, but in its practices in general we can see the coordination of tourist discourse and investment promotion. As Daly describes, it began as the idea of the Royal Dublin Society, which had held similar exhibitions in the years previous to the Famine. The success, Daly claims, of London's Great Exhibition of 1851 'encouraged a more ambitious approach, and in 1852 during the course of a national exhibition in Cork, the possibility of holding a major international exhibition in Dublin was mooted'. As Daly explains:

> Some days later William Dargan, a pioneer of Irish railway development, wrote to the Royal Dublin Society urging that such an exhibition should be given 'a character of more than usual prominence' and offering the society a sum of £20,000 to erect a suitable exhibition building. Dargan and his co-organizer, Dublin businessman Richard Turner, received considerable support from Irish railway interests, who saw the fair as a means of promoting tourism and restoring confidence in the Irish economy following the devastating famine of the 1840's; they also wished to assist economic development by publicizing the extent of Irish natural resources and introducing people to the wonders of new technology.[18]

The important aspect of the exhibition for my purposes here is its attempt to promote both tourism and 'economic development' at the same event. Of course, part of its project is to emphasize the putative post-political nature of Irish society, to demonstrate that an abundance of natural resources rather than abounding national resurgence was the focus of Irish society in the post-Famine years. Queen Victoria visited the event and in the same year and signed her name to the ancient Book of Kells housed at Trinity College in Dublin – as if it were the guest book of her hotel. In all, 1,156,232 visitors attended the exhibition. Most of them came from Great Britain. Thomas Cook led many successful tourist excursions to it. There were 1500 exhibits from Britain and Ireland, and 254 from overseas, including many other British colonies such as British Guiana, in which natural resources were the focus. In this sense, the exhibition was not only promoting tourism and investment in Ireland, but also in other British colonies at the same time. Ireland could be seen alongside, in the context of, these other colonies. This would be, perhaps, a more dramatic feature of the 1865 Exhibition in Dublin in which 2300 exhibits from 21 British colonies were set up.[19] But the same logic at least predominated.

Handbooks accompanying these fairs were produced, we know, in massive quantities. Special themed newspapers were also used as a means to promote tourism and investment. It was likely that every person to buy a tourist ticket that would enable them to attend these events would receive a guidebook to accompany it. Unfortunately, most of these throwaway guidebooks are no longer extant. But we can get a general sense of what would be contained in them by the exhibits offered at the exhibitions. It can be asserted, in any case, that the promotion of these exhibitions functioned to bring to Ireland vast quantities of English tourists on a scale unknown previous to the Famine. The exhibitions could function as the urban component of a tour of the picturesque countryside, the structures established to guide the tourist's gaze, to instruct the tourist, as the *Handbook* above does, about how to see Ireland now that the Famine had cleared the land. The exhibitions functioned to structure the gaze in such a way as to emphasize the 'commercial' as well as the picturesque aspects of Ireland.

10.2   From Murray's to *The Irish Tourist*

In 1864, when the English travel writer William Whittaker Barry was walking through County Wexford on a country road, he discovered that he was being followed by a constable. The constable eventually caught up with him and struck up a conversation, asking where he was going, where he had been, and so on. Barry finally comes to understand that the constable suspected him of being a Fenian outlaw, on the run. After dropping several hints, for example, asking what certain places were like for visitors, where they were located, and the like, Barry sees that the constable had not dropped his suspicions. At last, Barry, in desperation, decided upon another tactic to prove his innocence:

> I therefore produced Murray's Handbook, on the plea of looking for the places he mentioned. It now began to assume a worn appearance, consistent with and indeed only to be accounted for on ground of much travel, and I think its production served more than anything else to remove the constable's suspicions. While I was looking at the book he was busily employed peering over my shoulder and into the knapsack, evidently to discover if there were any revolvers there.[20]

The constable then wished him good day and returned in the direction from which he came. Barry, who was suspected of being a Fenian in almost every town he entered near the end of his tour – because of his bushy beard and worn clothes from two months of walking in Ireland – managed to evade arrest at least until he arrived back in England. There, his Murray's Handbook would not help him, and he was brought in for questioning after being trailed by a detective for some time. He had, apparently, fitted the description of James Stephens, the leader of the Fenian revolt, who had recently escaped from prison.[21]

While a tourist guidebook would serve as a pass, as proof of innocence in Ireland, as soon as the traveller crossed the Irish Sea, it lost its protective powers. As when theory travels but the conditions that enabled it do not, the guidebook retains its power only when used in the right context. Its power in Ireland was to prove that its possessor was not involved in subversive politics; this is because the guidebook was assumed to be 'non-political'. Taking this as a cue, I here analyse the expunging of politics from tourist discourse through an analysis of the first Murray's guide to Ireland, the guide Barry showed to that inquisitive member of the Royal Irish Constabulary.

By 1864, John Murray, the well-established London publisher of Scott and Byron, had almost single-handedly forged from the chaos of travel writing and gazetteers a new form of discourse: the tourist handbook. While scattered guidebooks had existed for at least sixty years previous to this time, Murray's innovation was to produce guidebooks to most countries on Earth. All of Europe was covered by his guidebook series, most British colonies, and other regions all were systematically described and placed into the framework of rationalized tourism.[22] It was the beginning of what would later explode into a major sector of the publishing industry. His guidebook series began in 1836 and by 1864 had been well established, with a team of writers sent out to survey and report upon all the countries covered in the series. Indeed, even by 1848, Murray had some sixty guides in his series.[23] At first, John Murray himself would write his guides and visit the locations covered in them; but when his company grew, his staff of anonymous writers grew with it. Notably, Ireland was very late to earn Murray's attention. In fact, guidebooks had been produced about nearly every country in Europe except Ireland by 1864. The *Handbook for Travellers in Ireland with Travelling Maps* was produced just in time for the Dublin Exhibition that would take place the following year.

In this first Murray's guide, we see the production of a *distanced writing subject*, one that can write from the position of a putative objectivity. Claims to objectivity when dealing with Ireland are almost always underwritten by a hidden or not-so-hidden partisanship. This first Murray's guide claims to give the facts of Ireland, for the convenience of tourists, while it simultaneously takes a clearly colonialist position in relation to these 'facts', maps, figures, and characterizations. This colonialist tone, which we detect throughout the guide, is eventually 'toned down', refined into more opaque potted histories, statistics, and directions in later printings. By 1912, when the last Murray's guide to Ireland was produced, the condescension and disparaging comments about Irish character, farming, and so on, that pocked the first guide, are wholly excised by its Irish Protestant editor, John Cooke (a Trinity College Dublin graduate). In other words, while the first guide would occasionally break into what can be accused of being openly political discourse, the last guide works even harder to cloak its political function. By the time that Muirhead's first *Blue Guide* was written about Ireland in 1931, which saw itself as a replacement for the Murray's guide (and says as much), 'objectivity' had been thoroughly established and guarded in the guidebook form's encounter with Ireland – colonialist objectivity, that is.

This particular perspective can be witnessed in several examples in the 1864 *Handbook*. In the preface, for example, we witness the following semi-Utopian vision of an Ireland settled by summering British tourists:

> The time will come when the annual stream of tourists will lead the way, and when wealthy Englishmen, one after another, in rapid succession, will seize the fairest spots, and fix here their summer quarters ... There are those who will not welcome such a change upon the spirit of that scene; but if we see in the beauty of Ireland even a surer heritage than in hidden mine or fertile soil, why may we not hope that it will again cover her land with pleasant homes, and a busy, contented, and

increasing people, such as we see in many other regions with nothing but their beauty and salubrity to recommend them?[24]

Utopian or not, in Murray's following introduction to Killarney, it appears that this vision of a future Ireland peopled by English tourists and supported wholly by the natural resource of 'beauty', has already been realized:

> The Lakes of Killarney can only be viewed with the eye of an artist or an angler, and not with any commercial intentions; were any such ever entertained, it is doubtful whether popular indignation of those dependent on the tourist district would even allow them to be tried.

Murray also presents for us a thesis on the effect of new technology upon culture:

> Ireland is becoming well supplied with railways, which have already effected incalculable good, and, as they increase, are likely to effect still more, by bringing fresh capital into the country, by cheapening the carriage of all marketable and agricultural produce, and by opening up what were formerly wild and unfrequented districts, to the approaches of civilization – breaking down the barriers of prejudice and ignorance, to which even the narrow-minded rancour fostered by party bigots must yield in course of time.[25]

There were thirty railway companies in Ireland when Murray was writing this. What is coded in his language, like 'bigot' and 'narrow-minded rancour', is not an attack upon the landlord class. It is one upon Fenianism, which was developing in pockets throughout the country, notably in places like Kerry (where Fenians successfully managed to seize the first intercontinental telegraph cable on Valencia Island in 1867). Railways spread 'good', they 'open up' 'wild' areas that were 'closed' to capitalist/colonialist penetration.

The 1912 Murray's guide deletes *all* of the quotations from John Murray that I treat in this essay. Slipping politics into the guidebook in this way would have violated the mature tourist handbook etiquette of the twentieth century. But the transgressions appear in bold in its early stage, even while cautioning tourists against political discussion:

> Be careful how you engage yourself in any discussion or opinion on party, and particularly religious, subjects. The traveller will soon find

out for himself that party spirit attains a pitch which is unknown in England …. The social features of Ireland are unfortunately so mixed up with political ones, that the tourist had better make his own observations on them, and keep them to himself.[26]

Perhaps this is the reason that the aforementioned constable who questioned William Whittaker Barry was not worried when he released Barry to his own devices having seen his Murray's guide. In any case, politics is reduced to 'pitch' here, with the emphasis on Irish 'orality', rather than reason, that had attended more than a century of colonialist discourse about Ireland by 1864. Murray is here urging his tourist to occupy the position of the *non-participant* observer. At the same time that Murray reproduces this model of objectivity – of the observer abstracted from the social – he seems not to trust its efficacy. But silence, somehow, is preferable.

We can understand this resort to silence by reading the subtext of Murray's preface which, like subtitles that cross the screen in the wrong place, shows itself inadvertently in moments like these. This subtext reads as paternalist racism. A later passage of his preface reveals this racism perhaps more clearly than anywhere else in the guide. It reads:

[The tourist] will find much to admire, especially in the hospitality of and warm-heartedness which seem to be every Irishman's birthright. He will also find some things to condemn; but he cannot fail to return home interested in Ireland's social progress, and with an earnest hope that she will some day thoroughly and truly feel the real love that England has for her, and that the Celt will come in time to consider that 'repale from the Sassenach' would be the worst thing that could happen to him.[27]

Hospitality is linked here with Celtic intransigence – an apparent contradiction. For what would a hospitable and warm-hearted Celt be doing refusing the 'love' of England? This contradiction is resolvable only with recourse to the idea of national character, which, applied specifically to the Irish context, takes its racist colours. Murray's version of the Celt, of course, is cliché. But as tourist discourse, it is a cliché that seizes the privilege of being mass produced; Murray sold 15,000 copies of this guide in its first edition. It would sell through eight more editions by 1912.[28]

As stated above, none of this colonialist subtext would stay inked between the lines of Murray's guide after John Cooke took over the editing of it in 1912. A brief note should be made on this latter guide, before examining the tourist magazine, *The Irish Tourist*. Cooke, in editing the Murray's guide for 1912, took it upon himself to anaesthetize the guide thoroughly, cutting out most of Murray's preface as well as rewording passages, such as Murray's attack on rundale farming in Gweedore, Co. Donegal. Cooke shows a faith in progress and in land redistribution schemes that is uncommon in tourist guides, yet retains a belief that British legislation will bring about what he calls a 'solution' to the 'Irish Question'. Cooke's efforts ultimately amount to a fashioning of the guide to conform with the conventions of guide writing that had, by 1912, fully evolved to a point of 'objectivity' in which the descriptive mode would dominate, and through which the interests of the colonial state's hegemony could be guarded.

After the incorporation of Ireland into the Murray's guide series, the most important event in Irish tourism development in the post-Famine decades is the publication of F. W. Crossley's *The Irish Tourist* penny magazine. Crossley, a railway owner and hotelier, would become the leading personality in the movement to rationalize tourism in Ireland. The first number of *The Irish Tourist* was published in June 1894. While surely not the first throwaway Irish tourist magazine, it remains the only one that managed not to be entirely thrown away, as many issues of it remain extant. It has a distinctly informal tone, and is firmly wedded to Unionism. I will focus below on a few examples that illustrate its general principles and which also help illustrate my general point in this essay about the split between explanation and description.

To begin, Crossley was committed to an understanding of tourism as a way to alleviate poverty in the countryside. It is the way of seeing tourism that has dominated to this day, where tourism is seen as, for example, the cure for politics in Northern Ireland and where tourist development is seen as an important part of Ireland's economy generally. Crossley puts it this way:

> The mission of the *Irish Tourist* is to make better known to the world this country's charm and beauty, and to attract multitudinous visitors to annually sojourn at our health and pleasure resorts, and thus leave with us that historic 'plethora of wealth' which might act as a panacea for Ireland's ills.[29]

This is a simple enough formula, and relies on the notion of 'attraction' (rather than, for example, production) to develop the industry.

It affirms dependency in the very moment it wants to solve the problem of poverty, not acknowledging the contradiction between encouraging endemic dependency and wealth production. In another number, the magazine explains further by citing a passage from the *London Standard* newspaper related to Achill Island, which was suffering from extreme poverty and emigration in 1894:

> With proper encouragement and enterprise the island might become the dairy farm and pleasure-ground of Great Britain, and the districts into which the money of the tourist could so easily be diverted are precisely those that are least hopeful from an agricultural point of view.

Then Crossley comments on this, affirming this programme: 'It is a notable fact that in those localities in Ireland where the scenic attractions are most striking the poverty is most marked'.[30] We have, of course, seen this kind of thinking before. It is inherited from the body of thinking represented by the post-Famine guidebook above, and furthermore by the Irish Tourist Association later; only, the twist here is that Crossley sees not the introduction of industries in the manufacturing sense of the term, but of the 'industry' of tourism as the answer to poverty in places of beauty. While earlier guides would try to attract 'capital' in the sense of investment, Crossley is trying to attract capital in the sense of spare change, the money deposited by tourists in places they visit. As Crossley puts it more directly a month later:

> The tourist season is in full swing. Visitors with purses well-filled are moving around. 'They have money and we have not / We *must* have, well, all they've got.' Now is the time to practise the art of catching and catering credibility for the passing crowd ... Please them, and they will purchase liberally.[31]

I highlight Crossley's logic of dependency here because the very same logic will prevail in tourism promotion after the foundation of the Free State and the settler state in the North. Crossley would not be involved in the foundation of either the Ulster Tourist Development Association in Belfast or the Irish Tourist Association in the Free State. He did, however, start an agency he called 'The Irish Tourist Association' in 1894, and successfully lobbied for British state funding for the promotion of tourism, though it was minimal in impact. Crossley's logic of dependency is the cul-de-sac into which the privileging of description instead of explanation leads Irish tourism. Able, finally, only to ask for help from outside, to 'attract' rather than to produce, to beg rather than to take, Crossley's version of tourism is still-born. Cloaking the political by appearing to be doing 'political' work like attracting tourists to poverty-stricken regions, Crossley shows us the limits of tourist discourse. To solve the problem of poverty, it begs for tourists to come and be a 'panacea'. This is as 'political' as it can get because it is strapped into the straightjacket of description, 'objectivity', and, finally, an assumption that power lies elsewhere.

Notes

1. All of my statistics here are based upon the incomplete, but authoritative and immensely useful, *Irish Travel Writing: A Bibliography* (Wolfhound Press: Dublin, 1996) by John McVeagh. Because his listings are not placed in historical sequence, but are alphabetized, it may be helpful to see the statistics as I have compiled from them. In the nineteenth century, 730 travelogues about Ireland were published. Sixty-four appear in the decade 1820–30; 99 in the decade 1830–40; 85 between 1840 and 1850; and 100 between 1850 and 1860. The figures drop off to between 64 and 82 for the remaining decades of the nineteenth century. In the decade 1900–10, 78 travelogues appear; 60 appear between 1910 and 1920; and 83 appear between 1920 and 1930. All of these statistics should be taken as provisional, as bibliographical work on Irish travel writing is currently in its infancy. It is quite likely that, in the periods where there was a great deal of activity, more books were published than have been accounted for.
2. Karl Marx, *Capital* (New York: Penguin, 1996), 665.
3. James Buzard, *The Beaten Track: European Tourism, Literature, and the Ways to 'Culture', 1800–1918* (Oxford: Clarendon Press, 1993), 53.
4. Buzard, *The Beaten Track*, 53.
5. *The Irish Tourist's Illustrated Handbook for Visitors to Ireland in 1852 with Numerous Maps*, 2nd edn (Dublin: Office of the National Illustrated Library, 227 Strand, M'Gashan, Sackville St., 1852), 1.
6. *The Irish Tourist's Illustrated Handbook*, 1.
7. See Sir John Carr, *The Stranger in Ireland; or, A Tour in the Southern and Western Parts of that Country in the Year 1805* (London: Richard Phillips, 1806); and Mr and Mrs S. C. Hall, *Ireland: It's Scenery, Character, &c.*, 3 vols (New York: R. Worthington Importers, 1842?).
8. See William Wilson, *The Post Chaise Companion or Traveller's Directory through Ireland* (Dublin: J. & J. H. Fleming, 1810).
9. Sir Francis Bond Head, *A Fortnight in Ireland* (London: John Murray, 1852).
10. See the following handbooks and guidebooks: *Handbook to Galway, Connemara, and the Irish Highlands*, Profusely illustrated by Jas. Mahony, Esq. (London: George Routledge and Co., 1854); *Handbook of the Harbour of and City of Cork* (Cork: Bradford & Co., 1852); *Guide to the Irish Highlands* (London: Edward Stanford, 1861); *Killarney from the Summit of Mangerton* (Dublin: James McGlashan, 1851); *Picturesque Guide to the Lakes of Killarney* (Dublin: Hodges

and Smith, 1851); *The Ulster Railway Handbook, and Travellers Companion of the Way* (Belfast: George Phillips, 1848); *Black's Guide to Dublin and the Wicklow Mountains* (Edinburgh: Adam and Charles Black, 1854); *Black's Guide to Killarney and the South of Ireland* (Edinburgh: Adam and Charles Black, 1854), and so on.

11. Kevin Whelan, 'The Modern Landscape: from Plantation to Present', in *Atlas of the Irish Rural Landscape*, ed. F. H. A. Aalen, Kevin Whelan, and Matthew Stout (Cork: Cork University Press, 1997), 91.

12. I mean this literally. As Whelan says, 'The linearisation of landscape spread the ladder farms over the west of Ireland, obliterating the earlier informal networks of the rundale system' ('The Modern Landscape', 91).

13. See Stephen Copley and Peter Garside, eds, *The Politics of the Picturesque: Literature, Landscape and Aesthetics since 1770* (Cambridge: Cambridge University Press, 1994), 1.

14. Copley and Garside, eds, *The Politics of the Picturesque*, 1.

15. *The Irish Tourist's Illustrated Handbook*, 9.

16. *The Irish Tourist's Illustrated Handbook*, 9, 10.

17. *The Irish Tourist's Illustrated Handbook*, 10.

18. Mary E. Daly, *A Social and Economic History of Ireland since 1800* (Dublin: Educational Company of Ireland, 1981), 9, 10.

19. Daly, *A Social and Economic History*, 31.

20. William Whittaker Barry, *A Walking Tour Round Ireland in 1865* (London: Methuen, 1867), 312.

21. Barry, *A Walking Tour Round Ireland*, 399.

22. See Buzard's thorough explanation of the beginning of Murray's guides series in his *The Beaten Track*, 71–9.

23. Buzard, *The Beaten Track*, 71.

24. *Handbook for Travellers in Ireland* (London: John Murray, 1864), i.

25. *Handbook for Travellers*, xx, xxxvii.

26. *Handbook for Travellers*, lxi.

27. *Handbook for Travellers*, lxi.

28. *Handbook for Travellers*, 1912, i.

29. *The Irish Tourist* 1.1 (June 1894), 1.

30. *The Irish Tourist* 1.2 (July 1894), 33.

31. *The Irish Tourist* 1.3 (August 1894), 5.

11
Meeting Kate Kearney at Killarney: Performances of the Touring Subject, 1850–1914

K. J. James

Throughout the nineteenth century, thousands of tourists to the district of Killarney in south-west Ireland (see Illustration 11.1) snaked their way, by foot or mounted on ponies, through the Gap of Dunloe – a barren, rocky defile – following a bridle-path of some seven-and-a-half miles through the Gap, opening onto the Black Valley, in a sensually-engrossing tourist spectacle. A landscape depicted as forbidding and sublime in romantic-era travel narratives later became the setting for a series of extraordinary performances enacted by tourists, a formidable hostess at a profitably-situated cottage, buglers, fiddlers, and a boisterous band of so-called 'mountain dew girls' deeper within the recess. Armed with containers of putatively illicit whiskey ('poitín', or 'mountain dew') and fresh goat's-milk, the local women offered a potent concoction for tourists to imbibe. Their model – and, some asserted, their forebear – was the legendary Killarney siren, Kate Kearney. Kate was an oft-referenced figure in Victorian popular culture whose presence permeated the Gap. A tour of the Gap and encounters with her putative descendant became an essential part of 'doing' Killarney (as it was colloquially known), typically as part of a day-tour that encompassed the iconic Lakes of Killarney and other sites in the vicinity – perhaps ruins at Aghadoe or Ross Castle, the Dunloe caves (discovered in 1838), the Purple Mountain, a magnificent precipice called the 'Eagle's Nest' situated within the Long Range, the Old Weir Bridge near the celebrated 'Meeting of the Waters', and Innisfallen, the small island in the Lower Lake made famous by the poet Thomas Moore's famous ode.[1]

In exploring contours of these embodied tourist practices – and in particular corporeal movements to and within the deep defile, along with various gestures and tastes which were part of the choreography of an encounter with Kate's 'granddaughter' – it is instructive to examine

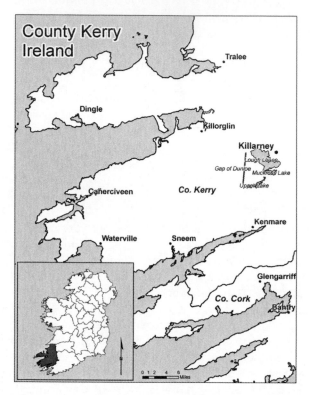

Illustration 11.1 'Map of Ireland and Detailed Map of County Kerry, showing Principal Tourist Resorts' (2011). Map created by Joshua MacFadyen. © K. J. James.

how the performance of 'tasteful' travel changed between the first dec-ades of the nineteenth century, an era explored recently by William H. A. Williams in his study of early Killarney tourism,[2] and the years after the Famine of the 1840s, how discourses of the sublime were implicated in this development, and how the self-characterized 'cultivated' travel-ler narrated social distance both from natives and fellow visitors in an era of increased tourist traffic. Indeed, 'mass tourism' served as a discur-sive foil for the refined traveller, who framed it as a spurious set of prac-tices devoid of reflexivity, signalling a limited capacity for discernment and superficial, ill-judged engagement with the toured culture.[3] This representation of mass tourism is too often reproduced uncritically, and hurriedly, in scholarship on tourism. The result is a concept tethered to a narrative of the 'homogenization' and 'standardization' of tourist practices, effected through the inexorable rise and pervasive influence of Thomas Cook and package holidays; resulting accounts elide the complexity, nuance, and diversity inherent in modern tourism.[4]

Discourses of personal refinement and discrimination, even if they were expressed by travellers to the Gap through promiscuous and repetitive deployment of the stock language of the sublime, and denigration of two creatures of mass tourism – the unoriginal and undiscerning tourist and the pestering, often wily native – were critical to how authorial sophistication was projected through travelogues, and to how their touring enterprise was framed. While this has been cast as a largely British practice, or one framed by Irish guidebook-writers for a British audience,[5] it was common to Americans, Canadians, continental Europeans, and many Irish travellers, too; indeed they often issued the most scathing critiques of peasant culture, echoing Dinah Maria Craik (the daughter of an Irishman) who recorded her encounter with an Irish beggar at the Gap, whom she scolded: 'I am Irish, and you make me ashamed of my country. What would my husband say to me if I went gadding about like this, instead of doing my work in-doors? Go home, and do *your* work'.[6] In terms of the travellers' accounts of bodily engagement with Killarney natives, social and cultural distance was expressed not by eschewing the conventions of native hospitality, but by performing and then commenting wryly on them, or referring disparagingly to Kate Kearney's reputed granddaughter, frequently employing her body as a canvas on which travellers projected incredulity at her claims of descent. Meetings with her were widely prefigured in myriad texts, and embodied encounters were realized at the entrance to the Gap of Dunloe (see Illustration 11.2). Guidebooks reminded readers that Sydney Owenson, later Lady Morgan, had given Kate Kearney immortal life in popular song:

> OH, did you not hear of Kate Kearney?
> She lives on the banks of Killarney:
> From the glance of her eye, shun danger, and fly,
> For fatal's the glance of Kate Kearney.
>
> For that eye is so modestly beaming,
> You ne'er think of mischief she's dreaming;
> Yet, oh! I can tell how fatal the spell
> That lurks in the eye of Kate Kearney.
>
> Oh, should you e'er meet this Kate Kearney,
> Who lives on the banks of Killarney,

Illustration 11.2   'Kate Kearney at the Gap of Dunloe', postcard, n.d., postmarked 1904. Source: K. J. James private collection.

> Beware of her smile, for many a wile
> Lies hid in the smile of Kate Kearney.
>
> Tho' she looks so bewitchingly simple,
> Yet there's mischief in every dimple;
> And who dares inhale her sighs' spicy gale,
> Must die by the breath of Kate Kearney.[7]

Owenson's Kate was an ambiguous enchantress – both beguiling and menacing. Penned in the first decade of the nineteenth century, and set to a traditional air – 'The Beardless Boy'[8] – Owenson's melody and lyrics spawned a variety of often-comical adaptations. The exploits of Kearney's putative descendants in Killarney were colourfully recounted in the pages of leading British and American periodicals, and in widely read travelogues, including Thomas Carlyle's account of a Killarney tour in 1849.[9] In addition to lyrical and literary incarnations which implanted her within popular culture, the embodied Kate Kearney became central to an experience in which excursionists were invited to enter a world of illusion and allusion, affecting surprise and disbelief as they 'met' this icon of Victorian popular culture and tasted her hallmark beverage. Writers who narrated their experiences in this Rabelaisian enclave produced mocking appraisals of the 'granddaughter's' genealogy. Indeed, their scepticism was an implicit assertion of social and cultural authority in relation to her, the denizens of Killarney, and the conventions of mass tourism generally.

11.1 Performing tasteful travel in pre-Famine Killarney

The social performances described above were strongly associated with the conventions of Killarney tourism in the post-Famine period, and with specific ways in which Irish culture was commodified for the touring public at the Gap. Especially after 1850, the Gap tour was codified in ways which embedded it firmly within expanding structures of commercial tourism – betokened by the arrival of the railway in Killarney and by the proliferation of hotels there. In contrast, from the late eighteenth century through the 1840s, and especially in the first three decades of the nineteenth century, travellers to the Gap of Dunloe articulated their encounter with the landscape with explicit reference to the ideal of the sublime. However, references to this category declined and, from the mid-nineteenth century, other sensations and distinctive social practices became ever more prominent tropes in narratives of the Gap tour. This did not imply a complete homogenization of tourist experiences, a standardization of practices, or indeed an altogether new performance (indeed Anne Plumptre, writing in the second decade of the nineteenth century, had despaired at Killarney, and at the Giant's Causeway, of the 'ingenious devices the people about have, each to pluck a feather out of the pigeon's wing'[10]). But it offered writers new devices to narrate their erudition and sophistication. This was especially true as they recounted a landscape teeming with mendicants and a tour which breached precepts of romantic travel.

From the mid-eighteenth century until the eve of the Famine, codes attached to the sublime underpinned writers' self-identification as tasteful travellers.[11] Romanticism grounded the traveller's relationship to the landscape in terms of powerful, spontaneous, deep, and internally-derived emotional responses drawn from the 'liberated imagination', which in descriptions of the Gap centred on the sublime.[12] Narratives of travel, domestic as well as foreign, provided a framework for the articulation of these qualities. England, Wales, Scotland, and Ireland furnished many English writers with places which they recounted as extraordinary, especially as the home tour became a fashionable middle-class performance after the 1770s and in subsequent decades when European conflict constrained continental sojourns, and as the classical focus of the Grand Tour diminished in influence. Though romanticism had a transatlantic form, it was also expressed within the parameters of national cultures, which furnished histories, politics, mythologies, and other literary forms and thematic materials through which distinctive national expressions were forged.[13] While there were myriad motivations behind tours, a search for 'inspiring' domestic landscapes was surely among the most prominent – and in the rugged mountains of the Scottish Highlands, in Snowdonia, and at the Gap of Dunloe many tourists in Britain satisfied their desire to behold peaks, precipices, and deep recesses which presented awesome scenery, induced profound sensations, and produced narratives of intense personal emotional engagement with an elemental landscape. Many of these topographic features had attracted scant attention (or in fact opprobrium) in previous eras; but what travellers may have once held as barren landscapes now became invested with fearsome emotional power.[14]

The category of the sublime had a long history stretching back to antiquity, and had various late-seventeenth century, eighteenth-century, and romantic elaborations. In the romantic period it was grounded in the individual's encounter with an external object that initially overwhelmed reason and understanding. The consequent intense, inexpressible emotional response hinted at powers that lay beyond the limits of understanding.[15] Qualities of the sublime in nature – the discourse most frequently invoked in descriptions of the Gap tour – were expounded by thinkers such as John Dennis, Joseph Addison, and Edmund Burke; indeed the latter's famous work *A Philosophical Enquiry into the Origins of Our Ideas of the Sublime and Beautiful* (1757) was a landmark elaboration of aesthetic theory in which Burke delineated the interactions of cognition, sensation, and the external object which produced the sublime: an ideal rooted in passions evoked by that which is 'in any sort terrible' in nature.[16] 'The passion caused by the great and sublime in *nature*', Burke wrote, 'when those causes operate most powerfully, is Astonishment; and astonishment is that state of the soul, in which all its motions are suspended, with some degree of horror'. If 'astonishment' was the 'effect of the sublime in its highest degree', its inferior effects were 'admiration, reverence and respect'.[17] The terrible, which evoked fear, assumed primacy in Burke's doctrine of the sublime;[18] indeed terror constituted 'the ruling principle of the sublime'.[19] The sublime was manifest in the response to vastness, or 'greatness of dimension', and also to the qualities of '[d]ifficulty' (as evinced by Stonehenge) and '[m]agnificence'.[20] Certain qualities of light and colour might also elicit such a response, with Burke writing that 'among colours, such as are soft, or cheerful, (except perhaps a strong red which is cheerful) are unfit to produce grand images. An immense mountain covered with a shining green turf, is nothing in this respect, to one dark and gloomy; the cloudy sky is more grand than the blue; and night more sublime and solemn than day'.[21] Yet Burke also contended that the eye was 'not the only organ of sensation, by which a sublime passion may be produced', and wrote that 'excessive loudness', such as that produced by 'vast cataracts, raging storms, thunder, or artillery', could awaken the same passions and sensations as the terrible landscape.[22] Sudden and intermittent sound might also have the capacity of producing the sublime, as could the cries of animals; while taste and smell might also have this effect, in Burke's opinion only '[e]xcessive bitters, and intolerable stenches' were productive of truly 'grand' sensations.[23] Burke's ideal of the sublime, then, was very much grounded in emotional responses to the visual. Techniques associated with contemporary landscape evaluation according to another ideal – the picturesque – implicated technologies such as the Claude Glass in practices which framed the external world as a composition.[24]

Certainly romantic-era travellers found the Gap to be an exemplar of sublimity in nature, even if, as William H. A. Williams has noted, they may have expounded on their affective response to landscapes without formal knowledge of the theories which underpinned it.[25] Their language evoked deep sensation, reverence, and a degree of terror. If such raw emotions were associated with views of the deep recess at Dunloe, Killarney offered a veritable feast for the aesthetic traveller. The prolific author Sir Richard Colt Hoare, in his 1806 *Journal of a Tour in Ireland*, described Killarney as offering a variety of scenery:

> I have seen no spot more adapted for the school of a landscape artist than KILLARNEY; and where he may study all the component parts of a fine picture with greater advantage. The rocks that bound the shores of MUCRUSS and the Lower Lake, with their harmonious tints, and luxuriant decoration of foliage, stand unrivalled, both in form and colouring. The character of the mountains is as grand and

varied, as the lakes in which they reflect their rugged summits; and the inconstant state of the climate subjects each to the most sudden changes, and produces the most admirable effects of light and shade imaginable. Here, in short, in this western *Tempe*, the artist will find every thing he can possibly wish: the *beautiful* in the Lower, and Mucruss Lakes; the *sublime* in the Upper Lake; *variety* in the river that connects the lakes, and the *savage* in the mountains that form the Pass of Dunloe.[26]

Critical to this visual framing of the 'savage' Gap was the identification of 'views' offered at specific stages on an excursionist's journey through the pass. They signposted elements of the landscape which guided the traveller towards specific practices of observation; they in turn corresponded to particular aesthetic categories, especially the picturesque and the sublime. In 1822, for instance, George Nelson Smith published a guide to the district of Killarney divided principally into 'stations', which offered especially pleasing and panoramic views of scenery in the district (an especially common picturesque practice). He represented the 'Gap of Dunlow' as awe-inspiring, wild, and savage:

This wonderful scene appears a frightful chasm, when seen from the Tralee road at the distance of ten miles; but it must be closely examined by those who desire to be acquainted with its stupendous details. Immense blocks of rock rent from the overhanging masses of the precipice, and precipitated down its ruined sides, lie scattered about, so as completely to choke up the defile. The entire is the mighty work of unassisted nature.[27]

With its treacherous topography, the Gap served as Killarney's signal awe-inspiring landscape. Romantic travel writing foregrounded deeply personal engagement, emotional and physical, with its elemental features. Thus narrators often adopted the reverential voice of the solitary traveller in the face of these testaments to the unfathomable act of Creation, even when accompanied by others on their tours. Complementary representational techniques were also evident in contemporary landscape painting. While sites in Killarney had been popular subjects of painting since the eighteenth century, frequently assembled in collections which highlighted 'scenic spots', or panoramic views of the Killarney lakes,[28] the Gap was often represented by visual artists as solitary and majestic. Watercolourists such as George Robson employed light to dramatic effect, inserting a lone figure in the landscape – a technique which also dramatized the grandeur of the place. What Carla Briggs has described as 'figures diminished' by the 'vastness' of the Gap was a recurrent theme.[29] Through these techniques, painters composed images which were complementary to prose narratives of the solitary traveller facing a grand, elemental landscape.

Writers narrated the presence of other people in the Gap sparingly; when they figured in narratives, it was often in ways that complemented the dominant aesthetic framing of the site. The artist Theresa Cornwallis ('Mrs Frederic West'), for instance, touring in 1846 with the purpose of exhorting English countrymen to follow in her footsteps, described the ascent into the Gap as a 'magnificent specimen' of the sublime, 'wild and cultureless – it seems to be the very end of the world'.[30] Commenting on the landscape of jagged rocks and moorland and Alpine plants, she also located a representative pastoral figure there.[31] West observed a herd of goats 'skipping about over the crags', and caught site of their shepherd: 'His brown garments and slouch hat were wondrous picturesque, the sharp dark eye peering out from its shadow; and I wished for the pencil of Salvator Rosa, or Rosa da Tivoli, to sketch him off with his shaggy charge'.[32] The solitary shepherd was integral to West's picturesque prose composition – positioned in a site otherwise portrayed as quintessentially sublime.

Though it underpinned many narratives of the Gap landscape, the sublime quality of the defile was debated. Some depictions, such as West's, detected picturesque qualities there. Others disputed the Gap's sublime character altogether. In a series of letters on travels published in 1827, for instance, the writer Nathaniel Hazeltine Carter, recounting his tour through Europe, opined that the site did not, for him, evoke fear or indeed the range of raw emotions expressed by other writers. Indeed Killarney offered little more than diminutive versions of other sites:

> In the exaggerated descriptions of the scenery about these lakes, it is stated among other things, that persons have entered the gap of Dunloe, and were so terrified at the precipices overhanging them, as to retreat without venturing through. They must have had weak nerves, if there be the least foundation for the report. We experienced nothing like terror. The scene is grand, but cannot be considered awful. In sublimity, it is far inferior to the Notch in the White Hills of New-Hampshire. The Saco is a much finer river, than the streamlet hurrying down the rocky pass of Dunloe, and M'Gilly Cuddy's Reeks

and Purple Mountain are mere mole hills, in comparison with Mount Washington.[33]

If its sublime character was contested, another aspect of the Gap attracted near-universal scorn: the disruptive presence of local men and women who pressed themselves upon the traveller, offering articles and services, and intruding upon the tourist's gaze. Their presence could not be elided, or subsumed within an aesthetic narrative, as West's shepherd had been. Indeed, as one traveller wrote in 1837 of a trip through the Gap and Killarney's lake: 'The only alloy to this glorious scene was the sight of the miserable peasantry, who, seeing our boat passing over the Lake, had run down from Mangerton and the other hills, to offer us goat's milk and "poteen". They seemed poor and wretched in the extreme, and formed a melancholy contrast with the heavenly spot they inhabited.'[34] This intrusion – which did not merely desecrate the scene, but constituted an unwelcome embodied intrusion, with attendant, unpalatable smells, tastes, and touches – was to become a dominant theme in travel accounts in the post-Famine period, and eventually became the principal conceit of the refined traveller's excursion narrative. This development reflected how John Urry's 'romantic gaze', grounded in the desire to establish a solitary and privileged frame, became destabilized.[35] Other sights and sensations underscored the carnivalesque features of the post-Famine Gap tour. Yet the recovery of the romantic gaze and a related narrative of solitary travel and emotional engagement remained an imperative in many travel accounts; indeed, writers employed the embodied encounter with Kate Kearney's 'granddaughter' to critique the raucous and disruptive circus that prevailed at the Gap of Dunloe and narrate its defilement.

11.2   '[T]all, bold, and greedy, with the gait of a mountaineer': Taste and tourist performances at Kate Kearney's cottage

The Famine years in Ireland marked a turning point in narrating the Gap landscape, introducing or codifying distinctive protocols of sociality and sensorial engagement. The social, economic, and cultural impacts of the Famine were indelibly etched on travellers' narratives of the country in the decades following that calamity. They nourished new narratives which privileged eyewitness accounts – first-hand observations of rural Irish social life, many of which drew attention to aspects of 'low' culture, the peasant *habitus* – as well as offering an enumeration of ruined abbeys, castles, and other markers of an eclipsed Irish 'high' culture. These accounts also tended to provide greater direction to multi-sensorial apprehension of places such as the Gap of Dunloe – and to forms of sociality there, which included reflections by writers on the experience of encountering both fellow excursionists and the bands of locals who pressed their attentions on them. The implication of all five senses in the tour, from the taste of mountain dew to the sensations of the bumpy jaunting-car ride, to the cacophony of voices pleading for the tourist's pocket-change, featured prominently in descriptions, and evaluations, of the excursion. Few travellers found occasion for solitary contemplation and intense engagement with awe-inspiring scenery. There were several reasons that this narrative changed: one was that the Famine was an event of such profound and enduring social and cultural consequence that it disrupted any narrative of Killarney as a place of fixed and enduring rural culture. This impacted on productions of its landscapes as expressions of constant qualities. The years immediately after the Famine also witnessed the development of commercial systems exemplified by the conducted excursion, in which tourists, many strangers to each other, were guided in large groups from site to site, making Killarney doubly-congested to the frustrated romantic traveller: overrun by mendicants and 'mere tourists' alike. These developments were linked to the expanding infrastructure for travel, signalled by railways, hotels, and a plethora of guidebooks, including those which directed tourists to spots of scenic beauty and which were sometimes concerned with how a tour might be effected with minimal expenditure, so that Killarney might be done by 'everyman'. Far from placing tourists under a hegemonic commercial structure, however (Thomas Cook and Son, for instance, competed with other large firms as well as with local operators), this era witnessed an expansion of tourist practices, from sporting tourism to those associated with the putative curative properties of climate, water, and devotional pilgrimage. But the signature allure of the Gap was a legendary seductress; it was an enclave of engrossing cultural performances, centred on Kate Kearney's eponymous abode.

The tourist's arrival at the entrance to the Gap initiated an encounter in which boundaries blurred between past and present, fact and legend, scripted and spontaneous performance. These were extensively and playfully explored in guidebooks and travelogues, which gave travellers considerable guidance on how to perform the 'meeting' with Kate's descendant. Insofar as they may be considered 'literary' tourists, many excursionists visiting the Gap were familiar with Owenson's poem

through short excerpts printed in guidebooks,[36] and through allusions to it in travel writings by authors who 'introduced' them to Kate
Kearney and delineated her 'customs' in colourful prose. In fact, few
tourists encountered anyone resembling the enchantress of Owenson's
song. The sentimentalized figure of Killarney lore was embodied by an
altogether different figure whom travellers met at Kate's famous cottage.
The resulting sensationalized accounts of meeting Kate's 'granddaughter' mixed irony and abhorrence at the spectacle. In a lengthy footnote,
Anna Maria and Samuel Carter Hall, authors of a well-known account
of a tour in Killarney, counselled tourists that they would encounter
Kate's 'granddaughter' at the Gap. She was the hostess of 'Kate Kearney's
Cottage'.

> The grand-daughter – herself the mamma of a fine family, Irish in
> number and in growth – is not unworthy the high fame of her grand-
> dame. She is what in Ireland is called a 'fine fla-hu-lagh woman' –
> meaning that she has 'blood and bone,' but as for the 'beauty' – we
> shall not be ungallant enough to question her legitimate right. The
> Tourist will find cakes and goat's-milk at her cottage, which neat-
> ness and order might very much improve. The cottage is close to the
> entrance to the Gap of Dunloe, so that he will be sure to see her: for he
> may be quite certain that she will be at hand with her – 'offerings'.[37]

Here the putative 'granddaughter's' body became a site for the Halls
to evaluate features of the Irish peasantry, including its fecundity. But
in addition to embodying a representative peasant figure, she was also
narrated as a unique character. Claiming improbable lineal descent
from the apocryphal beauty about whom Sydney Owenson wrote her
song, Kearney's 'granddaughter' inhabited the 'ancestral' abode at the
approach to the Gap, which the Halls found in less than salubrious
condition. Tourists' arrival at the cottage marked the point at which
they entered a socially distinct space. There, Kate's 'descendant' initiated them into the customs of the country. While many women in the
local tourist sector suggested that they had some ancestral connection
with the 'real' Kate Kearney, her 'granddaughter' offered her cottage
as tangible evidence of this lineage, calculating that it would resonate
with the touring public. Nonetheless, her claims aroused strong scepticism and led to assessments of the Gap which often depicted her as part
of the grubby commercialization of the district and an emblem of its
aesthetic decay. To writers desiring to narrate both social and cultural
distance from her and to cast themselves as impervious to native wiles,

the woman's deportment exemplified an Irish predilection to exaggerate and flatter for the guileless tourist's shilling. They described such persistent beggary as ubiquitous. Charles Mackay wrote in the *Illustrated London News* in 1849 that before approaching the cottage, a 'granddaughter' had already pressed mountain dew upon the party. 'The relationship', he commented wryly, 'which, as our very accurate and conscientious guide informed us, is real, and not pretended, is anything but unprofitable to her'. At Kate Kearney's Cottage the party found 'some new claimants upon our loose change', before entering the Spartan abode, furnished only with two chairs and decorated with a picture of Saint Patrick.[38] As the cottage became the critical physical marker of the beginning of the Gap tour, guidebooks, such as Murray's *Handbook*, assessed the 'granddaughter's' claims to lineal descent with marked scepticism, and described her sedulous attention to passing tourists:

> She offers hospitality, of which the tourist is expected to partake; being the first instalment of successive troops of attendant Hebes, who press their attentions on him, which tend to destroy the charm of the solitary grandeur of the gap by their ceaseless gabble and importunities.[39]

While most guidebooks noted wryly that the 'granddaughter' had succeeded in establishing a profitable trade on the site of her putative forebear's abode, C. S. Ward, in the *Thorough Guide*, identified her as the wife of Daniel Moriarty, proprietor of 'Kate Kearney's Cottage', where, he cautioned readers, '"milk and whiskey" troubles are in full force!':

> **Kate Kearney.** No one now (1888) living remembers to have seen this person, who is reputed to have been strikingly beautiful, to have sold potheen to tourists, and to have died about the beginning of the present century. Her house, levelled long ago, was near the slate house, 'Kate Kearney's cottage,' where Daniel Moriarty now holds a spirit license, &c., and Mrs. D. M. has adopted 'Kate Kearney' as a kind of trade-mark. Sometimes it is given out that she is the original, sometimes a daughter or near relative, but her maiden name was Burke, and the relationship needs proving. Mrs. M., who in her day was not a bad-looking woman (she is now well aged), sells her own photographs as Kate's.[40]

Ward's commentary broadly hinted that Moriarty's attempts to establish proprietorship over Kearney's 'trade-mark' was an effort to tap growing tourist interest in the site. Indeed, her practice of assuming Kate's persona for souvenir photographs also attested to the considerable licence which tourists granted her to impersonate this improbable ancestor. But the playful tone of guidebooks contrasted with the disdainful remarks of writers who waxed grandiloquently about the putative heiress's claims, and searched her body in vain for marks of authenticity. This assertion of travel writers' reason and judgment was an implicit critique of the barter, banter, and impertinent begging which they lamented as a scar upon the district. It reflected their efforts to distance themselves from prevailing practices in the tourist enclave, and implicitly suggested that were such trappings stripped away, one might recover an unmediated, solitary encounter with a primordial landscape.

One trope in post-Famine tourist narratives was to contrast the putative descendant with the romantic image of her forebear, described by one guidebook as a beauty with Spanish blood coursing through her veins.[41] The traveller recounted intense disappointment at detecting the woman's blatant deceit and recorded profound indignation that a woman of so few personal charms would exact money on the basis of such claims. Indeed, the 'granddaughter's' hideous body offered a canvas upon which caustic appraisals of authenticity were assessed. An account in the *Danbury News* offered one traveller's vivid description of the descendant, laced with acerbic humour:

> The next day I did the Gap of Dunloe. But it was gloomy and imposing was the Gap, and it rained nearly all the time, so there was some satisfaction about it. However, there was one feature – not of the Gap, as it is just out of it – which pleased me amazingly. This was the maid who occupies Kate Kearney's cottage, and sells photographs and potheen. I got some of the potheen. It isn't so pleasant, as a beverage, as camphene, but it is more dangerous. But the maid interested me. I had heard so much of the wondrous beauty of Kate Kearney that I was glad indeed to look upon the present occupant of the cottage, who is a direct descendant of Kate. Her name is Kearney, too, which struck me as being singular, for obvious reasons. Miss Kearney came to the door of the cabin on my application, and smiled, when she saw me, displaying two rows of teeth as she did so – one in each row. Then she had freckles, and coarse red hair, and a scar over her left eye, and one foot turned in, and a voice like a file, and she squinted. I withered before her glance. 'Are you a descendant of the beautiful

Kate Kearney?' 'Yis, sir.' 'Is Kate dead?' 'Miny years ago, sir.' 'Thank Heaven!' I ejaculated. 'Rig up a flowing bowl.'[42]

In evaluating the 'granddaughter's' claims, travel writers contrasted the bewitching forebear of legend and lore with the ugly, pertinacious hag – the embodiment of nature despoiled. Their embodied encounters were occasions to narrate surprise and disappointment that she bore no resemblance to the sentimental image conjured by romantic lore, stage-plays, operas, and postcards – a figure depicted as a comely, healthy denizen of the green hills – and then to express then suspicion at her mercenary motives. This was not the only place, as Nicola J. Watson has ably shown, where tourists in a romantic landscape found the 'force of sentiment' associated with a fictive figure lacking.[43] Indeed, the literal unavailability of the romantic Kate became a trope of the frustrated traveller's narrative: it offered an occasion to lament the eclipse of romantic travel, with its repertoire of mental practices and emotional modes of engagement grounded in the personal, 'unmediated' apprehensions of landscape.

As the woman's body was inscribed with increasingly virulent commentary, writers found ever-more florid ways to condemn her fraudulence and portray it is a marker of Killarney's desecration. In this way, the body became a canvas on which the tasteful traveller demonstrated aesthetic discrimination as well as expressive acumen. E. K. Washington, in his published memoir of travels to Europe from the United States, described the 'granddaughter's' mountain dew as 'perfectly execrable' and the 'granddaughter' as 'an ugly old Irish witch-faced hag – notwithstanding her ancestor was remarkable for her beauty'.[44] His invocation of the hag as a denizen of Dunloe reflected a trope through which the Gap was cast, like the body of the woman herself, as a locus of the grotesque and a site of carnival. It also conflated her with a heavily gendered representative figure of Irish rural culture – the crone – which appeared frequently in Irish travel accounts, most often as a character who aggressively exploited the tourist trade as a hawker or vendor, and who extracted pocket-change from excursionists to sites, at toll-gates, and in exchange for small wares. This figure merged with the supposed descendant of Kate in an 1852 account of a 'Week in Ireland', serialized in the *Manchester Guardian*; the author remarked that Kate's 'granddaughter' was famous for her 'truly Irish power of blessing and cursing'.[45] Indeed, readers were advised that a small piece of silver in exchange for her libation would earn the traveller a blessing, which the author transliterated in heavy brogue, with a warning that she would imprecate a curse upon any traveller who refused to share in her hospitality, or worse, offered only sixpence in return.

This exposition on the 'granddaughter' as a cursing hag, whose claims to Kate's blood-line were preposterous, tapped gendered notions of the sinister and the superstitious; they also evoked a stock figure in sublime landscapes, which dramatized their quality, perhaps in travellers' grasping efforts to position her within that idiom.[46] In a similar vein, the Canadian traveller Canniff Haight represented Kate's 'granddaughter' as a witch when recounting his visit to Kate Kearney's cottage. The woman whom he encountered in the flesh was a disappointing contrast to the figure of his mind's-eye. Haight remarked: 'Our dreams of the beautiful Kate were of brief duration, for we had scarcely got abreast of the cottage when there streamed out of it a dozen or more squalid wretches, who gave chase with shouts and swooped down upon us like so many starved eagles'.[47] Restating the predatory metaphor, he described how, upon disembarking from his jaunting car at the entrance to the Gap, the assembled beggars 'huddled and howled like a pack of wolves round me'. Bewailing the futility of his efforts to outride the mob, and regarding both his pony and guide as accomplices in this ambush, Haight described how the 'hungry pack' descended on him, 'howling and shrieking after me'.[48]

Not all post-Famine descriptions of Kate Kearney's employed discourses of animality, or invoked imagery of the hag, though most suggested that she was preying on tourists to some extent, and in so doing represented her as a specimen of the ubiquitous Killarney beggars who defiled the landscape. Travellers commented on the extent to which she 'hounded' them until they reluctantly 'gave in' to her demands for money. This was often coupled with assessments of her embodied practices which cast them as uninviting – even mildly threatening – and disruptive to tasteful travel practices. A piece in *The Scotsman* in 1871, for instance, recounted a meeting with Kate Kearney's 'granddaughter', a woman who 'has as much of "Meg Merrilies" in her as we saw in Ireland', being 'tall, bold, and greedy, with the gait of a mountaineer'; when the party was at a safe distance from her, they remarked that as she strode up to their car to welcome them to the Gap, they felt that her spell was 'as likely to be that of a witch as of a fairy'.[49] Caustic commentary was embedded within a comical narrative in which the author constituted himself as a 'sceptical' outsider fully cognizant of the wily 'granddaughter's' ruse. In *Harper's New Monthly Magazine*, for instance, the American writer Junius Henri Browne's disparaging remarks were laced with humour. This constituted an assertion of his intelligence, erudition, and authority over the artful peasant:

> Near by is a solitary hostelry kept by a putative grand-daughter of the apocryphal Kate Kearney. Kate is reputed to have been extremely lovely; but if she were lovely, if she ever existed, and if the young woman I saw was her daughter's daughter, the young woman is a most striking illustration of the theory that beauty is not hereditary.[50]

The body of the 'granddaughter' thus became a canvas upon which the wider features of the Gap carnival, and the most unpalatable features of Irish tourist culture, were evaluated. Narratives of the encounter between tourist and 'hostess' underscored how, in appearance and gesture, Kate's 'granddaughter' transgressed the romantic images of her putative forebear, and how, in her vulgarity and 'extortion', she also violated ideals of rural feminine hospitality. In this respect, they were expositions on gender, class, and Irish rurality. Moreover, ruminations on the granddaughter's artful but unconvincing ruse became grandilo-quent expressions of authorial distance from both her and the wider Gap carnival, assertions of reason, judgment, erudition, and taste, and lamentations on the ravages of mass tourism in Killarney.

11.3   Conclusion

When the writer Burton E. Stevenson lifted a glass of mountain dew to his lips at the well-appointed Kate Kearney's Cottage, he recounted in a 1914 travelogue that he drank the famous libation 'in the interests of this narrative' at a bar now staffed by playful barmaids willing to indulge the tourist's imagination.[51] The popular narrative of the Gap entailed the tourists' immersion in a place in which past and present, and fact and fiction were blended as generously as mountain dew and goat's-milk. Echoing widespread refrains of playful scepticism, Burton remarked mischievously that the neighbourhood of Kate Kearney's cottage, where he enjoyed his beverage, was 'a long way from the "banks of Killarney"' where Owenson's song placed its protagonist, and contended that the whiskey he imbibed 'is supposed to be surreptitious, but of course it has paid the tax like any other'.[52] In mapping the contours of the Gap tour onto the popular imagination, writers prefigured practices associated with Kate's mountain hospitality. Many excursionists approached the colourful human cavalry at the Gap mixing resignation and trepida-tion with prurience. Bereft of occasions to demonstrate connoisseurship through the language of aesthetics in landscape appraisal, 'tasteful' travellers found advantage in the Gap carnival, and especially in the embodied encounter with Kate's reputed descendant; indeed, they grounded their Gap travelogues in caustic appraisals of the granddaughter's claims, which were belied by her grotesque body and an altogether disenchanting personal manner. In these narratives, accounts of the embodied encounter offered ways of narrating the duplicity of the woman and the despoiled character of Killarney. They were also strategies to establish the authority of a visitor to the Gap attempting in vain to enact precepts of romantic travel and find moments of the elusive sublime in a Rabelaisian enclave, amidst the vulgar trappings of mass tourism.

Notes

1. See, for instance, tours outlined in John Cooke, ed., *Handbook for Travellers in Ireland*, 5th edn (London: John Murray, 1896), 423–9.
2. William H. A. Williams, *Creating Irish Tourism: The First Century, 1750–1850* (London: Anthem Press, 2010), 129–50.
3. James Buzard, *The Beaten Track: European Tourism, Literature, and the Ways to 'Culture', 1800–1918* (Oxford: Clarendon Press, 1993). The literature on Irish travel writing is impressive in scope and quality: see Glenn Hooper, *Travel Writing and Ireland, 1760–1860: Culture, History, Politics* (Basingstoke: Palgrave Macmillan, 2005); Ina Ferris, *The Romantic National Tale and the Question of Ireland* (Cambridge: Cambridge University Press, 2002), especially chapter 1, 'Civic Travels: the Irish Tour and the New United Kingdom', 18–45; Melissa Fegan, *Literature and the Irish Famine, 1845–1919* (Oxford: Clarendon Press, 2002). Valuable 'readings' of the landscape have been offered by William H. A. Williams in *Creating Irish Tourism*, and in *Tourism, Landscape, and the Irish Character: British Travel Writers in Pre-Famine Ireland* (Madison: University of Wisconsin Press, 2008); see also Elizabeth Meloy, 'Touring Connemara: Learning to Read a Landscape of Ruins, 1850–1860', *New Hibernia Review/ Irish Éireannach Nua* 13.3 (2009), 21–46.
4. John K. Walton, 'Prospects in Tourism History: Evolution, State of Play and Future Developments', *Tourism Management* 30 (2009), 783–93.
5. Susan Kroeg, 'Cockney Tourists, Irish Guides, and the Invention of the Emerald Isle', *Éire-Ireland* 44.3–4 (2009), 200–28.
6. 'The Author of *John Halifax, Gentleman*', *About Money and Other Things: A Gift-Book* (New York: Harper & Brothers, 1887), 224–5.
7. *A Select Collection of Songs; or, an Appendage to the Piano-Forte. Containing the Names of the Authors, Composers, Publishers, and Principal Singers* ... (Newcastle upon Tyne: S. Hodgson, 1806), 213. Here, the author of the song is not identified.
8. See *Songs of Ireland: 100 Favorite Irish Songs*, compiled and arranged by J. Bodewalt Lampe (New York: Remick Music Corp., 1916), 61.
9. Thomas Carlyle, *Reminiscences of My Irish Journey in 1849* (New York: Harper & Brothers, 1882), 117–27. Carlyle's wider travels in Ireland are discussed in

David Nally, '"Eternity's commissioner": Thomas Carlyle, the Great Irish Famine and the Geopolitics of Travel', *Journal of Historical Geography* 32 (2006), 313–35.

10. Anne Plumptre, *Narrative of a Residence in Ireland during the Summer of 1814, and that of 1815* (London: Printed for Henry Colburn, 1817), 273–4.

11. See Williams, *Creating Irish Tourism*, especially chapter 4, 'The Sublime and the Picturesque in the Irish Landscape', 69–88, and chapter 5, 'Picturesque Tourist Sites in Ireland', 89–106.

12. Claire Connolly, 'Irish Romanticism, 1800–1830', in *The Cambridge History of Irish Literature*, ed. Margaret Kelleher and Philip O'Leary, vol. 1: to 1890 (Cambridge: Cambridge University Press, 2006), 407–48. See also Tom Dunne, 'Haunted by History: Irish Romantic Writing, 1800–50', in *Romanticism in National Context*, ed. Roy Porter and Mikuláš Teich (Cambridge: Cambridge University Press, 1988), 68–91.

13. Carl Thompson, 'Travel Writing', in *Romanticism: An Oxford Guide*, ed. Nicholas Roe (Oxford: Oxford University Press, 2005), 555–66.

14. See the classic study by Marjorie Hope Nicolson, *Mountain Gloom and Mountain Glory: The Development of the Aesthetics of the Infinite* (Ithaca: Cornell University Press, 1959); for an examination of this development in Scottish travel writing, see Katherine Haldane Grenier, *Tourism and Identity in Scotland, 1770–1914: Creating Caledonia* (Aldershot: Ashgate, 2005), 21–3.

15. Philip Shaw, *The Sublime* (Abingdon: Routledge, 2006), 2–3. See also Thomas Weiskel, *The Romantic Sublime: Studies in the Structure and Psychology of Transcendence* (Baltimore: The Johns Hopkins University Press, 1976).

16. Edmund Burke, *A Philosophical Enquiry into the Origin of Our Ideas of the Sublime and Beautiful. The Second Edition. With an Introductory Discourse Concerning Taste, and Several Other Additions* (London: Printed for R. and J. Dodsley, 1759), 58.

17. Burke, *A Philosophical Enquiry*, 95, 96.

18. Burke, *A Philosophical Enquiry*, 96.

19. Burke, *A Philosophical Enquiry*, 97.

20. Burke, *A Philosophical Enquiry*, 127–9, 139–43.

21. Burke, *A Philosophical Enquiry*, 149.

22. Burke, *A Philosophical Enquiry*, 150–1.

23. Burke, *A Philosophical Enquiry*, 156.

24. Michael Haldrup and Jonas Larsen, 'Material Cultures of Tourism', *Leisure Studies* 25.3 (2006), 275–89. See also Malcolm Andrews, *The Search for the Picturesque: Landscape Aesthetics and Tourism in Britain, 1760-1800* (Stanford, CA: Stanford University Press, 1989).

25. Williams, *Creating Irish Tourism*, 76.

26. Sir Richard Colt Hoare, Bart., *Journal of a Tour in Ireland, A.D. 1806* (London & Dublin: 'Printed for W. Miller, Albemarle Street, and for J. Archer, and M. Mahon, Dublin', 1807), 80–1.

27. G. N. Smith, *Killarney, and the Surrounding Scenery: being a Complete Itinerary of the Lakes* (Dublin: Printed for Johnston and Deas, 1822), 163.

28. Carla Briggs, 'The Landscape Painters', in *Killarney: History & Heritage*, ed. Jim Larner (Wilton, Cork: The Collins Press, 2005), 145–55.

29. Briggs, 'The Landscape Painters', 153–4.

30. Mrs Frederic West, *A Summer Visit to Ireland in 1846* (London: Richard Bentley, 1847), 97.
31. For a discussion of typical pastoral figures, see Andrews, *The Search for the Picturesque*, 25.
32. West, *A Summer Visit*, 97–8.
33. N. H. Carter, *Letters from Europe, Comprising the Journal of a Tour through Ireland, England, Scotland, France, Italy, and Switzerland, in the Years 1825, '26 and '27*, 2 vols (New York: G. & C. Carvill, 1827), 1: 29.
34. 'J. K.', *Letters to the North, from A Traveller in the South* (Belfast & Dublin: Hodgson; Milliken and Son, 1837), 68–9. For evidence that the author may in fact be James Emerson Tennent, MP for Belfast and travel writer, see C. J. Woods, *Travellers' Accounts as Source-Material for Irish Historians* (Dublin: Four Courts Press, 2009), 122–3.
35. See, for instructive comparison, the case of Niagara, as discussed in John Urry, *The Tourist Gaze*, 2nd edn (London: Sage, 2002), 55–6. His discussion of the two gazes is found on 42–4.
36. See, for instance, R. M. Ballantyne, *The Lakes of Killarney* (London: T. Nelson and Sons, 1869), 65.
37. Mr & Mrs S. C. Hall, *A Week at Killarney, with Descriptions of the Routes thither from Dublin, Cork, &c.* (London: Virtue Brothers and Co., 1865), 110.
38. *Illustrated London News* (4 August 1849).
39. Cooke, ed., *Handbook*, 425.
40. C. S. Ward, *Ireland (Part II.) East, West, and South, including Dublin and Howth*, 3rd edn (London: Dulau & Co., 1895), 113.
41. *Southern Ireland: Its Lakes and Landscapes. The New Fishguard Route*, rev. edn (London: Great Western Railway, 1906), 40.
42. Qtd in *Bristol Mercury and West Counties Advertiser*, Issue 4432 (20 March 1875), 6.
43. Nicola J. Watson, *The Literary Tourist: Readers and Places in Romantic & Victorian Britain* (Basingstoke: Palgrave Macmillan, 2006), 132.
44. E. K. Washington, *Echoes of Europe; or, World Pictures of Travel* (Philadelphia: James Challen & Son, 1860), 249.
45. *Manchester Guardian* (11 August 1852).
46. Ian Ousby, *The Englishman's England: Taste, Travel and the Rise of Tourism* (Cambridge: Cambridge University Press, 1990), 167.
47. Canniff Haight, *Here and There in the Home Land. England, Scotland and Ireland, as Seen by a Canadian* (Toronto: William Briggs, 1895), 553.
48. Haight, *Here and There*, 554.
49. *The Scotsman* (6 October 1871).
50. 'Pictures of Ireland', *Harper's New Monthly Magazine* 42.250 (March 1871), 496–514; this quotation appears on 510.
51. Burton E. Stevenson, *The Charm of Ireland* (New York: Dodd, Mead and Co., 1914), 181–2.
52. Stevenson, *Charm of Ireland*, 181, 182.

12

'The Romance of the Road': Narratives of Motoring in England, 1896–1930

Esme Coulbert

The introduction of the motor car at the turn of the twentieth century revolutionized travel in Britain. In the nineteenth century the railway had dominated transport, to a large extent controlling travel between its network of stations. The invention of the automobile liberated domestic travellers from railway timetables and predetermined destinations. Guides devoted to motor tourism attested to its burgeoning popularity, while narratives welcomed a new-found freedom of mobility and individual liberty in a way that captured the enthusiasm of the early motoring movement. But the car also evoked ambivalent feelings about the relationship between humans and technology, and, more broadly, about the author's and the car's position in the post-Victorian industrial age. In his study of automotive cultural history, Sean O'Connell argues that 'the car and the motorist were used as both critiques and celebrations of modernity', and these, so prevalent in motor travel narratives, will be analysed here in the context of travel writing and the home tour.[1]

Anxieties in the narratives of popular contemporary travel writers H. V. Morton and J. J. Hissey highlight familiar travel writing concerns about tourism's damage to the landscape, the social and economic state of England, and the separate identity of 'travellers' as distinguished from the droves of passengers alighting at train stations. Focusing on the works of Hissey, Robert Shackleton, Morton, J. E. Vincent, and, briefly, Maud M. Stawell, this discussion will explore how these writers provide 'new modes of constituting knowledge and subjectivity' while re-imagining familiar home tour concerns.[2] Common preoccupations, such as fears of industrialism, the idealization of pastoral landscapes, and class-based prejudices against working class tourism, abound in the writing of this period. As this essay will emphasize, these issues all have earlier eighteenth- and nineteenth-century precedents in travel writing.

12.1   Overview

In 1896, the Locomotives on Highways Act removed the last legal obstacles to the use of 'horseless carriages' on British roads. Road journeys soon offered opportunities to test a car's commercial viability. Henry Sturmey's *On an Autocar through the Length and Breadth of the Land* (1899) is primarily motivated by such inquiries, and aimed to publicize the car and its technological potential. Sturmey and his team of Daimler engineers drove from John O'Groats to Land's End, before returning to the Daimler factory in Coventry. His narrative prioritizes the effectiveness of the car, and public reactions to it, over the beauties of the landscape. Not surprisingly, Sturmey co-founded and edited *The Autocar* magazine, first published in 1895, which regularly featured articles about the endurance tests of various models and engines, and car performance trials over some of Britain's most challenging landscapes. The magazine publicized automotive capabilities as far exceeding previous transport, and represented motor travel as a new way of perceiving the British Isles.

Before the First World War the car was a luxury item affordable only to the most affluent social classes, and the marketing ethos of British car manufacturers reflected this; advertising emphasized sumptuous and spacious interiors, and 'refinement' and 'dignity' were key descriptors.[3] However, there were some upper-middle class car-owning families, such as Maud M. Stawell's, whose travelogue *Motor Tours in the West Country* (1910) will be discussed briefly below.[4] Practically abandoned during the war years, motor touring revived after 1918, and the car became more attainable to the middle classes who 'began to identify car ownership as a necessity rather than a luxury'[5] (see Illustration 12.1). The number of cars on the road increased at a tremendous rate: in 1919 there were 110,000, compared with 315,000 in 1922.[6] Doctors, farmers, carriers, and even enterprising postmen were able to expand and diversify their businesses through the use of motorized transport.[7] Nor were the lower-middle classes entirely excluded from the motoring movement, as charabancs and motorcycles provided cheaper and popular alternatives for those wanting to tour.

The motoring craze gave rise to new patterns of tourism such as weekend camping and caravanning. *The Autocar* abounds in adverts for tents and caravans that one could easily attach to the back of the car for weekend getaways, a practice known as 'gypsying'; one of Morton's friends even referred to himself and his wife as the 'new gypsies'.[8] The car made it easy to evade weekday responsibilities and slip into an imaginary semi-nomadism at the weekend. Visiting American motor

THE CAR OF THE MODERNS

HILLMAN WIZARD FIVE-SEATER FAMILY SALOON £270

Illustration 12.1 'The Car of the Moderns: Hillman Wizard Five-Seater Family Saloon £270', front cover of double-sided advertisement brochure (1930). Source: Coventry Transport Museum.

tourist J. E. Vincent observes in *Through East Anglia in a Motor Car* (1907) the ease with which he can escape from town: 'Staying so long as seems pleasant and no longer, you may be transported when you please, rapidly and pleasantly, to scenes you have reason to believe to be worthy of your regard'.[9] The car could propel a family from their doorstep to the coast or countryside and gave the illusion of freedom and abandon that we now associate with the decadence of the inter-war years. In Evelyn Waugh's *Brideshead Revisited* (1945), Sebastian Flyte and Charles Ryder borrow a friend's 'two-seater Morris-Cowley' for an extravagant afternoon excursion into the country. Sebastian explains to Charles: 'I've got a motor-car and a basket of strawberries and a bottle of Château Peyraguey – which isn't a wine you've ever tasted, so don't pretend. It's heaven with strawberries'.[10] He adds a moment later: 'The motor-car is the property of a man called Hardcastle. Return the bits to him if I kill myself; I'm not very good at driving'. The narrator then reflects dreamily that they 'were soon in the open country on the Botley Road; open country was easily reached in those days'.[11] During the 1930s, the car's use extended even to the lower classes. As motoring became the most popular form of travel, it no longer possessed the novelty that was evident in earlier travelogues.[12]

12.2   By road and by rail

In the early period of the motoring movement, comparisons with rail travel were inevitable. Motoring narratives analysed the differences in practical arrangements, view, experience, and journey with an awareness that they had brought new perspectives and variation to home tour writing. The American Robert Shackleton notes in *Touring Great Britain* (1917) that travelling by motor car offered a more comprehensive view of the country:

> [T]he traveler who goes up and down the country by rail, stopping at the various famous places, gets the impression that Ann Hathaway's cottage is almost the sole survival of the ancient, picturesque cottages, whereas, on a motor tour through the country, one sees hundreds of such cottages and becomes a connoisseur of their beauty.[13]

Shackleton clearly advocates the car as a means of acculturation and of aesthetic, geographic, and historical judgment. He suggests that an experienced traveller and a good judge of 'taste' would recognize that Ann Hathaway's cottage is far from exceptional, and he therefore downgrades the objects of literary tourism. Shackleton also asserts that the traveller by rail is only ever capable of obtaining restricted views. Vincent agrees, stating that guidebooks written prior to the invention of the motor car

> were compiled by men who travelled by train from place to place, obtaining no view of the country often – for deep cuttings destroy all joy of the eye for the railway passenger – and at best only a partial view, for the use of men and women condemned to the like method of travel.[14]

James Buzard notes how Charles Dickens and Dante Gabriel Rossetti, contemporary critics of rail travel, felt that it produced on its passengers 'a degree of passivity' and an 'odd combination of movement and dormancy'.[15] In an automobile the traveller becomes an active participant in the journey, as opposed to the more passive role of train passengers, estranged from physical and geographical changes by their relative inertia. Wolfgang Schivelbusch, in his influential work *The Railway Journey: The Industrialization of Space and Time*, notes that many contemporary writers, including Ruskin, compare the role of the train passenger to a parcel, an object shifted from place to place.[16]

A frequent complaint of pre-war motorists is of being covered in dust from poor road surfaces. One was also exposed to the weather. When these experiences are compared with travelling by railway carriage, motoring seems to possess a certain ruggedness, and evince the driver's and passenger's willingness to get extremely dirty.[17] This new mode of travel also modifies narratives and itineraries, which become more spontaneous. J. J. Hissey makes the point of never following a planned route, taking whatever road he thinks looks like a pleasant drive. He frequently delights in his chance discovery of rural locations. Hissey's publications are exclusively about touring in the British Isles, his output amounting to fourteen books on the subject between 1884 and 1917, incorporating journeys made by horse-drawn coach and dog-cart to automobile.

In the narratives, cars and horse-drawn coaches frequently encounter each other, sometimes violently.[18] Metaphorically, this might represent the collision of two epochs, as the horse-powered age met the motor age. Contemporary comparisons usually focus on the robustness of cars compared to horses, which become fatigued over long distances and when climbing steep inclines. Motorists often stressed that motoring allowed them to see more in one day. Vincent writes of the motorist:

> There is now practically no limit save that of his personal choice and his physical endurance, to the distance he may go, and he need never be troubled, as the horseman must be from time to time, by doubts whether his pleasure may not be causing pain to the organism which carries him willingly from place to place.[19]

Vincent refers to the car as an 'organism', a whole constructed of interdependent components. However, the extract elides car and horse; the 'organism' encompasses both the natural and man-made. Vincent's argument here is that the motorist can now transcend animal limitations and become an accomplice to the machine, even a vital part of its working components. Thus mechanized, human boundaries are extended. The motorist feels empowered and independent, yet the excitement of rushing along in control of one's vehicle could be both frightening and addictive. This response recalls that of Thomas De Quincey, who apostrophizes the harmony of driver and animal in 'The English Mail-Coach, or the Glory of Motion' (1849; rev.1854), yet both De Quincey and his motorist descendants identify a common enemy in the railways which 'disconnected man's heart from the ministers of his locomotion'.[20]

The novel experience of driving a motor car, particularly at high speed, forms a central part of Hissey's travel narrative. He manages to capture the full range of emotions that he feels when going at top speed:

> It was quite wrong, but there was nobody to see ... hurt or put to inconvenience, so we 'let the motor out' and broke the law – greatly to our enjoyment. The motor, like a thing of life, appeared to enter into the spirit of the thing. We opened wide the throttle. She bounded forth responsively, rejoicing in unaccustomed liberty ... Chic, chic, chic went the engines with ever-increasing rapidity. The distance seemed to rush at us; the miles became yards. Downhill we dashed with a whirl of dust; up on the other side we raced at the pace we had descended. The chic, chic of the engines was soon lost in one harsh, continuous roar – we were flying! One horizon succeeded the other in rapid, bewildering succession. Our eyes were on ... the wonderful distance that ceaselessly came rushing to us. For a time a strange illusion took place; it was as though the car were standing still, and the country it was that went hurtling past. There is a joy in speed, and poetry in it, and danger in it too. But a rush at full speed in a motor car over a lonely road, and through a deserted country, wide and open, is an experience to be ever afterwards remembered. Truly, for such a moment life *is* worth living, and optimism is rampant![21]

Inverting Vincent's observations, Hissey described the automobile's transition from machine to animal, 'a thing of life' that roars, and later as 'she'. He also suggests that the creature shares his adventure; its natural behaviour is to break loose, like an unbroken horse. For Hissey, the thrill of taking the automobile to excessive speeds combined with its animal wildness, forms part of the allure of motoring, a dangerous and 'unaccustomed liberty'.[22] Horses, their equipage, and stables were part of affluent households; aligning the car with the horse therefore assists in integrating it into familiar domestic environments.

Hissey also compares motoring to flying. Such analogies are frequent in motoring narratives, as aviation and motoring were closely associated. Car manufacturers such as Rolls-Royce later produced aeroplanes, and marketing strategies in the 1920s emphasized the link. For Hissey, speed creates an awareness of the subjective nature of spatio-temporal distance; at velocity, Hissey confesses that he is unable to judge whether he or the landscape is moving. Schivelbusch discusses similar impressions among rail travellers: '"Annihilation of time and space" was the *topos* which the early nineteenth century used to describe the new situation into which the railroad placed natural space after depriving it of its hitherto absolute powers'.[23] In this respect, the distortion of time and distance is inherited from the railway journey and transferred to the mechanical and synthetic aspects of the car. Shackleton notes how the car 'annihilates distance', evoking its machine-like efficiency.[24] Hissey's observation that perspective and motion transgress boundaries between self and the object world are frequent in the narratives of automobile travel in this period. For his part, Vincent describes 'the [motorist's] sheer ecstasy of motion' and 'the road which seems to flow to meet him … to open before him as if by magic'.[25]

12.3   Representations of landscape

The way that these travellers represent landscape is remarkable for its awareness of motor travel's effect on perception. Although there are similarities between coach and rail travel narratives, coach travel lacks the speed and practicalities of the motor car, and rail travel lacks individualized transportation and the driver's freedom to travel where he or she pleases. Hissey describes his observations from a motor car:

> We rejoiced in our temporary triumph over space and steepness, in the ever-rapid unfolding of the country, in the dash uphill, in the constant and sudden changes of scenery like those of a theatre. It was as though we were passing though some vast picture-gallery – only the pictures were realities. For the nonce we were content to take a broad, general view of scenery, to the neglect of details. The eye had not time to grasp everything, as when travelling fast you only obtain impressions.[26]

Hissey's art metaphors create an impression of unreality; his descriptions are like distant and nuanced reels of images rather than detailed and measured observations.[27] Vincent emphasizes that such perception has a mnemonic function:

> The motorist is not an infatuated adjunct of a hurtling machine; rather he is one who, passing through scenes rapidly, learns to observe and to think more quickly than others, storing, as on a photographic film, memories to be unfolded and developed later, and by no means averse to linger in here and there a spot promoting easy reflection.[28]

In the first sentence, Vincent separates his human identity from the car, a move that may be contextualized by larger anxieties about the possible post World War I dehumanization of the population.[29] (The paradox of the car as a celebration of modern technology and a signifier of human decline will be discussed later.) Vincent then describes the human mind as a metaphor of machine-like efficiency; in the everyday use of machines, the brain and memory begin to function like a machine.

Horizons also play an important and symbolic role in the narratives. Robert Shackleton comments: 'Fourteen miles of splendid pleasure and with an added sense of the great horizons of motoring! – the ever-changing horizons that are such a keen and constant delight'.[30] To him they represent the developments and prospects of the future, and the transience and 'ever-changing' perspectives of the immediate present. Chasing and endlessly pursuing these horizons at high speed evokes the infinite possibilities of the open road, and transgresses the boundaries of distance and time.

'The open road' is a buzz-phrase in travelogues and other motoring literature well into the 1930s. It suggests opportunity, an enticing prospect, chance possibilities, and ultimately adventure (or misadventure).[31] The phrase was not only used in travelogues to capture the essence of motoring wanderlust, but also became a slogan in motor industry propaganda, part of the discourse of getting off the beaten track (see Illustration 12.2). It imaginatively visualized the escaping of limitations and constraints.

12.4   Touring in the countryside

The direction of movement in motoring travelogues is always beyond the city – usually London where most of them begin – in pursuit of an archaic and pastoral idyll. The physical and imaginary movement

Illustration 12.2 'Old Cottages off the Beaten Track in Sussex', from *The Autocar* 63.1760 (26 July 1929), facing page 160. © LAT Photographic.

of the motoring populace into rural space can be read as a way of distancing oneself from, and openly deploring, industrialism. Buzard explains that 'self-exemption is something which individuals living in modern societies feel they can "do" about modernity and its corrosive effects on culture'.[32] In the countryside, motor tourists are caught in a paradox of imagining themselves as active anti-industrialists. However, they also promote a modern tourist culture that leaves its mark on rural landscapes.

Anxiety about the ill-effects of industrialization is particularly prevalent in the works of H. V. Morton, whose travelogues of motor tours around the British Isles were tremendously popular in the late 1920s. Morton's work is characterized by a nostalgic longing for a pre-industrial age with pastoral landscapes and buildings, for example his description of the eighteenth-century Sandwell Hall in West Bromwich in *The Call of England* (1928). He describes the 'Old England' of Sandwell Hall threatened and encroached upon by nearby coal mines as

> an epitome of that new England, which is yet so young, the England that came out of steam as the genii in the fairy-tale sprang out of the bottle.
>
> It has swept away many lovely things, it has planted its pit shafts in deer parks, it has driven its railway lines through the place where hounds once met on cold winter mornings; and before it the Old England has retreated rather mournfully, understanding it as little as old Sandwell Hall understands the coal mines.[33]

Morton notes the sense of irreconcilable distance between the past and the present as industry and technology left evidence of their labours in the landscapes of the Black Country. The car is caught between the benevolent intentions of touring in the countryside and malevolent signs of the industrial twentieth century. Along with the new techniques of mass production, more aggressive approaches towards tourism and consumerism became apparent. As the popularity of motoring in the countryside increased, car manufacturers and businesses catering to motorists were quick to exploit this leisure trend. Hissey describes the deleterious effects on the landscape of 'modern' consumerism in Britain when he comments:

> During our journey we observed many a pleasing bit of village architecture thus spoilt as a picture by glaring plaques of crudely-coloured enamelled iron attached to them, setting forth the virtues, real or

otherwise, of somebody's soap, some other body's ointments or pills, and the like. One day we may discover the value of the picturesque and take measures against its spoliation, for nothing now is sacred to the enterprising advertiser.[34]

The landscape has become a marketplace where brands are advertised. This new aggressive and blatant consumer culture evoked a feeling of disenchantment with modernity, one that led travel writers in Britain to lament the decay of traditional crafts and artisan skills. Morton frequently reports on what he believes to be the last of these trades, for example the last treen bowl turner, whose trade, Morton supposes, dates back to the days of Alfred the Great: 'To say that eight hundred years seemed to have stopped at the door conveys nothing. The room was an Anglo-Saxon workshop! Probably the same sort of shed existed also in Ancient Egypt'.[35] The interest in traditional crafts can also be recognized in the Arts and Crafts movement then at the height of its popularity.

Similar reactions to modernity occur in travel writing as early as the eighteenth century, and again during the proliferation of the railways. According to Carl Thompson,

the figure of the 'tourist' becomes entangled with debates about modernity, and with anxieties about the apparently deleterious effects of the modernizing forces at work in British society (and subsequently, the world). The new tourism, born from the Industrial, Consumer, and Transport Revolutions, was very much a product of these modernizing forces – and so, perhaps not altogether surprisingly, the 'tourist' became as much an emblem of the 'modern', in Romantic-era discourse, as the enclosed field, the turnpike road, or the macadamized road surface.[36]

The desire to discover a pre-industrial Britain, devoid of the realities of modern commercialism, is common in the narratives of motor journeys. Hissey despised the advertising billboard that plagued the countryside, while contemporary appeals to aesthetic taste, notably in the pages of *The Autocar*, successfully influenced legislation to prevent such desecrations. Hissey, among others, reproached tourism as detrimental to natural landscapes and communities, threatening the pastoral idyll which motorists desperately sought.[37]

However, this complaint becomes more vocal in the 1920s when cheap fares on charabancs permitted working-class people to join the motoring population. In the nineteenth century, Thomas Cook helped develop a market in affordable working-class holidays and excursions. Charabancs and shared-ownership of motorized transport continued this trend. Writers like Morton believed that this lower class of traveller had neither the education nor taste to appreciate the country in picturesque terms, contributing to 'the vulgarisation of the countryside'.[38] For many, the automobile was now providing mobility to those whose mobility should be restricted. As Buzard remarks, 'The place that is endangered by ease of access is a sacred precinct in danger of violation; its vanishing or soon-to-vanish quality of being "untouched" becomes a subject for elegiac travellers' reveries'.[39] For the elite who had exclusive access to motoring during the pre-war period, the erosion of class privilege in the 1920s threatened the pastoral sanctuaries that they, through money and social exclusion, had sought to 'protect'. Buzard observes that this argument was present a century earlier in rail travel, notably when proposals were made to extend the rail network into the Lake District.

Motor tourism stimulated a rediscovery of the countryside, with an enthusiasm summed up by the title of Hissey's 1906 travelogue *Untravelled England*. Hissey himself felt that this title didn't accurately reflect his methods: 'That we set forth in search of unfrequented spots is true, but it is also true that in doing so we had to pass, now and again, over familiar ground and through familiar places, so my title cannot logically be defended'.[40] This combination of familiarity and novelty does in fact characterize many early motoring travelogues. 'Owen John' (a pseudonym) writes in his regular feature 'On The Road' in *The Autocar* of 1929: 'To-day ... one carries not only one's beaten track, but also one's own locomotive and carriage – and sleeping car, too, very often – with one'.[41] John acknowledges that motor tours in Britain are unoriginal in their ambitions, and the popularity of day-trips and more prolonged journeys in cars testify to such claims. Catherine Mee usefully details how the phenomenon of 'getting off the beaten track' to confirm one's status as 'traveller' rather than 'tourist' has a long history in the travel writing genre.[42] Tied in with these distinctions are claims to acculturation – demonstrating one's experience and knowledge acquired from travel. It can only be achieved by pursuing roads yet untravelled to capture the 'true' or 'real' country and people.[43] Therefore, the car becomes the means to 'culture', and exclusivity of landscape and destination; a tour catered to and delivered by the individual. Touring by motor car in its early days was a novelty that distinguished the individual 'traveller' from the plurality of railway 'tourists'. Before the First World War, the opportunity to make a motor tour was almost all that was needed to proclaim oneself an anti-tourist.[44] However, during the 1920s, the serious travellers had to go further afield to style themselves as such. Thus continental motor tours of Europe, Australia, and Africa became popular among the more affluent class of motorist.

12.5 Motoring ambitions

Hissey and Shackleton share the same motives for undertaking their motor tours: leisure and pleasure. In Shackleton's travelogue *Touring Great Britain*, the tour was to be 'a royal summer. It was six weeks of superb liberty, six weeks of kaleidoscopic paradise. ... It was six weeks of motoring, and of so motoring as to get at the very heart and essence of England and Scotland and Wales'. Interlaced with this decadent and luxurious summer tour is a serious attempt to compile 'every variety of scenery, every variety of castled and churchly charm, the towers, the cottages, the stately homes, the places of historical and literary note. ... There was no waste of time, nor was there omission of anything essential'.[45] Although Hissey and Shackleton both undertake their tours through similar motives, Shackleton's voracious consumption of landscape and landmarks is antithetical to Hissey's objectives in *Untravelled England*, which prioritize the track less beaten and seek rural 'discoveries'. In contrast, Vincent's *Through East Anglia in a Motor Car* (1907) takes the approach more closely associated with a guidebook. In early twentieth-century motor-tour writing, the car becomes a component of the narrative through its performance capabilities and the occasions when it breaks down. For Vincent, car travel forms the purpose for the journey itself, particularly since he asserts that there are no guidebooks that satisfy the motor tourist. He writes: 'A new method of travel, in fact, brings in its train the need for a new species of guide-book'.[46] Vincent foregrounds the practicalities of motoring and touring, offering guidance and advice for those wishing to emulate his road trip.

Maud M. Stawell's travelogue *Motor Tours in the West Country* (1910) harbours similar ambitions to those of Vincent. Stawell wrote a series of four regional tours for motorists between 1909 and 1926 that combine the functions of prescriptive guidebook and travelogue. However, her narratives consist more of historical impressions formed at locations than observations of those locations as she saw them. In this respect Stawell's narratives can be read through Buzard's theory of 'saturation', whereby 'the great importance repeatedly attached by travel-writers to the impacted meaning and pathos of history they found in antique settings seemed to militate against any precise observance of the actually existing life in those settings'.[47] When Stawell does pause to comment on details of motoring, the narrative is jolted back into the domain of the motoring guidebook, and the reader is reminded of the car's presence and function on the tour. In such moments, the paradox of juxtaposing information about this newly developed technology with an historical tour becomes apparent. The motor car is the grounding force that retrieves Stawell's narrative from historical reverie and brings it back to 1910.

The rediscovery of England in the motor travelogues of the period 1896 to 1930 constituted an examination of the present and a cata-logue of the past. Present concerns included frequent comment on the Agricultural Depression and the new wave of manufacture and indus-try. These were interwoven with anecdotes of local legends, myths, the broader historical relevance of a location, and ecclesiastical tourism. Writers are drawn into a dialectic between a rural past and the hyper-modern; their travelogues attempt to negotiate a line of continuity between pre-industrial England and the technological present. In this way, the travel writing of this genre becomes a quest for a new form of national and cultural identity. Perceiving one's heritage involved rede-fining England in a way that extended beyond Shakespeare's birthplace, Stonehenge, Warwick Castle, and monastic ruins, to include common-place rural villages as well. Some writers surveyed the various medieval market crosses in agricultural towns, while others, like Hissey, chose more eclectic subjects such as Tudor fireplaces in old farmhouses. All recognized and celebrated the traditional skills and crafts of artisans still seemingly unaffected by large-scale industrialism. It is also apparent, particularly in the work of Morton, that some believed that England's economic and cultural health depended on the relative health of its rural population and agriculture.[48] For these writers, industrialization came at the cost of rural life, with organic communities displaced by intensive industry.[49]

The Arcadian myth of an antiquated rural English retreat is a theme that recurs throughout the travelogues of this period, and also manifests itself in writers' language. From Stawell referring to Cornwall as the 'Land of Faery', to Reginald Wellbye frequently describing as 'sylvan' any type of woodland scene, all the travelogues succumb to this roman-tic pastoral nostalgia.[50] Paul Fussell identifies pastoral images of Arcadia as a key trope of interwar travel writing more generally:

> Pastoral has built into it a natural retrograde emotion. It is instinct with elegy. To the degree that literary travel between the wars

constitutes an implicit rejection of industrialism and everything implied by the concept 'modern northern Europe', it is a celebration of a Golden Age, and recalling the Ideal Places of Waugh, Auden and Priestley, we can locate that Golden Age in the middle of the preceding century. One travels to experience the past, and travel is thus an adventure in time as well as distance.[51]

The phantom of romantic rural lifestyle that Hissey and Morton try to capture is embedded within this 'elegy' for an English Arcadia. Old buildings and old trades and crafts are its emblematic remnants.

12.6 Conclusion

In motor-journey narratives written between 1896 and 1930, we witness a mechanically powered renaissance of the home tour, whereby the car driver feels invested with new freedoms to roam. Canonical sites such as Tintern and Fountains Abbey had become so thronged with 'trippers' and 'charries' that the sites themselves had to be altered to accommodate visitor numbers. Stawell's travelogues exemplify the modern companion to touring by car, combining generic guidebook information with advice about road conditions and scenic routes. Her narratives also respond to the new scope and requirements of the motorized home tour: where to obtain petrol, which villages or estates would not admit cars, what hills were not advisable to attempt, and where one was better off simply garaging the car and walking.

The multitude of motoring publications at the turn of the twentieth century, including motoring guides and travel narratives, reflect the desirability of touring for leisure, rather than for attaining knowledge of a particular 'culture', people, or landscape. For those wishing to escape the 'herding instinct' that is so much despised in contemporary editions of *The Autocar*, the countryside becomes an open park to the motor traveller. The car brings almost limitless access to areas of the British Isles that were previously only visited by determined travellers, those who could travel from railway stations by coach to remote destinations. With no planned destination, hotel or inn, or even direction, the journey of the home tour restores an aspect of adventure and the unknown that was crucial to the ideology of getting 'off the beaten track'. There were limits as cars are restricted to existing roads. However, farm roads and mountain tracks were all potential touring routes that the car could exploit. Driving off the track provided misadventure, uncertainty, opportunism, and most importantly the empowering thrill of motoring so well captured in these narratives. The new species of 'motor tourist' felt that they were able to see nature in more personal and non-prescriptive ways, as drivers were invested with new liberties to discover landscape for themselves. These writers saw the car 'opening up' the countryside for the purposes of knowing and exploring one's own country, but also as a way of getting back to England's Arcadian past; a means to escape the regimen of industrialism.

Notes

I would like to thank Tim Youngs, Carl Thompson, and Benjamin Colbert for their advice on earlier drafts of this essay. I would like to extend my thanks to The Coventry Transport Museum for the help of their archivists, and for unlimited access to the archive and collections. This essay is a result of research funded by an Arts and Humanities Research Council Collaborative Doctoral Award.

1. Sean O'Connell, *The Car in British Society: Class, Gender and Motoring* (Manchester: Manchester University Press, 1998), ix. O'Connell analyses social patterns of car ownership and provides a cultural history of motoring in general rather than an analysis of motor narratives.
2. Deborah Clarke, 'Domesticating the Car: Women's Road Trips', *Studies in American Fiction* 32.1 (2004), 101–28. Clarke describes how women undertaking road journeys had to learn new skills of perception to negotiate their liberation from domestic space.
3. This can be seen in almost any car advertisement featured in *The Autocar*. After the war, more exclusive brands such as Armstrong Siddeley (see the 1928 Armstrong-Siddeley sales brochure for the 'Richmond Enclosed Limousine') and Rolls Royce continued marketing the 'luxuriousness' of their cars to distinguish themselves from cheaper mass-manufacturers such as Morris, Ford, and Hillman, whose larger clientele came from the new car-owning middle classes.
4. O'Connell notes how some families increased their income from women seeking work outside the household, enabling them to own a car (*The Car in British Society*, 34).
5. During the First World War most cars were commissioned by the army to help on the front line. Some car owners, including many women, went with their vehicles to France as drivers (O'Connell, *The Car in British Society*, 49). O'Connell attributes increasing ownership after the war to rising disposable family income, combined with decreasing car prices. He also notes that manufacturers began to offer finance and monthly payment schemes (20).
6. Peter Thorold, *The Motoring Age: The Automobile and Britain, 1896-1939* (London: Profile Books Ltd, 2003), 88. Thorold bases his figures on the number of cars licensed in these years.
7. See O'Connell, *The Car in British Society*, passim; for the entrepreneurship of a rural postman, see Thorold, *The Motoring Age*, 104.
8. H. V. Morton, *In Search of England* (London: Methuen & Co., 1931), 260.
9. J. E. Vincent, *Through East Anglia in a Motor Car* (London: Methuen, 1907), 31.

10. Evelyn Waugh, *Brideshead Revisited* (London: Penguin, 2008), 18.
11. Waugh, *Brideshead*, 19.
12. O'Connell, *The Car in British Society*, 33–4, 37–8. O'Connell indicates that working-class owners shared cars with other families. By 1939, one in five families owned a car (2). These facts emphasize greater diversity of car ownership in the 1930s than in the 1920s.
13. Robert Shackleton, *Touring Great Britain* (Philadelphia: Penn Publishing Company, 1923), 211–2.
14. Vincent, *Through East Anglia*, xix.
15. James Buzard, *The Beaten Track: European Tourism, Literature, and the Ways to 'Culture' 1800–1918* (Oxford: Oxford University Press, 2001), 42–3.
16. Wolfgang Schivelbusch, *The Railway Journey: The Industrialization of Time and Space in the Nineteenth Century* (Berkeley, CA: University of California Press, 1986), xiv, 38.
17. An article in *The Autocar* called 'A Winter Day Run by "The Maid of Orleans"' details the harsh driving conditions during a Scottish winter, and the provisions needed to undertake such motor journeys (*The Autocar*, 17 February 1906, 200).
18. Motoring pioneer S. F. Edge recounts in his memoirs frequent violent exchanges with coach drivers on roads. See his account of a physical fight ensuing after he was deliberately struck with a coach driver's whip. *My Motoring Reminiscences* (London: G. T. Foulis & Co., 1934), 8.
19. Vincent, *Through East Anglia*, 157.
20. Thomas De Quincey, 'The English Mail-Coach, or The Glory of Motion', in *Confessions of an English Opium-Eater and Other Writings* (Oxford: Oxford University Press, 2008), 194.
21. J. J. Hissey, *Untravelled England* (London: Macmillan, 1906), 427.
22. Up until 1930 when all speed limits were abolished, most drivers frequently broke the law, and it is easy to understand why. Thorold's *The Motoring Age* gives the speed limits as 4 mph in open country and 2 mph in towns by 1865, 12 mph in 1896, and 20 mph from 1903 to 1930 (8, 16, 50, 206).
23. Schivelbusch, *The Railway Journey*, 10.
24. Shackleton, *Touring Great Britain*, 54.
25. Vincent, *Through East Anglia*, xx.
26. Hissey, *Untravelled England*, 357.
27. It is possible that Hissey is deliberately alluding to the moving pictures of early cinema impressions here, but the link is not conclusive.
28. Vincent, *Through East Anglia*, 227.
29. In *The Call of England* (London: Methuen & Co., 1936), H. V. Morton attacks the capitalist ethic behind the dehumanization of the working population and declares that 'machinery is a vampire that sucks the blood of humanity' (180).
30. Shackleton, *Touring Great Britain*, 38.
31. The *OED* defines the phrase as: 'A country road, or a main road outside the urban areas, where unimpeded driving is possible. In figurative contexts: freedom of movement'. Interestingly, it also notes: 'This word was first included in *New English Dictionary*, 1903, as a subentry of "open, adj."', right at the beginning of the motoring movement. 'Open road, n. and adj.', *Oxford English Dictionary*, Third edition (2009), Web, 21 January 2011.
32. Buzard, *The Beaten Track*, 335.

33. Morton, *The Call of England*, 201.
34. Hissey, *Untravelled England*, 18–19.
35. Morton, *In Search of England*, 8–9.
36. Carl Thompson, *The Suffering Traveller and the Romantic Imagination* (Oxford: Oxford University Press, 2007), 41.
37. See Buzard, *The Beaten Track*, and Ian Ousby, *The Englishman's England* (London: Pimlico, 2002).
38. Morton, *In Search of England*, viii.
39. Buzard, *The Beaten Track*, 40.
40. Hissey, *Untravelled England*, vii.
41. Owen John, 'On The Road', *The Autocar* (28 June 1929), 1326.
42. Catherine Mee, '"*Che brutta invenzione il turismo!*": Tourism and Anti-tourism in Current French and Italian Travel Writing', *Comparative Critical Studies* 4.2 (2007), 269–82.
43. Buzard, *The Beaten Track*, 6, 9.
44. The term 'anti-tourist' is here used in Buzard's definition of the term, whereby the notion hinges solely on self-representation. He writes: 'Snobbish "anti-tourism", an element of modern tourism from the start, has offered an important, even exemplary way of regarding one's own cultural experiences as authentic and unique, setting them against a backdrop of always assumed tourist vulgarity, repetition, and ignorance'. *The Beaten Track*, 5, 94–5.
45. Shackleton, *Touring Great Britain*, 1.
46. Vincent, *Through East Anglia*, xix.
47. Buzard, *The Beaten Track*, 187.
48. An argument developed by C. R. Perry, 'In Search of H. V. Morton: Travel Writing and Cultural Values in the First Age of British Democracy', *Twentieth Century British History* 10.4 (1999), 441–2.
49. Buzard, *The Beaten Track*, 18, 25.
50. Stawell, Maud M. *Motor Tours in the West Country* (London: Hodder and Stoughton, 1910), 162; Reginald Wellbye, *Picturesque Touring Areas in the British Isles* (Cheltenham and London: Ed. J. Burrow & Co. Ltd., [1930]), 65, 96 [et passim].
51. Paul Fussell, *Abroad: British Literary Traveling Between the Wars* (New York: Oxford University Press, 1982), 210.

13
Home Truths: Language, Slowness, and Microspection

Michael Cronin

It has long been acknowledged that one of the paradoxes of contemporary travel is that travellers often want to see what they already know. Going to see the original of Notre Dame cathedral or the Parthenon or the Colosseum is to empirically verify what are already familiar sights from visual reproductions, cinema, or television.[1] It is this familiar paradox that is challenged by the practice of travel writers travelling on home ground. It is precisely because they are assumed to already know what they want to see that the practice appears particularly pointless, as if the explicit object of the project was to highlight the textually predictable semiotics of tourism. For the enterprise to appear credible there must be a sense in which what seeing reveals is not so much what is already known as what remains remarkably unknown precisely because it is assumed to be known. The Purloined Letters of the travellers' insights are hidden in the most obvious of places, home.

In order to make sense of or bring attention to these Letters, the writers must engage in some form of defamiliarization. They must defamiliarize for themselves what is taken to be known or familiar, their own country, and in case of their compatriots as potential implied readers, defamiliarize a country they assume they know. A core element of assumed familiarity is language itself. Language is typically used for the circulation of meaning within a community, and speaking the idiom of the community implies a level of knowledge or access to the life and history of the community that is denied to those who do not master the idiom. It is precisely the desire for this knowledge or access that has been long held to be a rationale for foreign language acquisition.[2] Thus, if the home tour involves a necessary element of linguistic defamiliarization, that unsettling effect must inform the very medium in which the writers communicate their experiences, language itself. In a sense, the travel writers are obliged to engage in a foreignizing rather than a domesticating form of translation, where they must make the familiar foreign not through contact with the foreign but through engagement with the familiar.

This essay examines two travel accounts, both written by Irish travel writers about areas of their own country, *A Connacht Journey* by Desmond Fennell published in 1987 and *Walking along the Border* by Colm Tóibín, published the same year. Both accounts refer to journeys that were undertaken a year earlier. The purpose of the examination of these home tours is to establish how language features in the process of the re-presentation of Ireland for the writers and for their readers and how these acts of translation of place in the same historical period point up larger issues around the relationship between travel, experience, and language. As language and translation are bound up with questions of mobility, the essay will further explore how the mode of transport chosen opens up new perspectives on the experience of place in late modernity.

John Zilcosky, in an investigation of the nature of travel writing, wants to explore how the genre:

> circulates 'mimetic capital' about others. I mean 'capital' here, in the doubled economic/cultural sense. Requiring new resources and markets, capital encourages travel to far-flung places, and these travels produce representations that in turn become commodities (souvenirs) and cultural capital (knowledge).[3]

In the case of writers travelling through their own countries, they are producing mimetic capital of a different kind. They are not travelling to 'far-flung' places and if they are producing representations, the question is who is this capital for? Are they native informants letting the outside reader-ethnographer know what it is the natives really think about the place or are they engaged in a conversation with other natives about the very nature of the representations of the land of their birth? One way of investigating the nature of representation is to interrogate what is being represented and what is the language used to describe it.

13.1   Naming

For both Fennell and Tóibín, the choice of destination on their home tour is not innocent. Tóibín's choice is most obviously charged. He is walking along the contested border between Northern Ireland and the

Republic of Ireland in 1986 when the military conflict was still claiming lives and any possibility of ceasefire or peace seemed a distinctly
remote possibility. He does not offer any prefatory explanation or jus-
tification as to why he undertook the trip, as if the Border was in itself
a sufficiently contested concept to warrant further investigation. The
liminal nature of the border is repeatedly expressed through an insta-
bility around naming. The very first line of the account, 'As I walked
out of Derry towards the border',[4] points to the inescapable politics of
language in the Irish borderlands. Derry is the city officially known as
Londonderry, the name that appears on UK maps and weather forecasts.
Derry is the name used by the nationalist inhabitants of the city and on
maps and weather forecasts in the Republic of Ireland. As Tóibín makes
his way along the border, he is moving as much through language as
through time and space. Just as history and territory are contested and
fought over by the different armed factions present, so too the words
used to describe the lands through which the traveller moves carry their
own political and emotive charge. Northern Ireland is variously called
Northern Ireland, the North, the Six Counties, Ulster, or (part of the)
United Kingdom. The Republic of Ireland is referred to as the Republic
of Ireland, the South, the Free State, (part of) Ireland, or more specifically, in terms of the counties Tóibín travels through, Ulster, in the sense
of the nine counties that make up the historical province of Ulster. The
border as a territorial frontier doubles up as a political fault line through
the language of denomination. The shifting appellations show that it
is not only what is to be represented that is problematic – the nature
and origins of conflict – but the very words themselves do not so much
neutrally describe as actively articulate particular representations of the
conflict. As travel writing is primarily a creation of the written word, the
very medium of expression in this context cannot escape the shadow
of the self-reflexive.

Desmond Fennell is equally preoccupied with borders, differently ori-
ented. His journey to the western province of Ireland, Connacht, brings
its own charged indecisiveness around naming:

> Around the middle of the nineteenth century, Connacht – or 'the
> West of Ireland' – again became the subject of myth. It was depicted
> as the essential, real and historical Ireland: different from the human
> norm, rural/agricultural, poor, traditional and wild. Or rather, it was
> depicted as the former because it was seen and depicted as the lat-
> ter. It had all begun with Ireland's being seen – by comparison with
> 'normal, urban/manufacturing, rich, modern, civilised' England – as

different, rural/agricultural, poor, traditional and wild. Then, because the latter description seemed to apply more to the West of Ireland than to the East, the West was depicted as Ireland *par excellence*.[5]

In colonial shorthand, Connacht becomes the West which, in turn, becomes Ireland, an abbreviated topography which is subsequently internalized by Irish East Coast post-colonial elites. Connacht's shifting status as a political signifier is bound up with the fluctuating boundaries of the 'West' itself. In one understanding, it includes all of the western coastal areas and so takes in West Cork, Kerry, Clare, and Donegal. In another, it is specifically all of the land west of Ireland's longest river, the Shannon. In another, it is primarily deemed to cover the most westerly parts of the province of Connacht, namely, Connemara and the Aran Islands.[6] Travelling through the present-day province of Connacht, Fennell is continuously alert to the connotative baggage of the East/West divide, connotations that repeatedly stalk denominations.

He arrives by air in the province, a statement in itself, as he repeatedly challenges the representation of Connacht as the benighted site of the pre-modern. Fennell is scathing in his dismissal of Dublin-based commentators who derided the construction of an international airport near a site of religious pilgrimage and reputed apparition of the Virgin Mary, Knock. However, as he cycles out of the airport, he looks back to see what is, in his view, a betrayal of place by language. His ticket issued in Manchester calls the airport 'Connacht' Airport, it is popularly known as 'Knock Airport', but when he is some distance from the main terminal building, he notes with dismay over the entrance, a large sign reading 'Connaught' airport:

> 'Connaught', even in small print, is a very ugly word both in appearance and in the suggestiveness of the 'naught' part – a spelling, moreover, which leads ignorant people to pronounce the word 'Connawt' – but in letters several feet high it is awful; it is menacing like a black cloud.[7]

The spelling of the word has its origins in the practice of English officials in Ireland to anglicize Gaelic place-names. The name of the airport was initially to be 'Connacht Airport' but, as the manager of the airport explains to Fennell, it was changed to 'Connaught' at the behest of two representatives from the Irish Department of Communications on the airport's board of management. As for Tóibín in the North, for Fennell in the West, naming is never without consequences. Not only are names constantly mutating (the airport, the reader is told in a footnote, is now the 'Horan International Airport') but the language of toponymic description must itself be parsed for the historico-political tensions of allegiance. The spelling is further evidence for Fennell of the acute culture cringe affecting Dublin political and administrative elites whose very orthographic preferences display lingering colonial habits of linguistic deference.

At stake here is the status of translation as a way of engaging with the troubled relationship between land, mobility, language, and power. Stating a preference for 'Connacht' is to invoke the historical aura of the source language, the Gaelic language previously widely spoken in the province. The refusal to translate is a return to the originary force of the native language. However, one of the crueller paradoxes of language shift is that what was once familiar now becomes foreign so that the retention of the original Gaelic name for a majority Anglophone population exoticizes, at a certain level, the place it describes. When the population translates itself into another language, the former mother tongue is no longer target but source. It is an unfamiliar object in need of translation. The Anglicization practice of the colonizer, dutifully continued on by the public servants of an independent Ireland, points up the translation dilemma for the colonized and their descendants. What the transliteration of 'Connaught' attempts to do is give a conventional English-language form to an Irish place-name. It is a translation that prioritizes form over content, a form of transliteration that accords primacy to the signifier. The word appears English but like 'Booterstown' (suburb of South Dublin) or 'Ballintubber' (site of a well-known abbey in County Mayo) the names are perfectly meaningless in English. What they might signify, in the absence of a knowledge of Gaelic, is a mystery. In a sense, these transliterations have all the appearance of translations, in their conventionalized English-language form, but they singularly fail to work as translations, in that they convey nothing about the meaning of the words that are 'translated'.

In one respect, the experience of the Irish traveller is not particularly unique. If the Sorbonne Professor Brichot dwells at such length on questions of toponymy in Marcel Proust's *Sodome et Gomorrhe*, it is because he assumes, no doubt correctly, that with the passage of time and the shift from Latin and/or regional languages to French that French place-names have become opaque to many French speakers.[8] However, there is a sense in the Irish accounts that the scale of toponymic translation has been so historically recent and so geographically widespread that the travel writer must in a sense double up as a translator. The transliterated opacity of the place-names is a kind of haunting, a stark reminder of what has been lost and a continual challenge to the narrator (accepted or rejected) to engage in an act or acts of retrieval for the reader. Prosper Merimée once observed that, *'rien de plus ennuyeux qu'un paysage anonyme'*[9] ['nothing more boring than an anonymous landscape']. As pilots have intuited in their narratives from the cockpit, the act of naming and situating the landscape invests a scene with human interest. What was formerly an illegible jigsaw seen from a great height becomes charged with the connotative power of the place and association. Closer to earth, the Irish travellers on home ground know that not so much anonymous as all too familiar landscapes require their own, particular form of translation.

13.2 Deceleration

Wilfred Thesiger in *Arabian Sands* comments favourably on the slowness of movement of the nomadic tribe he accompanied: 'In this way there was time to notice things ... There was time to collect a plant or look at a rock. The very slowness of our march diminished its monotony. I thought how terribly boring it would be to rush about this country in a car'.[10] Colm Tóibín explicitly describes his own mode of travel with its own inevitable implication of slowness:

> I had made certain arrangements with myself about walking. I had made rules. All progress along the border must be on foot, I had agreed. If I wanted to go and see something that was off my route I could do so by taxi or I could hitch a lift, but every move towards my ultimate destination, Newry, must be on foot, except if there was danger, and then I would do anything – hire a helicopter if necessary – to get out fast.[11]

One consequence of the mode of travel along a border that is not always clearly signposted is that Tóibín engages in conversations with locals as he looks for directions. It is not simply orientation, however, that provides the trigger for talk as the writer slowly winds his way along the border. Wherever he goes, his curiosity about the cultures and identities of the communities living along the border leads to a ceaseless flow of conversation (punctuated in places by more ominous silences), alternately reported as direct or indirect speech. In Lough Derg, a celebrated site of pilgrimage, he notes that the 'most important thing that

I discovered was that you could talk: there was no rule of silence'.[12] In a sense, what Tóibín reveals in his journey along the Irish border is the close relationship between mode of travel and density of language interaction.

As time slows down to follow the traveller on foot, and space expands to reveal the embedded detail of the walker's environment, human encounters when they occur cannot be easily ignored. The medium of the encounter is language and so language takes on a presence that takes precedence over the visual. Though the account has a number of, sometimes lengthy, descriptive passages, the main focus of the account is on information that is retailed to the travel writer in narrative form, such as the accounts of experiences of workers like Rose McCullough who were hired as young children at Fairs to work on farms. As if to acknowledge an implicit division of labour, *Walking Along the Border* is illustrated with photographs taken by Tony O'Shea. Even if the relationship between the photographs and the text is more oblique than explicit, there is a clear sense in which Tóibín's account is primarily concerned with information that is conveyed through human speech. Part of this concern relates to the very territory Tóibín is attempting to negotiate. The significance of the border rests on the very different ways in which it is viewed – for unionists a bulwark of protection, for nationalists a sign of division. Tóibín's travels are primarily a way of eliciting different stories about what the Border means for the different communities in terms of their experiences of the conflict, whether this be talking to relatives of young paramilitaries killed by the British Army or the families and relatives of members of the security forces assassinated by the IRA.

By walking along the border, the narrative density of conflicting loyalties becomes palpable as the writer is obliged to cover almost every square foot of the contested ground. A particularly vivid example of the contrast between the panoptic shorthand of the visual and the extended narrative of the linguistic is offered in the final chapter of the book entitled 'Surviving South Armagh'. On the second page of the chapter, there is a full-length photograph of South Armagh, taken from a British Army helicopter, the river bisecting the photograph indicating the presence of the border. On the previous page, Tóibín had written about meeting a local Sinn Féin representative, Jim McAllister, who had shown Tóibín one of his poems:

> It was about being arrested by the British army and being taken by helicopter to the base in Bessbrook, across his world, his territory,

the places he knew; which those who had arrested him would never know and had no claim to.[13]

South Armagh during the Troubles was an area where the British army would not move about on foot because of the danger, and the very act of walking by Tóibín is doubly suspect. Suspect for the army who keep him continually under surveillance from observation posts and helicopters and suspect for those with monochrome views of the conflict as he recounts the tragic human stories of Protestants and Catholics of different national allegiances caught up in the violence. What is an empty, silent landscape from the air becomes a dense, mutinous medley of voices on the ground.

Desmond Fennell is equally committed to deceleration as a way of revealing the inner tensions and complexities of another contested territory, the West. His main mode of transport is the bicycle and the consequences of his choice are ironically hinted at when he accompanies a local businessman, P. J. Carey, in his car to visit Carey's factory in north-west Mayo:

> Back on the Bangor road, he said, 'Don't ask me what village or townland we're passing through, I never know. I have my eyes always on the road, thinking of how I could be using this time to make money'.[14]

In Carey's home tour what matters is time, speed, and money. As a local agent of entrepreneurial modernity, slowness and topographic detail are, at worst, obstacles and, at best, distractions. The slower times goes, the less money comes in. Fennell is sympathetic to Carey's involvement in local development and is scathing about urban romanticists who want the rural population to remain hostage to poverty-stricken quaintness. However, his preferred mode of transport makes him very aware of what 'village or townland' he is passing through and *A Connacht Journey* diligently logs the precise location of his movement through the province. As with Tóibín, as time slows, words flow. It is possible, moreover, to link the experiments in time-space decompression in Fennell's and Tóibín's home tours with broader conceptual shifts in late modernity.

13.3 Microspection

The French anthropologist Marc Augé in developing a rationale for '*l'anthropologie du proche*'[15] ('the anthropology of the near') not surprisingly looked to the familiar ethnographic coordinates of space and time. If anthropology was fundamentally about the business of deciding who others were and what it was that made them other, then it could not ignore the dramatic acceleration in the transformation of space and time which determined '*une réflexion renouvelée et méthodique sur la catégorie de l'altérité*'[16] ['a renewed and methodical reflection on the category of otherness']. In sketching out the changes that inform late modernity, Augé refers allusively to '*changements d'échelle, change-ments de paramètres*'[17] ['changes of scale, change in parameters'] which underlie the emergence of spatial concerns in the age of '*surmodernité*' ['supermodernity'], but not much is added by way of explanation as to what these changes in scale or shifts in parameter might involve. In the light of Augé's fundamental concern with thinking through new notions of space and time, we can explore how the shift in scale implicit in a particular understanding of the '*anthropologie du proche*' and exemplified in the travels of Tóibín and Fennell has interesting consequences for contemporary understandings of mobility in a global age.

Anthony Giddens famously, if not particularly memorably, defined globalization as 'the intensification of worldwide social relations which link distant localities in such a way that local happenings are shaped by events occurring many miles away and vice versa'.[18] The emergence of international institutions (IMF, World Bank, World Trade Organization (WTO)), the spread of global brands (McDonalds, Starbucks), heightened environmental awareness (Chernobyl, the Brundtland report (1987), UN reports on climate change), worldwide protest movements (Vietnam, anti-globalization protests) are seen as both causes and symptoms of the 'intensification of worldwide social relations'. In the context of travel, time-space convergence at a national level in the nineteenth century and the first half of the twentieth century is facilitated notably through the construction of railways and road networks. Time-space convergence at a global level in the second half of the twentieth century is enabled through the exponential growth in air travel and the proliferation of information technology (IT) and telecommunications networks. As the time taken to travel distances is greatly reduced, it has become habitual to speak of time-space compression as a central feature of the phenomenon of globalization.

The last two centuries might therefore be termed the era of *macro-modernity*, where the emphasis has been on assembling the overarching infrastructures which allow time-space compression to become a reality. So the most commonly invoked paradigm of our age is the planet as 'a shrinking world'. The collapse of Soviet communism and economic reforms in China further added to the sense of the rise of one System under Market.[19] From this perspective, not only is the world smaller but, to borrow Thomas Friedman's coinage, the earth is flatter. For Friedman, the world is conceived of as a level playing field, where all compete, however unequally, for the spoils of free trade.[20]

The advent of globalization and globalizing processes is not, of course, always or inevitably, seen as a benign development. From the rise of the anti-globalization movement in the 1990s to the meltdown of financial markets at the end of the first decade of the twenty-first century, globalization has become a synonym for a plethora of ills, financial, ecological, social, and political.[21] One constant is the contention that what globalization entails is an irretrievable loss of innocence, a death sentence for diversity and the spread of what I have called elsewhere 'clonialism', the viral spread of corporate, hegemonic sameness.[22] As the world shrinks, so do our possibilities for exploring, preserving, and promoting difference. The global villages begin to resemble each other in dispiritingly predictable ways, carbon copy model towns presided over by brand uniformity. Pedestrianized zones offer the same glossy retail experience whatever the continent.

Contemporary experience and the accounts of Fennell and Tóibín can, however, be approached in another way and this is through the prism of what might be termed *micro-modernity*. By this I mean that by starting the analysis from the standpoint of the local, the nearby, the proximate, the micro, we can conceive of the local not as a point of arrival, the parachute drop for global forces, but as a point of departure, an opening out rather than a closing down, a way of re-enchanting a world grown weary of the jeremiads of cultural entropists. The world of micro-modernity, in a sense, potentially challenges the orthodoxies of global macro-modernity. Whereas previously emancipation has been thought of as a going further, faster, it is now possible to think of liberation as going deeper, slower. In other words, the shift of perspective implicit in the accounts points to a new politics of *microspection* which seeks to expand possibilities, not reduce them, and which offer the opportunity to reconfigure positively the social, economic, and political experience of the fundamentals of space and time in late modernity.

When Italo Calvino's Mr Palomar enters a cheese shop in Paris he is enchanted by what he finds:

> Behind every cheese there is a pasture of different green under a different sky: meadows caked with the salt of the tides of Normandy deposit every evening; meadows scented with aromas in the windy

sunlight of Provence; there are different flocks with their stablings and their transhumances; there are secret processes handed down over centuries. This shop is a museum: Mr Palomar visiting it, feels, as he does in the Louvre, behind every displayed object the presence of the civilization that has given it form and takes form from it.[23]

A random visit to a Parisian shop becomes a dramatic journey through space and time. A local shop becomes a secular stargate, a portal into the geography and history of an entire nation. Palomar's epiphany gives vivid expression to a distinction set up by the French travel theorist Jean-Didier Urbain between exotic travel and endotic travel.[24] Exotic travel is defined as the more conventional mode of thinking about travel where travel is seen to involve leaving the prosaic world of the everyday for a distant place, even if the notion of 'distance' can vary through time. Exotic travel implies leaving familiar surroundings for a place which is generally situated at some remove from the routine world of the traveller. From the perspective of macro-modernity, where far becomes ever nearer through improvements in forms of transportation, it becomes all the more commonplace to equate travel with going far. Endotic travel, on the other hand, is an exercise in staying close by, not leaving the familiar and travelling interstitially through a world that is assumed to be known. Endotic travel is, in a sense, the mobile site of micro-modernity. It is also another definition of what the home tour involves for travel writers like Colm Tóibín and Desmond Fennell.

There are three different strands informing the practice of endotic travel. The first strand is the exploration of what Georges Perec has called the 'infra-ordinary'.[25] Perec explores the teeming detail of confined spaces in works such as *Espèces d'espaces* (1974), *Tentative d'épuisement d'un lieu parisien* (1982), or *L'Infra-ordinaire* (1989). In *Espèces d'espaces*, the narrative focus moves from the bed to the bedroom to the apartment to the apartment building to the street to the town and eventually to the cosmos. In this reverse Google map, the cursor of the writerly eye pulls back from spatial minutiae to a picture which is constructed on a larger and larger scale.[26] The primary aim of Perec's method is to make evident the sheer scale of the 'infra-ordinary', the encyclopaedic density of things going on in our immediate surrounding which generally pass unnoticed. This approach is evident in *Tentative d'épuisement d'un lieu parisien* where the narrator compulsorily lists all the goings on in and around the Café de la Mairie near the Saint Sulpice church in Paris.[27]

The second strand is an ethnology of proximity expressed in a tradition of writing which goes from Montesquieu's *Lettres Persanes* to Marc Augé's *La Traversée du Luxembourg* and *Un Ethnologue dans le métro*.[28] In this ethnographic practice, the usual poles of enquiry are reversed so that it is the domestic not the foreign which becomes the focus of analytic enquiry. In Montesquieu's famous conceit, he presents French society and mores as if they were being observed from the viewpoint of Persian visitors. The familiar is exoticized through this foreignizing practice and along the way the French writer points up the disturbing shortcomings of a putatively 'civilized' society. Marc Augé, for his part, in elaborating his own *'anthropologie du proche'* which I mentioned at the outset, treats the Parisian underground in *Un ethnologue dans le metro* or a Parisian municipal park in *La Traversée du Luxembourg* as if they were an unknown and hitherto unexplored ethnographic terrain, familiar worlds rendered other through the probing inquisitiveness of the professional ethnographer. There is clearly a sense in which both *Walking Along the Border* and *A Connacht Journey* participate in this ethnology of proximity as Fennell and Tóibín like Augé apply their writerly and analytic skills to the domestic rather than the foreign.

The third strand contributing to endotic travel practices is interstitial travel writing. Interstitial travel writing makes its point of departure its point of arrival. One of the earliest examples is Xavier de Maistre's *Voyage autour de ma chambre* (1794). In this account de Maistre treats his bedroom in Paris as if it were a vast, uncharted, and perilous territory where moving from his bed to a chair has all the adventure of an expedition on the high seas. A more recent example is François Maspero's *Les Passagers du Roissy Express* (1990). In this travel account Maspero spends two months with the photographer Anaïk Frantz doing a journey that normally takes forty-five minutes. They stop off at each of the stations on the way to central Paris and what are revealed are whole other worlds normally invisible to the traveller hurtling through seemingly featureless spaces on the way from the airport to the city.[29]

What these different strands share is that they are all strategies of defamiliarization, strategies that are central to the functioning of the home tour. They compel the reader to look afresh, to call into question the taken for granted, to take on board the infinitely receding complexity of the putatively routine or prosaic. They suggest that shrinkage is not a matter of scale but of vision. Worlds do not so much shrink as our vision of them. A narrowing of focus, a reduction in scale can in fact lead to an expansion of insight, an unleashing of interpretive and imaginative possibilities often smothered by the large-scale, long-range hubris of the macro-modern.

What endotic travel might involve in routine, everyday life is best captured in Stuart Hall's notion of 'vernacular cosmopolitanism'.[30] Hall argues that the most notable shift in societies in many parts of the globe in the latter half of the twentieth century has been the rapid, internal differentiation of societies. In other words, whereas formerly the foreign, the exotic, the other was held to be over the border or beyond the mountains or over the sea, now the other is next door, or across the street, or in the same office. Globalized patterns of migration and the creation of supranational structures like the European Union have meant that a great many places, in particular, but not only, cities, are host to peoples with many different linguistic and cultural backgrounds. This, indeed, is one of the most salient features in Maspero's decelerated odyssey through the stations on the line from Roissy airport to the city centre. He comes into contact with migrants speaking a plurality of languages and bringing with them a variety of spoken and unspoken histories. They are bearers of what James Clifford has called 'travel stories' which he distinguishes from 'travel literature in the bourgeois sense'.[31] The stories are multiple in expression and different in origin but crucially they are close to hand. Slowing down involves an opening up. What endotic practices reveal ultimately is the potentially endless complexity of the everyday lifeworld.

13.4 Difference

As both the accounts discussed in this essay were published before the advent of extensive inward migration to Ireland during the period of the Celtic Tiger, the notion of 'vernacular cosmopolitanism' could only with difficulty be applied to an island that was experiencing high levels of outward migration, both North and South, a phenomenon that is repeatedly referred to, particularly in *A Connacht Journey*. However, the endotic nature of the home tour can reveal differences that are vivid and real and that are not necessarily predicated on the more easily identified patterns of recent inward migration. Colm Tóibín frequently finds that he does not know whether he is in the North or the South. The landscape looks the same. Same fields, same livestock, same rain. It is only when people open their mouths and speak does he know where he is. Part of knowing where he is involves knowing whether he is in a predominantly nationalist or unionist area. Flags – tricolours or Union Jacks – are occasional visual boundary markers but generally it is detailed, local, oral testimony that maps out the terrain of difference for the traveller. When Tóibín meets a taxi driver in County Tyrone he observes:

> I guessed by the taxi driver's name that he was a Protestant, and as he drove me out towards the Hunting Lodge [small hotel] I asked him if there were pubs in Castlederg he wouldn't go into. These days, there were, he said. Things were bitterly divided now. The young people were completely separated into different camps, which had not been the case for their parents. There was a time when Catholics and Protestants lived in a kind of harmony in Castlederg.[32]

It is language which fills in the seemingly inexhaustible detail of demarcation and antagonism. In this endotic travelling, the local is neither simple nor cosy, but complex and fractious.

For Desmond Fennell the differences are similarly made manifest through language, though language can also conceal the very differences that are suggested by the invocation of the cosmopolitan. At one point, listening to a radio news bulletin, Fennell reflects, 'It struck me, half-listening to the Western voices in the bar: these people never hear their own accents reading the news in English on the national broadcasting service – Northern and English accents yes, but Western ones never'.[33] The voices of those around him are literally silenced by the national broadcaster with its inherited prejudices about the inhabitants of Connacht. In Fennell's case, the writer's project is as much about making these voices heard as it is about learning from them. In the context of a politics of microspection, what emerges is the burgeoning complexity of the Western province, the expanding worlds of insight so that at one point Fennell himself confesses, 'Once again, as on so many occasions, I thought how little I knew about Ireland'.[34] One of the occasions of surprise is in the town of Boyle in County Roscommon when Fennell is listening to Irish traditional music in a pub:

> A man had sat down on the other side of me, and I had judged by his accent that he was a Westerner. He turned out to be a German engineer who had thrown up his career and settled near Boyle only six months previously; and the plump, little woman beside him, who brought us all a drink, was his wife.[35]

The German engineer, Hall's vernacular cosmopolitan, is one of the newcomers to the area, alongside more established residents like Erwin, the German goldsmith, and his Swiss girlfriend Vitta. As Fennell moves through the region north of Boyle and south of the town of Sligo, he claims that 'through the '70s and '80s, and through the interaction of immigrant and native elements, a surge of collective self-possession and self-confidence had been taking place'.[36] This self-possession and self-confidence is invisible in Fennell's view to the macro-modern condescension of the East Coast but is revealed from the perspective of micro-modernity implicit in his endotic home tour.

Gabriella Nouzeillies discussing the vogue for forms of extreme physical hardship in contemporary travel accounts makes the observation that

> In modern times, reality and authenticity are thought to be elsewhere, in other eras and other cultures. For backpackers the nomad is not only the indigenous Other to be visited, but represents as well an idealized form of travel that brings liberation from the constraints of modern society and its artificial hollowness.[37]

This contention ignores the reality of endotic travel, the practice of the home tour which engages with 'reality and authenticity' not 'elsewhere' but close to hand, near to home. Indeed, what emerges from the accounts both situated on the same island in the same time period and published the same year is the extent to which the reality or authenticity of home can prove to be the most elusive of all. Colm Tóibín may be an Irish writer born in Ireland but what his border journeyings reveal is the inauthenticity and unreality of his assumptions about life on both sides of the Irish border. In a hotel he comes across a glossy society magazine called *The Ulster Tatler* and he observes, 'Over the next few months, I was to discover that things were, in fact, rather different from the world depicted in *The Ulster Tatler*'.[38] What he discovers is that the island that might be broadly described as his 'home' was very different not only from the roseate view of *The Ulster Tatler* but from views that he himself might have held before embarking on the journey. Similarly, Desmond Fennell, who had spent a number of years living and working in the West of Ireland, finds out again and again how little he knows about home, about Ireland. It is the authenticity of the multiple realities he encounters in what he assumed to be broadly familiar territory that is most startling to him, and by extension, it is assumed, to his readers. Part of the challenge, indeed, of *Walking Along the Border* and *A Connacht Journey* is to invite readers to see what they think they already know and to reveal through language, deceleration, and microspection how seeing can reveal the blindness of home truths.

Notes

1. Jonathan Culler, *Framing the Sign: Criticism and Its Institutions* (Oxford: Blackwell, 1988), 153–67.
2. Pierre Judet de la Combe and Heinz Wismann, *L'Avenir des langues: repenser les humanités* (Paris: Éditions du Cerf, 2004), 31–43.
3. John Zilcosky, 'Writing Travel', 1–22, Introduction in *Writing Travel: The Poetics and Politics of the Modern Journey*, ed. John Zilcosky (Toronto: University of Toronto Press, 2008), 10.
4. Colm Tóibín, *Walking along the Border* (London: Queen Anne Press, 1987), 9.
5. Desmond Fennell, *A Connacht Journey* (Dublin: Gill and Macmillan, 1987), 1.
6. Micheál Ó Conghaile, *Conamara agus Árainn 1880–1980: Gnéithe den Stair Shóisialta* (Béal an Daingin: Cló Iar-Chonnachta, 1988).
7. Fennell, *Connacht Journey*, 11.
8. Marcel Proust, *A la recherche du temps perdu* (Paris: Gallimard, 1999), 1346–492.
9. Prosper Mérimée, 'Colomba', *Romans et nouvelles*, vol. 2 (Paris: Garnier, 1967), 149.
10. Wilfred Thesiger, *Arabian Sands* (Harmondsworth: Penguin, 1991), 54.
11. Tóibín, *Walking*, 12.
12. Tóibín, *Walking*, 41.
13. Tóibín, *Walking*, 141.
14. Fennell, *Connacht Journey*, 45.
15. Marc Augé, *Non-Lieux: Introduction à une anthropologie de la surmodernité* (Seuil: Paris, 1992), 15.
16. Augé, *Non-Lieux*, 35.
17. Augé, *Non-Lieux*, 49.
18. Anthony Giddens, *The Consequences of Modernity* (Stanford: Stanford University Press, 1990), 64.
19. Francis Fukuyama, *The End of History and the Last Man* (London: Hamish Hamilton, 1992).
20. Thomas Friedman, *The World is Flat: The Globalized World in the Twenty-First Century* (London: Penguin, 2006).
21. Naomi Klein, *The Shock Doctrine: The Rise of Disaster Capitalism* (London: Penguin, 2007).
22. Michael Cronin, *Translation and Globalization* (London and New York: Routledge, 2003), 128.
23. Italo Calvino, *Mr. Palomar*, trans. William Weaver (London: Picador, 1986), 66.
24. Jean-Didier Urbain, *Secrets de voyage: menteurs, imposteurs et autres voyageurs immédiats* (Paris: Payot, 1998), 217–32.
25. Georges Perec, *L'infra-ordinaire* (Paris: Seuil, 1989).
26. Georges Perec, *Espèces d'espaces* (Paris: Galilée, 1974).
27. Georges Perec, *Tentative d'épuisement d'un lieu parisien* (Paris: Bourgois, 1982).
28. See Charles de Secondat Montesquieu, *Lettres Persanes* (Paris: Garnier-Flammarion, 1964), originally published 1724; Marc Augé, *La Traversée du Luxembourg* (Paris: Hachette, 1985) and *Un ethnologue dans le métro* (Paris: Hachette, 1986).

29. François Maspero, *Les Passagers du Roissy Express* (Paris: Seuil, 1990).
30. Stuart Hall, 'Political Belonging in a World of Multiple Identities', 25–31, in *Conceiving Cosmopolitanism: Theory, Context, and Practice*, ed. Steven Vertovec and Robin Cohen (Oxford: Oxford University Press, 2002), 30.
31. James Clifford, 'Travelling Cultures', 96–111, in *Cultural Studies*, ed. Lawrence Grossberg, Cary Nelson, and Paula A. Treichler (London: Routledge, 1992), 110.
32. Tóibín, *Walking*, 32.
33. Fennell, *Connacht Journey*, 101.
34. Fennell, *Connacht Journey*, 126.
35. Fennell, *Connacht Journey*, 116.
36. Fennell, *Connacht Journey*, 110.
37. Gabriela Nouzeillies, 'Touching the Real: Alternative Travel and Landscapes of Fear', 195–210, in Zilcosky, ed., *Writing Travel*, 196.
38. Tóibín, *Walking*, 16.

Bibliography

Primary sources

Abbott, Jacob. *A Summer in Scotland*. Dublin: J. MGlashan, 1849.

About Money and Other Things: A Gift-Book. New York: Harper & Brothers, 1887.

Adomnan of Iona. *Life of St. Columba*. Trans. Richard Sharpe. New York: Penguin, 1995.

Anderson, George and Peter Anderson. *Guide to the Highlands and Western Islands of Scotland*. Edinburgh: A. and C. Black, 1863.

Archenholz, Johann Wilhelm von. *A Picture of England: Containing a Description of the Laws, Customs, and Manners of England*. Trans. fr. German. London: E. Jeffery, 1789.

Ashworth, John Harvey. *A Saxon in Ireland, or the Rambles of an Englishman in Search of a Settlement in the West of Ireland*. London: John Murray, 1851.

Austen, Jane. *Lady Susan/The Watsons/Sanditon*. Ed. Margaret Drabble. London: Penguin, 1974.

Ayton, Richard and William Daniell. *A Voyage Round Great Britain, Undertaken in the Summer of the Year 1813 … By Richard Ayton. With a Series of Views … Drawn and Engraved by William Daniell, A. R. A*. 8 vols. London, 1814–25.

Ayton, Richard. *Essays and Sketches of Character*. London: Taylor and Hessey, 1825.

Badcock, John. *Letters from London: Observations of a Russian during a Residence in England of Ten Months*. London: Badcock, 1816.

Baikie, James. *The Charm of the Scott Country*. London: A. and C. Black, 1927.

Ballantyne, R. M. *The Lakes of Killarney*. London: T. Nelson and Sons, 1869.

Barrow, John. *A Tour Round Ireland*. London: John Murray, 1836.

Barry, William Whittaker. *A Walking Tour Round Ireland in 1865*. London: Methuen, 1867.

Beale, Anne. *The Vale of the Towey, or Sketches in South Wales*. London: Longman, Brown, Green, and Longmans, 1844.

Bent, William. *London Catalogue of Books with Their Sizes and Prices*. London: W. Bent, 1799.

Black's Guide to Dublin and the Wicklow Mountains. Edinburgh: A. and C. Black, 1854.

Black's Guide to Killarney and the South of Ireland. Edinburgh: A. and C. Black, 1854.

Black's Picturesque Tourist of Scotland. Edinburgh: A. and C. Black, 1871.

Black's Shilling Guide to Edinburgh and its Environs. Edinburgh: A. and C. Black, 1853.

Blake Family of Renvyle House. *Letters from the Irish Highlands* [1825]. Ed. Kevin Whelan Clifden. Galway: Gibbons Publications, 1995.

Boswell, James. *Life of Johnson*. Ed. R. W. Chapman. Oxford and New York: Oxford University Press, 1998.

Bowman, J. E. *The Highlands and Islands: A Nineteenth-Century Tour*. Introduction by Elaine M. E. Barry. New York: Hippocrene Books, 1986.

Brayley, Edward Wedlake and John Britton. *The Beauties of England and Wales; or, Delineations, Topographical, Historical, and Descriptive, of Each County*. 18 vols. London, 1801–18.

Brewer, James Norris. *Introduction to the Original Delineations, Topographical, Historical, and Descriptive, Intituled The Beauties of England and Wales*. London: J. Harris, et al., 1818.

Burke, Edmund. *A Philosophical Enquiry into the Origin of Our Ideas of the Sublime and Beautiful. The Second Edition. With an Introductory Discourse Concerning Taste, and Several Other Additions*. 2nd edn. London: R. and J. Dodsley, 1759.

Bush, John. *Hibernia Curiosa*. Dublin: J. Potts and J. Williams, 1769.

Campbell, Thomas. *A Philosophical Survey of the South of Ireland*. London: W. Strahan and T. Cadell, 1777.

Carlyle, Thomas. *Reminiscences of My Irish Journey in 1849*. New York: Harper and Brothers, 1882.

Carr, Sir John. *The Stranger in Ireland; or, A Tour in the Southern and Western Parts of that Country in the Year 1805*. London: Richard Phillips, 1806.

Carter, Nathaniel Hazeltine. *Letters from Europe, Comprising the Journal of a Tour through Ireland, England, Scotland, France, Italy, and Switzerland, in the Years 1825, '26 and '27*. 2 vols. New York: G. and C. Carvill, 1827.

Chatterton, Lady Henrietta. *Rambles in the South of Ireland during the Year 1838*. 2 vols. London: Saunders, Otley, 1839.

Cliffe, Charles Frederick. *The Book of South Wales: the Bristol Channel, Monmouthshire, and the Wye*. 2nd edn. London: Hamilton, Adams, and Co., 1848.

Cook, Thomas. *Cook's Scottish Tourist Practical Directory: A Guide to the Principal Tourist Routes, Conveyances and Special Ticket Arrangements*. London: Thos. Cook, 1866.

Cowper, William. *The Poems of William Cowper*. Ed. John D. Baird and Charles Ryskamp. 2 vols. Oxford: Clarendon Press, 1980.

Crabbe, George. *The Complete Poetical Works*. Ed. Norma Dalrymple-Champneys and Arthur Pollard. 3 vols. Oxford: Clarendon Press, 1988.

Crockett, W. S. *Footsteps of Scott*. Edinburgh and London: T. N. Foulis, 1908.

———. *The Scott Country*. London: A. and C. Black, 1902.

Croker, T. Croften. *Researches in the South of Ireland*. London: John Murray, 1824.

Cromwell, Thomas K. *Excursions through Ireland, Comprising Topographical and Historical Delineations of Leinster*. 3 vols. London: Longman, Hurst, Rees, Brown, 1820.

Defoe, Daniel. *A Tour through the Whole Island of Great Britain*. Harmondsworth: Penguin, 1971.

De Quincey, Thomas. *Confessions of an English Opium-Eater and Other Writings*. Oxford: Oxford University Press, 2008.

Description of the Lakes of Killarney, and the Surrounding Scenery. London: W. H. Smith and Son, 1849.

Dumont, Pierre Étienne Louis. *Letters Containing an Account of the Late Revolution in France, and Observations on the Constitution, Laws, Manners and Institutions of the English; Written during the Author's Residence at Versailles, Paris, and London*. Trans. fr. German of Henry Frederic Greenvelt [i.e. trans. fr. French, by Samuel Romilly and James Scarlett]. London: J. Johnson, 1792.

Dunton, John. *Teague Land: Or A Merry Ramble to the Wild Irish (1698)*. Ed. Andrew Carpenter. Dublin: Four Courts, 2003.

Eastwood, Thomas S. Badger. *Ivanhoe-land; Being Notes on Men and Books Connected with the Town and Neighbourhood of Rotherham, in the County of York.* Rotherham: A. Gilling, 1865.

Edwards, O. M. *Cartrefi Cymru (The Homes of Wales).* Wrecsam: Hughes a'i Fab, 1896.

Edwards, O. M. *Clych Adgof: Penodau yn hanes fy addysg (The Bells of Memory: Chapters in the History of My Education).* Caernarfon: Swyddfa 'Cymru', 1906.

———. *Tro i'r gogledd [A Trip to the North].* Caernarfon: Swyddfa 'Cymru', 1907.

———. *Tro i'r de [A Trip to the South].* Caernarfon: Swyddfa 'Cymru', 1907.

Eyre-Todd, George. *Scotland Picturesque and Traditional.* 2nd edn. Glasgow: Gowans and Gray, 1906.

Faujas de Saint-Fond, Barthelemi. *Travels in England, Scotland, and the Hebrides.* Trans. fr. French. 2 vols. London: James Ridgway, 1799.

Fennell, Desmond. *A Connacht Journey.* Dublin: Gill and Macmillan, 1987.

Ferguson, Malcolm. *A Trip from Callander to Staffa and Iona.* Dundee: John Leng and Co., 1894.

Fontane, Theodor. *Ein Sommer in London.* Dessau: Katz, 1854.

Forster, Georg. *Ansichten vom Niederrhein.* Ed. Gerhard Steiner. Leipzig: Dietrich'sche Verlagsbuchhandlung, 1979.

Forster, John Reinold [Johann Reinhold]. *Observations Made During a Voyage Round the World.* London: G. Robinson, 1778.

Franklin's Itinerary for the Trosachs and the Royal Route through the Highlands of Scotland. Edinburgh and Glasgow: John Menzies, [1877].

Gilpin, William. *Observations on the Coasts of Hampshire, Sussex, and Kent, Relative Chiefly to Picturesque Beauty: Made in the Summer of the Year 1774.* London: T. Cadell and W. Davies, 1804.

———. *Observations on the River Wye, and Several Parts of South Wales.* London: R. Blamire, 1782.

Giraldus Cambrensis. *The Description of Wales*, 2, Etext, *Munseys*, Web; original Latin edition: *Itinerarium Kambriae* (1191).

Goede, Christian August Gottlieb. *The Stranger in England; or, Travels in Great Britain.* Trans. fr. German. 3 vols. London: Mathews and Leigh, 1807.

Gordon-Cumming, Constance F. *In the Hebrides.* London: Chatto and Windus, 1883.

Grant, Elizabeth. *Memoirs of a Highland Lady.* Edinburgh: R. and R. Clark, 1897.

Gray, W. Forbes. *The Scott Centenary Handbook: A Guide to Edinburgh, Abbotsford, and the 'Rob Roy' Country.* Edinburgh: Grant and Murray, 1932.

Grose, Francis. *The Antiquities of England and Wales.* 4 vols. London: S. Hooper, 1772–6.

Guide to the Irish Highlands. London: Edward Stanford, 1861.

Haight, Canniff. *Here and There in the Homeland. England, Scotland and Ireland, as Seen by a Canadian.* Toronto: William Briggs, 1895.

Hall, Anna Maria and Samuel Carter Hall. *Hall's Ireland: Mr. and Mrs. Hall's Tour of 1840.* Condensed edn. Ed. Michael Scott. 2 vols. London: Sphere, 1984.

———. *Ireland: It's Scenery, Character, &c.* 3 vols. New York: R. Worthington Importers, [1842?].

———. *A Week at Killarney, with Descriptions of the Routes Thither.* London: Virtue Brothers and Co., 1865.

Handbook for Travellers in Ireland. Ed. John Cooke. London: John Murray, 1864.

Handbook of the Harbour of and City of Cork. Cork: Bradford and Co., 1852.

Handbook to Galway, Connemara, and the Irish Highlands, Profusely illustrated by Jas. Mahony, Esq. London: George Routledge and Co., 1854.

Head, Francis Bond. *A Fortnight in Ireland.* London: John Murray, 1852.

Heath, Charles. *Excursion down the Wye, from Ross to Monmouth.* Monmouth: [Charles Heath], 1796.

———. *Historical and Descriptive Accounts of the Ancient and Present State of Tintern Abbey.* Monmouth: [Charles Heath], 1801.

———. *Historical and Descriptive Accounts of the Ancient and Present State of Ragland Castle.* [New edn.] Monmouth: [Charles Heath], 1819.

Heely, Joseph. *Description of Hagley Park.* London: Printed for the Author, 1777.

Heine, Heinrich. *Reisebilder.* Ed. Jost Perfahl. München: Winkler Verlag, 1969.

Hissey, J. J. *Untravelled England.* London: Macmillan, 1906.

Hoare, Richard Colt. *Journal of a Tour in Ireland, A.D. 1806.* London and Dublin: W. Miller; J. Archer, 1807.

Howitt, William. *Homes and Haunts of the Most Celebrated British Poets.* 2 vols. London: Richard Bentley, 1847.

Inglis, Henry D. *A Journey throughout Ireland, during the Spring, Summer, and Autumn of 1834.* 3rd edn. 2 vols. London: Whittaker, 1835.

Ireland, Samuel. *Picturesque Views on the River Wye, from its Source at Plinlimmon Hill, to its Junction with the Severn below Chepstow.* London: R. Faulder and T. Egerton, 1797.

The Irish Tourist's Illustrated Handbook for Visitors to Ireland in 1852 with Numerous Maps. 2nd edn. Dublin: M'Gashan, 1852.

Irving, Washington. *Abbotsford and Newstead Abbey.* Paris: A. W. Galignani, 1835.

'J. K.', *Letters to the North, from A Traveller in the South.* Belfast and Dublin: Hodgson; Milliken and Son, 1837.

Johnson, James. *The Recess, or Autumnal Relaxation in the Highlands and Lowlands.* London: Longman, Rees, Orme, Brown, Green, and Longman, 1834.

Johnson, Samuel and James Boswell. *A Journey to the Western Islands of Scotland* and *The Journal of a Tour to the Hebrides* [1775, 1786]. Ed. Peter Levi. Harmondsworth: Penguin, 1984.

Killarney from the Summit of Mangerton. Dublin: James McGlashan, 1851.

Kinglake, Alexander William. *Eothen: Traces of Travel Brought Home From the East.* London: Picador Travel Classics, 1995.

The Land of Scott Guidebook. Galashiels: A. Walker and Son, c. 1903.

Landscape-Historical Illustrations of Scotland, and the Waverley Novels: from drawings by J. M. W. Turner, Balmer, Bentley, Chisholm, Hart, Harding, McClise [sic], Melville etc etc. Comic Illustrations by G. Cruikshank. Descriptions by the Rev. G. N. Wright M.A. etc. 2 vols. London: Fisher, Son and Co., 1836.

Lizars, William Home. *Lizars's Scottish Tourist.* Edinburgh: W. H. Lizars, 1840.

London and Paris, or Comparative Sketches. By the Marquis de Vermont and Sir Charles Darnley, Bart. London: Longman, Hurst, Rees, Orme, Brown, and Green, 1823.

Luckombe, Philip. *A Tour through Ireland in 1779.* London: T. Lowndes, 1780.

Lumsden and Son's Guide to the Romantic Scenery of Loch Lomond, Loch-Kethurin, The Trossachs, &c. 3rd edn. Glasgow, 1838.

MacBrayne, David, pub. *Summer Tours in Scotland.* [New edn.] Glasgow, 1896.

MacCulloch, John. *The Highlands and Western Isles of Scotland, Containing Descriptions of Their Scenery and Antiquities ... Founded as a Series of Annual*

Journeys between the Years 1811 and 1821, and Forming a Universal Guide to that Country, in Letters to Sir Walter Scott, Bart. 4 vols. London: Longman, Hurst, Rees, Orme, Brown, and Green, 1824.

Macready, William Charles. *Macready's Reminiscences, and Selections from His Diaries and Letters.* Ed. Sir Frederick Pollock. 2 vols. London: Macmillan & Co., 1875.

Marshall, Matthew. *Legh Richmond.* London: Religious Tract Society, 1893.

Maspero, François. *Les Passagers du Roissy Express.* Paris: Seuil, 1990.

Mavor, William. *The British Tourist's, or, Traveller's Pocket Companion, through England, Wales, Scotland, and Ireland.* 3rd edn. London: Richard Phillips, 1809.

Meister, Jacques-Henri, ed. *Correspondance littéraire, philosophique et critique, addressée à un souverain d'Allemagne ... par Le Baron de Grimm et par Diderot.* Vol. 5, pt 3. Paris: F. Buisson, 1813.

———. *Letters Written during a Residence in England.* Trans. fr. French. London: Longman and Rees, 1799.

———. *Souvenirs d'un voyage en Angleterre.* Paris: Chez Gatty, 1791.

Menzies, John, pub. *Menzies' Tourist's Pocket Guide for Scotland.* Edinburgh, 1853.

Mérimée, Prosper. *Romans et nouvelles.* Ed. Maurice Parturier. 2 vols. Paris: Garnier, 1967.

Montesquieu, Charles de Secondat. *Lettres Persanes.* Paris: Garnier-Flammarion, 1964.

Morgan, Mary. *A Tour to Milford Haven, in the Year 1791. By Mrs Morgan.* London: John Stockdale, 1795.

Moritz, Karl Phillip. *Travels Chiefly on Foot, through Several Parts of England, in 1782.* Trans. fr. German. London: G. G. and J. Robinson, 1795.

Morton, H. V. *The Call of England.* London: Methuen and Co., 1936.

———. *In Search of England.* London: Methuen and Co., 1931.

Napier, George G. *The Homes and Haunts of Sir Walter Scott.* Glasgow: James Maclehose and Sons, 1897.

Nicholson, George. *The Cambrian Traveller's Guide and Pocket Companion.* Stourport: George Nicholson, 1808.

Nodier, Jean Emmanuel Charles. *Promenade from Dieppe to the Mountains of Scotland.* Trans. fr. French. Edinburgh: William Blackwood; London: T. Cadell, 1822.

Noel, Baptist Wriothesley. *Notes on a Short Tour through the Midland Counties of Ireland in the Summer of 1836.* London: J. Nisbet, 1837.

Olcutt, Charles S. *The Country of Sir Walter Scott.* London: Cassell and Co., 1913.

Oliver and Boyd's Scottish Tourist. Edinburgh: Oliver and Boyd, 1860.

Osborne, Sydney Godolphin. *Gleanings of the West of Ireland.* London: T. and W. Boone, 1850.

Otway, Caesar. *Sketches in Erris and Tyrawly.* Dublin: William Curry, Jun.; London: Longman, Orme, and Co., 1841.

———. *Sketches in Ireland: Descriptive of Interesting, and Hitherto Unnoticed Districts, in the North and South.* Dublin: William Curry, Jun., 1827.

———. *A Tour of Connaught; Comprising Sketches of Clonmacnoise, Joyce Country, and Achill.* Dublin: William Curry, Jun., 1839.

Ovid. *Ovid's Metamorphoses, in Fifteen Books. Translated by Mr. Dryden, Mr. Addison ... and Other Eminent Hands.* 4th edn. 2 vols. London: J. and R. Tonson, 1736.

Pasquin, Anthony [pseud. of John Williams]. *The New Brighton Guide; or, Companion for Young Ladies and Gentlemen to All the Watering-Places in Great Britain.* London: H. D. Symonds and T. Bellamy, 1796.

Patmore, Peter George. *Letters on England. By Victoire, Count de Soligny.* 2 vols. London: Henry Colburn, 1823.

Pennant, Thomas. *Arctic Zoology.* 2 vols. London: Henry Hughs, 1784–85.

———. *British Zoology.* 4 vols. London: Benjamin White, 1768–70.

———. *The Literary Life of Thomas Pennant Esq., by Himself* [1793]. Dublin: J. Christie, 1821.

———. *Outlines of the Globe.* 4 vols. London, 1798–1800.

———. *A Tour in Scotland MDCCLXIX.* Chester: John Monk, 1771.

———. *A Tour in Scotland and Voyage to the Hebrides.* 2 vols. Chester: John Monk, 1774.

Pernot, François Alexandre. *Vues pittoresques de l'Ecosse, avec un texte explicatif extrait en grand dessinées d'après Nature.* Bruxelles: Wahlen et Dewasme, 1827.

Pichot, Joseph Jean Marie Charles Amédée. *Historical and Literary Tour of a Foreigner in England and Scotland.* Trans. fr. French. 2 vols. London: Saunders and Otley, 1825.

Picturesque Guide to the Lakes of Killarney. Dublin: Hodges and Smith, 1851.

Plumptre, Anne. *Narrative of a Residence in Ireland during the Summer of 1814, and that of 1815.* London: Henry Colburn, 1817.

Price, Uvedale. *An Essay on the Picturesque, as Compared with the Sublime and the Beautiful, and, on the Use of Studying Pictures, for the Purpose of Improving Real Landscape.* London: J. Robson, 1794.

Proust, Marcel. *A la recherche du temps perdu.* Paris: Gallimard, 1999.

Puckler-Muskau, Hermann. *Tour in England, Ireland and France in the Years 1826, 1827, 1828 and 1829 ... in a Series of Letters by a German Prince.* Philadelphia: Carey, Lea and Blanchard, 1833.

Radcliffe, Ann. *A Journey Made in the Summer of 1794, through Holland and the Western Frontier of Germany, with a Return down the Rhine: to Which Are Added, Observations During a Tour to the Lakes of Lancashire, Westmoreland, and Cumberland.* Dublin: William Porter, et al., 1795.

Reid, Thomas. *Travels in Ireland in the Year 1822.* London: Longman, Hurst, Rees, Orme, and Brown, 1823.

Ritchie, Leitch. *Ireland, Picturesque and Romantic.* 2 vols. London: Longman, Rees, Orme, Brown, Green, and Longman, 1837.

Russell, Richard. *Dissertation on the Use of Sea Water in the Diseases of the Glands.* 4th edn. London: W. Owen, 1760.

Schopenhauer, Johanna. *Reise nach England.* Ed. Konrad Paul. Berlin-Ost: Buchclub 65, 1982.

Scott, John. *A Visit to Paris in 1814; Being a Review of the Moral, Political, Intellectual and Social Condition of the French Capital.* 2nd edn. London: Longman, Hurst, Rees, Orme, and Brown. 1815.

Scott, Walter. *The Journal of Walter Scott, 1825–32.* New edn. Edinburgh: Douglas & Foulis, 1927.

Shackleton, Robert. *Touring Great Britain.* Philadelphia: Penn Publishing Company, 1923.

Sharp, William. *Literary Geography.* London: Pall Mall, 1907.

Shaw, Stebbing. *A Tour to the West of England, in 1788*. London: Robson and Clarke, 1789.

Shelley, Frances, Lady. *The Diary of Frances Lady Shelley 1787–1817*. Ed. Richard Edgcumbe. 2 vols. London: John Murray, 1912.

Shelley, Mary Wollstonecraft. *The Letters of Mary Wollstonecraft Shelley*. Ed. Betty T. Bennett. 3 vols. Baltimore and London: The Johns Hopkins University Press, 1980–88.

Shelley, Percy Bysshe. *Poetical Works*. Ed. Thomas Hutchinson, corr. G. M. Matthews. Oxford and New York: Oxford University Press, 1970.

Simond, Louis. *Journal of a Tour and Residence in Great Britain: During the Years 1810 and 1811. By a French Traveller*. 2 vols. Edinburgh: A. Constable, 1815.

Silliman, Benjamin. *A Journal of Travels in England, Holland and Scotland, and of Two Passages over the Atlantic in the Years 1805 and 1806*. 2 vols. New York: Ezra Sargeant, 1810.

Smith, Charlotte. *The Poems of Charlotte Smith*. Ed. Stuart Curran. New York and Oxford: Oxford University Press, 1993.

Smith, G. N. *Killarney, and the Surrounding Scenery: being a Complete Itinerary of the Lakes*. Dublin: Printed for Johnston and Deas, 1822.

Smith, Henry EcRoyd. *The History of Coningsborough Castle, with Glimpses of Ivanhoe-land*. Worksop: Robert White, 1887.

Smollett, Tobias. *The Expedition of Humphrey Clinker*. Ed. Angus Ross. London: Penguin, 1985.

Southern Ireland: Its Lakes and Landscapes. The New Fighguard Route. Revised edn. London: Great Western Railway, 1906.

Southey, Robert. 'Art. XII. 1. *Letters from Albion to a Friend on the Continent* ... '. *Quarterly Review* 15.30 (July 1816), 537–74.

———. *Essays, Moral and Political, by Robert Southey*. 2 vols. London: John Murray, 1832.

———. *Letters from England: by Don Manuel Alvarez Espriella. Translated from the Spanish*. 3 vols. London: Longman, Hurst, Rees and Orme, 1807.

The Sportsman in Ireland, with his Summer Route through the Highlands of Scotland by a Cosmopolite. 2 vols. London: Henry Colburn, 1840.

Stawell, Maud M. *Motor Tours in the West Country*. London: Hodder and Stoughton, 1910.

Stevenson, Burton E. *The Charm of Ireland*. New York: Dodd, Mead and Co., 1914.

Stoddart, John. *Remarks on Local Scenery and Manners in Scotland during the Years 1799 and 1800*. 2 vols. London: William Miller, 1801.

Sturmey, Henry. *On an Autocar through the Length and Breadth of the Land*. London: Lliffe, Sons, and Sturmey, [1899].

Sylvan's Pictorial Handbook to the Scenery of the Caledonian Canal, the Isle of Staffa, etc. etc. London: John Johnstone, 1848.

Teilo, Gwilym. *Llandeilo Vawr and its Neighbourhood, Past and Present*. Llandeilo: D. W. and G. Jones, 1858.

Tennyson, Alfred, Lord. *Idylls of the King*. London: Macmillan, 1889.

Thackeray, William Makepeace. *The Irish Sketch Book: 1842*. London: Chapman and Hall, 1857.

Thesiger, Wilfred. *Arabian Sands*. Harmondsworth: Penguin, 1991.

Thomas, Bertha. *Picture Tales from Welsh Hills*. Chicago: F. G. Browne and Co., London: T. Fisher Unwin, 1913.

———. *Stranger within the Gates*. Ed. Kirsti Bohata. Dinas Powys: Honno, 2008.

Tilt, Charles. *Illustrations: Landscape, Historical and Antiquarian to the Poetic Works of Sir Walter Scott, Bart*. London: Charles Tilt, Chapman, and Hall, 1834.

Tóibín, Colm. *Walking Along the Border*. London: Queen Anne Press, 1987.

Twiss, Richard. *A Tour of Ireland in 1775 with a Map, and a View of the Salmon-Leap at Ballyshannon*. London: Robson, Walker, Robinson, Kearsly, 1776.

The Ulster Railway Handbook, and Travellers Companion of the Way. Belfast: George Phillips, 1848.

Victoria. *More Leaves from the Journal of a Life in the Highlands from 1862–1882*. London: Smith, Elder and Co., 1884.

Vincent, J. E. *Through East Anglia in a Motor Car*. London: Methuen, 1907.

Voltaire. *Lettres Philosophiques*. Ed. René Pomeau. Paris: GF Flammarion, 1964.

Ward, C. S. *Ireland (Part II.) East, West, and South, Including Dublin and Howth*. 3rd edn. London: Dulau and Co., 1895.

Washington, E. K. *Echoes of Europe; or, World Pictures of Travel*. Philadelphia: James Challen and Son, 1860.

Waugh, Evelyn. *Brideshead Revisited*. London: Penguin, 2008.

Wellbye, Reginald. *Picturesque Touring Areas in the British Isles*. Cheltenham and London: Ed. J. Burrow and Co. Ltd., [1930].

West, Mrs Frederic. *A Summer Visit to Ireland in 1846*. London: Richard Bentley, 1847.

West, Thomas. *A Guide to the Lakes: Dedicated to the Lovers of Landscape Studies, and to All Who Have Visited, or Intend to Visit the Lakes in Cumberland, Westmoreland, and Lancashire*. London: Richardson and Urquhart, 1778.

White, George Preston. *A Tour in Connemara, with Remarks on its Great Physical Capacities*. London: W. H. Smith and Son, 1849.

Wilson, John Marius. *The Land of Scott; or, Tourist's Guide to Abbotsford, the Country of the Tweed and Its Tributaries, and St Mary's Loch*. London: Nelson, 1858.

Wilson, William. *The Post Chaise Companion or Traveller's Directory through Ireland*. Dublin: J. and J. H. Fleming, 1810.

Winter, William. *Over the Border*. New York: Moffat, Yard and Co., 1911.

Wordsworth, William. *William Wordsworth*. Ed. Stephen Gill. Oxford: Oxford University Press, 1984.

Secondary sources

Adler, Judith. 'Origins of Sightseeing'. *Annals of Tourism Research* 16 (1989), 7–29.

Anderson, Benedict. *Imagined Communities*. London and New York: Verso, 1991.

Andrews, Malcolm. *The Search for the Picturesque: Landscape Aesthetics and Tourism in Britain, 1760–1800*. Stanford: Stanford University Press, 1989.

Arnold, Matthew. *On the Study of Celtic Literature*. London: Smith, Elder and Co, 1867.

Augé, Marc. *Un Ethnologue dans le métro*. Paris: Hachette, 1986.

———. *Non-Lieux: Introduction à une anthropologie de la surmodernité*. Seuil: Paris, 1992.

———. *La Traversée du Luxembourg*. Paris: Hachette, 1985.

Barnes, Julian. *Something to Declare*. London: Picador, 2002.

Bending, Stephen. 'The True Rust of the Baron's Sword: Ruins and the National Landscape'. *Producing the Past: Aspects of Antiquarian Culture and Practice 1700–1850*. Ed. Martin Myrone and Lucy Peltz. Aldershot: Ashgate, 1999. 83–93.

Bermingham, Ann. *Landscape and Ideology: The English Rustic Tradition, 1740–1860*. Berkeley: University of California Press, 1986.

Brendon, Piers. *Thomas Cook: 150 Years of Popular Tourism*. London: Secker and Warburg, 1991.

Brietenbach, Esther. *Empire and Scottish Society: The Impact of Foreign Missions at Home, c. 1790 to 1914*. Edinburgh: Edinburgh University Press, 2009.

Briggs, Carla. 'The Landscape Painters'. *Killarney: History & Heritage*. Ed. Jim Larner. Wilton, Cork: The Collins Press, 2005. 145–55.

Burrows, Simon. 'The Cultural Politics of Exile: French Emigré Literary Journalism in London, 1793–1814'. *Journal of European Studies* 29.2 (June 1999), 157–77.

Burrows, Simon. 'Émigré journalists and publishers'. *An Oxford Companion to the Romantic Age: British Culture 1776-1832*. Ed. Iain McCalman. Oxford: Oxford University Press, 1999. 495–6.

Burwick, Frederick. *Thomas De Quincey: Knowledge and Power*. New York: Palgrave Macmillan, 2001.

Buzard, James. *The Beaten Track: European Tourism, Literature, and the Ways to 'Culture'*. Oxford: Clarendon Press, 1993.

Calvino, Italo. *Invisible Cities*. Trans. William Weaver. London: Vintage, 1997.

Chalmers, Alan. 'Scottish Prospects: Thomas Pennant, Samuel Johnson, and the Possibilities of Narrative'. *Historical Boundaries, Narrative Forms: Essays on British Literature in the Long Eighteenth Century*. Ed. Lorna Clymer and Roeber Mayer. Newark: University of Delaware Press, 2007. 199–214.

Chard, Chloe. 'Introduction'. *Transports: Travel, Pleasure, and Imaginative Geography, 1600–1830*. Ed. Chloe Chard and Helen Langdon. New Haven: Yale University, 1998. 1–29.

Clarke, Deborah. 'Domesticating the Car: Women's Road Trips'. *Studies in American Fiction* 32.1 (2004), 101–28.

Clifford, James. 'Travelling Cultures'. *Cultural Studies*. Ed. Lawrence Grossberg, Cary Nelson, and Paula A. Treichler. London: Routledge, 1992. 96–111.

Colbert, Benjamin. 'Aesthetics of Enclosure: Agricultural Tourism and the Place of the Picturesque'. *European Romantic Review* 13.1 (March 2002), 23–34.

———. *Shelley's Eye: Travel Writing and Aesthetic Vision*. Aldershot: Ashgate, 2005.

Colley, Linda. *Britons: Forging the Nation 1707–1837*. London: Pimlico, 2003.

Connolly, Claire. 'Irish Romanticism, 1800–1830'. *The Cambridge History of Irish Literature*. Ed. Margaret Kelleher and Philip O'Leary. Vol. 1: to 1890. Cambridge: Cambridge University Press, 2006. 407–48.

Copley, Stephen and Peter Garside, eds. *The Politics of the Picturesque: Literature, Landscape and Aesthetics since 1770*. Cambridge: Cambridge University Press, 1994.

Corbin, Alain. *The Lure of the Sea: The Discovery of the Seaside, 1750–1840*. Trans. Jocelyn Phelps. London: Penguin, 1995.

Corrigan, Gordon. *Wellington: A Military Life*. London: Continuum, 2001.

Cronin, Michael. *Irish Tourism: Image, Culture and Identity*. Bristol: Channel View Publications, 2003.

———. 'Global Questions and Local Visions: A Microcosmopolitan Perspective'. *Beyond the Difference: Welsh Literature in Comparative Contexts: Essays for*

M. Wynn Thomas at Sixty. Ed. Alyce von Rothkirch and Daniel Williams. Cardiff: University of Wales Press, 2004. 186–202.

———. *Translation and Globalization*. London and New York: Routledge, 2003.

Culler, Jonathan. *Framing the Sign: Criticism and Its Institutions*. Oxford: Blackwell, 1988.

Daly, Mary E. *A Social and Economic History of Ireland since 1800*. Dublin: Educational Company of Ireland, 1981.

Davies, Damien Walford. *Presences that Disturb: Models of Romantic Identity in the Literature and Culture of the 1790s*. Cardiff: University of Wales Press, 2002.

Dearnley, Moira. 'I Came Hither, A Stranger: A View of Wales in the Novels of Anne Beale (1815–1900)'. *The New Welsh Review* 1.4 (Spring 1989), 27–32.

Derrida, Jacques. *On Cosmopolitanism and Forgiveness*. Trans. Mark Dooley and Michael Hughes, with a preface by Simon Critchley and Richard Kearney. London: Routledge, 2001.

Donnelly Jr., James S. *The Great Irish Potato Famine*. Stroud: Sutton, 2001.

Drayton, Richard. *Nature's Government: Science, Imperial Britain, and the 'Improvement' of the World*. New Haven and London: Yale University Press, 2000.

Dunne, Tom. 'Haunted by History: Irish Romantic Writing, 1800–50'. *Romanticism in National Context*. Ed. Roy Porter and Mikuláš Teich. Cambridge: Cambridge University Press, 1988. 68–91.

Durie, Alastair. *Scotland for the Holidays: A History of Tourism in Scotland, 1780–1939*. East Linton: Tuckwell, 2003.

Fegan, Melissa. *Literature and the Irish Famine, 1845–1919*. Oxford: Clarendon Press, 2002.

Ferris, Ina. *The Romantic National Tale and the Question of Ireland*. Cambridge: Cambridge University Press, 2002.

Friedman, Thomas. *The World is Flat: The Globalized World in the Twenty-First Century*. London: Penguin, 2006.

Fukuyama, Francis. *The End of History and the Last Man*. London: Hamish Hamilton, 1992.

Fulford, Tim. *Landscape, Liberty, and Authority: Poetry, Criticism, and Politics from Thomson to Wordsworth*. Cambridge: Cambridge University Press, 1996.

Fussell, Paul. *Abroad: British Literary Traveling Between the Wars*. New York: Oxford University Press, 1982.

Ghiobúin, Mealla Ní. *Dugort, Achill Island 1831–1861: The Rise and Fall of a Missionary Community*. Dublin: Irish Academic Press, 2001.

Giddens, Anthony. *The Consequences of Modernity*. Stanford: Stanford University Press, 1990.

Glendening, John. *The High Road: Romantic Tourism, Scotland, and Literature 1720–1820*. London: Macmillan, 1997.

Gold, John R. and Margaret M. Gold. *Imagining Scotland. Tradition, Representation and Promotion in Scottish Tourism since 1750*. Aldershot: Scolar Press, 1995.

Gray, Fred. *Designing the Seaside: Architecture, Society and Nature*. London: Reaktion Books, 2006.

Grenier, Katherine Haldane. *Tourism and Identity in Scotland, 1770–1914: Creating Caledonia*. Aldershot: Ashgate, 2005.

Grubenmann, Yvonne de Athayde. *Un Cosmopolite Suisse: Jacques-Henri Meister (1744–1826)*. Geneva: Librairie E. Droz, 1954.

Hagglund, Betty. *Tourists and Travellers: Women's Non-fictional Writings about Scotland, 1770–1830*. Bristol: Channel View Publications, 2010.

Haldrup, Michael and Jonas Larsen. 'Material Cultures of Tourism'. *Leisure Studies* 25.3 (2006), 275–89.

Hall, Stuart. 'Political Belonging in a World of Multiple Identities'. *Conceiving Cosmopolitanism: Theory, Context, and Practice*. Ed. Steven Vertovec and Robin Cohen. Oxford: Oxford University Press, 2002. 25–31.

Hammersley, Rachel. *French Revolutionaries and English Republicans: The Cordeliers Club, 1790–1794*. Woodbridge: Boydell Press for the Royal Historical Society, 2005.

Hill, Richard. 'The Illustration of the Waverley Novels: Scott and Popular Illustrated Fiction'. *Scottish Literary Review* 1.1 (Spring/Summer 2009), 69–88.

Holloway, James and Lindsay Etherington. *The Discovery of Scotland: The Appreciation of Scottish Scenery through Two Centuries of Painting*. Edinburgh: National Gallery of Scotland, 1978.

Hooper, Glen. *Travel Writing and Ireland, 1760–1860*. Basingstoke: Palgrave Macmillan, 2005.

Horgan, Donal. *The Victorian Visitor in Ireland: Irish Tourism 1840–1910*. Cork: Imagimedia, 2002.

Janowitz, Anne. *England's Ruins: Poetic Purpose and the National Landscape*. Oxford: Blackwell, 1990.

Jemielity, Thomas. 'Thomas Pennant's Scottish *Tours* and [Samuel Johnson's] *A Journey to the Western Isles of Scotland*'. *Fresh Reflections on Samuel Johnson: Essays in Criticism*. Ed. Prem Nath. Troy: Whitston, 1987. 312–27.

Jones, Ifano. *A History of Printers and Printing in Wales to 1810 and of Successive and Related Printers to 1923. Also, A History of Printing in Monmouthshire*. Cardiff: William Lewis, 1925.

Judet de la Combe, Pierre and Heinz Wismann. *L'Avenir des langues: repenser les humanités*. Paris: Éditions du Cerf, 2004.

Kahan, Jeffrey. *Reforging Shakespeare: The Story of a Theatrical Scandal*. London: Lehigh University Press, 1998.

Kinsley, Zoë. '"In Moody Sadness, on the Giddy Brink": Liminality and Home Tour Travel'. *Mapping Liminalities: Thresholds in Cultural and Literary Texts*. Ed. Lucy Kay, Zoë Kinsley, Terry Phillips, and Alan Roughley. Bern: Peter Lang, 2007. 41–68.

———. *Women Writing the Home Tour, 1682–1812*. Aldershot: Ashgate, 2008.

Klein, Naomi. *The Shock Doctrine: The Rise of Disaster Capitalism*. London: Penguin, 2007.

Kroeg, Susan. 'Cockney Tourists, Irish Guides, and the Invention of the Emerald Isle'. *Éire-Ireland* 44.3–4 (2009), 200–28.

Lemprière, J. *A Classical Dictionary; Containing a Copious Account of all the Proper Names Mentioned in Ancient Authors*. 11th edn. London: T. Cadell and W. Davies, 1820.

Levi, Peter. 'Introduction'. *A Journey to the Western Islands of Scotland* and *The Journal of a Tour to the Hebrides* [1775, 1786]. By Samuel Johnson and James Boswell. Ed. Peter Levi. Harmondsworth: Penguin, 1984.

Lynch, Michael. *Scotland: A New History*. London: Pimlico, 1991.

MacCannell, Dean. *The Tourist: A New Theory of the Leisure Class*. Berkeley: University of California Press, 1999.

McKay, K. D. *A Vision of Greatness: The History of Milford Haven, 1790–1990*. Haverfordwest: Brace Harvest Associates, 1989.

McVeagh, John. *Irish Travel Writing: A Bibliography*. Dublin: Wolfhound, 1996.

Mandler, Peter. *The Rise and Fall of the Stately Home*. New Haven: Yale University Press, 1997.

Matheson, C. S. *Enchanting Ruin: Tintern Abbey and Romantic Tourism in Wales*. Ann Arbor: University of Michigan, Special Collections Library, 2008.

Maxwell, Richard. 'Walter Scott, Historical Fiction, and the Genesis of the Victorian Illustrated Book'. *The Victorian Illustrated Book*. Ed. Richard Maxwell. Charlottesville and London: University Press of Virginia, 2002. 1–51.

Mee, Catherine. '"Che brutta invenzione il turismo!": Tourism and Anti-tourism in Current French and Italian Travel Writing'. *Comparative Critical Studies* 4.2 (2007), 269–82.

Meloy, Elizabeth. 'Touring Connemara: Learning to Read a Landscape of Ruins, 1850–1860'. *New Hibernia Review/Irish Éireannach Nua* 13.3 (2009), 21–46.

Mitchell, Julian. *The Wye Tour and its Artists*. Chepstow: Chepstow Museum, 2010.

Moir, Esther. *The Discovery of Britain: The English Tourists 1540–1840*. London: Routledge and Kegan Paul, 1964.

Mueller-Vollmer, Kurt. 'On Germany: Germaine de Staël and the Internationalization of Romanticism'. *The Spirit of Poesy*. Ed. Richard Block. Evanston: Northwestern University Press, 2000. 150–66.

Nally, David. '"Eternity's commissioner": Thomas Carlyle, the Great Irish Famine and the Geopolitics of Travel'. *Journal of Historical Geography* 32 (2006), 313–35.

Nath, Prem, ed. *Fresh Reflections on Samuel Johnson: Essays in Criticism*. Troy: Whitston Publishing Co., 1987.

Nicolson, Marjorie Hope. *Mountain Gloom and Mountain Glory: The Development of the Aesthetics of the Infinite*. Ithaca: Cornell University Press, 1959.

Nouzeillies, Gabriela. 'Touching the Real: Alternative Travel and Landscapes of Fear'. *Writing Travel: The Poetics and Politics of the Modern Journey*. Ed. John Zilcosky. Toronto: University of Toronto Press, 2008. 195–210.

O'Connell, Sean. *The Car in British Society: Class, Gender and Motoring*. Manchester: Manchester University Press, 1998.

Ó Conghaile, Micheál. *Conamara agus Árainn 1880–1980: Gnéithe den Stair Shóisialta*. Béal an Daingin: Cló Iar-Chonnachta, 1988.

Ó Gráda, Cormac. *Ireland: A New Economic History 1780–1939*. Oxford: Clarendon Press, 1995.

Ousby, Ian. *The Englishman's England: Taste, Travel and the Rise of Tourism*. Cambridge: Cambridge University Press, 1990.

Paz, D. G. *Popular Anti-Catholicism in Mid-Victorian England*. Stanford: Stanford University Press, 1992.

Perec, Georges. *Espèces d'espaces*. Paris: Galilée, 1974.

———. *L'infra-ordinaire*. Paris: Seuil, 1989.

———. *Tentative d'épuisement d'un lieu parisien*. Paris: Bourgois, 1982.

Perry, C. R. 'In Search of H. V. Morton: Travel Writing and Cultural Values in the First Age of British Democracy'. *Twentieth-Century British History* 10.4 (1999), 431–56.

Pitchford, Susan. *Identity Tourism: Imaging and Imagining the Nation*. Bingley: Emerald Group, 2008.

Pittock, Murray, ed. *The Reception of Sir Walter Scott in Europe*. London: Continuum, 2006.

————. 'Scott and the British Tourist'. *English Romanticism and the Celtic World.* Ed. Gerard Carruthers and Alan Rawes. Cambridge: Cambridge University Press, 2003. 151–66.

Pudney, John. *The Thomas Cook Story.* London: Michael Joseph, 1953.

Reports of the Commissioners of Inquiry into the State of Education in Wales. London: William Clowes, 1848.

Robinson, Matthew. 'Salmacis and Hermaphroditus: When Two Become One (Ovid, *Met.* 4.285–388)'. *The Classical Quarterly,* New Series 49.1 (1999), 212–23.

Schivelbusch, Wolfgang. *The Railway Journey: The Industrialization of Time and Space in the Nineteenth Century.* Berkeley: University of California Press, 1986.

Shaw, Philip. *The Sublime.* Abingdon: Routledge, 2006.

Shields, Rob. *Places on the Margin: Alternative Geographies of Modernity.* London and New York: Routledge, 1991.

Smith, Anthony D. *National Identity.* Harmondsworth: Penguin, 1991.

Smyth, Alfred P. *Warlords and Holy Men. Scotland, AD 80–1000.* Edinburgh: Edinburgh University Press, 1984.

Soubigou, Gilles. 'French Portraits of Sir Walter Scott: Images of the Great Unknown'. *Scottish Studies Review* 7.1 (Spring 2006), 24–37.

Swinglehurst, Edmund. *Cook's Tours: The Story of Popular Travel.* Poole: Blandford Press, 1982.

Szerszynski, Bronislaw and John Urry. 'Visuality, Mobility and the Cosmopolitan: Inhabiting the World from Afar'. *The British Journal of Sociology* 57.1 (2006), 113–31.

Thomas, Keith. *Man and the Natural World.* London: Allen Lane, 1983.

Thompson, Carl. *The Suffering Traveller and the Romantic Imagination.* Oxford: Oxford University Press, 2007.

————. 'Travel Writing'. *Romanticism: An Oxford Guide.* Ed. Nicholas Roe. Oxford: Oxford University Press, 2005. 555–66.

Thorold, Peter. *The Motoring Age: The Automobile and Britain, 1896–1939.* London: Profile Books Ltd, 2003.

Travis, John. 'Continuity and Change in English Sea-bathing, 1730–1900: A Case of Swimming with the Tide'. *Recreation and the Sea.* Ed. Stephen Fisher. Exeter: University of Exeter Press, 1997. 8–35.

Urbain, Jean-Didier. *At the Beach.* Trans. Catherine Porter. Minneapolis: University of Minnesota Press, 2003.

————. *Secrets de voyage: menteurs, imposteurs et autres voyageurs immédiats.* Paris: Payot, 1998.

Urry, John. *The Tourist Gaze.* 2nd edn. London: Sage, 2002.

Walton, John K. 'Prospects in Tourism History: Evolution, State of Play and Future Developments'. *Tourism Management* 30 (2009), 783–93.

Watson, Nicola J., ed. *Literary Tourism and Nineteenth-Century Culture.* Basingstoke: Palgrave Macmillan, 2009.

————. *The Literary Tourist: Readers and Places in Romantic and Victorian Britain.* Basingstoke: Palgrave Macmillan, 2006.

————. 'Readers of Romantic Locality: Tourists, Loch Katrine and *The Lady of the Lake*'. *Romantic Localities: Europe Writes Place.* Ed. Christoph Bode and Jacqueline Labbe. London: Pickering and Chatto, 2010.

Weiskel, Thomas. *The Romantic Sublime: Studies in the Structure and Psychology of Transcendence*. Baltimore and London: The Johns Hopkins University Press, 1976.

Wellek, René. *A History of Modern Criticism 1750–1950*. Vol. 2: The Romantic Age. London: Jonathan Cape, 1970.

Whelan, Kevin. 'The Modern Landscape: from Plantation to Present'. *Atlas of the Irish Rural Landscape*. Ed. F. H. A. Aalen, Kevin Whelan, and Matthew Stout. Cork: Cork University Press, 1997. 67–103.

———. 'Settlement Patterns in the West of Ireland in the Pre-Famine Period'. *Decoding the Landscape: Papers Read at the Inaugural Conference of the Centre for Landscape Studies*. Ed. Timothy Collins. Galway: Centre for Landscape Studies, 1994. 60–78.

Whelan, Irene. *The Bible War in Ireland: The 'Second Reformation' and the Polarization of Protestant-Catholic Relations, 1800–1840*. Dublin: Lilliput, 2005.

Williams, William H. A. *Creating Irish Tourism: The First Century, 1750–1850*. London: Anthem, 2010.

———. *Tourism, Landscape and Irish Character: British Travel Writers in Pre-Famine Ireland*. Madison: University of Wisconsin, 2008.

Williams, William Proctor and Craig S. Abbot. *An Introduction to Bibliographical and Textual Studies*. New York: MLA, 2009.

Withers, Charles W. J. 'Introduction'. *A Tour in Scotland and Voyage to the Hebrides 1772 [1774]*. By Thomas Pennant. Ed. Andrew Simmons. Edinburgh: Birlinn, 1998.

Withey, Lynne. *Grand Tours and Cook's Tours*. New York: William Morrow, 1997.

Wohlgemut, Esther. *Romantic Cosmopolitanism*. Basingstoke: Palgrave Macmillan, 2009.

Wollen, Peter. 'The Cosmopolitan Ideal in the Arts'. *Travellers' Tales: Narratives of Home and Displacement*. Ed. George Robertson, et al. London: Routledge, 1994.

Woods, C. J. *Travellers' Accounts as Source-Material for Irish Historians*. Dublin: Four Courts Press, 2009.

Zilcosky, John. 'Writing Travel'. *Writing Travel: The Poetics and Politics of the Modern Journey*. Ed. John Zilcosky. Toronto: University of Toronto Press, 2008. 3–21.

Index

A

Abbotsford   135, 137, 138, 139, 140,
    141, 144, 146
Abbott, Jacob, *A Summer in
    Scotland*   130 n46
acculturation (*see also* culture)   204,
    212
accuracy   63, 95 n18, 139, 193, 212
Act of Union (*see under* Ireland and
    Scotland)
Addison, Joseph   39, 48 n26, 186
Adler, Judith   112 n4
advertising   10, 15, 55, 76, 82 n24,
    140, 168–9, 202, 203, 211, 216
    n3
aesthetics (*see also* landscape,
    picturesque, sublime)   2, 3, 5,
    9–10, 12 n8, 14, 20–1, 23–28,
    34–5, 40–1, 44–5, 51, 52–5, 60,
    69, 75, 97, 107–8, 134, 148,
    165, 167–8,
    186–90, 192, 195, 198, 199
    n14, 204, 211
aestheticization and
    commodification   41, 115,
    136, 168, 185, 220
allusion   24, 39, 49 n29, 79, 85, 92,
    136, 185, 192
Africa   16, 102, 213
Agee, James   95 n18
Agricola   24
agriculture (*see also* tourism)   3, 5,
    12 n8, 15–16, 20, 32, 102, 104,
    106–9, 134, 167–8, 170, 175,
    178, 214, 221–22
Alien Acts   69
alienation   68–9, 80, 102, 109, 160
    politics of   68, 71
Anderson, Benedict, *Imagined
    Communities*   13, 28 n1
Anderson, George and Peter, *Guide to
    the Highlands*   119, 129 n19,
    130 n19

Andrews, Malcolm   12 n10, 65 n2,
    199 n24, 200 n31
Anglicanism   94, 125
Anglo-mania   85
anthropology (*see also*
    ethnography)   87, 226–7, 230,
    234 n15
anti-Catholicism   102–3, 108–9, 119,
    117 n21, 171
antiquarianism   4, 14–15, 21–2, 24,
    25, 50, 52–3, 56, 61–2, 63, 65
    n5, 98–9, 120, 135, 139, 144,
    146 n25
Antrim   98, 109
anxiety   36, 43–4, 68, 76, 117, 135,
    143, 149, 201, 208, 210–11
Archenholz, Johann Wilhelm
    von   73, 83 n27
    Picture of England   70
Argyll, Duke of   26, 116, 119, 125, 128
Arndt, Ernst Moritz   87
Arnold, Matthew   148, 149, 161,
    162 n5
Arthur's Seat   132, 133
Arts and Crafts movement   211
Ashworth, John Henry, *A Saxon in
    Ireland*   111, 113 n30
Augé, Marc   226–7, 230, 234 n15–17,
    234 n28
Augustine   91, 119
Austen, Jane   33, 47 n8
    Sense and Sensibility   62
authenticity   194, 233
    of body   194
    of English character   86
    of experience   2, 218 n44
    of home   233
    of travel and traveller   121
autobiography   7, 58, 60, 150, 162 n19
Autocar (magazine)   202, 209, 211–12,
    215, 216 n3, 217 n17, 218 n41
automobile   201–218
Ayrshire   134

B
Badcock, John. *Letters from
    London* 70, 71
Baikie, James, *The Charm of the Scott
    Country* 141
Baird, John D. 47 n1
Ballantyne, R. M., *The Lakes of
    Killarney* 200 n36
Balquihidder 137
Band of Hope Review 128
Banks, Joseph, Sir 14, 15, 16, 25, 28
    n2, 72, 82 n20
Barnes, Julian 85, 95 n3
Barrow, John 110, 111
    Tour round Ireland 110, 113
    n29
Barry, William Whittaker 172, 180
    n20
Bath 86, 90
bathing machine 33, 40
beach 6, 31–3, 37, 38, 40–1, 45, 47
    n8, 49 n29, 121
Beale, Anne 153, 161, 162 n7
    The Pennant Family 149
    The Vale of the Towey 147–8, 157,
    158
Beckford, William 75–6
beggars 8, 92, 105–6, 115, 123, 183,
    193–4, 196
Bending, Stephen 53, 65 n5
Bennett, Betty T. 75 n3
Bennett, William 110
Bermingham, Ann 5, 12 n19
Birmingham 86–7, 89
Black, Adam and Charles
    Black's Guide to Dublin 180 n10
    Black's Guide to Killarney 180 n10
    *Black's Picturesque Tourist of
    Scotland* 116, 119, 122, 129
    n19
    *Black's Shilling Guide to
    Edinburgh* 140
Blackwood's Edinburgh Magazine 80
Black Country 210
Blake, Henry (and Blake
    family) 110–11
    Letters from the Irish Highlands 112
    n9
Blake, William 90

body 36–47, 79, 183, 185, 190, 192,
    194–5
    as canvas 194–5, 197
    as grotesque 194, 198
    as site of carnival 195
    landscape compared to 19
Bonaparte, Napoleon 35, 68, 72,
    80, 92
borders 2, 3, 11, 21, 25, 26, 27, 77,
    109, 136, 137, 140, 142, 144,
    145 n16, 160, 220–1, 224–5,
    230, 231, 233
Borm, Jan 7
Boswell, James 14, 19, 85, 95 n4
Boulton, James 90
Bowman, J. E. 121
    Highlands and Islands 130 n37
Brayley, Edward Wedlake 4
Brewer, James Norris 4–5, 12 n15
Brietenbach, Esther 130 n27
Briggs, Carla 189, 199 n28
Britton, John 4
Browne, Junius Henri 196–7
Buffon, comte de 28 n2
Builth Wells 153
Burns, Robert 134, 144 n7
Burke, Edmund 71, 77
    *A Philosophical Enquiry into ... the
    Sublime and the Beautiful* 168,
    186–7, 199 n16
Burt, Edmund 16
Burwick, Frederick 84 n54
Bush, John
    Hibernia Curiosa 97
Buzard, James, *The Beaten Track* 12
    n16, 69, 81 n4, 130 n35, 130
    n50, 165, 179 n3, 180 n22, 198
    n3, 205, 210, 212, 213, 218 n44
    'cultural accreditation' 4
    'saturation' 213
Byron, George Gordon, Lord 69, 80,
    173

C
Calvinism 86, 119
Calvino, Italo 1, 11 n2, 228,
    234 n23
Campbell, Thomas
    Philosophical Survey 97

canals 101
Carlyle, Thomas 185, 198 n9
carnivalesque 190, 195, 197–8
Carr, Sir John
  A Stranger in Ireland 166, 179 n7
Carter, Nathaniel Hazeltine
  Letters from Europe 189–90, 200 n33
Cashel, Rock of 98
Catholic Emancipation 92, 102
Catholicism (*see also* religion) 100,
  102–3, 105, 109, 112 n11, 119,
  129 n22, 171, 226, 232
celebrity 136
Celtic church 119
Celtism 4, 9, 14, 17, 24, 119, 144
  n5, 148, 162 n5, 176, 231
Chalmers, Alan 18, 29 n4
Chambers, Robert 145 n9
Chambers, William 129 n7, 130 n42
Chamisso, Adelbert von 87
Chapman, Robin 155, 157, 162 n26
Chard, Chloe 112 n4
Chatterton, Henrietta, Lady 107
  Rambles in the South of Ireland 113
  n21
Chaucer, Geoffrey 2
charity 8, 71, 74, 114–5, 123–4
Chepstow 52, 63
Chepstow-Tintern turnpike 52
Chester 21, 169
children 8, 42, 43, 90, 105, 106,
  114–15, 121–22, 125, 126,
  127–8, 148, 150, 155, 160, 225
Christianity 8, 93, 115, 117–20,
  124–27
Church of England (*see* Anglicanism)
city 87, 88–90, 100, 221, 230–1
  vs. country 10, 77–8, 87, 88–9,
  122, 208
civilization 2, 19, 24, 118, 119, 133,
  168, 170, 175, 221, 229, 230
'civilizing mission', so-called 119–20,
  127
class (*see* social class)
Claude Glass 187
Cliffe, Charles Frederick 48 n17
Clifford, James 231, 235 n31
'clonialism' 228
Clymer, Lorna 29 n4

coasts (*see* Tourism)
coenaesthetic 41, 43
Colbert, Benjamin 7, 8, 11, 12 n8,
  216
Coleridge, Samuel Taylor 79
Colley, Linda 48 n16, 82 n11
colonialism (*see also* 'clonialism';
  imperialism) 14, 16, 18, 19,
  29 n10, 71, 102, 111, 150, 152,
  168, 170, 172–3, 222–3
Columba, St 8, 22, 115, 117–21, 123,
  125, 127, 129 n3
commerce and commercialization 3,
  5, 8, 10, 26, 35, 44, 48 n19,
  57–8, 70, 73, 75, 77–8, 86, 91,
  115, 126, 138, 169–70, 172,
  175, 185, 191–2, 202, 211
Connaught (*see also* Ireland) 99,
  101, 222–3
Connemara (*see also* Ireland) 101–2,
  110–11, 179 n10, 198 n3, 222
consumerism 134, 136, 138, 210–11,
  213
Cook, James 6, 14–15, 22
  Voyages of the *Endeavour* 14
  Voyage round the World 86
Cook, Thomas 8, 10, 115, 122–8,
  130 n50, 130 n56, 145 n16,
  165, 172, 183, 191, 211
  Cook's Excursionist 8–9, 127, 130 n39
Cooke, John 174, 176–7, 198 n1
Constable, Archibald 138
Copley, Stephen 168, 180 n13
Corbin, Alain 6, 12 n20, 34, 43, 47
  n9, 48 n23, 49 n30, 49 n38
Connacht (Knock) 11, 104, 220–3,
  226, 230, 231–2
Connolly, Claire 199 n12
Cork 171, 179 n10
Cornwall 214
Cornwallis, Theresa (*also known as*
  Mrs Frederic West) 110, 189
Correspondance littéraire 72–4, 82
  n23, 82 n26
Corrigan, Gordon 83 n45
cosmopolitanism 7–8, 68–9, 70, 73,
  74, 75, 77, 79, 81 n5, 82 n12,
  82 n16, 82 n22, 151, 162 n18,
  231–2, 235 n30

insular 7, 70, 78
micro- 2, 11 n3
vernacular c. 231
Coulbert, Esme 10, 11
countryside 18–21, 23, 27, 99, 106,
107, 136, 165, 167, 169, 172,
177, 203–4, 208–13, 215, 216
Cowper, William
'Retirement' 31–2, 33, 46, 47, 47
n1, 47 n8
The Task 31
Crabbe, George 34, 47 n11
Craik, Dinah Maria 183
Craven, Elizabeth, margravine of
Anspach 74–5, 77, 83 n27,
83 n33
Crockett, W. S. 146 n34
Scott Country 141, 143, 144 n4
Croker, T. Crofton
Researches in the South of Ireland 99
Cromwell, Thomas K.
Excursions through Ireland 105, 112
n17
Cronin, Michael 2, 11, 11 n3, 12
n11, 234 n22
Crossley, R. W.
The Irish Tourist (magazine) 177–8
Culdees 119
Culler, Jonathan 234 n1
culture 3, 12 n17, 14, 17, 19, 24, 28
n1, 35, 52, 54, 69–70, 72, 76,
77, 80–1, 82 n12, 85, 86, 89,
92, 94–5, 99, 102, 107, 109,
122–4, 128, 132, 134, 148,
150–5, 159–61, 164, 166–8,
170–1, 175, 181–3, 185–6,
189–92, 195, 197, 201, 210–12,
214–15, 216 n1, 218 n44, 220,
223–4, 228, 231, 233
cultural nationalism 154–5
curiosity 14, 15, 16–18, 20, 25, 42,
52, 54, 58, 60, 65, 97, 102, 147,
224
Curran, Stuart 47 n10

D
D., W. 'Abbey Church of Iona' 129
n20
Dallas, Alexander 102

Dal Riata 115
Daly, Mary E. 171, 180 n18
Daniell, William 4, 6, 11 n3, 32–3,
46, 47 n4, 47 n5
Dargan, William 171
Davies, Damian Walford 61, 67 n38
Dearnley, Moira 149, 162 n9, 162
n10
defamiliarization 11, 43, 219, 220
Defoe, Daniel 5, 13–16, 20
Robinson Crusoe 46
Tour through the Whole Island 5,
13, 18, 21, 23, 29 n13, 29 n15,
30 n29, 89, 96 n25
'True-born Englishman' 13
De Maistre, Xavier
Voyage autour de ma chambre 230
Dennis, John 186
depopulation 10, 126, 164–5
De Quincey, Thomas 79, 84 n54,
206, 217 n20
Derrida, Jacques 151, 157, 162 n18
Derry 221
desire 21, 31–2, 40–1, 43–4, 51, 60,
94, 186, 211
Dettelbach, Michael 30 n52
Dickens, Charles 92, 205
Dickson, M. F. 104, 112 n14
Diderot, Denis 72, 76, 82 n26, 83
n40
Donnelly, James S., Jr 112 n15
Dover 34, 35, 86
Drayton, Richard 29 n10
Druid 17, 24, 151
Dryburgh Abbey 135, 139, 140, 144
Dublin 101, 169, 170–2, 174, 222,
223
Dufferin, Lord 165
Dumont, Pierre Étienne Louis
Letters 70, 81 n10
Dunne, Tom 199 n12
Dunton, John 101, 112 n8
Durie, Alastair J. 12 n11, 129 n5

E
East, John (Rev.)
Notes and Glimpses of Ireland 110
Eastwood, Thomas S. Badger
Ivanhoe-land 142, 146 n32

economy   5, 6, 8–9, 13, 16, 27, 29,
        48 n19, 94, 97, 99–104, 106,
        108, 111, 114–15, 121, 125–8,
        164, 165, 167, 171, 177, 190,
        201, 214, 220, 227–8
Edinburgh   77, 132–3, 137, 140, 144
        n3
Edinburgh Review   77
Edwards, Owen Morgan   147, 148,
        151–5, 157–8, 160–1, 172 n19
    *Cartrefi Cymru (The Homes of
        Wales)*   155, 162 n26, 162 n28,
        163 n31
    Tro i'r De (A Trip to the South)   152,
        158
    *Tro i'r Gogledd (A Trip to the
        North)*   152, 154, 158, 160
emigration   9, 69, 71, 73, 77, 81 n7,
        83 n27, 103, 104, 105, 110,
        111, 164–5, 178
enclosure (*see also* landscape)   5, 12
        n8, 20, 55, 103, 107–8, 211
Encumbered Estates Act   111
Engels, Friedrich   90
England (*see also individual places*)
        2–5, 7, 9, 10, 13, 18–19, 21, 28,
        32, 35, 68, 70–4, 76, 78, 81,
        85–96, 98, 103, 104, 105, 107,
        108, 115, 137, 142, 150, 160,
        176, 201–18, 221
English character   86
    as homely   91
    as resistance to the foreign   86
Enlightenment   53, 70, 71, 85, 91
epistolary travelogue   18, 36
eroticism   41–2
Etherington, Lindsay   135, 145 n10
ethnography (*see also*
        anthropology)   4, 7, 17, 28,
        220, 227
    of proximity   11, 230
Evangelicalism   102, 118, 120
Evans, Walker   96 n18
Eyre-Todd, George   129 n4
exoticism   18, 223, 229–31
expatriate   68, 77
exploration   14, 16, 18, 32, 34, 41,
        46, 89, 98, 101, 230
    Pacific   6

F
Faujas de Saint-Fond, Barthélemi,
        Travels in England   69, 72, 82
        n18, 82 n20
Fegan, Melissa   198 n3
Fenianism   172–3, 175
Fennell, Desmond, *Connaught
        Journey*   11, 220–3, 226–30,
        232–3, 234 n5
Ferguson, Malcolm, *A Trip from
        Callander to Staffa and
        Iona*   129 n11
Ferris, Ina   8, 12 n21, 198 n3
fisheries   8, 15, 20, 25, 27, 33, 110,
        124–8
Fletcher, Alexander   124
Fontane, Theodor, *Ein Sommer in
        London*   93–4, 96 n44
Fonthill Abbey   75–6
foreignness, perception /
        representation / experience
        of   2, 7, 8, 11, 26, 68–81,
        85–95, 119, 148, 170, 219–20,
        223, 230–1
Forster, Georg,   7, 95 n4
    Ansichten von Niederrhein   85, 86–7,
        88, 89, 90, 94, 95 n5, 95 n7
Forster, Johann Reinhold   30 n52
France (*see also* Paris)   77, 85, 93,
        134, 216 n5
    compared with England /
        Britain   35, 69, 71–4, 76,
        77–81, 84 n57, 85, 91–2
    Revolution in   3, 35, 68, 73–6, 99
    Gallophobia and   70, 72, 79, 82 n11
    manners and customs of   35, 74,
        78–81, 88
    Post-revolutionary   7–8, 70, 79–80
*Franklin's Itinerary for the
        Trossachs*   145 n16
Frantz, Anaïk   230
Friedman, Thomas   228, 234 n20
Fukuyama, Francis   234 n19
Fulford, Tim   5, 12 n18

G
Gaelic (*see* language)
Galway   102, 108,
Gap of Dunloe   181–98

Garside, Peter 168, 180 n13
gaze 14, 19, 38–9, 60, 107, 128, 172, 190, 200 n35
gender 3, 33, 37–43, 195–7
geology 25, 29 n22,
George III, King of Great Britain 15
George, David Lloyd 161
Gerald of Wales (*see* Gerallt Gymro)
Gerallt Gymro 2, 147, 161
German accounts of Britain 7, 66 n25, 70, 73, 81 n10, 85–96, 232
Giant's Causeway 98, 185
Giddens, Anthony 227, 234 n18
Gilpin, William 34, 36, 56, 59, 63
Observations on the Coasts of Hampshire 35, 48 n14
Observations on the River Wye 51
Glasgow 132, 135, 139
Glendening, John 12 n11, 135–6, 145 n11, 145 n14
globalization 11, 16, 227–8, 231
Goede, Christian, *Stranger in England* 70
Goethe, Wolfgang von 87
Gold, John R. and Margaret M. Gold 129 n5
Goldsmith, Oliver 7
Gordon-Cumming, Constance F., *In the Hebrides* 129 n10
Gosse, Edmund, 'Journal in Scotland' 121–2, 130 n38
Gothic 53, 132, 148
Graham, Patrick 137
Gramich, Katie 2, 9
Grand Tour (*see* tourism)
Grant, Elizabeth, *Memoirs of a Highland Lady* 136, 145 n13
Gray, Fred 47 n7
Gray, Thomas 51
Gray, William Forbes 145 n18
Great Britain (*see* England, Ireland, Wales, Scotland)
Great Industrial Exhibition (Dublin) 171–2, 174
Grenier, Katherine Haldane 8, 12 n11, 129 n5, 199 n14
Greville, Charles Francis 37
Griffin, Phillip, of Hadnock 61, 62, 67 n41

Griffiths, Ann 156–7
Griffiths, Ralph 29 n14
Grimm, Friedrich, Baron von 72, 82 n26
Grose, Francis, *Antiquities of England and Wales* 52, 53, 56
Grosley, Pierre Jean, *Londres* 71
Grubenmann, Yvonne de Athoyde 82 n22, 83 n40
Guest, Harriet 30 n52
guidebook 2, 4–6, 16, 21, 50–67, 78, 90, 115, 118, 119, 121, 122, 125, 129 n8, 134–5, 141, 145 n16, 160, 164–80, 183–4, 188, 191–4, 201, 204, 213, 214, 215
guides 2, 7, 9, 116, 117, 121, 137, 188, 191, 193

H
Hagglund, Betty 12 n11
Hagley Hall 60, 67 n33, 87
Haight, Canniff, *Here and There in the Home Land* 196, 200 n47
Haldrup, Michael 199 n24
Hall, Samuel Carter, and Anna Maria Hall 101, 109, 112 n7
Ireland, Its Scenery, and Character 110, 166, 179 n7
Week at Killarney 192, 200 n37
Hall, Stuart 231–2, 235 n30
Haines, W. H. 66 n14
Hammersley, Rachel 73, 83 n31
Hamilton, Sir William 37
Haverfordwest 36, 38, 42
Head, Frances Bond, *A Fortnight in Ireland* 167, 171, 179 n9
Heath, Charles 6–7, 50–67
Historical and Descriptive Account ... Tintern Abbey 6, 50–67
Heath's Picturesque Annual (1835) 139, 140
Hebrides 8, 15, 17, 18, 21, 22, 25, 69, 114–31, 142
Heely, Joseph (*see also* Hagley Hall)
Description of Hagley Park 67 n33
Heine, Heinrich 7, 87
Reisebilder 85, 91–4
Hill, Richard 146 n26

Hissey, J. J. *Untravelled England* 201, 205–7, 210–13, 214, 215, 217 n27
Hoare, Richard Colt, *Journal of a Tour in Ireland* 99, 187, 199 n26
Holloway, James 135, 145 n10
Holyhead 169
home tour (*see* tourism)
Hooper, Glenn 12 n11, 100, 109, 111 n2, 198 n3
Horgan, Donal 12 n11
hospitality 106, 151, 157, 176, 183, 193, 196, 197
Howitt, William, *Homes and Haunts of the Most Celebrated British Poets* 134, 137, 144 n6, 145 n9
Hughes, Mrs, of Uffington 137
Humboldt, Alexander von 86, 87
hybridity 53, 58, 71, 72, 77, 79, 137, 147, 154, 155

I
Icolmkill (*see* Iona)
identity 6, 13, 157, 201
   British 32, 77, 150
   hybrid 77
   local 35
   micro-cosmopolitan 2
   mobile 70
   multiple 11, 235 n30
   national 3, 7, 18–19, 21, 35, 70, 74, 119, 133, 157, 161, 214
   personal 68
   Scottish 119, 133
   tourism and 3
   transcultural 81
   transnational 71–2, 79
   Welsh 150–1
illustration 9, 32, 54, 58, 60, 65 n9, 73, 138–41, 145 n20, 146 n26, 146 n32, 165, 225
imagination 3, 5, 13–14, 16, 17–18, 21, 37, 39, 41, 42, 92, 102, 117, 133–5, 138, 143, 165, 185–6, 197, 202, 208, 210, 230–1
imperialism (*see also* colonialism) 3, 6, 15, 28, 69, 100, 120, 151

improvement 5–6, 15–16, 18–20, 22–3, 25–8, 29 n10, 80, 93, 108, 110, 126, 128, 168, 170, 229
industry; industrialization 3, 5, 8, 10, 15–16, 48 n19, 86, 87, 89–90, 94, 101, 103, 105, 115, 117, 126, 128, 151, 161, 164, 165, 167, 171, 173, 177, 178, 201, 205, 208, 210–11, 214–16
Inglis, Henry D., *Journey throughout Ireland* 102, 103, 110, 111, 112 n7
Innisfallen 181
Iona 8–9, 22, 114–31
Ireland (*see also individual places*) 3, 97–113, 164–200, 219–35
   Act of Union and 3, 8, 9, 97, 100, 103, 107, 109, 166, 169, 177
   clachans in 104–5, 106, 168
   colonial discourse on 102, 168
   demographics of 103–4
   famine / Great Famine in 9, 97, 102–4, 110–11. 126, 164–80, 182, 190–8
   Free State of 171, 178, 221
   Northern 177, 220–1
   poverty in 5, 8, 100, 102, 105–7, 109–10, 111, 177–9, 226
   Republic of 171, 221
   West of 98, 101, 102, 107, 110, 111, 112 n13, 180, n11, 221–2
Ireland, Samuel, *Picturesque Views on the River Wye* 61, 63–4
Ireland, William Henry
   Shakespeare forgeries of 63
Irish Tourist Association 178
Irish Tourist's Illustrated Handbook 165–6, 168–9, 179 n5
Irving, Washington, *Abbotsford and Newstead Abbey* 146 n23
Isle of Wight 34, 48 n12

J
Jacobite rebellion 25, 136
James, K. J. 10
Janowitz, Anne 21, 29 n27
Jeffrey, Francis 77, 79
Jemielity, Thomas 29 n4
Johnson, James, *The Recess* 129 n2

Johnson, Samuel   14, 16, 20, 21, 29
    n4, 85, 86, 87, 95 n4, 118, 120
  Journey to the Western Islands of
    Scotland   29 n3, 29 n4
Jones, Ifano   66 n11
Judet de la Combe, Pierre   234 n2

K

K., J., *Letters to the North*   200 n34
Kahan, Jeffrey   67 n46
Kamtschatka   17
Kay, Lucy   47 n11
Kearney, Kate   10, 181–200
Kelso   27
Kenilworth Castle   142
Kent   35, 48 n12, 89, 119
Kerry   175, 182, 222
Killarney   3, 10, 98, 169, 175, 179
    n10, 181–200
Kinglake, Alexander William,
    Eothen   93
Kinsley, Zoë   6, 11, 12 n10, 12 n11,
    47 n11
Klein, Naomi   234 n21
Kroeg, Susan   198 n5

L

labour   3, 5, 62, 90, 105–6, 154, 170,
    210, 225
Lake District (English)   1, 3, 4, 12 n14,
    21, 34, 48 n12, 68, 69, 212
landscape   13–30, 133–46, 181–200
  aesthetics of   2–3, 5, 10, 14, 23, 26–8,
    34, 46. 97, 102, 107–8, 111 n2,
    164–5, 168, 185–9, 198
  affective response to   18, 31, 44,
    185–7, 195
  associations of history and fiction
    with   4, 25, 78, 118, 133–46,
    157
  naming and   224
  painting of   32, 138
  representations of   20, 21, 23, 90,
    108, 207–8
  religion and   103, 112 n12
  textualization of   4
    (*see also* coast, illustration,
    improvement, picturesque,
    sublime, *and individual places*)

Landscape-Historical Illustrations of
    Scotland   139, 141
Landseer, Edwin   138, 146 n23
language   3, 11, 43, 75, 120, 122,
    127, 134, 159, 175, 219–35
  English   35
  French   35, 69, 78, 93
  Gaelic   14
  Welsh   147–9, 152–3
  (*see also* translation)
Larsen, Jonas   199 n24
Leinster   108, 109
Lessing, Gottfried   87
Levi, Peter   29 n3
liberty   7, 73, 77, 79, 82 n24, 91,
    93–4, 95 n2, 201, 206, 213
liminality   6, 11, 19, 32, 34–5, 221
Linnaeus, Carl   28 n2
Lizars, William Home, *Lizars's Scottish*
    Tourist   130 n30
Loch Katrine   135, 137, 139, 140,
    143
Loch Lomond   137, 140, 145 n16
Lockhart, John Gibson   138
London   19, 69, 70, 72, 74, 77, 80,
    86, 87–8, 89, 90–2, 105, 124,
    137, 141, 158–9, 208
London and Paris, or Comparative
    Sketches   70, 80
Londonderry (*see also* Ireland)   109,
    221
Luckombe, Philip, *Tour through*
    Ireland   97
Lynch, Michael   130 n24

M

McBrayne's Shipping Company   115,
    129 n8
MacCannell, Dean   4, 11 n7,
MacCulloch, John, *Highlands and*
    Western Isles of Scotland   146 n25
MacDonald, Flora   25
MacKay, Charles   193
McKay, K. D.   48 n18
Macpherson, James, *Ossian*   14, 80,
    134
Macready, William Charles   137, 145
    n17
macro-modernity (*see* modernity)

McVeagh, John, *Irish Travel Writing: a Bibliography* 111 n1, 179 n1
Manchester 90, 222
Mandler, Peter 111 n3
Manners, John, Lord 110
manuscripts
circulation of 51
relationship between print and 72
Martin, Martin 16
Marx, Karl 164–5, 179 n2
masculinity 31, 43, 46, 126
Maspero, François, *Les Passagers du Roissy Express* 230–1
mass tourism (*see also* Cook, Thomas) 165, 176, 182–5, 197–8
Matheson, C.S. 6–7, 65 n2
Mavor, William, *Travels through England* 69, 81 n9
Mayer, Roeber 29 n4
Mayo 102, 103, 223, 226
Maxwell, Richard 146 n26
mechanization 205–6
Meister, Jacques-Henri, *Letters Written during a Residence* 7, 70, 72–8, 80–1, 82 n22, 82 n23, 82 n25, 83 n27, 83 n33, 83 n40
Meloy, Elizabeth 198 n3
Melrose Abbey 138, 140
Menzie's Tourist's Pocket Guide to Scotland 129 n23
mercantilism 19, 23
Merimée, Prosper 224, 234 n9
micro-modernity (*see* modernity)
'microspection' 11, 219–35
migration (*see* emigration)
Milford Haven 6, 31, 36–46, 48 n19
missionaries 112 n11, 115, 119–20, 125, 127
Mitchell, Julian 65 n2
mobility 2, 7, 10, 44, 70, 201, 212, 220–1, 227, 229
modernity 2, 3, 5, 6, 10, 14, 15–20, 22, 24, 25, 68–9, 75, 80, 118, 155, 161, 165, 201, 203, 208, 210–11, 220–1, 226–33
hyper- 214
macro- 227–9, 231, 233
micro- 11, 228–9, 233

Moir, Esther 2, 11 n5, 12 n11, 29 n12
monasticism 4, 52–3, 56, 99, 115, 119–20, 214
Monmouthshire 50–67
Montagu, Elizabeth 38
Montesquieu, Charles Secondat, *Lettres Persanes* 7, 230, 234 n28
Moore, Thomas 181
Morgan, Mary 6, 31–49
Moriarty, Daniel 193
Moritz, Karl Philipp, *Travels Chiefly on Foot* 71, 94, 96 n49
Morton, H. V. 201–2, 210–14, 217 n29
Motor tourism (*see* tourism)
motoring 201–18
Mueller-Vollmer, Kurt 70, 82 n12
Mull, island/Sound of 115, 125, 127
Munster 101, 108, 109
Murray, John
guidebook series of 180 n22
Handbook for Travellers in Ireland 172–9, 193, 198 n1
Muskau, Hermann Pückler, *Tour in England* 66 n25

N
Nally, David 199 n9
Nangle, Edward (Rev.) 102
Nath, Prem 29 n4
nation (*see also* England, Ireland, Wales, Scotland) 2, 3–4, 10, 34, 80, 88, 92, 99, 133, 144, 157, 229
-building 12–30, 161
of tourists 1, 7, 9
national character (*see* identity)
national identity (*see* identity)
nationalism 9, 28, 35, 70, 98, 154–5, 158, 221, 225, 231
natural history 14–15, 17, 18, 20–1, 72
nature (*see also* landscape) 15, 21, 23, 25, 28, 34, 35, 44, 46, 53, 97, 98, 99, 117, 156, 186, 195, 216
as other 19, 107–8
return to 155

state of 20, 22–4, 27
  sublime in (*see* sublime)
Nicholson, Asenath 110
Nicholson, George, *Cambrian
  Traveller's Guide* 65 n4
Nicolson, Marjorie Hope 199
  n14
Ní Ghiobúin, Mealla 112 n11
Nodier, Jean Emmanuel Charles,
  Promenade from Dieppe 80, 84
  n58
Noel, Baptist Wriothesley (Rev.), *Notes
  on a Short Tour* 102, 109, 112
  n10
Norfolk 44
Nouzeillies, Gabriella 233, 235 n37

O
Oban 115, 117
objectivity 15, 81 n10, 174, 176,
  177, 179
Ó Conghaile, Michael 234 n6
O'Connell, Daniel 98, 102, 107
O'Connell, Sean 201, 216 n1, 216
  n4, 216 n5, 217 n12
Ó Gráda, Cormac 105, 113 n20
Olcutt, Charles, *The Country of Sir
  Walter Scott* 141, 145 n15
Oldbuck, Jonathan, 'A Visit to
  Iona' 117, 129 n9
Oliver and Boyd's Scottish Tourist
  145 n16
open road 10, 208, 217 n31
Osborne, Sydney Godolphin (Rev.),
  *Gleanings of the West of
  Ireland* 110
O'Shea, Tony 225
Ossian (*see* Macpherson)
otherness 2, 9, 19, 27, 70, 77, 147,
  151, 158–9, 161, 220, 227, 230,
  231, 233
Otway, Caesar (Rev.) 103
  Sketches in Erris and Tyrawly 99
  Sketches in Ireland 99
  Tour in Connaught 99
Ousby, Ian 2, 11 n4, 12, n11, 200
  n46, 218 n37
Overton, J. H., 'A Cruise among the
  Hebrides' 129 n17

Ovid 39–41, 44, 48 n26, 49 n42
Owenson, Sydney (Lady Morgan) 10,
  183–4, 191–2, 197

P
Pacific (*see* exploration)
Pantycelyn, William Williams (hymn
  writer) 153
Paris 72, 74, 80, 92, 93, 228–30
pastoral 10, 167, 189, 200 n31, 201,
  208, 210–12, 214
Patagonia 22
Patmore, Peter George, *Letters on
  England* 70, 80, 84 n59
patriotism 15, 18, 21, 35, 77, 79,
  118, 154–55
Paz, D. G. 129 n22
peasantry (*see also* social class) 5,
  9, 10, 102, 104–8, 110, 148–9,
  151, 183, 190–2, 197
pedestrianism 11, 52, 53, 101, 147,
  157, 172–3, 180 n20, 221,
  224–6, 228,
Pembrokeshire 36–9, 44, 46, 147
Pennant, Thomas 5–6, 13–30
Perec, Georges 229, 234 n25
Pernot, François Alexander, *Vues
  pittoresque de l'Ecosse* 139, 146
  n27
Perthshire 20
Phelps, Jocelyn 47 n9
Phillips, Terry 47 n11
Pichot, Joseph Jean Marie Charles
  Amédée, *Historical and Literary
  Tour of a Foreigner* 80–1, 84
  n60, 137, 145 n19
picturesque 2–5, 6, 9, 12 n8, 12 n10,
  15, 17, 21, 23–4, 27–8, 52, 53,
  58, 61, 63, 64, 65 n2, 86, 89,
  97–100, 102, 106, 107, 119,
  134, 139, 140, 160, 164, 166,
  168–70, 172, 187–9, 204, 211,
  212
Pitchford, Susan 3, 12 n12
Pittock, Murray 134, 144 n5
Plumptre, Anne, *Narrative of a
  Residence in Ireland* 99, 185,
  199 n10
Polo, Marco 1

Pope, Alexander   89
popular culture   32–3, 53, 132, 166, 181, 185, 197
poverty   5, 8, 15, 19, 26–7, 88, 92, 100, 102, 105–7, 109–10, 111, 114–5, 121–3, 126–8, 177–9, 226
Presbyterianism   119
Price, Uvedale   26–7, 30 n48
primitivism   19, 23–4, 80, 148, 150
Protestantism   100, 102–3, 105, 109, 119, 157, 171, 174, 226, 232
Proust, Marcel   223, 234 n8
proximity   14, 19, 27, 35, 118, 151, 228, 230
Pudney, John   130 n50

Q
Quarterly Review   71, 82 n13

R
racism   151, 170, 171, 176
Radcliffe, Ann   34–5, 36, 46, 48 n12
Ragland Castle   57,
railways   10, 101, 111, 132, 153, 164, 167, 169, 170, 171, 175, 177, 185, 191, 201, 204–7, 210, 211, 212, 215, 217 n16, 227
Rebecca Riots   150
Reformation
  English   102
  Scottish   119
Reichard, Heinrich August Ottokar   73, 83 n27
Reid, Thomas, *Travels in Ireland*   99
religion (*see also* monasticism, missionaries, *and under denominations*)   8, 22, 53, 75, 92, 109, 114, 117–18, 120–1, 126, 128, 155, 156, 175
  as cultural colonialism   102
  Celtic   24
  Ireland and   99
  liberty and   91, 92, 93
  militant Irish Protestantism
  pilgrimage and   2, 222
  Scotland and   114–16
resorts   3, 31, 33, 40, 42, 46, 57, 177, 182

Richardson, Dorothy   46, 49 n45
Richmond, Legh   125, 128
Ritchie, Leitch, *Ireland*   99, 107, 112 n16
road (*see also* open road)   2, 10, 16, 19, 20, 29 n24, 44, 50, 52, 53, 98, 101, 105, 106, 169, 172, 201–18, 226, 227
Robinson, Matthew   38, 41, 49 n32
Robson, George   188
Romantic
  fascination with decay   99
  gaze   190
  internationalism   70, 82 n12
  irony   75
  travel and traveller   20, 53, 58, 67 n2, 148, 150, 181, 185, 187, 191, 195, 198, 214
Romanticism   9, 20, 25, 32, 33, 36, 43, 46, 50, 52, 59, 60, 65 n2, 69, 135, 185, 186, 188, 199 n12, 211
  French   81, 85
  visual culture and   52
Romans   17, 24, 53,
Rosa, Salvator   189
Rossetti, Dante Gabriel   205
Rothkirch, Alyce von   11 n3
Roughley, Alan   47 n11
Rousseau, Jean Jacques   78
ruins   8, 51, 52–5, 58–9, 61–4, 66 n10, 73, 98–100, 117–18, 122, 123, 126, 128, 140, 141–2, 181, 188, 191, 214
Ruskin, John   34, 205
Russell, Richard   48 n22
Russell, Thomas, 'Sonnet X'   115
Ryskamp, Charles   47 n1

S
St Columba   8, 22, 115, 117–21, 123, 125, 127
Schiller, Johann Christoph Freidrich von   87
Schetky, John   139
Schopenhauer, Arthur   87
Schopenhauer, Johanna, *Reise durch England und Schottland*   7, 85, 87–91, 94

science 3, 14, 17, 25, 72, 82, n21, 87, 117
Scotland (*see also individual places*) 2, 3, 4, 6, 8, 9, 12 n11, 13–30, 80, 87, 89, 91, 98, 104, 114–31, 132–46, 165, 170, 186, 213
  Act of Union (1707) and 3, 13, 21
  Highlands of 1, 3, 5–6, 14, 16, 18–20, 22, 26, 80, 114, 117, 119, 121–2, 124, 126, 128, 135–6, 186
Scott, John, *Visit to Paris* 78–9, 84 n57, 92
Scott, Michael 112 n7
Scott, Walter 9, 78, 79, 80, 132–46, 173
  hybrid tours based on works of 135–44
  monuments and statues of 132–3
  'Scott country' and 9, 132–46
  Waverly novels, stage adaptations of 139
  Works
    Chronicles of the Canongate 137
    'Eve of St John' 136
    'Glen Finglas' 136
    Heart of Midlothian 137, 140
    Ivanhoe 137, 142, 146 n32
    Kenilworth 142
    Legend of Montrose 137
    Lady of the Lake 78, 135
    Marmion 136, 137–8
    Minstrelsy of the Scottish Border 136, 143
    Old Mortality 137
    Rob Roy 136–8, 139, 140
    Waverley 133, 135–6, 137–8, 140, 141
sea-bathing 6, 33, 36–43, 46, 47 n8, 154
self-discovery 33–4, 59–60, 70
sexuality 6, 39–42, 46, 49 n29
Shackleton, Robert, *Touring Great Britain* 201, 204–5, 207, 208, 213
Shakespeare, William 37, 63, 67 n46, 74, 83 n27, 94, 214
  Cymbeline 37
  Macbeth 20, 24

Sharp, William 142–3, 146 n33
Sharpe, Richard 129 n3
Shaw, George Bernard, *John Bull's Other Island* 165
Shaw, Philip 199 n15
Shaw, Stebbing, *Tour to the West of England* 67 n28
Shelley, Frances, Lady, *Diary* 133, 144 n2
Shelley, Mary Wollstonecraft 68, 81 n3
Shelley, Percy Bysshe 34, 80
  'A Vision of the Sea' 47 n11
  Alastor 68–9, 81 n1
Shields, Rob 47 n3
sightseeing 2, 112 n4, 116–7, 120, 122–4, 128, 160
Silliman, Benjamin, *Journal of Travels in England* 71
Simmons, Andrew 29 n6
Simmons, Jack 83 n48
Simond, Louis, *Journal of a Tour* 51, 65 n3, 69, 70, 71–2, 77–81, 84 n57
Skye 24–5, 124, 126
Smailholm tower 136, 140, 143
Smith, Anthony D. 155, 162 n27
Smith, Charlotte 46
  Elegiac Sonnets 34, 47 n10, 47 n11
  The Emigrants 69
Smith, George Nelson, *Killarney, and the Surrounding Scenery* 188, 199 n27
Smith, Henry EcRoyd 146 n32
Smollett, Tobias 33,
  Expedition of Humphrey Clinker 47 n8, 91
Smyth, Alfred P. 129 n3
Snowdonia 186
sociability 56–7, 90
social class 2, 3, 4–5, 7, 9, 10, 71, 88–9, 90, 99, 105, 107, 121–22, 124, 126, 128, 143, 149–50, 154–5, 159, 161, 164, 166, 175, 186, 197, 201, 202, 204, 211–13, 216 n3, 217 n12
Society for the Relief and Encouragement of the Poor Fisherman in the Highlands and Islands 8, 112, 124–8

Soubigou, Gilles　146 n22
Southern Ireland: Its Lakes and
　Landscapes　200 n41
souvenir　12, 44, 127, 194, 220
South Armagh　225–6
South Seas　16, 28, 95 n4
Southey, Robert　70–2, 79–80
　'Accounts of England by Foreign
　　Travellers'　70–2, 82 n13
　Letters from England　7, 70, 78, 83
　　n48
spas　3, 134, 153
Sportsman in Ireland　101, 112 n7
Staël, Germain, Madame de　68, 72,
　74, 78, 82 n12
Staffa　14, 25, 115, 117
state of nature (*see* nature)
Stawell, Maud M., *Motor Tours in the*
　West Country　201, 202,
　213–15, 218 n50
steam power　10, 52, 80, 90, 93, 101,
　116, 117, 120, 121, 122, 128,
　167, 169, 210
Steiner, Gerhard　87, 95 n5
Stendhal　74
Stephens, James　173
Sterne, Laurence　94
Stevenson, Burton E., *The Charm of*
　Ireland　197, 200 n51
Stoddart, John, *Remarks on Local*
　Scenery　136, 145 n12
sublime　6, 9, 33–4, 43, 46, 97–8,
　100, 107, 134, 148, 150, 168,
　181, 182, 183, 184, 185–90,
　196, 198
Sunderland (Scotland)　24, 27
Swinglehurst, Edmund　130 n50
Sylvan's Pictorial Handbook to the
　Scenery of the Caledonian
　Canal　118, 129 n15
Szerszynski, Bronislaw　69, 81 n5

T
Tacitus　24
Talfourd, Thomas Noon　48 n12
Teilo, Gwilym, *Llandeilo Vawr and Its*
　Neighbourhood　149, 162 n8
temperance movement　124–5
Tennsyon, Alfred, Lord　148

Thackeray, William Makepeace, *Irish*
　Sketch Book　101, 103, 108,
　110, 112 n7
Thames　18, 71, 73, 89, 91
Thesiger, Wilfred　224, 234 n10
Thomas, Bertha　158, 160–1, 163 n32
Thomas, Keith　29 n9
Thomas, Nicholas　30 n52
Thompson, Carl　199 n13, 211, 216,
　218 n36
Thompson, Spurgeon　9–10, 11
Tilt, Charles, *Illustrations ... to the*
　Poetic Works of Sir Walter
　Scott　139
time　10, 11, 27, 29 n22, 99, 120,
　133, 205, 207, 208, 215, 221,
　225, 226–31
time-space convergence　11, 226, 227
Tintern Abbey　3, 6–7, 50–67, 215
Tipperary　108
Tóibín, Colm, *Walking along the*
　Border　11, 220–2, 224–33
Tonypandy riots　161
topography　5, 6, 15, 18, 19, 20–1, 25,
　54, 56, 57–8, 62, 65, 138–9, 141,
　155, 186, 188, 222, 226
topographical illustration　138–9
tourism
　as industry　10, 114–15, 127, 164,
　　172, 177–8
　as ritual　99, 122
　capitalism and　167–72
　modernity and (*see also*
　　modernity)　5, 17–18, 211
　semiotics of　219
　types of
　　agricultural　3
　　Borderland (Scotland)　145 n16
　　coastal　12 n10, 33–40, 46, 48
　　　n12, 154
　　cycling　158
　　disaster　110
　　estate　98
　　Grand Tour　2, 8, 18, 99–100
　　home tour　1–4, 12 n11, 13, 15,
　　　31, 32–4, 69–70, 85, 91, 98,
　　　147, 186, 201, 204, 215,
　　　219–20, 226, 229–31
　　identity　3–4, 12 n12

literary   3, 37, 48 n21, 78, 122,
132–46, 191–2, 195, 204
mass   5, 9, 165, 176, 182–5,
197–8
motor   10, 201–18
package   10
pedestrian   52, 53
'petite tour'   8, 100, 106
picturesque   3, 12 n10, 15, 17,
20–1, 27, 52, 58, 63–4, 98, 107,
172
religious   102–3, 118–19
tourist
culture   99, 210
day-tripper as   181
national identity and   1, 19
'tourist amnesia'   105
'tourist gaze' (*see also* gaze)   107, 128,
172, 190
tourists vs. travellers   2, 212
Towey valley   148–51, 153
translation   7, 11, 38, 68–84, 134,
158, 220, 223–4
transliteration   196, 223–4
transnationalism   70–2, 79
travel
as leisure   2, 5, 33, 56, 62, 210,
213, 215
British propensity to   1, 7, 9, 78
deceleration and   11, 224–6
itineraries of   1, 2, 55, 103, 110,
134, 135–40, 205
moral benefits of   127–8
rail (*see* railways)
relation of experience to   2, 4, 31–4,
37, 38, 45–6, 50, 59–60, 65, 78,
117, 120, 134, 136, 151, 159,
206, 215, 218 n44, 220
relation of language to   220
steamboat (*see* steam power)
travel writing
accuracy of (*see* accuracy)
definitions of   50, 75
fiction and   48 n21, 69–70, 80, 83
n40, 132–46, 158
French   70, 71–3, 77–81
genre and   7, 50, 56–8, 64, 69–71,
77, 147, 151, 166, 212, 214,
220

German   85–95
illustrated (*see* illustration)
interstitial   230
intertextuality and   68
Irish   107–11, 198 n3
politics and   18, 34, 80, 90, 166,
171, 173, 177
printing and publication of   51,
54–5, 56, 57, 59, 61, 64, 66
n15, 67 n29, 73, 78, 83 n33
representations of labour in (*see*
labour)
representations of poverty in (*see*
poverty)
Romantic (*see* Romantic)
self-reflexivity of   155, 221
Travis, John   48 n23
Trossachs   78, 136, 140, 145 n16
Tuke, James Hack   110
Turner, J. M. W.   138–9, 145 n20
Turner, Richard   171
Twiss, Richard, *Tour of Ireland*   97,
101, 112 n8

U
Ulster   100–1, 104, 108–9, 221
Ulster Tatler   233
Ulster Tourist Development
Association (Belfast)   178
Urbain, Jean-Didier   38, 48 n25, 229
distinction between exotic and
endotic travel   229–33
Urry, John   69, 81 n5, 190, 200 n35

V
Vandeul, Marie-Angélique   83 n40
Victoria (Queen)   98, 124, 140,
171–2
Victorian Period   9, 10, 85, 108, 115,
117, 119, 126, 132–4, 148, 181,
185
Vincent, J. E., *Through East Anglia in a
Motor Car*   201, 203–8, 213
Virgil   24
visual culture   52, 107, 139, 187,
188, 209
Voltaire   28
Candide   85
Lettres philosophiques   95 n2

voyages (*see also* Cook, James) 4, 14, 15, 16, 18, 21, 22, 25, 32, 76, 86, 95 n4
voyeurism 11, 40–1

W
Wales (*see also individual places*) 6, 9, 13, 14, 31–49, 50–67, 98, 147–63, 186, 213
  Anglicization and 149, 155
  as birthplace of domestic tourism 50–1
  'Blue Book' reports on 148, 151
  Celticism and 17, 148
  colonial relationship with England of 150
  links with United States of 9, 152, 160
  nationalism in 9
  peripheries and 17, 21, 26
  territorialization and 18
Welsh language 147, 149, 151, 152, 153, 159, 161
Welshness 19, 149–51, 155, 161
Walton, John K. 198 n4
Walpole, Horace 28
Ward, C. S., *The Thorough Guide* 193–4
Washington, E. K., *Echoes of Europe* 195, 200 n44
Watson, Nicola J. 9, 12 n9, 12 n11, 48 n21, 78, 84 n52, 144 n7, 145 n10, 145 n14, 195, 200 n43
Waugh, Evelyn 203, 215
Weiskel, Thomas 199 n15
Wellek, René 83 n36
West, Frederic, Mrs. (Theresa Cornwallis West), *A Summer Visit to Ireland* 110, 189–90, 200 n30
West, Thomas 4, 12 n14
Whelan, Irene 112 n11
Whelan, Kevin 112 n9, 112 n13, 167, 180 n11, 180 n12
White, George Preston, *Tour in Connemara* 110–11
White, Gilbert 28
Wicklow 98, 169
Williams, Daniel 11 n3

Williams, David, *Hist. of Monmouthshire* 61–3, 64, 67 n36, 67 n41
Williams, David (Rev.), of Llandyfeisant 148
Williams, John (pseud. Anthony Pasquin) 40–1, 49 n31
Williams, William (hymn writer) 157
Williams, William H. A. 8, 11, 12 n11, 111 n2, 111–2 n3, 112 n4, 112 n12, 112 n13, 112 n18, 112 n19, 113 n26, 113 n31, 182, 187, 198 n2, 198 n3, 199 n11, 199n25
Williams, William Proctor 66 n15
Wilmot, Sarah Anne 65, 67 n50
Wilson, John Marius, *Land of Scott* 141
Wilson, William, *Post Chaise Companion* 179 n8
Winter, William, *Over the Border* 120, 130 n32
Wismann, Heinz 234 n2
Withers, Charles W. T. 29 n6
Wohlgemut, Esther 70, 82 n12
women 31–49, 181–200
  agency and 159
  as motor tourists 216 n2, 216n6
  fashion and 74
  'New Woman' fiction and 158
  of Jura 17
  represented as hag, crone, or witch 195–6
  sea-bathing and 6, 31–49
  writing by 12 n11, 31
Wood, Gillen d'Arcy 138, 145 n20
Woods, C. J. 200 n34
Wordsworth, William 79, 138
  'The Brothers' 69, 81 n6
  The Excursion 68
  'Iona (upon landing)' 114–15, 121, 122, 123
Wye River 1, 3, 6, 50–3, 55, 60–3, 65 n2, 153
Y
Yarrow river 138
Yates, William Holt, *Ivanhoe Illustrated* 146 n32
Z
Zilcosky, John 220, 234 n3